LISTENING TO THE CURLEW

LISTENING TO THE CURLEW

IAN SHERRY

LAGAN PRESS
BELFAST
2011

Published by
Lagan Press
Unit 45
Westlink Enterprise Centre
30-50 Distillery Street
Belfast BT12 5BJ
e-mail: lagan-press@e-books.org.uk
web: lagan-press.org.uk

ARTS
COUNCIL
of Northern Ireland

ISBN: 978 1 904652 05 2 (pbk)
978 1 904652 06 9 (hbk)
Author: Sherry, Ian
Title: Listening to the Curlew
2011

To Stasia

Mick Wilson was comfortable in Magills' kitchen, dozing gently in a cushioned limbo, slouched in Oul' Paddy's fireside chair. Blissfully unconscious of having usurped a sacrosanct position, he nursed his bowl of whiskey and idly teased feathers from the broken stitching at his hand. He always liked the smell of Magills'; it was the faint whiff of tar and paraffin, flour on the griddle, and the scent of washing soda from the people in the house. He looked absent-mindedly at the tuft of curved feathers he had extracted, ruefully slipped them into his pocket, smoothed the damage in the upholstery, and drained the last of the delft bowl.

Only then did he realise that there was an awkward silence, a sort of dense vacuum, aggravated by Betty's mother rattling the plates on the dresser, and her grandmother persisting in grinding the fanbellows wheel. 'The Fans' became the focus of his fuddled musing. The big wheel was now rounded shoulders with hands clasped at the navel, the encased bellows a perfectly circular pot belly and hips, a squat and voluptuous black woman whom he looked at for a while, until the joint of the leather strap scurrying round the circuit of the hoop and the spindle began to hypnotise him. The half-inch of raised overlay and stitching, round and round it went; a mouse on a cinder track, it could never get off. For some reason it reminded him of his own subliminal treadmill, his recurring dream. He was inching along a narrow spiral pathway on a vast cavern wall. Purgatory was how he interpreted it. A sheer rock face, dropping to the abyss below him and rising to infinity above. He could see himself, a tiny figure, one of thousands, millions even, in an endless shuffling queue. On and on, that was the 'mouse's' fate, driven by the old woman, her hand clasping the ash handle, her fingers 'blackthorn', her nails 'glazed November sloes'. She was part of it, fused to it, a dark bundle slumped in the corner, forever in the shade of the primrose Aladdin lamp, measuring her time in slow rotations, and breathing life into the fire.

God in Heaven! He woke with a start. What was he thinking of? He must have been dreaming. In a fluid movement he sprang from the chair and tossed the bowl, spiralling from his cupped hands, up to where it almost tipped the thatch. Then, catching it, he reached back and placed it on the table, where Betty was washing the dishes in an earthenware crock. He felt silly, so, shoving his hands deep into his trouser pockets, he stomped his feet on the hearthstone and, without a word, walked out.

The three women looked at one another and nodded in resigned relief.

Outside, the frost and moonlight revived Mick. Oul' Paddy, flanked by Arthur Keenan and Joe Marley, were down at the garden wall. Even with their backs to him, Mick could see they were drunk. In an uninhibited huddle, shuffling, standing too close to one another, and striking matches for already lit pipes. Smoke wafted gently skywards, wisps of goats' hair drawn to a full moon.

It was the whiskey that had done it. Had they come on home after four or five bottles of stout, they would have been all right. Mick shook his head and smiled. The whiskey, instigated by the news of Stephen Flavin, that's what had done the harm. Such an apology! Who in their right mind would have given Stephen Flavin a job as a porter in the railway station in Warrenpoint? Such a hallion! It was the talk of the pub—seems that some unfortunate traveller, a gentleman, all tweed coat, kid gloves and polite airs, had stepped off the train, and in a petulant display of self-importance, had commanded the bold Flavin to fetch his luggage, post-haste.

'The luggage, my man, and be smart about it!' he had barked. Orders delivered in a tone and demeanour that so enraged Stephen, so reminded him of his sojourn in the army, that he drew his breath, stripped his teeth, and, with eyes bulging, swaggered up tight against the passenger and spat, 'Go and shite!'—an edict so shocking, it took a moment to register, before the gentleman practically ran to the stationmaster's office and blurted out his complaint. Stopping short of repeating the vulgarity verbatim, while nonetheless conveying enough indignation to have the errant porter called. It was a belligerent Stephen who, far from showing contrition, further horrified all present with an apology that took the form of an aggressive finger-stabbing: 'Do you see, you. I told you to go and shite! Well you needn't bother your arse!' Even thinking about it made Mick laugh.

At Magills' doorstep, Mick took a minute to look down the valley. Idly he wondered if there was any truth in the talk that the people in the hills had been driven out of lowland farms hundreds of years ago, banished from mountains of soil. May Shannon said that's why they call the Keenans 'The Parchies'. Seems it should have been 'The Parcels', a consequence of some old ancestor of theirs lamenting, 'I used to have acres of good land, now I only have parcels of hungry ground.'

In the dark blue light, the country was 'easy looked at', the clumps of sycamore and Scots pine muffling the whitewash and thatch of every farm. At night, houses were homes, and fields and hedgerows a pattern drawn blindfold by man's hand on God's original design. The moon was right at his eye level, perched above Carlingford, silver fissures slashed the Lough, and dark shadows highlighted the craigs of Slieve Foy. It was eerily quiet. In front of him a schooner slept in the bay at Rosetta; to his near left, a raven coughed on Spallick, and on his far right, over in Carrigs, a fox was crying in the whins. Not a dirge, but confident bold yelps, challenging the country's hunters: their shotguns, lurchers, terriers, light crowbars and short spades. He was an aboriginal posing on his haunches, as he stretched his head to Heaven, and (in keeping with the exaggerations of local speech, where 'the street' was the hard footing between the dwelling and the outbuildings, 'the country at large' was the four or five neighbouring houses, and 'the world and their wives' was the populace within a radius of a mile) praised himself, his vixen, and all his line.

But praise is tricky, easily misconstrued. And not only self-praise. Cream over-whipped can turn sour, as Arthur and Joe well knew. They were men who more or less devoted themselves to the diplomatic wiles of weddings, funerals, markets and fairs, and were astute enough to know that they weren't doing that well. The situation was different from bringing people together in a bargain. Standard phrases like 'If you bid a man half what he asks, you haven't insulted him' or 'You'll divide it between you' didn't seem much good. Certainly they could not jostle Paddy Magill, could not grab him by the coat and shout, 'Come on now, hold out your hand.' That was their dilemma; it wasn't as simple as that. While their job was to heap praise on Mick Wilson—after all, they were his supporters in 'asking for' Betty—it was nevertheless impossible to give the thing the real *alluagh-dulluia*, what with Magill knowing him so well. Knowing everything about him, 'seed, breed and generation', scrutinising every turn of him, from when he was a child. Sure didn't Mick spend half his time about it, and for fear that wasn't bad enough, to put the tin hat on it, hadn't they carried out the same function three years before? Then he'd 'asked' and didn't take the older sister Maysie, a folly that certainly hadn't done her a button of harm, because it had spurred Hugh Connolly to stop dithering and make her the mistress of Bay View Farm. But sweet mother of God, this really was the height of nonsense, a calamity sparked when they all fell in with one another at the binder demonstration in Hogg's big flat field, and then spent the heel of the evening drinking in the town.

'He's the boy can sing "The Rose of Mooncoin",' Arthur ventured. Safe enough ground since it was Paddy's favourite song, and Mick had done it proud, not once, but twice, first in Riley's Bar, and again, at Paddy's request, at the horse well in the Dark Place on the way home. On both occasions, Magill had slaughtered it by joining in. Not just the chorus, but random lines and even single words: 'lovely' and 'mooncoin' he highlighted, printed in huge matt black grotesque capital letters, with a gulder of an out-of-tune roar.

'And you can give it a bit of lift yourself,' Arthur continued. But his blether had the blessing of falling on deaf ears, because no sooner had they heard Mick pulling the big door after him than Paddy repaired to the house, leaving the suitor and his two mentors to continue on up the road, unsure if the idea of 'asking for' Betty got any further than Arthur's vague matchmaking in the pub. However, Joe felt that, as bad as they had done, it wasn't as bad as the time they had gone down to Hilltown with Stephen Flavin. They couldn't believe where he was taking them, ramstam, to one of the best grocery businesses in the parish, to 'ask for' the daughter of the house. Such a debacle! 'Well, he can certainly get no worse,' Arthur found himself babbling to the girl's father, in a parody of marriage brokering, where the irrepressible suitor still got the wife.

In the moonlight, the three of them, abreast, the full width of the road, threaded the unsteady measure of men who have had too much to drink. Re-righting themselves as they bumped into each other, they waltzed over the bridge at Roark's Glen, where Joe, mumbling and cursing about Hugh Shevlin, was lucky not to fall in. 'It's a disgrace, a disgrace on the whole country,' he ranted, 'and every man in it. Such a thing to do!'

'I didn't think it was that bad,' Arthur said. 'It's not as if he stole something.'

'What! Not that bad?' Joe roared, rocking back on his heels, his fists clenched. 'A man arrested for being drunk. Just drunk. If he was any sort of man at all, it should have been drunk and disorderly; that's a proper charge. Arrested for fighting, not for sitting meekly on your arse.' And he was still carping, as on up the road they went, under the Holly Rock, and down Craigarian loanin and into Wilsons' street, a setting for much shaking of hands, 'good luck's, and pacifying of the dog, before Mick eventually went into the house. But not before Joe, who couldn't help starting a rumour or, failing that, adding to a story to make it worse, lamented, 'Jasus, it was awful what Stephen said to the Protestant Bishop in the railway station in Warrenpoint.'

Then he and Arthur followed the little path between the gable of Wilsons' house and the high wall of Pulnafrog. Down the fields to the stepping stones, where Joe insisted on lighting a skelp of a whin to look for a salmon, before crossing into the Wee Holms and heading up to the Far Road. And on that of all nights, Arthur, who was very freakish, didn't see a ghost. Not even a light in the fairy domain of The Clornies, a following foot, nor a 'grey woman' leaving an isolated thorn.

Maggie turned on her side, tucked the clothes round her rump, tightened the sheet under her oxter, and tried to get back to sleep after the dog's barking and the craic out at Wilsons', and endeavoured to dispel her unease … about Owen in London, his daughter in France, and the sound of the foot on the street foreboding the McGrains.

A new autumn day dawned in the valley, casting a cool grey light on Knockbarragh and Drumreagh, treating them at first both equally, as they reared, one to the west, one to the east, of the valley floor. Two long rectangular townlands stitched together at the river, their steep sides reflecting a road with fertile land below it, rough pasture, heather and craigs above. It was an inclined valley, its floor rising in an eight-mile thrust from sea level to fifteen hundred feet at its watershed in The Bog. A valley of infinite contrasts, reflecting its micro-climates: woodland, arable land, cropping rock, pasture and heath. It was a place that even the sun did not treat equally, warming first Carraigs on the upper reaches of Knockbarragh, then sliding down the mountain face, crossing the river to Craigarran, and taking in the rest of Drumreagh.

But it stayed longest on Craigarran, a *clachan* of three farmsteads perched just above the river on the lower slopes of Loughinmore. A precinct of tiny fields, streams, rights of way and double stone walls, which afforded views of the entire glen of the river tumbling from the Bog to the Lough, and the mountains climbing to the horizon on both sides. Craigarran sat on a neat plateau, structured by nature, inviting further modifications by man. You could not stand in it without a sense of what had gone before. This had been a place of habitation for millennia, a prehistoric earthwork, evolving through ring fort, motte-and-bailey, to communal rath. Now its faintly defined outer terraces enfolded the sloped crescents of smaller raths, standing stones, the cashel of Pulnafrog, and paving suggesting the lintels of a souterrain or chambered grave. Every twist and turn, mound and depression, had the stamp of man's labour. Generation upon generation of sweat and industry, and in the case of 'The Needle', here was an expression of spiritualism and art. Heaven knows what culture had sponsored it: an eight-foot standing stone, extensively chiselled with an interlacing pattern and stamped with a perfectly circular fist-sized hole through its head. A high priest metamorphosed and put to practical use as a central support in the carthouse wall.

And not all the ancient monuments were within the earthwork. The river, like the drumlin, was naturally structured. It had 'The Pots', a string of deep pools stocked with good trout in summer and resting salmon during their late autumn run. Starting from the waterfall at the Gorum Rocks, it flowed through 'The Forty Foot' and 'Puldavy' to more accessible ponds, one on each side of the Stepping Stones: the seven stout defenders of man's right to cross— three original wisdom teeth of living rock, and four artificial molars that had been transported, prised and crowbarred, to fill the gaps. The Stepping Stones was a causeway over the river to a suburb of Craigarran: the Wee Holms. Five acres of raised flood plain, a curious pleasure ground of paths and clearings and rampant blackthorn, underpinning sycamore, oak, and less majestic trees. The Wee Holms also had its archaeology: Crahuggily, a huge boulder cogged up three-legged pot-style on lesser stones. And over from it, central to the entire area, a faint circular enclosure, a burnished rath, 'The Rabbits' Green', striking for its lack of shrubbery, a distinct oval which, apart from a profusion of snowdrops in January, remained as closely cropped verdant grass.

The Holms was a place of enchantment, carpeted with primrose and bluebell where the wary turned their coats inside out to cross. It was a sanctuary for the fabled 'Black Pig'; a place for the great boar to come and rest and plan further ructions, brooding in the impenetrable thickets, his bloodshot eyes following the movement of everyone who passed. It was where the team of small black men came out from under Crahuggily— lithe and energetic, they played football in the arena before returning to their world deep under the stone.

The entire domain was a haven for the paranormal. The headrig of Craigarran's river field had a chimera, 'The Bauchinborough', a candy-striped marquee, an exotic linen cathedral that materialised, pulsating strange music and revelry, rationalising the four trumpeting bull elephants elaborately attired and shackled at its door. Haybag's Stone Horse was a feature: a great ghost stallion that galloped the loanins on November nights, carrying Holy Souls from purgatory. Drumreagh and Knockbarragh men allowed a little respite in their mortal playground as a consequence of our prayers. Then there were the hoards of fairy gold hidden in the double stone ditches and, more tangible, the sacred chalice and paten concealed by a persecuted priest during penal times.

All this rested on the inhabitants, particularly after dark, when ghosts of every form roamed, kept alive by an oral tradition related round the fire; when clumps of ancient rhododendron and laurel sheltered them as they slipped from one bolt-hole to another in the shadow of stone embankments and reproving trees.

It was easy to believe anything in this almost deserted manor of the Wilsons and the McGrains—two distinct families in close proximity, neither at war nor at peace and, only because of the Wilsons' diplomacy, in a delicate permanent truce. Residents for as long as anyone could know, these people, different in stature and outlook, never interbred and kept themselves apart, cultivating different alliances, even down to never going to the same Sunday Mass. Now, through emigration and stifling social nuances, they were clan branches almost at the end of their line. Mick's father, John, could remember the present three houses each with children in them, the place a whirlwind of activity, occupied by as many as nineteen people, and dressed cornerstones in structured positions pointed to a history of many houses more. Now the two occupied dwellings, thirty yards of semi-detached stone and clay terrace, harboured only three: Mick and his father to the east, on the loanin side, and Maggie McGrain, a wicked pismire of a spinster in her seventieth year, residing in the half pointing to the river, due west. The other dwelling, a little removed from the rest, and across a stone-channelled stream, was unoccupied, and had been for several years. It was the property of Craigarran's exiled miscreant, the parish's very own lost soul, 'The Divil', as Arthur loved to call him: the man who had had the effrontery to marry an Englishwoman in a registry office, the formerly pilloried, now almost forgotten, Owen McGrain. He was Maggie's first cousin, her adopted brother, and John's friend.

The three of them had gone to school together and, even then, she had kept an eye on him, through a blur of skipping and ring-a-ring-a-rosies, of the penny catechism and the times tables, until they had left, aged twelve. That was when Maggie went to her short but incident-packed service employed by the Thompson-Smythes of Clooneevan. John and Owen, in an altogether more docile vein, were hired for three years as farm labourers to Tollertons of Clonallon, then they wrought a couple more in Scotland, before Owen went down to London, and in his own words, 'Met my blossom in a boozer', and made the city his life. As indeed his 'kicking over the traces' in marrying outside the church ordained he must. He had come home again only once, twenty-eight years before, four weeks after his mother and father, Pat and Tessy, died, she in the morning, he draining the spuds at dinnertime, keeled over on the big granite slab in front of the door. And Oul' Joe Marley, who had just been

[17]

sympathising with him about Tessy, heard the commotion from Wilsons' street, rushed back, and jumped astride the corpse now on the settle-bed, still warm! and had Pat by the lapels, and was pulling him up and down and shouting, 'Patrick Mary McGrain, born on or about the fifteenth of August in Craigarran in the townland of Drumreagh. A parishioner of Kilbroney in the diocese of Dromore. A good man at buildin' a stack or mowin' or saltin' a crock of herrings. A melodeon player, a shepherd and horseman, who for years and years drank nothin' but an odd bottle of stout.' And then falling silent, for he had begun to realise what the shock of the whole thing had done to him. Of his being talking to a man one minute and him being dead the next; and, sensing where he was, and ashamed of himself, he knelt down and, leaning his head on the edge of the settle-bed at Paddy's ribs, said, 'Jesus, Mary, and Joseph, Pat, you're dead!'

Nobody had ever seen anything like the two funerals going down the road. A sombre pageant of Lightbody's hearse, in tandem with McAnuff's, drafted in from Warrenpoint, the cortege forming a tribunal that split between pious souls who whispered, 'Wasn't it nice for them to get away together? Pat and Tessy were always so close. Poor Owen, I think it's worse when you can't get home,' and a 'free Barabbas' faction who mumbled, 'Sweet Jesus. Marrying in a registry office! Is it any wonder his mother's heart was scalded? Such an action, he killed the both o' them. You'd think he'd at least have the decency to come home.' And when he did come home for the 'month's mind', they were the very people who said, 'What the hell took him? You'd think he'd have the decency to stay where he was. And did you see him, with a pair of pearl rosary beads? There's no shame in him … at Mass!'

But Maggie had a welcome for him, and on that evening, as she watched him idly strolling the loanins, her heart bled, for she knew it was a reflective goodbye to Craigarran, and indeed the next day, taking only 'The Music Box', he went drinking with John Wilson to Newry, and never came back. He had one child, a daughter about the same age as Mick, a spoiled, headstrong girl if Maggie was to be believed, and according to Joe Marley, who even then couldn't help starting a rumour, was the spitting image of Dinny Coyle.

Dinny was a relative of theirs, a gouger, who portrayed in his appearance and disposition all the worst characteristics of the breed. Stand-offish by nature, he was then inclined to be snappy and aggressive when drawn into the company of other men. He was particularly hairy. A grey black shock encroached on his forehead, and bristles and curls crept up his neck and flourished on the backs of his hands. He made an awful hash of shaving; random tussocks sprouted from his face and added to the presence of a man who could have laced his shirt with the hairs on his chest. Arthur accurately described Dinny as 'like something caught in a trap'. A hell of a grulsh of a boyo, thick-set, but difficult to tell just how thick-set, because he always wore a wardrobe of old clothes. You could count his age from the rings of gansies round his neck. He was a figure who positively cried out for a nickname, but other than Joe Marley occasionally referring to him as 'the hairy-arsed schoolboy', people left it at that. Dinny was an honorary Craigarran man, almost a fourth resident if you counted the time he spent there serving as Maggie's factotum, and the custodian of Owen's house.

The deal was that, in a complex charter, where he was serving-boy, crown prince and drudge, Dinny kept the place clean, did a few turns for Maggie, and had the use of Owen's land. She never crossed the stream to put her foot on the property, but saw to it that he whitewashed the outside of the house, maintained the thatch, and mowed the grass round the door of her Uncle Pat's. He was allowed to go in only at set times, and then under strict instructions, to further whitewash and blacken the hearth, and light the fire. He was a man who may have looked a bit Neanderthal to the casual observer, but those who knew Dinny never doubted that he was smart, keeping well in with Maggie, telling her titbits of news, and always being on her side in the imaginary war she waged against Mick and John, manufacturing a bit of propaganda and, if need be, reminding her of past outrages, when he thought that things were going off the boil. She liked a full and detailed report on the Wilsons' movements.

Nothing pleased her better than talk about girls being let down by Mick, of him 'makin' a pig's ass of himself by askin' them' and then 'throwin' them up'. It was all grist to the mill.

Dinny pursued a stewarding policy of neglecting Owen's land, of keeping the stone ditches in such bad repair that no field could be taken for conacre. What with the ditches at the river, particularly the march ditches between the Coyles and the McGrains practically non-existent, one got the visual impression of it all being the same parcel of land. Dinny had almost a squatter's right to it; consequently an outsider couldn't possibly 'come in' to a nice eight acres that, at very little money, was inevitably heading in the direction of being permanently added to the Coyle farm.

The morning sun stepped out from behind the shoulder of Ballynagelty, and smiled full-faced on the back terrace of the Wilsons' and McGrains' houses. It warmed them, intensifying the colours of the thatch and the daubing, and the subtle shades of independence which showed they were detached. It was an autumn sun, its declination such that it shone right through the Wilsons' windows, highlighting the grain in any stick of furniture it struck, and dancing on the brass trimmings of the dresser and the glazed finish of the delft dogs. A cylindrical beam introduced itself in the kitchen, a rainbow, not multi-coloured by reflections in droplets of water, but mono-coloured from suspended specks of oaten flour and minuscule particles of soil. And it remained there, casting patterns of brilliance and shade on the earthen floor and walls, while leaving the whitewash and tar of the hearth in a twilight, which gave the glow of the fire a special warmth. All this—the sun, the fire, the shadows—enhanced a very old kitchen, a place in harmony with itself, settled with cobwebs, crickets and mice.

Mick wasn't long out of bed. Enveloped in a cloud of dust, he performed the morning ritual of beating his woollen socks off the hearthstone, teasing and twisting them, transforming them from warm, soil-encrusted hardboard fused by a night at the fire, to pliable knitwear he could put on his feet. He had the contented, tousled appearance of a man at ease with the world, in that sublime happy state of thinking about nothing. A primate, stretching gently into the day after a good night's sleep, yawning in additional gulps of oxygen, as his father, a ponderous 'silverback', came in the door.

'Sufferin' Christ! My good God, man, I suppose what Maggie tells me is true,' he murmured. A stage whisper, not really addressed to anyone, just a frustrated exclamation as he shuffled his arthritic frame up the earthen floor. At the top of the table John Wilson sat. He pushed back Mick's breakfast dishes: the willow-patterned porridge bowl, the white plate with the circular ochre traces of swept-up fried eggs, the cup (no saucer) and the jug of milk. Absent-mindedly he moved the palm of his hand over the surface of the table, making semi-circles of particles of fried soda bread. Then he crouched forward, his gnarled hands clutching the wooden sides, the very straps of his braces cutting into his shoulders with the tension of his pose, and he cried. Not tears of salt and water, but just audible sobs of dry emotion, 'Jasus! Jasus! Jasus!'—a prayer torn from the depths of a powerful frame. Frequently he put up his hands and rubbed the tufts of white hair on the sides of his bald head, an unconscious attempt to keep the news that Maggie had told him out of his brain.

Seldom had he seen her in such good form. 'Aw, my God! Sweet mother of God, Mick, how could you do it again?'

His voice was slow, calm and tortured.

'Arthur Keenan and Joe Marley have you for a complete lug. No they haven't, you're doing it all yourself. You're the laughing stock of the country and so am I. Have I to go back again to Paddy Magill, make a fool of myself with a bottle of whiskey, and tell him there's another of his daughters you've "asked for" and won't take?'

He stopped and looked round at Mick, unperturbed and lacing his boots, prompting him with a nod and direct eye contact. Getting no response, he went on, 'An awful fine wee girl. Sure everyone knows about you anyway and nobody takes you seriously. You have asked every woman in five or six townlands, and threw them all up. You get mad drunk in the town, and then go running with another bottle of whiskey to some man's house. Sweet God, when are you going to get sense?'

His father's anguish seemed to mean little to Mick. He quietly reached over and took the final mouthful from the cup of tea, put on his coat, opened the half-door and went out, leaving his father slumped at the table with the dishes to wash. Outside, three speckled hens and a half-pheasant rooster picked titbits in the street, a black and white dog walked over wagging its tail, and the dun mare snorted a welcome from the stable stall. All this Mick Wilson took as his due. Before him the frost was lifting in the valley like a giant theatre curtain, rising on the panorama of the mountains and the Lough. The autumn colours, convivial in morning sunshine, smiled with a vibrancy far beyond depiction by any mortal's art. Hues of brown, red and green, from heather, grass, rowan, sycamore and whin, deepened in colour where the oakwood swept along the shore. The country was covered in a huge tweed coat. It was nature at its most vivid, lost to Mick, because he had been used to it all his life.

He was also used to Maggie McGrain. She stood, as always, four square behind the splendid iron gates that she had engaged McElhenny to forge for her. Resolute in design, they were painted green, with white tips on the uprights, and swung from stout pillars built by James Moore—an assertion of boundary Maggie reinforced by constantly touching up the ironwork, and keeping the masonry sparkling with applications of liquid lime. For Craigarran they were a new feature, blocking off Maggie's area from the rest of the street. Recently she had taken to not coming out from behind them, to walking down the back fields and over the stepping stones to the Far Road, if she wanted to go to the town. Her sense of territory extended to taking the postman to task for leaning his bicycle against the gates, and threatening John Wilson with court action if his hens strayed through the bars over to her side.

Maggie was in many ways a handsome woman for her years, square of shoulder and forehead, with a thick thatch of pulled-back grey hair. Healthy as a moorhen, and not too tall. She had a voice like stone chippings in a tin bucket, and with it she shouted from behind a pair of folded arms: 'You'll not take her either, Mickey Wilson, you're not a man at all. Dinny Coyle told me this morning, when you were still lying in your bed, that them two drunken scuts, Keenan and Marley, called to his house last night. You asked another daughter of Paddy Magill's to marry you. Well, you've asked every woman in the parish and you never got one yet. Not a one would take you if your father went back to make a real match. When Luke comes home from America, he'll get the farm. You have nothing. You couldn't graze a buck goat; you don't own as much grass as would wipe your arse! There's not a woman in the country would pish in the same field as you. Do you hear me? Are you listening to me? Pish in the same field as you!'

That said, she rolled up her sleeves, and squared herself in her regulation pinny and ankle-high rubber boots. Then, revelling in an old woman's prerogative to be vulgar, she widened her stance, again folded her arms, and stuck out her chest, challenging Mick to fight. But it was futile, water off a duck's back, only provoking a cheery, 'You're right there, Maggie!', an offhand dismissal that further frustrated her, giving rise to a firm 'You impudent skittering monkey!' as she turned in disgust from the gate and repaired to the house.

When Mick went to the back of the carthouse for a bucket of corn, there was a small black mouse in the barrel. He could hear it (even before he saw it): the light swish of its scamperings as his shadow fell over its world. It was jumping now, futile, exhausted leaps of six inches, trying to run up the concave interior, then somersaulting back on the corn. A tiny vertebrate, bloated with hard tack, probably thirsty, trapped and vulnerable, with no way of knowing that the hands enfolding it were obligingly lifting it out.

From the carthouse door, his father watched, saw him lean into the barrel, gently roll his shoulders, then straighten to place the mouse up on the wall. Even as a small boy, he wouldn't hurt anything. You never knew what to make of him, caring as he did about everything, while caring about nothing at all ... He wasn't like anyone else.

Luke was different. He'd have given the mouse a bat of something, without a second thought. But Mick wouldn't. And who under God would go around the country asking for women they didn't want? John Wilson shuffled a bit closer and stood at the wheel of the upturned cart, his great frame encroaching on his son's space, blocking the passage between the hub and the wall.

'The next woman you ask, you'll marry her, my boy,' he said in the most measured of tones. 'Upon my soul you will!'—an edict sealed by the knuckles of his right hand, white where he gripped the twelve o'clock spoke of the wheel, and his left hand pounding the interlacing pattern of 'The Needle' in the wall. That was all he said ... but it was enough.

Mick, carrying the bucket of corn, pushed up between the dun mare and the black horse. Not a man in the country would have ventured into the stable, never mind brush up the mare's side. She gathered herself, humped her back, swished her tail and pawed a hole in the hard blue clay with her right front foot. Her neck was arched, her eyes flashed, and her long ears lay back against a flaxen mane. Her coat was shining and, as she rippled her muscles, areas on her flanks changed from bay to black to shore brown. She tossed her head above the manger, and then swung it like a serpent to snap her teeth at imaginary foes between her shoulder and her knees. Full bred, fifteen hands three, whalebone, half-racing thoroughbred, the rest hackney and Irish draught, she had the temperament of an asp and was the trickiest foal to ever squeal, kick and snap its way through Hilltown's Hollentine Fair. John sobered the next morning to find he had bought her and the mother—a catastrophe lightened only by the sight of Cyril Morris coming down the loanin, desperate to buy back, certainly not the foal, but his good draught mare. Then Mick took to her, trained, cajoled and mastered as a six-quarter, but never broken. She responded to his offhand confidence with a readiness to go through the eye of a needle at his command.

As he halved the bucket of oats in the box at the mare's head, he passed no more remarks on her antics than he did on the stoic stance of the black cob, running his hand from her withers to her rump as he came down the stable, then making her change her footing as he graped up the bedding and renewed it with dry straw.

He had the two of them out on the street, the mare harnessed and standing peevishly as he groomed the black cob, polishing his coat with quick licks of the dandy brush, driving waves of dust and short stubble down the broad of his back to waft over his rump and shimmy to the ground. Stopping, he put his hand on the cob's withers as his attention was caught by the faint dry clash of a shod hoof, and the sight of a horse and rider crossing the granite lintels of Roark's Bridge and, trotting on up the road, passing the Holly Rock. The new priest, he thought, watching the dark figure bobbing sedately in the saddle, on the chestnut Mick had seen in McElhenny's forge. It was more the horse he recognised: a placid animal, a big slack old heavy hunter with a stiff action, coming up the road. What was he doing? It was not like this man of the cloth to practise his ministry so far from the town. Even Mick could feel the country's apprehension, a different sort of apprehension than felt at the sight of a doctor or a policeman. More a sad final melancholy, the man on the big horse trailed up the road. Everyone saluted him, and breathed a glad sigh as he went past, a spiritual ruler turning down Craigarran loanin, under the vigilant eye of all on the Far Road.

Maggie and John observed him. She seemed petrified, straightening her pinny, wiping imaginary flour off her apron, fidgeting forward, getting herself ready for the dreadful news the priest was bearing. To Mick's amazement, she opened the gate and, with an unconscious lateral movement, sidled over to join his father at the door. She was hypnotised, her head up, transfixed by the dapper figure on the horse. Mick held the dun mare, thwarting any unsavoury antics, as the big chestnut walked past. An animal that wouldn't know how to be bad to you, but an ungainly oul' hure, elevating his rider to a lofty position, from where he nodded piously to his parishioner, and was saluted in return. A vicar robed in soft black leather, sporting as fine a riding habit as Craigarran had ever seen, and displaying an equally exquisite bridle and saddle and an unnecessary martingale on his horse, Father Bennett was a classical scholar, a bespectacled professional Christian who loved academia and had a sense of his own destiny within the hierarchy of the church.

He had been a short time in the parish, but as a former principal of the seminary in Newry, he knew what he was about. On his very first Sunday, he came down off the altar and told Lady Jennifer Moss that she must move over and no longer keep the entire front seat to herself. This ruthless, premeditated sally created an eruption, splashing nitroglycerine on every object of devotion, and caused a schism between the Church and the last of the local Catholic dynasty, as Lady Jennifer dramatically flounced out. Certainly he had lost a patron, undoubtedly he had rattled the Bishop, but he had gained the complete support of the rest of his congregation and, more importantly, clasped a tight grip on the parish himself.

When Mick's father took the three steps forward, the three measured, stilted paces, to catch the bridle of the chestnut and assist the priest down, Father Bennett was well enough informed to grace him with a quiet 'Thank you, John,' a polite murmur that deemed to accept not only the courtesy, but the allegiance and 'Freedom of Craigarran' as well. Then he further composed himself, meticulously took off his pigskin gloves, put them into his pocket, smoothed down the flap, and tapping together the tips of the five fingers of each hand, not flat as if joined in prayer, but more to form a dome, moved towards Maggie, frozen at the Wilsons' door. He bowed his head slightly, and in a quiet consolatory tone, said, 'I am very sorry,

Maggie. I have distressing news for you. I have been informed by letter that your cousin Owen is dead. *Requiescat in pace.*' And allowing a further pause: 'His remains will be arriving at Warrenpoint station tomorrow evening on the seven-thirty train.'

Mick could not help but admire the man's professionalism: his gentle, sympathetic delivery, and his use of the bit of Latin to dignify the occasion and elevate himself. It was a performance that would normally have drawn the recipient to him, respectfully in awe, conveying that someone of his stature was far too important to be involved with such a mundane event. However, that wasn't Maggie's attitude. In the pause after '*Requiescat in pace*', she had come right back to herself, to take control of the situation, and in so doing, reminded Mick of nothing as much as an old priest herself, an adept archbishop, patiently listening to Father Bennett's confessions, weary of hearing the same old tired sins.

'I know, I know, I know,' she whispered, detached from his disclosures, never altering her distant gaze. 'I knew it … I knew it … I knew it: it was Owen's foot on the street all week, and the faint lilt of the music from him playing The Box. It's the foot on the street and the music that follows us,' she confided. 'It's the step on the street and the music. The Banshee doesn't follow the McGrains.'

Her words, like cold winter mizzle, settled on Craigarran. It settled on the men, on the horses; it settled quizzically on Mick. What would the new priest think of it all? he thought, and for a space even the three hens stopped picking lime from the whitewashed wall.

Then John Wilson started time again, when, with one hand behind his back, he led the chestnut the few steps up to Maggie, and with the other shook her by the hand. 'It seems no time since we were running up the fields together,' he said.

'To school,' she murmured, as he smiled, nodded and eased back against the shoulder of the big horse. Pushing him a little—he was not an animal to spin on a sixpence—he had to be cajoled back and forward to turn him around, to lead him over and tie the leather reins through the loop of a horseshoe cemented into the byre wall. It was a show of good manners, a pretence that the horse might be spirited enough to bolt, when it was inconceivable that he would even think of running away.

Then, abruptly, Maggie shook herself, blew her nose in her apron, squared her shoulders and headed down the street. John Wilson knew to shuffle after her, and with little option open to him, so too did the parish priest. The three of them in a line: Maggie pugnacious and determined, John stilted and resigned, and the cleric curiously pigeon-toed and pippety-poppety. Past Mick and the horses, past the end gable of the house, and right to the latticed hazel gate of Pulnafrog, where, as she had done ten thousand times before, Maggie lifted the fastening fashioned from an old bucket handle, and stepped within the cashel's walls. John Wilson held back to allow the priest to go before him, and then the little procession moved on, over the mossy grass and burnished cropping rock that carpeted and flagged the enclosure's floor.

Timothy Bennett had never sensed anything like it. Not at Newgrange, not at Navan, this comparatively small stone circle with the well at its centre pulsed with energy from the past. It was now his turn to stop and allow John Wilson to go on; to take time to stand, while his scholar's mind dwelt on this place, and he sensed that it in turn studied him. Who were these surveyors, architects, builders, who put their stamp on this drumlin, in this valley, long before Christ? This was the world of the Seanchus Mor and *The Annals of the Four Masters*. It was ... and then a very sobering thought ... all his readings in ancient Brehon Law and in O'Donovan's translations of eighth-century Irish life were inadequate. This place had existed long before that; this cashel was but a part of a far greater settlement. He could only begin to imagine the outer bawn, pile-driven with vertical timbers, a vast stockade. Nobody really knew anything about the people who once had lived within its sphere. That was why there were myths and legends to fill the void and reconcile an infinitely more spectacular habitat than now. Certainly this place overlooking the site of the *Táin Bó Cuailnge* was worthy of Cuchulain, a fitting haven for the Achilles of the Irish Gaels. And Father Bennett walked over and placed his hands on the peak of the lintels, which formed a cowl over the well.

Maggie was now kneeling at the Thorn Altar, the natural oratory fashioned from a great boulder clasped by the roots of an ancient thorn, a tree gnarled and perpetually hungry, wicked from a lifetime of fighting for sustenance beneath the rocks and clay of the cashel's southern wall. 'In the name of the Father, the Son, and the Holy Ghost,' she murmured, as she knelt on the chiselled kneeler under the canopy of red haws. 'The first glorious mystery, the Resurrection of the Dead,' her voice rising and falling unconsciously as she caressed the thorn's dark talons, and looked down at the Lough. It was something of the slightest touch of a rebuff to Father Bennett, who would normally be asked to recite the rosary himself.

In a quiet ritual, Mick took the harness off the dun mare: the hems, the collar, the traces. Then he removed the bridles from both horses, and, holding them just by the mane, walked them over to Cullinatee, the wee field at the back of Owen's house, and, slowly, not in any rush to get saying the rosary, he red up the things before joining the others at the Thorn Altar in Pulnafrog. It was where the families from the three houses had always prayed: a mother for the safe return of a son, for a daughter at childbirth, for an ill relative, and, more joyously, for 'the May devotions'. He felt a little shiver at the back of his neck. 'The May devotions!' He was a child—they were all there, his mother was singing, her head up, looking down at the Lough. 'Oh Mary, we crown you with blossoms today; Queen of the Angels and Queen of the May.' Looking at his father and Maggie, Mick was struck by how close they really were. Her shouting and complaining were little more than affection in another form. They had been together for almost every day of their entire lives. The little dramas of sheep breaking into her fields, or hens on the wrong side of her gate, were nothing—all forgotten in the sadness of the loss of Owen. He looked at them praying and, out of the corner of his eye, could see Dinny, no doubt sent over by Alice, peeping, juking and hiding, too odd to come out.

Then there was what Father Bennett would call 'a quiet moment of reflection', after Maggie gave out the last 'Glory be', after their unison 'Amen'. And in a decent space he began to talk. 'His daughter's in France,' he told them, 'nursing the troops in the Great War.' His delivery was in a quiet confession-box tone, and gave the impression that he did not entirely approve—a sort of weary 'if everyone had stayed at home and said their prayers, and minded their own business, and not got above their station, things would be all right'.

'I don't think she knows yet; priorities change in carnage.'

He leaned back, entwined his fingers while rubbing his hands, and began to interact a bit more. 'I had a comprehensive letter from the Abbot of the Dominican Monastery in Peckham Rye. They are in charge of the arrangements and are complying with Owen's wishes to have his remains sent home. Reading between the lines, I gather Owen in life seldom came home; estranged from his family ... mixed marriage. Perhaps you could cast further light?' And he tilted his head, looked over his glasses, and waited for Maggie's response.

In time, reluctantly and very slowly, it came. 'An Englishwoman. He married her in a registry office. A Protestant. Sure when Uncle Pat and Tessy were alive, he couldn't come home. And to this day'— she was warming to her subject—'I blame the bastards that was workin' with him. God forgive me for cursin'. And their carryin' home tales and writin' home dirt. It broke his mother's and his father's hearts. They were ashamed of him, and him all they had. They died on the same day. Jesus, will I ever forget Joe Marley? He went simple. Simple. Lightbody had to engage McAnuff from the Point. Two hearses goin' down the road. Everybody said it killed Tessy, but I used to watch him, standin' lookin' into the ground, sometimes for hours on end, doing nothin'. He took it the hardest. They know themselves whose fault it was, and it wasn't entirely Owen's. It killed Uncle Pat.'

None of it was news to Mick; it had rolled over him a hundred times. But he knew why Maggie was death on the tale-carriers. He had all but forgotten 'The Tumbler'. 'It seems that when Billy Tomelty first came home from America in the summer of seventy-one, he came up from Ballyvalley and "asked for" Maggie, and she liked him, and the match was made. And then them that was away with him said he'd raked Chicago, and the rumours spread, even in 'Americky' letters, and it got to Maggie's mother and father. Seems there was a shockin' furore. They had to watch the river; she would have drowned herself. Anyway, it was all off.'

'We went away together,' John said, 'Me, Anthony Green, and Owen.' He was talking to no one in particular, just going over things with himself. 'To Scotland. Then the two of them went to the tunnelling in London. After a time Anthony joined the Order and,' smiling wearily at Maggie, 'Owen met his blossom in a boozer.'

'Met his blossom in a boozer,' Maggie repeated. 'Wasn't married when he was home for my father's funeral. It was God sent him. I don't know what I'd have done without him. And I didn't forget him for it.'

'Anthony and him remained very close,' John continued. 'He's in that monastery in Peckham Rye.'

'I see,' said Father Bennett, ' ... as through a glass darkly,' and he pushed each hand up the other sleeve and purposefully tripped back to his horse.

Mick had met Brother Anthony, a mountain of a man with rosy cheeks, wearing a brown cloak, sandals, and no socks. An anomaly, a man with all the restrictions of religious life and none of the advantages of being a priest. He would call into Craigarran when he was home for his holidays, doing the rounds of the neighbours, and collecting a few shillings for his cause, taking a long time to talk to John, and telling him he would pray for Luke. It was a strange life, a brother, neither fish nor fowl, caught in a limbo between revered cleric and vagrant holy man. Mick was still pondering it all as he held the chair, and John held the horse, and Maggie held her own counsel, and Father Bennett put on his gloves and composed himself, aligned his glasses, and got ready to prepare to ease up on the horse. What did Geordy Lyons think of Father Bennett? Mick wondered. 'The Vinegar Man', whose tirades against the clergy shocked even Mick.

'God's workers are very poor workers,' he'd start. 'It's the mothers

[31]

that spoil them. Spoiled! As soon as any skittering monkey says he has a vocation for the priesthood, he gets the best bite in the house, the warmest, cleanest, softest stitch of clothes. Then, should he go to the monastery … when he comes home for his holidays … home for his *holidays*! … the mother gets all dressed up and trails with him round the neighbours, the best china's took out, he's sat like a delft ornament in the parlour. It's not right! What happened to fasting and sackcloth and living among the poor?'

And in a swish of soft leather, Father Bennett did get up on the horse.

And Mick again thought of Brother Anthony. No doubt he was fine within his own group. A strict, regimented life in cloisters, the monastery's output of prayers somehow easing our voyage in this vale of tears. But out in the world? Even Mick's father was uncomfortable with him, not sure how he should act—more comfortable with Pilgrim Dan, the blind tramp who stayed the night and collected money for Lough Derg; more comfortable even with Father Bennett. At least with him he knew where he was.

Watching the big chestnut go up the loanin, Mick could only suppress a smile at the Vinegar Man's other tirade: 'Do you see them in the Stations of the Cross? The Apostles! In swathes of muslin, in petticoats. How in the name of Christ could they help Jesus, dressed as they were in women's clothes?'

Maggie went back into the house, and John said quietly, 'Maybe you'll take a walk over to Shannons'?' He could just as readily have said the place-name, 'Coolnafrankey', or the Shannons' nickname, 'The Foxes'. Mick put his hands in his pockets and stepped over the stream, strolling past Owen's, and out the first familiar quarter-mile of loanin to Tievegorm—'Wilson's plan', the arable field and rough grazing (totalling six acres) that ran from the loanin to the river, and was registered in Mick's name. From here on he ran a gauntlet of unchecked red bracken and bramble, tipping his coat until he got to his godmother's. As May Shannon never tired of telling him, 'I carried you up the chapel in my arms.'

Coolnafrankey and the Shannons were waning; Dan was nearly as stiff as his father, Rosie kept herself to the near loanins, and May made no effort to trim her beard, and stayed in the house. Only Sailor was as handsome as ever, and Mick knew never to say that because he was Rosie's, and it would be a slight on May's plainer Shep.

'Good God, look at the height of you. You'll smoke a cigarette? Ahh, ma sound Mick.'

They greeted him, and after a pious 'God rest his soul', Rosie and May began tearing strips off Owen, saying, 'A good beating with a sock full of shite would have helped him,' a vulgarity The Oul' Fox countered with a reflective, 'Every man knows how to kiss his own wife,' as Mick composed himself, and sat on the settle-bed smoking the cigarette. And all the while Sailor practised the Alexander Technique and Shep slouched in a bundle of matted hair.

By dinnertime the word was out: Owen is dead; they are going to bury him at home. The daughter is in France. Over in Brannigan's big meadow, Stephen Flavin, Arthur Keenan, Joe Marley and Old Tom himself were gathering potatoes, bursting the drills with the grey horse and plough and further working the soil with clats: innovative hand-held grapnels fashioned by bending the central prongs of an old graipe. It was a placid drudgery that Flavin allayed by holding court, telling the company about his time in the army and his posting to Gibraltar, and how Owen's daughter was probably a nudist. Sparking a chorus of, 'A what? A nudist? Surely not!' as everybody stopped clatting their drill.

'Yes,' Flavin said. 'People who run about with no clothes on, not a stitch—that's what they do in the summertime in France. Not a rhonean on them.' They had only got over this intelligence and started clatting again, when Joe said, 'It's the truth, because I've seen a picture of her Maggie keeps in the drawer.' Arthur and Stephen nearly pissed themselves laughing. But Old Tom, who wouldn't say 'gooseberry' because it had hair on it, jumped up and said, 'In the name of God, stop such talk! There'll be no luck. The prudders will rot in the pits,' and he looked at the three of them and solemnly stressed, 'Never ... ever ... say ... the ... likes ... of ... that ... again.'

The scents of bootblacking, camphor and coal tar soap swirled in Wilsons' kitchen as the two men bustled to get ready to collect the remains from the railway station in Warrenpoint. 'There was far too much high spirits at Charlie Rosin's wake,' John said. 'A bit of a song and a step of a dance was decent, but after the neighbours left, you young people who sat up all night went clean mad. I know Charlie had nobody, but it was beyond all latitude—sittin' the corpse outside so you could get more space to dance in the room. Men so drunk they completely forgot about him. What did Jem Sullivan think when he came over at daylight? Charlie in his shroud, propped at the holly tree in the street, the house full of men puttin' Bedlam to shame. It was the talk of the country, and not a bit of wonder. Sobriety was the feature most missed. Youse found a bit of bacon in the man's dresser, hair on it the length of your arm, and you fried it with eggs stolen from Rooney's hens. Then, Holy Mother of God, man, when we were followin' the hearse by Lennon's corner, we met you comin' up, driving poor Charlie's pony and a cart, full of drink. You never got to the funeral at all. Nor did half the neighbours. Sufferin' Christ, you drew them back with you.'

John was never confrontational, but he always told Mick what he expected in a roundabout way. His voice drifted off as he began musing to himself. 'Charlie, good rest to him (and God knows he had plenty of it when he was here), didn't break too many pick-shafts. Said he couldn't go up to fix the roof when it was raining, and he couldn't see where the hole was, to go up and fix it when it was dry. He never got too caught up in work, but he was decent. That's all that matters at the end of it, if you're decent. "Give his hands back to his maker the way he got them." It was a good one. Only The Vinegar Man could have thought of it at the grave.'

A wedding can bring out the best in some women, but Mick could see that it was a funeral which brought the best out in Maggie McGrain. To keep her right, a close relative would have to die at least once a week. She came through the gates in a black costume and hat, with the serenity of a clipper gliding up the Lough. A seasoned actress, who had been banished to the chorus, suddenly feted and demanded by her public at centre stage. Mick wondered how anyone could possibly hold a funeral if Maggie wasn't there.

Earlier in the day he had washed the stiff-wheeled cart and greased the axles, polished the harness and cut three suitable laths to support the coffin. Then, well on in the evening, with the black cob brushed and combed, and the front board of the cart detached and placed back a bit to form a seat, the last remaining residents of Craigarran set off to meet the train.

John Wilson drove, with Maggie in the middle, and Mick on the other side. At the top of the loanin, three more carts fell in behind, starting a procession down the broad road. They were joined by others at every house, people who had only heard of the deceased, and a few who had known him sixty years before as a boy. It was a tradition, really little to do with Owen, who had never attended a local funeral or a wake. It had to do with Maggie. It was to her that the whole country was now paying its respects, showing her how important she was, in the inclined head of every adult, and the upturned, quizzical face of every child.

At the 'Dark Place', a brooding crescent of unfenced ground, there was always a gypsy encampment—travelling people, claiming an oasis beneath a canopy of mature trees at the side of the road. This time it was the McDonaghs, a clan somewhere below caravan-dwelling aristocrat, but well above begging tinker—itinerant artisans making and selling tin cans, clothes pegs and, now and again, trading a horse. They were an extended family of spirited adults and ragged children who disdained permanancy and stone, and opted for

[35]

temporary shelters of hazel poles and oilcloth. Crouched at cauldrons bubbling on fires of seasoned oak, they boiled, brewed and further pigmented their innards and outers with smoke, while a solid punch of a coloured stallion, two mares, an ill-disposed grey gelding and a black jack-donkey, picked fresh grass from between the dead nettles and thistles on the verge. Around the trees a menagerie of smaller animals loitered, as streetwise and bohemian as the gypsies themselves. An old man in a dishevelled tweed suit, felt hat, and open-mouthed boots, stood hunched in the entrance to a tent, a shelter perilously vulnerable, tangential as it was to the edge of the road. He was for all the world a shaman, revered and erudite, contemplative at the entrance of his cave, eyeing every horse in the cavalcade as it came up, looking for style, power, arthritis, broken wind. Straightening himself, as in his fancy he is sitting in the dickey of a gaily painted van, and with a pair of good leather reins is driving Wilsons' cob.

Huddie Mulligan was third in the line, an aged but spirited man, an endorsement that could have just as readily been applied to his mare. She was well cared for, a good hard dark bay in colour and, on this occasion, given a bit too much corn. Just as he came level with the tent, the mare started to gather herself and shy: flustered in the smoke, timorous at the general roadside activity, the proximity of the campfires and the particular antics of a scurrying pet pig. John motioned Mick to go back and steady her, but in that very instant the old tinker had her by the head.

'A fine tempery mare you have there, sir.'

'Aye,' said Huddie. 'She's only four.'

With the slightest movement of his thumb, the old tinker turned down the mare's lower lip and took the quickest glance at her mouth. 'She is indeed, sir,' he said, 'but you forgot to add the other score.'

The mare never broke her stride, and for the first time that day John Wilson smiled. He knew the mare's exact age was twenty-four. The string of horses and carts turned right at the village, and struck out along the coast road for Warrenpoint—a train powered by an orchestra: the percussion section was shod hooves, iron-rimmed wheels and draught chains, while the strings were lilting leather, and the horns impromptu horses' snorts. Along the well-maintained promenade they freewheeled, playing to substantial houses in four- and five-acre gardens, gentlemen's residences, one after the other on the land side, and occasionally sited where there was enough raised beach between high tide and the road wall.

On they trundled, past the monument, a splendid 100-foot plume of granite, erected to commemorate a Rostrevor man, Sir John Ross—an extravagance that, for fear it wasn't bad enough, is duplicated in Halifax, Nova Scotia—a matching pair, marking Ross's achievements in Egypt and America, where seemingly, in the latter's War of Independence, he was the only 'English General' to have any success.

Presently they were passing Clooneevan, a stately home, whitewashed yellow, sitting well back off the broad road. It was settled in a landscape of positioned trees, where the evening light pencilled its peaks and valleys in malleable lead. Brooding architecturally, it had secret underground passages, fish ponds in a walled garden, crags of cold stone steps and an ambience that Dracula would have loved.

To this sepia manor, Maggie had come fifty-seven years earlier, a slip of a girl, to 'do her service'. Her employers, the Thompson-Smythes, Bristol shippers trading to the Orient: old money, landed gentry, who, other than an occasional walk through the adjacent pleasure-grounds, took no interest in their two hundred acres of farm. They thought agriculture unfashionable and vulgar; their passion was class. They were aristocrats, entertaining lavishly the gentry from the Province: the Bowes-Lyons, the Brownlows, the Chichester-Clarkes. Here on 17 September 1864, on her very first evening, when taking a stone hot water bottle to the master bedroom, Maggie encountered a strange and unusual man, 'a stout butt of a fellow' as she put it. Dressed in a sort of priest's robe, he had a bald swathe on the top of his head, but enough hair for a pigtail to hang down his back. A wide sash reinforced his middle, and girded a scabbard for a sword. But there was no sword. It was a confident bucko who stood in front of her, his elbows splayed at right-angles to his trunk, his fists clenched at his kidneys as he puffed out his chest and addressed her sharply with the single word 'Hajima'.

'Hajima yourself,' she said, and to her surprise he took a step back, and for his first trick walked straight through the wall, directly into the master bedroom. Quick as she could, Maggie got to the door, opened it and followed but, no matter where she looked, high up or low down, in the wardrobes, behind the curtains, under the bed, he was nowhere to be found. Her story, though told quite matter-of-factly, had an alarming effect on the whole house, terrifying the servants, upsetting the Captain, and putting the fear of God into Mrs Thompson-Smythe, a woman to whom Maggie showed no deference, treating and talking to her as she would someone at home. 'He's like a playboy knows what he's after,' she confided. 'Like a boyo would strip a roost. A strong grulsh.'

Such observations increasingly horrified the Mistress, doubly upsetting her, firstly in the revelations, and secondly in the familiar way Maggie would walk up and give another uninvited opinion on the affair.

The corridor to the master bedroom, 'The Emperor's Walk', as Mrs Thompson-Smythe liked to call it, was a stifling tunnel of Chinese art. The Captain had brought back not just the objects, but the whiff of the Orient. The narrow walkway teemed with ghosts: concubines, eunuchs, serfs and noblemen, who wouldn't let go, couldn't let go, of displaced objects in their charge. A folding horseshoe recliner caught the eye, its frame of bamboo an exotic stick insect, adorned with engraved silver in Shinto design. Its delicate bone-structure contrasted with the quarter ton of ebony in the intricately carved chest and two chairs. Then there was the porcelain and ivory, a world of it. Vases, hand-painted in green and blue, illustrated legendary tales of a moustachioed noble, astride a high-stepping horse. One particularly beautiful oil jar, a perfect globe with flawless alabaster skin, standing five feet high, was decorated with soft fruits and blue finches. The figures in ivory were principally of Buddha and other deities, and the entire collection, lacquered pagodas, terracotta horses, and intricate carvings, reeked of an oriental mysticism and prompted the question: were these sacred items pilfered from hallowed shrines?

Then there was the sword, lying on polished marquetry, naked to the world, its blade of forged iron and steel burnished and chamfered to a surgically keen edge, its sharkskin handle fashioned in a diamond pattern, inlaid with a scattering of precious stones. It was a sacred object, a mystical samurai heirloom, now exhibited on a table, and exposed to a barbarian household's vulgar gaze.

'The bloody bugger's after the sword,' Maggie said to the Mistress, and, turning to the Captain, 'Did you hear me? Are you listening to me? The bloody bugger's after the sword. I think it's his. He already has a knife. It's in the folds of that white paper he is carrying. A gully knife.'

The blood drained from the Captain's face. Maggie's remarks had clearly triggered some terrible recollection and for an instant he was transfixed. Then he started to bark orders. 'To me! To me!' he shouted. A nervous figure, calling for the household staff, the yard staff, anybody. Rallying an expanding group of servants, who were astonished to see, right before their eyes, a reversal of roles, as, calm and supportive beside him, Mrs Thompson-Smythe actually became his strength. She never batted an eyelid as he decreed that he and his wife would henceforth occupy the guest suite on the first floor, that the contents of the master bedroom would be transferred there, and that all the oriental paraphernalia, the sword particularly, be taken from the corridor and put with the Chinaman in the emptied room. It startled everyone that the Captain should give credence to Maggie's story, that he should specifically mention a Chinaman, and send post-haste for Willie Lyons, a master carpenter, to lath the door and seal the entire East Indies collection therein.

His decree also extended to Maggie. She was to be kept permanently below stairs. The Captain's dalliance with spiritualism had convinced him that Maggie was a medium, a channel, and if she was given free rein, God knows what else she might conjure up while traipsing through the house.

That was on the first day of Maggie's tenure—a Thursday. On the Friday, when she saw Mrs Leeky and Wee Minny McAteer begin to trim the kidneys and dice the beef for a steak and kidney pie, she went clean mad. Bounding up the stairs, she burst into the drawing room to alarm the Captain and his visiting pastor, the Reverend Dean Simms. Ignoring them, she extracted what she took to be a seasoned sally rod from the display cabinet and, to their startled chagrin, burst out again, and three steps at a time returned down the stairs.

'Bitches a' Hell! Bitches a' Hell!' she branded poor Mrs Leeky and Wee Minny. Then, lashing the sally rod against the side of the jar tub and splintering it in fragments, she predicted hellfire and damnation for those who ate meat on the day our Saviour died; and far worse would befall those who prepared it. 'Hot pokers, hot pokers,' she shouted, 'and you know where he'll put them! Eating meat on Friday is a very dirty habit; it'll have to stop. You're either with me or against me.' Then, more quietly and threateningly, 'With me or against me, that's what Christ said, "Because you are lukewarm, I will spit you out of my mouth".'

She wouldn't even stay with them below stairs and kept on creating a dreadful furore. Leaving a distraught Mrs Leeky and Wee Minny to their consciences, she stormed once again up the front stairs, brushing aside the Mistress on the three-quarter landing beneath the fated second floor, driving the sole of her good stout shoe against Billy Lyons Senior's delicate lathing, and, on gaining entry, sitting and sulking in the 'Chinaman's Room'.

It was all too much for the Thompson-Smythes, who were by now really afraid of Maggie. In an uncharacteristic display of generosity, they stumped up a full sovereign, summoned the coachman with the pony and trap, and, insisting she keep her shoes, uniform and cape, implored her to go home for good, terrified lest she add to her legacy of a Chinaman, a sealed room, the torments of hellfire, and a broken Narwhal's horn, all in the space of two days. But it was the Narwhal's horn, smashed on the jar tub by Maggie, which vexed the Captain most. Even years after, when the sealed room was so established as to be unremarkable, he still pined for the beautiful Inuit carved treasure, a favourite conversation piece he held so dear.

It was a story well known to John, who drolly turned to Maggie at the wrought-iron gates and said, 'Will you go in?'

Giving him a wry smile, she replied, 'Sure it's only the Chinaman would know me now.'

The road to Warrenpoint was a familiar path to horses and men. Hill farm incomes were supplemented by carting coal from the docks, freight from the railway station, and jarveying from the Square. Better than that, Matty Doherty had for a time been the refuse collection man. His wife described his job as 'working in the rhubarbs', a mispronunciation of 'suburbs' that ruined her pretensions, a *faux pas* that would never have happened to the like of Warrenpoint. Here was a seaside resort that camouflaged a commercial heart, a town that was a seasoned professional, beguiling the public with effortless aplomb.

The Shore Road was now busy with other traffic, as people made their way home at the end of the working day. The procession eased over to allow a bread van with two horses, a carriage with a matching pair of 'steppers', and a motor car to pass. Waves of men on bicycles greeted them with shouts of 'How do, young fellas! Good girl yourself, Maggie!' as they came the other way. They were local stevedores who dug coal from the boats in the docks; their clothes, hands and faces were as black as the Earl of Hell's waistcoat. Often they had a fellow worker on the bicycle's bar.

From the corner at Summerhill, at the beginning of 'the rhubarbs', they were under the street lights. Foregoing the tradesman's entrance of the Back Road, they took the front boulevard, flowing past the three-storeyed terraces and the municipal baths and gardens, into the town, where the public lighting vitalised everyone, particularly those who were experiencing Warrenpoint by night for the first time. For the residents, the procession was equally captivating, riveting them to the pavement, and drawing them to their curtained dining-room windows as the carts went past. Senior members of the medical and legal professions broke the rule of a lifetime, interrupted their evening meal, and asked the servants, 'What are the country people doing in town?'

At the station, the cortège of fourteen horses and carts lined up in the yard and waited for the train. It was an unprecedented spectacle, bringing the people of Railway Avenue first to their windows, then to their doors, and further to collogue with their neighbours out on the street. From there they sent an emissary, and then a delegation, and when no one came back, they all went over to the carts themselves. Two old women knew Maggie and threw their arms around her, delight on their faces, as they chanted, 'Carrigs, Roosley, Sliver Roe,' a litany of childhood placenames they had clung to for nigh on fifty years. Huddie Mulligan (still preoccupied with the tinker) asked Mick, 'Like a good man, put your hand to the mare's head while I slip over to the Travellers' Bar,' but everyone else remained where they were, waiting stoically as a mark of respect to Owen McGrain. Not that it was any hardship, what with the diversion of the constant arrivals. By the time two policemen came, the small crowd of fifty had developed into a throng of three hundred or more. It seemed that everyone in the Point with the slightest connection to Craigarran, and many with none, had come to shake hands and make the visitors feel at home—an affinity bolstered by the last Friday in the month fair, the docks, the jaunting-car trade and, more often than not, tenuous ties of blood.

It was very manly to be smoking, posing serenely with a foot on the spoke of a wheel, or leaning on the shaft of a cart. To have a hand on a horse's withers, or on his rump, was extra good. Many smoked pipes and had a ritual of paring the plug, rubbing the shavings twixt heel and heart of hand, filling the bowl and solemnly lighting up. Others simply cut a whack off the compressed narcotic, and stuck it directly into their mouths. A few even did both. Peter Heaney, in a frenzy of puffing, chewing and spitting, prompted Maggie to remark, 'The wee bugger will go afire!'

Then the 'Bog King' arrived. No gathering in Warrenpoint was complete without the Morris Oxford, and Tom Cochrane, the ebullient chairman of the Urban and Rural District Council, and proprietor of the Crown Hotel. To say he merely arrived was to be blasé. Rather he transpired. In a whisper of tappets and tyres, he was amongst them, the champagne Buddha, bursting from his car. He was a powerful figure, as broad as he was long, resplendent in camel-hair coat, tweeds and brogues, smiling as always, showing the American gold in his teeth, swaggering up to Maggie, and doing something only he could have done. He threw his arms around her and gave her a bear hug. He wasn't that much taller than her, but his width and girth were such that he enfolded her and stretched her to point on her toes, unflinching in his exuberance as she scrunched up her face and kept her arms stiffly by her sides, publicly only tolerating him, while secretly delighted that he had known to do the right thing. When he let her go, and just for a moment became solemn and said he was sorry about Owen, she quietly inclined her head, while he too paused as a mark of respect, before roaring, 'The Talaigh' (John Wilson's nickname) as he welcomed him with laughter and the shaking of his hand. Then going right down the line— 'Dandy, Fox, Dasher,' rocking on his heels, greeting them all by their nicknames, a liberty that, no matter how rollicking, could have been carried out only by one of their own. A native of 'The Wasteland', who, having gone to school with them, knew to avoid 'Cadger' and other names of derision, sobriquets that (coming even from him) would offend. The 'Bog King' was a relative of Maggie's, and she delighted in calling him 'a polished rogue'.

It was difficult for the two policemen, new recruits in a new force, who had been sent round from the barracks to show a presence, only to find themselves broadly ignored. Gasogs, tall and thin, their uniforms hanging off them, their guns incongruous, they looked dreadfully young; second sons of prosperous Protestant farmers, naturally uneasy in the presence of so many Roman Catholics. Could the remains be a Republican? they asked themselves. Worse, could it be a crate of guns? And why had so many decent Warrenpoint people flocked to this mountain tribe? Tom Cochrane's presence was a puzzle, and a comfort, and the policemen began to think of what they should be doing, what they could be doing, when Insey Monday, an adult with the mind of a child, started running between the horses, spinning a tin hoop. It was a God-sent opportunity for the constables to do their duty and move him on. Inoffensively shooing Insey with their hands, it got them started, and was a springboard to stamp their authority on the proceedings, by standing guard at the head of the procession, one at each side of Wilsons' cob—a positive action they immediately regretted, thinking, what, with all the talk of Home Rule, Partition, Civil War, and rebels openly swaggering about with machine guns no more than a mile away across the Lough in Omeath, what are we doing—we two members of the Royal Irish Constabulary, being ornamental in front of a line of peasants, giving ourselves little room for manoeuvre, having taken this stance?

The assembly outside the station gathered itself as they saw the smoke from the train. Rising above the trees at Narrow Water, it signalled sight of the engine, and then its sound. A great black horse, pulling four carriages round the curve of the Lough, well within itself, and cantering with an easy rhythmic grace. From about half a mile out, it was reined in, steadied by the driver, and brought to a steaming, sweating halt, snorting and belching, in Warrenpoint station. Its arrival sparked a great flurry of excitement. Uniformed porters, with the noted exception of Stephen Flavin, blew whistles and shouted, while the Guard enthusiastically waved a green flag. Even before the train had quite stopped, people were tumbling out of the carriages. First a few linesmen in their gunsmoke tunics, then dark-suited businessmen, followed by young women with children, and finally, the matriarchs, dark 'shigs' of clothes with baskets, following the scurrying wave of travellers washing up the platform, frantic to get into the town.

It was a force about to be faced by an equally determined 'front row', rucking to get in. A team led by the resolute Maggie and her champion, the 'Bog King'—a prop forward the full width of the exit ramp, the tails of his camel-hair coat wafting behind him as he propelled his ward forward, his hand on her arm. John Wilson had opted to stay with the cavalcade, but one of the policemen, seeing his chance, moved over swiftly to join forces with Maggie, leaving his colleague outflanked and dejected. It was an entourage that was all too much for the commuters. They fell back and formed a stunned guard of honour for Maggie, who was undoubtedly a dignitary, seeing as she was being escorted by the policeman, and closely attended by Councillor Cochrane. Even Mr Shortall, the manager of the Provincial Bank in Lisburn, and Captain Haugh, a director of Clockley's paintworks in Belfast, stood back, mystified, subservient until the company had passed.

On down the platform they paraded, the perspiring train filling the air with the exotic mix of foundry and Turkish bath. Marvelling at the plush furnishing of the first-class carriage, they passed the second-class and the third and proceeded to the freight wagon at the rear. Here, spearheaded by Maggie, they formed a tightly packed fan of mourners, blessing themselves as the porter slid open the double doors.

It was not the setting they had expected. Certainly it wasn't what Maggie had expected. She had imagined a little cordoned-off area, a sort of side-altar, the coffin discreetly draped on trestles, not as it was, lying neglected and nondescript amongst a squabble of freight on the floor. Owen's remains being cheek by jowl with common chattel hurt Maggie, sparking in her an outrage at the railway authorities, and if it was divine retribution for him marrying the Englishwoman, then it extended to her being very displeased with God. But all this was only for a moment, because a twinkling clasp of Tara silver caught her eye, and through the bric-à-brac a small hexagonal rosewood box smiled at her, and made her heart soar. 'The melodeon!' she gasped. 'It's home. The Box.' It was the exquisite musical instrument, passed down the generations and played at the christenings, funerals and weddings of the McGrains, an integral part of their history linked to the near front handle of the coffin with a light chain.

It's holding hands with Owen, Maggie thought, and with the idea a desperate yearning rose in her. She too wanted to hold the melodeon. John Wilson, who had decided to shuffle after the procession, now saw the melodeon too, and knew exactly what Maggie was feeling; and just for an instant, in his mind's eye, he pictured her, young and laughing, her shoulders rolling and playing at his wedding. An exquisite pleasure exploded in his heart.

In that moment of contemplation, it was unthinkable that the porter, now in the freight wagon, should further add to Owen's indignity and drag the coffin along the floor. Mick, in a quick-witted spurt to prevent such a catastrophe, took two quick strides past Maggie and the policeman, and with the third, sprang through the wagon's opened doors, turning to offer an assisting hand, first to Arthur and Joe who had followed him, and then to Sonny Boy the Dandy, a representative from Sliver Roe.

They positioned themselves one at each corner of the coffin, Mick respectfully placed the melodeon on top of it, and in unison all four raised it to their shoulders in a smooth lift. Then they took three precise and co-ordinated steps across the freight wagon's floor, halted, swivelled and, supporting their charge at chest level, passed the coffin fluidly out on to the platform's sea of upstretched hands. There it was held, as Maggie produced a bottle of holy water, and desperately fumbled with the brown paper bung, secured so tightly that even John had trouble pulling it out.

'Lord have mercy on him. Lord have mercy on him,' Maggie beseeched, pouring the water on the palm of her hand and firing

[46]

great spring showers of it, to bless the coffin, the railway carriage, the policeman, the people, and to dampen any dust on half the platform as well. Then she reached high above her head, and with her right thumb made the sign of the cross by drawing together the droplets of water on the casket's highly polished prow. This was a prelude to the coffin with the melodeon on top being carried, shoulder-high, out of the station and placed in an elevated position on the three laths, which now braced the sides of Wilsons' cart. Everyone bowed their heads and blessed themselves, looked up under their eyes and wondered about the additional hexagonal package perched like a symbol of honour on top of the coffin. And Insey Monday spoke for many when he shouted, 'What's in the wee box?'

As the procession struck out along the coast, the moon was rising over the wood at Killowen, enormous in the illusion it gave before clearing the mountains, reflecting sunshine from the other side of the world, and casting fissures of gold on a waning tide. Going past Nuttall's gates, Paddy Magill struck up with, 'Once when I was delivering a load of dung to Nuttall's garden, the Major himself came out. He's a blether. Told me about his time in the army. Seems when he was in Abyssinia, he was a great man for leading advance parties through hostile territory. His ruse was to give the headman of the district a small gift, pretending it was a mere sample of the caravan-load of exquisite presents trundling in his wake. That's how he got safe passage! Then he rambled about India; how he prolonged a favourable posting by keeping Hindu/Muslim tensions on the boil. The bastard would secretly shoot a sacred cow! Could you believe such a heap of shite? He's pestering young Owen Millar when he delivers the milk. Jamenty father! he wants young Owen to have his appendix out, so as he'll be ready to join The Regiment overseas. Standard procedure with chloroform—that's what he says.'

[47]

'One impudent pup,' said Maggie, who had overheard and clearly disliked the Major. 'He was never really in the army. Just went to say hello to it one day. Then he recruited half the childer of the country with lies and bullshit, and sent them off to be slaughtered in France. It was he who recruited Stephen Flavin.'

'A relative of your own,' John prompted.

'Thank God Stephen got out of it before the war,' she continued. Then, nodding back towards Nuttall's, 'No thanks to that tramp.'

'Do you remember when Stephen wrote home asking his father to buy him out?' John said, 'And Oul' Terry, not sure what to do, went down to the parochial house where Father Byrne said, "Let him stay where he is; it'll make a man of him." And years after, and Stephen knowing that, and him lucky enough to be home and his time done, and Oul' Terry dead, God rest him, Father Byrne came up looking for money for Masses. "What for?" says Stephen. "To get your father out of purgatory," says Father Byrne. "Let him stay where he is; it'll make a man of him," says Stephen.'

Maggie, who had heard it all before, smiled, but she was really thinking of something else.

'I wonder who will come to meet Owen,' she said. 'When my father was dying, he told my mother he'd like her mother to meet him. I wonder, can the Englishwoman meet him? I hope she can.' A motor car they met stopped and the driver turned off the engine. Then he stepped out and stood to strict attention beside it, and only when the entire cortège had passed, did he get out the starting handle, crank up the engine, and again step up behind the wheel. Such was people's respect for a funeral that not one sinner in a vehicle or on a bicycle thought to pass; they all lined up like a string of herrings, foregoing their dinner, hungry, patient, saying their prayers.

At the Dark Place, the gypsies were more than ever outlandish. They seemed a foreign species, with the able-bodied amongst them finding it impossible to regiment themselves, to stand in any sort of line, to even momentarily remain still. In a studied scatter they bowed their heads, fluttering great manes of copper and straw as they twitched and shimmied their respects, making concentrated signs of the cross by tapping their chests. They were a people who needed freedom and movement to extract the oxygen from the air, who even for a few moments, bolstered with the best will in the world, still could not conform. Huddie Mulligan, leading the mare and prepared for the encounter, reached out to the crouching figure in the brown suit, with a purchase from The Travellers' Rest. It was a half-pint of whiskey, a treat for a chieftain, dues for the knowledge he held. And more than that, it was for the day that was in it, the knowing that you can't take it with you, and the kindness and the debt. It was also about a void bridged by old age, and an acceptance of that in a shy smile, a gentle inclination of the head, and a soft tinker's brogue whispering 'God bless you, sir.'

Only when the road started to rise for the mountains did they feel that they were bringing Owen home, as house after house took in their dogs, closed their big doors, and put out their lights as a mark of respect. There was something mystical in the scene, conjured from a time much further back, a combination of the people, the horses, the corpse, the moonlight, and a touch of early frost. It evoked ghosts. Local people long dead lining both sides of the road, and battalions of fairies, for once regimented, standing respectfully in columns, lines and squares, on the lee side of thorn hedges, and behind the whins and rushes on the knolls of every field.

The britchen on the black horse's rump moved rhythmically up and down as he climbed the hill, his shoulders bunched into the collar, his neck arched, leaving his head close to the ground. The great plates of his front feet reached forward, his breath visible as he pulled in more of the road's hard-packed till. Wilsons' black cob was heading for home. The muscles on his flanks rippled as he seemed to pull, not just the one cart with Mick, his father, Maggie and the coffin, but all the other carts, and the increasing stream of neighbours making up the cortège. He was drawing them through time, from a modern twentieth-century Warrenpoint, at sea level, to a high hinterland, where in Craigarran old traditions were enshrined. Every step he took, every contour he climbed, drew them back a little more. When they came over the ridge at the Holly Rock, they began to see the light from the oil lamp in the wake house, flickering through the hedges; the only light in the country not smothered for the night, not hidden from the world by the closing of the big door and the drawing of the blinds.

The cortège stopped amongst the crowd at the junction of the loanin. Willing hands stretched up to assist Maggie to terra firma, and willing shoulders were braced to carry the coffin to the house. It was an assembly of men from three parishes, amongst them solitary souls, and a few who were frankly odd. Dinny Mangan and the brother had walked four miles to hide and peep from behind a whin bush. They had washed and cleaned themselves up, put on their good clothes, only to find they couldn't come forward when they saw the crowd. Maggie caught a glimpse of them and, knowing their whole strain, went out of her way to speak to them, and thank them for being there.

Rosie Wilson's husband had come up from Carcullion. He shook hands with Maggie, reached across the cob's rump to greet his father-in-law, and then stood beside Mick. The bold Stephen Flavin, raw-boned and dangerous as always, returned Maggie's compliment of 'It's fine you look, Stephen, when you're washed and shaved and cleaned up,' with a growled 'Jasus, you're not so bad yourself, Maggie, when you're washed and shaved and cleaned up.' But he was still one of those she asked to carry the coffin. John noticed that it was men with a bit of life about them whom she chose to escort Owen. She wanted as pallbearers the drunken scuts, and of course Stephen, who although fifty, was still as irascible as a man of twenty-five.

Down the loanin they paced, Mick and Stephen, Joe and Arthur, with Maggie directly behind them, cradling the melodeon, leading five or six close neighbours, a buffer between John in the cart and the great swell of people from the junction at the road. There was a camaraderie in carrying the coffin, the arm around the shoulders, the careful smooth steps of the solemn dance: a set performed as the moon shone on the grain in the flat rock, and the infinite grades of gravel, milled by the grind of commerce over centuries past. At Pulnafrog they stopped, marking its sanctity, and Maggie turned round and nodded invitingly to John. It was a bit like when Biddy Cummings had sent the wedding invitation to her Uncle Barney in America. She knew he wasn't coming; he knew too, but after forty years of exile it was nice not to be forgotten, nice to be asked. But John wasn't content with just being asked. Rigid, assisted off the cart, gently pushed forward by Maggie with her hand in the small of his back, he carried the coffin a few paces before returning it to Mick, allowing more supple men to sweep it over the stream, and to McGrain's front door.

The house harboured a dozen of the most tenacious in-fighters in the two townlands, women who had triumphed over their sisters in the squabble about going to make ready the wake-house. Half the country, from slips of girls to grandmothers born during the Famine, were 'fit to be tied'. Old doting women, crucified with pains and blighted by cataracts, harridans, revelling in their permanency up in the corner at the fire, were desperate to get over to McGrain's house. It was partly because it was empty, and partly because as soon as Maggie went up the loanin, they had the ball at their own foot. But mostly it was because of the circumstances, the exotic agitation of Owen's remains coming home. It hypnotised them, like sixteen-year-old girls yearning to get to the crossroads dance, they craved to attend this once-in-a-lifetime international event. A mix of piety and party spiced with such scandal that Owen McGrain may yet be denied Christian burial; may have to be cremated! That's what they had to talk about. To gather, tie, stook, shig, and finally build in a stack. A gaggle of them were as busy as blue-arsed flies, cleaning, shining, scraping, transforming the house, turning it from an empty cold enclosure into a warm and welcoming home; a place with the fire lit, the hearth whitewashed and blackened, the smell of griddle bread, and porridge on the boil. They were adults 'playing house' in a setting to which they had brought extra delft, and linens, and religious paraphernalia, right down to St Bridget's crosses for hanging behind the doors. A tradition of Christian good neighbourliness, so claustrophobic it was often the recipe for a very dirty fight.

Maggie had sent Dinny for an ocean of whiskey. Liquid embers that warmed the older women but overheated Jane Corby, who for some reason did a handstand against the low gable wall, a display of athleticism that, while unusual, sat comfortably within the bounds of an event, where traditionally whiskey played an integral part. When Dan Darby died, all hands went clean mad; they were drunk for days. The cost of the funeral put the family on the road. They had to sell the place and move to Scotland, to pay for the drinks bill after the wake.

With a bit of manoeuvring, they got the coffin into the kitchen and turned. They then navigated the unwieldy object down to the room. Maggie never took her eye off the activity, supervising every tilt, angle and move, as they placed the coffin exactly central on the starched white linens, covering the wooden sheeting of the bed, changing the space from a haven of the living to a sepulchre for the dead.

The women, more subdued now in the presence of their commander-in-chief, occupied themselves with exactitude. Rosie Shannon lit the blessed candle and repositioned the saucer of holy water and the slip of pine, while Mary O'Hare plumbed and squared the drapes of linen and the covers of lace. Everything was exemplary, except for one glaring anomaly. The lid of the coffin had to remain closed. It was an impediment to the standard condolences of 'Doesn't he look well?' or 'Sure, he's exactly himself.'

However, now the judicious matron could trump the card of her more pushy sister. She brought sandwiches. Generously filled slices of commercially baked bread (a welcome change from home-baked wheaten bonnacks and soda farls) which she transported in a wicker basket, covered in the whitest of the white flour-bag teacloths, the edges picked in a delicate lacy design. Now she too could step into the inner circle of those making the tea.

All who could crowded into the house, women mostly, ready with their rosary beads, leaving a semi-circle of men, pipes slaked, hats off and heads bowed, standing round the door outside. 'First joyful mystery: the ascension into Heaven' sounded. It was the beginning of the five decades Maggie was giving out.

To the murmur of the responses in his ears, Mick Wilson slipped away. Down the fields behind the house, over the Stepping Stones and up to Finnegans' on the Far Road. As had been his pattern for the best part of two weeks, he nodded to Big Jim, the girls and Susan, and waited while she went to a drawer in the dresser, and took out a length of string and The Stone. Then they both went down to the room, where Peter, his head distorted and bandaged, his eyes bloodshot and pain-filled, was lying on the bed. With the cord, his mother measured his head in a number of great circles, a daily practice to see how much his skull had contracted. Then, holding The Stone against it, she said the prayer. Her eyes closed, her lips moving, concentrating, desperately storming heaven for a response, finishing with countless aspirations, and a dozen repetitions of 'Sweet heart of Jesus, look down in Thy love.'

Mick sat on the edge of the bed and, spreading his hands, gently clasped Peter's bandaged head. As if holding a ball, he applied a constant pressure, fusing together the damaged skull. Immediately it had an effect; and the tense figure began to relax, to close his eyes and seemingly to drift into sleep, a respite that comforted his mother and put a spring in her step, as she lightly tiptoed from the room, leaving Mick to talk.

He didn't trouble Peter with sympathetic platitudes; he just held his head and in a quiet voice related the country's news, going over the trip to Warrenpoint, Stephen Flavin's retort to Maggie, and the tinker telling the exact age of Huddie Mulligan's mare. This was a discipline of inertia, and Mick used it to test himself, exchanging the increasing pain of his forearms, neck and back for the agony of Peter's head, concluding with a bout of silent counting, a technique he used to block out his discomfort, until his frame began to tremble and it was no longer beneficial to go on.

As soon as Mick stepped out of Finnegans', he could hear the music of the wake. Distinct and clear, it drifted the half-mile: an orchestra of voices, song, clattering dance, and a melodeon's soft refrain. Far from drawing him to it, he felt detached and melancholic as he walked the milled surface of the Far Road. Oblivious to the steel grey panorama of the valley, he climbed down the stile in the bank and into the field above the Wee Holms. Not given to self-analysis, he still knew this oppressive feeling was one he had carried periodically since childhood. Then it was the fear of death that had numbed him; he'd wanted to know how old he was. That's what used to worry him; he didn't really know how old he was, because he didn't know how much of his life he had used up. Like a bellyful of wet turf, 'the feeling' lay on him, a great weight that had no nourishment, no outlook, no lift. It was the whoops of the dancers that had brought it on, Peter Finnegan's torment, and something vague about Owen being the last man in the line of the McGrains.

The Wee Holms had their spell on him. His thoughts drifted to when he was a child. His mother was lying in bed. Spring sunshine on the street. It must have been only days before she'd died. His father was standing with him.

'Sure what I have will do him no harm, John,' she said, putting her arms around Mick and patting his head. That's how big he was, a wee bit bigger than the bed. Even then she was looking for the postman. He could almost feel her squeezing him tighter and saying 'We'll say a Hail Mary for Luke.' Luke must have been a year in Scotland at the time. Somebody would have told him, but still he never wrote. How did his father carry it? How did Rose? It was strange how he was only now missing his mother ... twenty-five years on. At the time he was happy feeding the pet lambs, skitein' about Craigarran, and putting a harness on the goat. The feeling was denser now, darker, fed by the trees and the river and its own intensity, and it was no good turning his coat inside out. He missed her so much, missed the soothing balm of her hand on his head. A great weakness was dragging at him, calling for him to drop on his knees and cry. Instead, he walked over and placed his hands on the Crahuggily Rock. He spread his fingers and, pressing all his weight against it, allowed its granite grain to pitt his palms. Then lower down he stroked it gently, and knew that it was where his mother would have caressed it as she passed. Already he felt better.

Joe Marley always said that he got money there, and if he hadn't told anyone, they'd be slipping sovereigns out from under it for him still. Whatever about Joe, who said more than his prayers, it was easy to believe the legends of the place on such a night. The mass chalice, supposedly hidden in the river, the crocks of fairy gold, the black men playing football, and Haybag's stallion pirouetting on the Rabbits' Green. Mick didn't know if the mythical porcine demon (The Black Pig) was in residence, and looking at him. His only certainty was that this was where his grandmother had come to search and retrieve her boots, stolen by the fairies and invariably hidden here, in one of their unfathomable games.

His meandering thoughts were broken by a glimpse of a hare, and the faintest perfumed scent. Just for an instant it was with him, then it was gone: the exquisitely poised zephyr, and a tantalising familiar fragrance from the past. It stunned him, an apparition in pure clean delicate lines, flashed in a strobe of blue-grey light. That, and the faintest hint of lavender transported him back. Back … back … back … he couldn't quite grasp it, back to something, to somewhere, to a warm secure feeling he had experienced when he was a child. He fought against the rise in his spirits, against the absurd sense of having received some tangible blessing. Bemused and inexplicably elated, he headed back up the fields, past a bunch of ewes sleeping on the Boughinborough's pitch, round the corner of Pulnafrog, and over to Owen's house.

The wake had settled a bit; the first wave of the crowd had paid its respects and had now gone home, and those who remained were crammed inside. Twenty to twenty-five people, drinking whiskey, and smoking clay pipes: neighbours, brewing a warmth and vitality which enveloped Mick as he gently pushed past them and ducked his head to go down to the room. It was difficult to see, and only the cloaked red glimmer of a Sacred Heart lamp allowed him to dip the slip of pine in the crucible of holy water, and sprinkle the coffin lid.

[55]

'Lord, have mercy on him,' he murmured, as his eyes became accustomed to the gloom. He ignored a daughter of Barney McCreeche's and a fella from Trumley courting in the nook behind the door. Deciding to move to the gable end, Mick stood beside his father, Dan Shannon, and Joe Marley's father (Oul' Joe Marley), who were sitting on a plank supported at each end by an upturned crock.

'Oh, I'll never forget it,' Oul' Joe was saying. 'I'd only left him, only after shaking hands with him, saying how sorry I was about Tessy, when I heard the commotion from your street. I ran back and, Holy Jaysus, Paddy McGrain himself was dead. I shook him and shouted at him … all no good. Death's very sudden, even in an animal. It's very easy to take a life, but impossible to give it back.'

And for the umpteenth time, Mick's mind went back to the shock of that lovely September evening, when he had noticed the best black-faced tup ever they had, with a bit of a halt in his off back foot. Wanting to have him right for the Hallowentine fair, he mixed up a jampot of bluestone and teased him with a handful of oats into the wee pen in the field behind the house.

Such a sheep! Two hundredweight of muscle, stomping his foot and facing him before spinning and jumping the wall. Again he teased him in, and this time threw a rope over his head; making sure it was only round his horns, he tied him securely to the swing post of the gate. Passing no remarks on his buck-lepping, nor on his slouching back on his haunches, he began to dip the sheep's foot in the bluestone when he noticed that his tongue was out. Quick as he could, he loosened the rope, and, to his horror, found that he had not checked carefully enough and that the rope had indeed been under the tup's throat causing him to slump back unconscious and he knew the tup's life was on a knife's edge. He grabbed him by his horns and shook him, and the tup's tongue walloped about, and there were involuntary noises from his innards, and he pumped his belly, and lifted him up by the hind legs and bumped him on the ground, God knows how many times, and his shirt was soaked in sweat, and he knew. Jesus, the tup was dead!

A great sadness enveloped him, to think that this magnificent and vital animal had been teased into the pen, not once but twice, and carelessly choked. It had all happened so quickly. Distraught and exhausted, he walked round to the house and told his father, who quietly soothed him with 'These things happen. When your mother was here, I came home one Sunday from Mass and Communion, and passing the good goat, tied her, and came into the house for the milking tin, and walked straight back out to find her choked by the neck. I hadn't realised her front feet couldn't touch the ground. I'd tied her too high.'

Mick knew there was no reason why that should make him feel better, but it did, and he got the spade and walked back round to the wee pen, fully expecting the tup to have revived. But he was still dead.

Oul' Joe's voice brought him back to the present with 'How's young Finnegan?' and, not waiting for a reply, 'That low country's treacherous, shocking to think of it, a gasog of sixteen, kicked to ribbons and left for dead. It's all in his head, I believe. Big Jim's in an awful state and not a bit of wonder. What's the world coming to? Very bitter down there, and our own "lots" not that great either. I believe they're very decent people that hired him.' After a moment John murmured, 'Ah, he'll come on, please God,' while Dan, with a bit more lift in his voice, said, 'By the help of God,' and the three of them sat hunched, looking at the floor.

'Was that the child that Joe Trainer's jack-donkey locked his teeth in?'

'Aye, Peter, Big Jim and them had an awful time prising open its jaws.'

'Dinny reckoned that if anyone had had any brains, they would have shook pepper on its nose.'

'Pepper my arse! McElhenny said it was the worst brute to cross the forge door.'

'He said it was shoeing donkeys that made blacksmiths cross.'

'Well, he must have shoed an awful lot of them.'

'That piebald horse donkey we had, he would run at you and butt you with his head.'

'Well, that wouldn't be so bad; it's the spinning and kicking and biting lumps out of you that's more treacherous.'

'Did the child have to go to hospital that time?'

'No, no. Luckily enough, it had a big heavy coat on it.'

'I mind seeing that donkey over in Finnegans' field, when the mare was with it. It tore over to the gate, eee-awin, its ears back and its teeth stripped.'

'It was a dangerous brute.'

'Some innocent child home from Glasgow could go over to it and get destroyed.'

'That's the trouble.'

'Seems Joe always got some cub to run up the Chapel Hill in front of it, and it so vicious it would forget about the four tubs of coal in the cart, and bore after it, its heart set on tearin' the child apart.'

'For all the cross on its back, it's hard to see it getting down on its knees on Christmas night.'

'They say donkeys do that.'

'So they say.'

'McElhenny loves to tell how Joe, with a sup of drink on him, and not being able to get a child to tempt it, was lacing into it with a sally rod in front of the Parochial House. "Now now, Joe," the Monsignor scolded him, "surely you know that a donkey carried Our Saviour triumphant into Jerusalem?" "Well he might have, Father," slurred Joe, "but he wouldn't even have got to Kilbroney on this stubbon hure."'

'The daughter's in France, I believe.'

'Aye … aye … in the war.'

'Seems so now. Any further news?'

'No.'

'Did he ever write about her or anything? Did Maggie ever say anything about her?'

'No.'

'Was there ever a photo or anything sent?'

'No. Not as far as I know.'

'Hmmm! Strange, wasn't it? A strange job.'

At that, Isaac Walls put his head round the door and motioned Mick up to the kitchen, an action that prompted the three old men to get to their feet, shake themselves in their coats, and make ready to go. A ritual in itself. They stepped over to the coffin and contemplated the lid of it in a final silent prayer. Then, blessing themselves, they too went up to the kitchen to speak to Maggie.

Each in turn shook hands with her and she thanked them for coming. The four of them stood in a warm 'ring-a-ring-a-rosie'; it seemed no time since they had all been at school. Neighbours' children, pleased to be together, in comfortable equilibrium. In some vague way they were all enriched by the occasion, uplifted even, enjoying a sense of well-being that suddenly evaporated when Big Jim came in. He was desolate, silently shaking hands, not just with Maggie, but, absent-mindedly, with them all.

'You've got your own troubles,' they murmured, and she, knowing he would have no heart for the diversions, immediately thanked him for coming, granting, as it were, a dispensation which he seized with another handshake, and was gone.

'His heart's scalded,' said Maggie, and even the Oul' Fox was quiet, as he and John and Oul' Joe Marley went home.

It was a break in the night, an opportunity for those who were not staying until the morning also to leave a time when Isaac Walls handed Mick the measure of whiskey filled to the blue line in the porridge bowl that the second and final stage of the wake began.

Again Maggie had the melodeon on her knee, its dark leather straps clear against the raised veins on the backs of her hands. Sitting on a low chair by the fire, she started to play, her fingers deftly pressing the buttons, smoked ivory against the black of her nails. Rotating her shoulders in time with the music, not one to one with it, but exactly on every fourth beat, like a snake charmer with a cobra, she mesmerised the music box, and it in turn enchanted her. She willed it to tell her everything, to remind her of long-gone jollifications and to tease her with whispered secrets from her past. She played not the type of music they could dance to, but harmonies that were intricate lace; music that turned whiskey into laudanum, and made the kitchen happy to be sad. And she sang in a voice of dry red bracken, beautiful, brittle and cracked. She gave them the old songs, the familiar ones about famine and emigration, and the poteen-maker who 'left his blackbird clockin' on the hills of Mullaghmore'.

And just when they thought they knew everything about her voice, just when they thrilled to that element that was laced with mineral salts, she changed it, and in a new voice, rich and soft, sang:

The holms were bathed in blue and gold,
The river gently flowed,
My heart was full of happiness,
As we dallied in the glow.
The setting sun smiled down on us,
The joy I'll always know,
When you met me at the Stepping Stones,
For the dance at Sliver Roe.

As she sang, pearls of pure emotion ran down her face. This was her song; this was her pain, which she had held and nurtured for nigh on fifty years. She was proud of it, and the whole kitchen rocked in time with her, and May Hardy and Sally Lennon linked arms and allowed themselves the pleasure of crying too. Warm, sad and euphoric, they all gently followed her in the chorus of each second line and knew that for a moment Maggie had entrusted her heart to them, and they held it tenderly in the palms of their hands.

My heart was full of happiness ...
The joy I'll always know ...

... stopping, blowing her nose, and through her tears, smiling and rising it a bit,

When you held my hand and smiled at me,
And we danced at Sliver Roe.

Then she changed the tune, upping the tempo. May Hardy began a step of a dance. Unsure at first, it developed into a slow slip jig on the hearthstone. Then a hornpipe, in which Mick joined, followed by a fairy reel and 'The Siege of Ennis', which had them all involved, singing, laughing, drinking, forgetting the corpse and the cares of the world.

That is the wonderful irony about drink at a wake. Those who say their prayers, remain sober, helpful and dignified, are often looked upon as cold and aloof. Billy McKeever drank half a bottle of poteen and got so drunk he couldn't suck his thumb. He roared and shouted and sang and danced. Well, he grunted and slabbered in a vague rhythmic fashion that resembled song, while shuffling in the corner by the door of the room. Then he collapsed on the floor and cried: great floods of tears to join the dribbles at his mouth, and drop in a chain of honey and treacle globules, first on his shirt, and then on the floor. He sobbed praise and desperate expressions of grief. What a fine fella Owen was, how much he would miss him, how he felt he could not go on. Maggie was delighted, and came down the floor and stooped to cradle his head and further console him, putting aside the fact that Billy had never met Owen, and his emotion was the outpourings of one Maggie would normally describe as a drunken scut.

Poor Alfie Synge was a schoolfriend of Owen and could not get over the sight of his mate's coffin in the railway van. Seven hours later, very drunk, he was still talking to himself about it. 'You never get away from it, the brown box. You could live on the top of the mountain, hide along the shore, it knows where you are—always waiting for you, spoiling your life. Go to America, it's no good; go to London, it's all no good. We're just like a bun in a breadcart—we never know when we'll be lifted and took away.'

As the first slash of light cut the sky over Clermont, Maggie McGrain took a deep breath, straightened herself and felt very proud, gratified that she, a woman, had stayed up all night, done her duty and given her cousin a great wake; a real 'belt of the hammer' wake, with decent singing and dancing, whiskey for the neighbours, and plenty of craic. She was also delighted with the crowd that had come, with the bloodlines of the country which had surged to her banner, and underlined her standing in a dozen townlands.

With great deliberation she put the melodeon back in its box, making it comfortable, and closed the lid with the sad reverence of one who knew they would never play it again. For some reason she was relinquishing her title to it because, instead of keeping it herself, she handed it to Mick so he could put it up on the top of the dresser, leaving it waiting in an empty house.

The porridge pot on the crook was brought to the boil and, to the refrain of Maggie's 'Get that down your shirt', bowls of gruel were handed out. Most people ate it with a pinch of salt, a few added a splash of buttermilk, while Arthur Keenan, in an orgy of extravagance, added sweet milk to his, and a spoonful of sugar as well. It was a repast that occupied everyone in the kitchen and afforded Maggie a quiet moment with Owen down in the room, sprinkling the coffin with holy water and whispering 'Eternal rest grant to him, O Lord, and let perpetual light shine upon him. May he rest in peace. Amen.' While, like a mother fussing over a boy on his First Holy Communion day, telling him to stand straight, licking her hand to smooth down his hair, and positioning him in the middle of a coat two sizes too big, she fussed over Owen, brushing minute shives of thatch from the coffin lid, and repositioning everything on the wee table at the side of the bed.

Then, 'Dennis, where are you?' she shouted—a correct ceremonious address that had people glancing at each other. 'Come

[62]

down here this minute and sit with Owen. I'm going over to the house to do a few turns.'

Mick could see that it wasn't a task Dinny readily warmed to. Even in God's daylight, even with the lid closed on the coffin, he did not want to sit with the corpse. Not on his own. But he had to, because the matriarch of Craigarran was now thanking everyone (a directive to go home) and issuing a further decree.

'We'll bury him with my father. There wouldn't be room for him with Uncle Pat and Tessy; not with them being side by side.'

Mick, Arthur Keenan and Joe Marley, armed respectively with a spade, a pick and a shovel, headed off to dig the grave. The countryside looked different, clean and new, the touch of frost exposing a profusion of glistening cobwebs and turning the stream into liquid light. A still morning, perfectly calm, when God's hand was on the country, ordaining it slightly chilled and unscented, while He weighed everything in autumnal colours of red, purple and green, tinged with brown and white. Fresh daylight, when two hares boxing in Knockacullen, a fox sauntering across the loanin, and a weasel standing on the ditch, all resented the human intrusion. When even the hazel, rowan, thorn and holly arched their eyebrows and scolded the three men for violating this sacrosanct time when humans shouldn't be abroad. It was such a perfect morning, you just knew it would rain in the afternoon.

The three felt good. Tiredness would rest on them later in the day. The longer a family's history in a parish, the farther back in the cemetery will be their graves, and McGrains' plot was very far back. It was overshadowed by the ruins of St Bronagh's monastery, right in amongst the curiosities and the markers of uncut stone. Beside 'Wee Jimminy', the little pagan god refashioned as a crucifix when the new religion arrived. Cheek by jowl with the resting place of Giant

Murphy, with the high Celtic cross, and with the dressed stone obelisk, itself two foot square and eight foot high. Yet their grave was distinctive, a half-ton slab of granite with the single name 'McGrain' chiselled on its face. It was a robust statement, the seven heavily incised letters claiming clan possession, and reminding the living of the importance of the dead.

Striking powerful sharp strokes with the spade, Mick marked out the sods on the top of the ground. A rectangle, four feet wide by eight feet long, was lifted in sixteen squares and laid carefully aside. Then Arthur stepped into the space and started to pick the packed, sandy soil, loosening it, trimming the edges with the spade and, when he had a few shovelfuls, throwing it up on the side. God knows how many souls had been laid to rest there over the years, how many times the same soil had been shovelled in, and shovelled out, in that ritual in the chain of life, where in the normal course of things we bury the link in front of us and are in turn buried by the link behind. Craigarran had an observance of keeping their dead 'well up to the sun', and Mick knew that at his grandfather's funeral the legendary patriarch Canon McGurr had insisted the grave be eight foot deep. This edict was complied with until the actual interment, when his Grandmother Cassy saw the pile of soil and the hole in the ground. She went clean wild, grabbed a long-handled shovel and filled in about four feet before she would let the coffin go down. 'We're burying Terry, not sinking him!' she snapped at the Canon. Her tantrum so knocked him back on his pasterns, he visibly wilted and took refuge by saying the prayers.

James Scullion had seen a lot of graves opened in his time. Apart from six months working in Chancellor Maybury's wife's garden, an ordeal he never tired of recounting, he had hung about the graveyard all his life, opening a grave now and then for somebody who had nobody, and generally putting himself in charge of the dead.

'Jasus,' breathed Arthur. 'For fear Joe reading the headstones isn't bad enough, Scullion's looking over the wall.'

'"Patrick Murphy, Killowen, The Irish Giant",' Joe recited. '"This young man was admittedly the tallest man in the world at the time of his death, his exact height being eight foot one inch". He was born 15 June 1834 and died at Marseilles 18 April 1862. He was only twenty-eight. He was in a circus or something. The remains were embalmed, brought home and "interred in Kilbroney graveyard on 18 June 1862".'

'Look at this one. It has a heart on it, with an arrow through it, and a face. I suppose that's Christ's face. Then a rising sun with "IHS" in the middle. Other arrows pointing up, a chalice and "Memento Mori. Here lieth the body of Alan Crilly, son of Colin Crilly, who died the 9th day of December 1718, in the twelfth year of his age". God help people. Crilly's not a local name; it's not a name that I have ever heard before.'

'Talkin' about names,' Joe was smiling mischievously, 'have you ever thought how "The Vinegar Man's" name doesn't sound like one of us?'

'"The Vinegar Man?"' Mick asked.

'Geordy Lyons, you know—his real name. What sort of a name's that for a Catholic? Bit of a mix-up in the jerseys there somewhere. It's a wonder they didn't call him Brendan or something like that. Brendan Lyons. Now that sounds more like one of us. The other side of the house: if they have a bit of a suspect surname—say McWilliams – they balance it with Sammy or Ivor. You see, that's why "The Vinegar Man" is always getting the boots into the clergy. He's not really one of us.'

'Is that why he's forever going round the Stations of the Cross?' Mick countered.

'I see you're defending him,' Joe said with an even bigger smile. 'Wilson … I wouldn't be so sure about that. Wilson doesn't sound like one of us!'

At fifty paces from the graveside, James Scullion (now accompanied by Larry White, Maggie's emissary, with a bottle of whiskey) couldn't restrain himself. He must have felt Joe's readings to be a challenge.

'A big, strapping, bouncy woman in a long brown dress and a hood,' he shouted. 'Bare feet, walked unconcerned over whins and stones; she had a pair of rosary beads around her middle and a leather belt. Landed in Killowen, but stayed only the one night. Next ramstam.' James was now at the grave and in full swing, great sweeps of his arms pinpointing every location from the top of the mountain to the edge of the shore. 'Up to that house of Bohil Sweeney's in Levellyclonone, but couldn't settle herself there either. So down here she came—St Bronagh herself and six nuns—to build that chapel and convent, and convert our pagan forefathers.' It was sterling stuff. James made it sound like yesterday, rather than from a past of almost a thousand years.

At about four feet deep, the men started to look for other occupants of the grave. Down on their knees, brushing with their hands, wishing that James Scullion would stop giving advice, they gently tapped with a spade, and were relieved to find the previous coffin well positioned and preserved. Maggie's father, Peter Owen, was resting in the spot dug for him by Mick's father and Owen, who was now about to be buried himself. Continuing, they deepened the grave on the shore side, as Maggie had instructed, while James regaled them with the big wind of '39 that had blown away the fairies, the Famine of '48, and the finding of St Bronagh's bell in the bough of a tree. Standard fare, until he brought them up short with 'Do you see that headstone there?', pointing at the obelisk. 'It took twelve horses to pull that over the Chapel Hill. There's twenty-eight pillars the same as that in the structure of Liverpool Town Hall. I know Liverpool's a city, but they still call it the Town Hall. There's another four foot of that below the ground.'

'Who's it over?' Mick asked.

'It defines the final restin' place of a woman whose son pushed her over the mountain in a wheelbarrow from Kilcoo. It was a desperate bad night, and he stopped at Downeys' on the ridge of Crotlieve for a cup of tea. "Have you anyone with you?" they asked. "My mother," he said. "Your mother! Well, for the love of God, take her in." Well, when he brought in the coffin, it scared the livin' shite out of them. There was only room for it to be propped up straight in the wee house. He stayed that night; and the next day, after he'd buried her, he went straight to Redmond's stoneyard in Newry, and seen that stone. Redmond didn't want to sell it, but thinkin' yer man couldn't afford it, he asked ten shillings or whatever would have been a good price at the time. Well yer man surprised him, said he'd take it, and Redmond couldn't go back on his word. Funny, there's no mark or name or nothin' on it—just them bits of chamfers, but sure as we're bound for Alabama, there's twenty-eight more like it in the Liverpool Town Hall.'

From the pile of dry red earth, which Mick and Arthur and now Larry White had thrown out from the grave, because after his readings Joe had done little else but sit on Wee Jimminy and sup whiskey, the men silently picked any obvious fragments of bone. Nothing identifiable like a rib, a skull or a fibula, but little pieces of one or more skeletons that Mick could cup in his hands, and replace and cover in the bottom corner of the grave. Then he dusted one hand off the other, and the Craigarran men blessed themselves, and went over to rub their eyes with the water from St Bronagh's Well, because it had a cure in it. And James Scullion, pleased with his morning's work and having seen to it that they had done nothing wrong, went home. As soon as he was out of earshot, Arthur asked, 'Did any of you know we were bound for Alabama?' and they all smiled.

John didn't want to move. He craved to lie there in the heat, pain free, on the broad of his back. After all the years of chiding and cajoling Mick out of bed in the morning, now on his own, he didn't want to get up, didn't want to make the first movement that starts the day. But he was glad to have the night behind him. With Mick away, the loneliness had come back. The cold black terror that gripped him, his Uncle Joe must have been inflicted with it too, he thought. After Lizzie died, Joe would have done anything—drunk, céilied, slept in the loanin, anything but go into his own empty house. John was so ashamed of it, he couldn't tell anyone. It was getting worse, a great sadness that pulled him into a void of despair. It was as if his soul was panic-stricken at the thought of death, that it somehow knew about rejection in the final judgement and could feel the hopelessness of an eternal solitary confinement in Hell.

Throwing back the blankets, John slowly twisted on the hair mattress and gave his arthritis the pleasure of a long, low, torturous shout, 'Agh Christ!', something he would never have done if Mick had been there. Sitting on the side of his bed, he put on his dungarees and stuffed his feet into his boots, glad that he had had the presence of mind the night before to keep on his shirt and socks. His pains had never been worse; they were telling him it was going to rain. He sat there for a moment, a crouched study in sandstone, his passive exterior masking the turmoil in his head.

It was easier if you had nothing, John thought; you were just as well in a cotter house. Land only tied you. That's why Luke stayed in America. It was the freedom. Scotland was freedom: you were away from home, you had the ball at your own foot. But America! That was out of all latitude; there were no restrictions, no traditions, nothing. You could fly an aeroplane. But that was all grand when you were young. When you got on a bit, you wanted an anchor, a furrow to walk in. Freedom could be very lonely when you were old.

John's thoughts turned to Mick. He was a puzzle. When he told him that he had gone into Finley, the solicitor, and had the name on the deeds of 'Tievegorm' changed from John Wilson to Michael Wilson, not one blind bit of notice did Mick take. Mind you, that was all he told him; you don't tell anybody about your will. Well, not if you've left them something; it would be a sort of bringing them to heel. He'd left fifty pounds to Rosie and the children in 'Cullion, and the home place would go between Luke and Mick. Finley advised against it, thought it too complicated, but he worded it in such a way that Mick owned the house and land, but Luke, if he ever came home (sure he never would come home), at least would have a place to stay. His mother would have wanted that. Scrolls of parchment turned in the great sandstone head. Deeds, maps, wills, signed and witnessed on the best farm in the country—Finley's desk.

Down in the kitchen he put a handful of dry red bracken on the embers of the previous night's fire, raked over a bit of coal and, with a turn of the fans, rekindled a flame. He was glad there was water in the kettle on the crook; it meant he need bend one time less in the purgatory of making the porridge and the boiled eggs.

Outside, he wanted to get the 'turns' done before the crowd arrived. There was plenty of straw in the manger, so he got a bucket of water from the stream and, carefully keeping tight to the cob, left it at the head of the dun mare. Only then did he take the 'Black' out, give him a handful of oats in a bucket, and tie him to the stable door.

Back at the house, he poured a mug of hot water from the kettle, stropped his razor and sat at the head of the table to shave. Taking time to adjust the mirror, propping it against the sugar bowl, finding his focal length, then, with practised sweeping strokes, he removed foam and stubble as satisfactorily as he had once swung a scythe. That done, he put the tin basin on the chair, filled it with spring water from the bucket at the door, and in the great male tradition of snorting, grunting and blowing, cupped water in his hands and, bending just a little, scooped it up to wash his face, ears and neck. Up in his bedroom, he shuffled into his good suit and heavy black coat, beaten by only one thing: Mick wasn't there to tie his shoes.

Over the river, across the fields and down the loanin, men gathered for the lifting of the corpse. Unhurried in their best clothes, they congregated in Craigarran Street. Pat Quinlin, a gentle soul if ever there was one, was very taken with the black cob. Removing his coat to brush the horse, Pat displayed an unusual pair of drawers. Rising above his trousers nearly as far as his oxters, they were dark blue in colour and had white sheep interwoven in the cloth. James Lynus got so fascinated by the garment, he actually went over and plucked at it.

'He'd go up the cat's arse for news,' growled Stephen Flavin, as Pat explained to James, 'My sister sent them from Chicago. There's

[69]

a matching shirt with them; you're supposed to wear it and the drawers in bed.'

'A good kick on the hole would fairly help Lynus,' further counselled Flavin, while Pat, delighted with the quiet nature of the cob, laced into brushing and curry-combing him and knelt on his cap to groom the feathering on his legs. The horse, jet black with three white socks and a white blaze, had magnetism. Twelve hundredweight of controlled power, a perfectly balanced force, both handsome and beautiful, his mane and tail an exquisite plumage, almost unnaturally copious and ornamental, and, in the way James Lynus couldn't help pinching the American drawers, even reserved men couldn't resist touching the cob. Like Pat Quinlin, they wanted to be involved: getting the harness on him, the collar, hems, britchen, straddle, leading him the few paces across the street and backing him under the upturned cart. Drawing down the shafts, hooking the chains, tying the bellyband, and feeding the rope through the rings for the driving reins. Even Stephen Flavin seemed to have mellowed a bit because he jumped up and removed the front board to brace the sides farther back, forming a seat for Maggie and John.

There was a stark finality to seeing the hearse come up the road. Like a great black sheepdog, it had the power, even from that distance, to bunch the people and hunt them to Owen's door. There they resembled tall sheaves of dark rushes, standing passively, hats off, heads bowed, murmuring responses to Maggie's final prayers. Then, in groups of four, they lifted the coffin. Out of the house, over the stream, and to the cry of the curlew and bleats of a ewe, up Craigarran loanin for the last time and on to the main road. John and Maggie followed, sitting erect on the 'front board', both old enough to have put the dismay—because that is all it ever was—of Owen's death quietly behind them. Old enough to drift in a limbo, comfortable with mortality, allowing the coffin, the neighbours, the cob, even the rattle of the hubs and the grind of the big shod wheels to be on the periphery of their senses, as Maggie stooped and tied the scattered laces of John's shoes.

At the top of the loanin, a crowd had again gathered, drawing back a little to allow the coffin to change bearers and, as was the custom, be carried for a short way behind the hearse. The undertaker, William Lightbody, was on the dicky, while Joe Wallace paced beside the matched black horses, their plumed bridles contrasting with his stovepipe hat. Somehow his excessive formality galled Maggie.

'Isn't that Joe Wallace just too much of the monkey?' she said, and, to slight him even further, for she had somehow inexplicably taken umbrage against him, 'He's full o' shite.'

'Do you know anything about the daughter?' John asked, drawing her away from Joe, and at the same time satisfying a curiosity himself.

'No, very little. I knew the mother had died, but other than that he never wrote about them. I didn't know she was in the Army. Do they have women in the Army? ... Aw, sure she would know nothin' about us.'

As with the collection of the remains the evening before, each family stood at their gate. The men, their hats off as the carriage approached, blessed themselves and fell in behind, while the women, giving their children a lesson in basic courtesy, remained stoic and reverent, until everyone had passed. An increasing procession of neighbours walked leisurely to the town, murmuring quietly about the price of cattle, the continuing Troubles and, at the Dark Place, commenting on how the gypsies had gone, leaving, as always, rags on the bushes, embers of a fire and, on the trampled grass at the side of the road, varieties of animal dung.

Sherwood the chemist, who had walked up the road a piece to meet the cortège, stood to attention as it went past. Purposefully he fell in step with Wee John McGivern, 'Pinicky' as he was known. 'Dia duit a Seán,' he greeted, and the two of them rattled away to each other in Irish, a language Sherwood had acquired in the hallowed halls of Dublin's Trinity College, 'Pinicky' in the lowland fields of Scotland, working with people from Donegal.

Jimmy Kerr had a penchant for being insulted. Wearing a new blue suit, and right out of his pecking order in trying to take a rise out of Stephen Flavin, he said, 'You'd be a horse, Flavin, if you could dung when you were walking.' He was put in his place with, 'In my day, there was good men with no suits on them. Now there's good suits with no men in them. Keep well back.'

The procession had an unspoken format, a hierarchy within which every local knew his place. A family tree of relatives, interspersed with personal friends, where those closest to the hearse had the tightest links to the deceased. In rows they walked, five, six, or even as many as eight abreast. There was no formality in the number, but what did matter was that each row steadfastly maintained its distance from the row in front. In the natural rhythm of walking, this space was about a yard and a half, a distance that must never be allowed to increase and so break the procession into two or more parts.

At the corner of the town the horses were reined in, and momentarily stopped to allow the procession to take its final form. From the steps of the Chapel, Father Bennett surveyed the entire scene and signalled for the bell to be rung. He could see Maggie being assisted to alight elegantly from the cart, while John Wilson, pulsing independence, had his hands on the horse's rump and his knees on the shaft of the cart as he clambered awkwardly down. Then the two of them took their rightful place directly behind the hearse. It was when Father Bennett began to realise something else, a dawning on him with the ever-increasing numbers assembled at the corner of the town—Owen McGrain and Craigarran were much more important than he had previously thought. Shopkeepers, tradesmen, labourers still had their roots in the hills. Possession of land conferred nobility, and second sons and housefuls of daughters yearned for it still. From cotter homes they clung to scattered cornerstones, and lazy-beds, cherished links with ownership farther up the road.

Now, in a revision of his plan, a redistribution of troops as it were, Father Bennett dispatched an altar boy to have his curate, Father Hicks, also attend, while he continued to familiarise himself with every name as they walked up the street, have them right on the tip of his tongue for when the offerings were called. Yes, he acknowledged to himself, the effort he had put in over this last month had been worthwhile. He knew them all, not just Christian names and surnames, but the nicknames as well.

There were three or four prominent families who had flourished in the locality over the last couple of hundred years. Clans who stuck resolutely to half-a-dozen mainstream Christian names, a practice that left their branches needing to be further defined. Flaxies, Tailors, Dandies, Coits, Dashers and Parchies all walked up the street, nicknames that no longer had any relevance to the individual. The Dandies dressed soberly, the Tailors hadn't sewn on a button in their lives. Harmless titles, which for some bizarre reason could never be uttered in the presence of those holding them. Somehow this culture had defined that to catch the merest whiff of one's own supplementary name, even though it be flattering, was tantamount to a grievous offence.

It was a procession with a grey-black dress sense. A company that only Ian Cambry, in his cream trench coat, silk scarf and feathered hat, had the audacity to challenge, flouncing a frothy 'direct from Paris' style. Father Bennett thought of his nickname, the never-to-be-mentioned 'Lady Cambry', and smiled. Then, with the bells chiming, the horses pacing and tossing their plumes, and the procession up the street at its greatest swell, it started to sleet. Big, wet, grey flakes, landing and momentarily settling on the shoulders of heavy black coats, the cloth often mildewed and in places tinted gold and green; serge taken from a damp wardrobe and given a first airing that year.

Well back in the porch of the church, so as to avoid the rain, Father Bennett, flanked by his curate and three altar boys, met the coffin with holy water and prayers. Then, at an authoritative, measured pace, he led it up the aisle. A fastidious figure, his white alb and lace-trimmed surplice complementing his purple stole. He had the tallest boy carrying a high cross in front of him, the other two with ceremonial-issue candles at his elbows, and a forlorn Father Hicks in simple black soutane behind. They passed The Vinegar Man, who turned to Tommy Sloan and said, 'Just as well there's a good bit of stuff in that coffin. Maggie wouldn't want him in anything he'd wear the arse out of too quick.'

At the altar, Father Bennett turned, and waited soberly until everyone was settled, and the coffin had been placed on trestles in the nave. A conservative lot, he thought, observing their curious habit of crowding to 'the men's side' at St Joseph's altar, leaving just Maggie, John Wilson and a few women in a swathe of empty seating at Our Lady's altar, on the 'women's side'. 'Kindly be seated,' the priest said and climbed the five steps to the pulpit. He spread his hands on the marble coping, and began.

'Dearly Beloved, when Owen McGrain first left home nearly sixty years ago, he had no idea he would stay away for so long; no idea that England was where he would make his life. From stepping across the tiny stream at the bottom of the loanin, it was but a modicum of time before he found himself walking across the bridges of the mighty Thames. There he married, had a daughter, and developed staunch and faithful friends. Yet throughout all this, he never considered London to be his home. His heart always yearned for Craigarran, with its black soil, stone ditches and views of the sea.'

He paused, took off his glasses, pinched the bridge of his nose, replaced the glasses. He allowed another pause before continuing. 'In the same way, my dear people, our souls are never happy on this earth, no matter how long we stay. Our attachments are only temporary, and in the depths of ourselves we yearn to be united with dead loved ones and friends in the Kingdom of the Lord. That is where Owen is now and, let me assure you, the welcome you gave his earthly remains is as nothing compared to his triumphant entry into the Kingdom above.'

At this point Father Bennett slipped each hand up the opposite alb sleeve, and allowed for a very long pause—a studied, troubled pause within which he expected the congregation to grasp that while Owen McGrain had strayed from the straight and narrow, their parish priest was resolutely biting his tongue, and charitably letting all that pass.

'Finally,' he said, 'let me extend my sympathy to his cousin Maggie, his many close friends, and of course to his daughter, whom I am told is nursing the troops in the Great War in France. I know that Maggie would also like me to mention the splendid work done by the Franciscan Friars in Peckham, who sent Owen McGrain's body home.'

This congregation did not applaud in church, but from their demeanour the preacher could gauge a response to what he had said, and from the way Maggie had leaned forward and nodded her approval at the mention of her name, Father Bennett knew he had done well. It had been a tricky enough assignment and, back down on the altar, he began to prepare for the offering collection with a confidence borne from what had gone before. The felt-lined wooden plate was placed on the altar railings, the mourners lined up as if coming to Communion, and John Evans, the verger, got ready to shout out the names and amounts—a litany that Father Bennett would authorise, by repeating the names and offerings with aplomb. He would normally also enter each mourner's name, and his or her subscription, in the offerings book, a task delegated on this occasion to Father Hicks. It was a traditional, and in lots of ways universal, religious scene: priests and officials on the sacred ground of the altar, their followers presenting alms from the other side. There was also a direct correlation between the amounts of money subscribed and the volume of the verger's shout. Peter McEntee's sixpence was announced with just enough tone to be heard, while Oscar Morgan's half-crown registered almost a roar.

And so it went on—the sixpences, the shillings and the very occasional half-crown. Father Bennett, his thoughts drifting to a new motor car, automatically and absent-mindedly kept on calling out: 'Peter Hand, one and six; Alfie Sloan, a shilling; Dinny Boyle, two shillings; Lady Cambry, one and six.' He couldn't believe what he had just said! 'Ian Cambry!' he shouted, but it was too late. Sweet mother of God! The words 'Lady Cambry' were reverberating from every pillar in the Church. They even seemed to be coming from the pipes of the great organ, filling the entire space, numbing the congregation and shocking them to a point far beyond nervous laughter, where everyone instinctively held their breath. The curate, the altar boys, the verger, like Lot's wife, all turned to pillars of salt. Ian Cambry, one pace past the offering plate, was now rooted to the spot. He spun on his heels, stripped his teeth in a snarl, and glowered at the priest. Three seconds in such circumstances can be a long time. Then with a twist of his shoulders and a swish of his cream gabardine coat, he strode down the nave, out through the doors and into the porch, tossing his head and raising his right hand to flutter his red silk scarf. Again the line paying offerings continued to pass the spot where Father Bennett was standing, a sad, deflated figure, too dejected to call another name.

But it's an ill wind that blows no good for somebody and when everyone's attention was focused elsewhere, one of the altar boys, a skittering monkey of a young McArdle, seized the moment. An imp, who had asthma and used his complaint for devilment at every turn, slipped out to the vestry and dipped the charcoal that was to be used for burning the incense into the holy water, leaving poor Wee Davy Smyth unable to light it when it came to the final prayers. Davy's extra-long absence prompted Father Hicks to investigate, and the curate, not being able to light it himself, sent Wee Davy back across the altar to the nuns' oratory, where Sister Vincent, the Reverend Mother in charge of all the accoutrements of ceremony, had the key to the safe in the vestry wall. A very august chamber, securing the unconsecrated altar breads, the wine, the jewelled box of frankincense, several back-up gold-lined chalices, the monstrance, a King's ransom of ornaments, and the supply of charcoal discs in a brown paper bag.

And, just as the congregation was beginning to detect a pause in the ceremony, Wee Davy got back. Now Father Hicks, in a bit of a fluster, took out a new disc of charcoal, lit it, placed it in the thurible and swung it furiously. And in a time-saving exercise to prevent the parish priest being further detained by having to go up to the altar and introduce the smidgen of frankincense that Sister Vincent had left out for him, the curate took an extra large spoonful from the cache in hand, shook it on the now glowing ember, thrust the steaming globe on the end of the chains at poor Wee Davy, and pushed him in the direction of the coffin, out the vestry door. A small boy arrived on the altar swinging a silver fire box, belching pungent fumes—puffs that joined in clouds of goose down, and wafted in skelps of goats' hair, to jolt Father Bennett from his stupor, and choke even those in the bordering five pews who normally smoked War Horse plug. Everyone was stifled except Maggie, who inhaled deeply of the vapour and struck an even more erect pose as she registered her pleasure that no expense had been spared.

There was rain in torrents as they lowered the coffin into the grave. Great sheets of water moved up the valley from the Lough and drowned all things in their path. Every animal in the country was huddled behind a ditch, leaving only those at the burial in open ground. Maggie seemed immune to the downpour, standing square-shouldered and resolute at the end of the grave, John Wilson staunch beside her, defying it to aggravate his pains. But everyone else was miserable, cold and wet. Growler Lennon said that he wished Father Bennett had called out his nickname, so he too could huff and go home. The rain was dripping off caps and noses and running in streams through gullies, to soak singlets and drawers. Pints were absorbed in heavy black overcoats, and two umbrellas couldn't keep it off the priest's surplice, stole and soutane. It was almost pointless splashing holy water, so diluted was it by the deluge of rain. 'Happy the corpse' people said to each other, consoling themselves with the old adage 'Happy the corpse buried in the rain.'

'Happy?' said Jimmy Kerr; 'He must be really delighted. I'm dying to get out of it myself—it's a damn bad day,' a remark that didn't go down well with Tom Brannigan, who formally chastised him with, 'God never made a bad day! Never ... created ... a ... bad ... day.'

Father Bennett made short work of the prayers. He would have rattled through them even quicker, only Maggie was there. 'Dust thou art and into dust thou shalt return' seemed very hopeful of better weather, as he made the symbolic gesture with a few drops of wet gutters from the end of the spade. It signalled able-bodied mourners to start to fill in, shovelling, scraping, scooping the riddled red clay, now a quagmire of auburn slime. The 'filling in' was as much a tradition as carrying the coffin. Neighbours came forward with cavalier disregard for their best clothes. Tramping in slurry, wet at the ankles, and splattered to the knees, the turn-ups of wide-bottomed pinstripe trousers full. It wasn't a time to think of your good Sunday suit or light leather shoes. Life was short, what the hell about them they signalled, as they trimmed, patted, squared, put back the sods, and finally left a shovel and a spade crossed on the completed mound. And through it all, Father Bennett knew he must stay to finish off with a decade of the rosary, Maggie's bearing telling him that anything less, such as the abridged version of three Hail Marys, would not suffice.

John and Maggie sat silently in the cart, weary with the events of the past few days, and the persistence of the rain. Glad to go home, freewheeling down Rostrevor's newly tarmacadamed street, lulled by the percussive sound of the cob's steel-clad feet, a bass note created by the water compressed in the cavity between the frog of his foot and the flat surface of the road. It was the sound of willing hands being cupped and clapped together while scooping up fresh buttermilk from a dash churn. The black cob was taking them home, John to suffer stoically with his pains, and Maggie to her self-imposed isolation behind the gates.

⌒

It was comfortable sitting by the window of the Belfast, Gorraghwood Junction, to Warrenpoint train. So good to be afforded such easeful space that Lizzy McGrain dozed, drifting half-conscious as the country slipped past. Its field patterns were so similar to rural England that only the adjacent vacant plush red corduroy seats (so different from the austere furnishings of the packed London trains) reminded her that she was somewhere else. Here the gentle rocking of the carriage kept her on the border of moving into and out of sleep, a twilight giving rise to a swaddled feeling, numbing her against an abrasive world.

For some reason, her thoughts would dwell on a particular straight path on Clapham Common, a taut black ribbon stretched at an angle from the Balham Road. She was a child, secure between her mother and father, as they walked under the sycamores and chestnuts. Both held her hands, while she skipped and swung towards the copper oxide dome of the bandstand, her progress serenaded by trumpets and horns. Always there were the chess players, foreign-looking men in the shelter of the escallonia, crouched smoking over portable tables and chairs.

Lizzy felt sad, a gentle warm feeling to be wallowed in, almost enjoying the embers of the raw emotions she had felt before. The guilt of being in France when her father had died intermingled with the dreadful horrors of the war. She cringed with embarrassment at the uninvited image of Captain James Pointer, an officer in uniform, erect and aloof. She had joined the Voluntary Aid Detachment with the girlish fantasy of somehow linking up with him, blind to the gulf in status between the two-roomed flats of Elmhurst Mansions, Clapham North, and the real mansions of Holland Park. Her father had never wanted her to be a volunteer. Come to think of it, he had never wanted her to be part of anything, except of course the Catholic Church. Sunday after Sunday, attending Mass in the Friary, and afterwards tea with Brother Anthony. The endless reminiscence about Craigarran from that small room in Peckham Rye. Why did they not go back and have done with it? Then, too, why had she remained in France?

The sadness Lizzy was comfortable with began to turn to hurt. Why couldn't her father have breached the barriers and brought her and her mother to the place he had talked so much about? Was he like James Pointer, who had 'walked out' with her in Hyde Park, ultimately ashamed? Were they pariahs, suitable for companionship at a distance, never to be introduced to 'the virtuous caste'? She roused herself and shook her head. In her father's case, it was not true. He had stayed with them, rejecting the world of Craigarran he loved so much.

As Lizzy dozed, she felt neither excited nor driven to see that world, just resigned, allowing herself to be drawn. She knew so much about it, she could have documented every stone and tree. At the Clapham Common Church of England Girls' Primary School, she felt so Irish. Why? She, like her mother, was English-born and a Protestant to boot. It had to do with her father's teaching her the Catholic Catechism and the anomaly of her being re-baptised in the Friary in Peckham Rye. How ridiculous the nuances of Christian religions, she thought; how diligently they work to keep their congregations apart. How obscene for Christian clergymen in Britain and Germany to pray for the subjugation of their brethren on the other side; to usurp God. Even the common soldier knew that 'Fritzy' was the same as him, coming together at the Christmas ceasefire, kicking around a ball in no man's land, and exchanging cigarettes. Hadn't one soldier, a Londoner, met his German barber, the man who had cut his hair before the advent of war? Yet for some, religion was a great comfort, a source of fortitude through all the horrors; something men clung to when they had nothing else, and a base from which young women who had never so much as dried a spoon sprang to nurse the injured and the maimed.

Lizzy knew her reasons for volunteering were at best superficial: the vague romance she had envisaged with James Pointer, and her determination to show herself, and of course her father, how English she was. She wanted to drive a motorised ambulance, and come back to a London where she would be a lady, transformed from a serving girl. She had never got to drive, or directly nurse, the sick. But, looking back now, it was just as well. Often in the Catering Corps of General Hospital No.2 in Le Havre, she thanked God that she was not closer to the horror. Perhaps her mother's death had prompted her to go to the Front, her father's opposition compelling her when she got there to stay.

She shifted herself a little in the seat. Mrs Pointer had made her seem so important, promising to pay her wages until the hostilities had ceased. The Home Nursing Certificate training, before her posting in Le Havre, was great fun. Girls from factories and from below stairs mixing with the daughters of the rich, each enjoying the novelty of one another's company, smoothing pillows, making beds and concocting beef tea—shoulder to shoulder in the Voluntary Aid Camps on Epsom Downs. But equality amongst the volunteers lasted for only a short time.

After the first week, Emily Pointer and her friends were driving ambulances, had practised bandaging the officers' feigned injuries and had partied in their Banstead and Leatherhead homes. Girls 'released' by their employers peeled potatoes, made stew and looked forward to a trip to the perimeter fence to collect buckets of water, handed over by privates from the army camp.

'Gorraghwood Junction,' shouted the platform guard. 'Change for Dundalk, Drogheda, Dublin, and all points in between.'

Lizzy roused herself, sat up, tightened her mouth and took a deep breath. It can't be far now, she thought, as the Dublin passengers scurried along the platform and the goats looked down from their precarious perches on the quarried rock. Then, with two familiar jolts, they were off, slowly building momentum through the hazel and willow shrubbery and over a rise to reveal Newry and Carlingford Lough. A blue swan sweeping through the mountains, its neck the ship's canal, its head the busy docks. No sooner had they built up speed than they began to slow down again. Edward Street Station, where a few passengers got out; Bridge Street Station, where a dozen or more stepped on; then progressing through the salt marshes on the fringe of the town to the lock gates, and along the sloping masonry of the estuary wall.

'She was the postmistress.' The voices were from the two women who had just boarded, and now occupied seats in the next row but one. 'Very good to everyone, filled in their forms, everything! They went to her funeral because she'd got them the pension, signed their books.'

'And did they go into the Protestant Church?'

'No, no, no! They stood outside. But they went up to the Protestant graveyard with the remains.'

'And they went in?'

'Yes. They went in and stood back a bit from the service at the grave. Then, coming home, they got worried had they done the right thing, and went into the Parochial House.'

'But they hadn't gone into the Protestant Church!'

'No, but they had sort of took part in the Protestant service at the grave. Father Cummins said he couldn't give them absolution—it was a reserved sin. Only the Bishop could do that. So, the following morning the two of them had to walk from Roosley to the station in the Point, get the train to Edward Street, and walk up to the Bishop's house at Violet Hill. And them in their seventies.'

'What did he say?'

'I don't know.'

Whatever about the reserved sin, Lizzy's spirits lifted. With the sight of the Lough, the mountains and the wooded countryside, her melancholy vanished. She was free, free to see her father's resting place and free to move on. Perhaps to take a job as a telephonist in the exchange in Holborn, or a clerical assistant in Post Office headquarters at St Martin le Grande. For her the war had changed everything. Her expectations had altered. She could no longer settle at service. She wanted a rented room of her own.

As the train slowed at Narrow Water, she could almost have reached out and touched a schooner going by. An imposing thoroughbred, high in the water, pushed up by a summer breeze and a full tide. On its decks sailors worked, pulling ropes, adjusting rigging, enjoying the attention the passengers on the train were giving them as the boat was guided between the whitewashed stone pillars that marked the deepest water. Lizzy's mind turned to the navigation skills of the pilot and the achievement of marine engineers from centuries past. How could they have anchored such columns in this bottleneck of tides, a maelstrom at the head of Carlingford Lough? A sixty-yard width of churning current, galloping up the swan's neck at the rise, avalanching back at the fall, only placid for this fifteen minutes at each side of high tide. Here was a cross-section of history. A stone's throw to the north stood the sprawling 'new' castle, then the county road, the railway, the old castle shouldering The Narrows, and on the other side, predating everything, an ancient mound, now a pompadour of deciduous trees.

Here Lissara, the beautiful princess of the MacGuinness', had loved the wandering harper. A tragic romance was sealed when she had leapt from these battlements to perish with him in the dark waters below. Here, too, across The Narrows lay the ancient kingdom of Cooley, the realm of mountains and fertile plain, where Gaelic literature began. Where a century before the birth of Christ, Maeve of the Conflicts, the great warrior queen, raged out of Connaught with 50,000 warriors to capture Tarbh-Donn, Daire of Cooley's prize Dun Bull. In the oldest and grandest epic poem in the ancient language of Ireland, the *Táin Bó Cuailnge*, we are told of Maeve's onslaught, of Cuchalain's 'night after night, hanging on her force's flanks', and of wizardry and death.

Lizzy knew nothing of this, but she did know that the ornamentation of this fickle beauty had not been for nothing. Even on a pleasant summer evening, it had a sense of place, with the 'ivory tusks' snarling from the waters, the old castle bracing itself against The Narrows, and the mound, now the mattress of a heronry, where, as the train passed, powerful grey wings randomly beat out the end of the day.

It was exciting, nearing the end of her journey, to view the country from the familiar base of the train. There was always a little of London in the smell of steam, grease, smoke and the asthmatic sound. Not for the first time, she was reassured by the Post Office savings book in her bag: opening the clasp to have a peep, visualising the neat columns of figures, the pounds, shillings and pence, the accrued interest and the total amount. It was extraordinary that Mrs Pointer should have continued to pay her wage while she was on Voluntary Aid Detachment, that she should have walked round each month from her villa in Holland Park to the Post Office in Shepherd's Bush Road, during all the time Lizzy was in France. Lizzy always felt favoured by her, felt particularly special in the kitchen, when she was coached to bake fine dishes, from the recipes Mrs Pointer's daughter, Girlie, had brought home from her finishing school in the Swiss Alps.

She felt important when Mrs Pointer had encouraged her to write down the recipes. Lizzy knew that she had foolishly drifted into thinking that she was more than 'at service'; she was on the fringe of the family, almost hosting the tea dances in the drawing room, where the lower orders could gain entry by helping the war effort and donating a piece of brass. So much for the war effort. As if offering up a son and daughter was not enough, she paid for Lizzy to go as well, and suffered the added penance of having one servant less. It was all to do with a sense of duty, a family tradition in which Boy (James) Pointer and Girlie (Emily) Pointer were first packed off to boarding school, then Boy to the Regiment, and inevitably to war. And Girlie, too, was expected to do her duty and comply with her family's wishes that she marry and nurse Colonel Trench, the elderly recruiting officer, invalided out of active service with diabetes and one arm.

Lizzy reproached herself for constantly thinking about the Pointers, for still being part of the household, for still in a sense working for them, and for not yet having hewn a place in life for herself. She smiled at the irony of how she saw herself and how they probably saw her: a minion, a chattel so unimportant that, in front of her, they were themselves. But the money was nice, and it was decent of Mrs Pointer to still hand over the savings book to a servant who had just told her she no longer wished to be employed.

'"The Vinegar Man" says St Joseph mustn't have been much of a carpenter. What with the Blessed Virgin heavy with child, and her riding a donkey. Surely to God he could have cobbled up a bit of a cart.' This weighty theological observation posted by the woman in the seat but one in front, suddenly degenerated into an excited 'Gather up your parcels,' from her, as the train glided past a golf course and slowed for the final stop.

'Gather up your parcels!' This war cry created a false sense of urgency as everyone dashed to the leather straps, let down the windows, and reached out to open the doors, even before the train had quite stopped. Already the fleet of foot were galloping up the platform, causing a bottleneck at the turnstile, owing to the vanguard suddenly reverting to inertia and further blocking the exit, when their tickets had been collected and they cranked through the barrier to the outside.

If Euston Station was an estuary, then Warrenpoint was the beginnings of a very minor tributary, bubbling up from the ground. It had a covered platform and a buffer, signalling that this was the end of the line. The setting sun gave the single track, the paved footpaths and the fretwork on the roof a tinge of pink. A picture postcard with a warm wash, evoking for Lizzy images of France.

Lizzy was travelling light: the clothes she stood up in, a simple leather shopping bag, and a stout chest locked and further strapped. The porter, one of those men who not only wanted to be an engine driver but—from the amount of keys on his belt—a jailer as well, transferred the chest from the goods carriage to the left luggage store; and, unlike Stephen Flavin, the incumbent before him, he was polite and kind and touched his cap and wished Lizzy good day. As she walked out of the station and up the street, it struck her how much her father had talked of Craigarran and how little of anywhere else. Influenced by the London newspapers, she had expected low thatched roofs, ragged people, and perhaps a donkey and cart. In its place she was surprised to find a thriving port complementing a fashionable seaside resort. In a five-minute stroll she passed docks pilled with coal and timber, traipsed through funfairs and amusement arcades and strode the wide seafront promenade. The climate was 'Brightonesque', with guest house notices on Georgian terraces, a domed bandstand in the pleasure gardens, and an open air salt water swimming pool that lassoed a square of the tide. Who in London could envisage all this and a boutique displaying Paris fashions in an Irish town? It had already been worthwhile; her doubts of a wild goose chase evaporated as she perused the movement of the boats in the bay. The late evening sunshine illuminated not only the little black dress and strings of pearls in the window of the shop across the road, but the sails on an assortment of maritime craft. Pleasure skiffs

[85]

scurried in the inner bay, sloops plied their trade across the half-mile strip of water dividing Ulster from Leinster, and schooners, their names—*The Olive* and *The Oak*—emblazoned red and black on their bows, glided into the docks on a spring tide.

Lizzy was conscious of feeling free and uncommitted, delighting in the quaint habit of people greeting her as if she was someone they knew. She began to play a game of predicting the form the salute would take, assessing the books by the covers as they came along. A gentleman in a tweed overcoat and brown brogues would inevitably greet her with a polite 'good evening' and a doffed hat. Black suit, patent leather shoes and a flower suggested a retired soldier, and was confirmed by a crisp salute; while mismatched coat and trousers, flat cap and dungarees meant local tradesman, and voiced a cheery 'Hello'. She walked just far enough to see the mountains touch the shore at Rostrevor, and the splendid residences that decorated the curve of the bay. She had never seen so many trees. It was like the park in Berkeley Square, replicated again and again. Whisked green egg-whites rolled along the Lough. Miles of arboretum were stippled with a splash of red terracotta tile here, a stroke of steel grey Bangor blue slate there.

Lizzy stood for a moment at the steps down to the 'Rowing Boats For Hire' pitch, and then walked back towards the ivy-clad hotel in the square. It had caught her eye and triggered a memory. The arched Olde English script proclaiming 'The Crown Hotel' had reminded her of a dreary lethargic time, of droned conversations, seemingly going on for hours, in a threadbare monastic room. Certainly nothing then had conveyed the appeal of the place. How beautiful it was, surely Elizabethan, with its lathes painted black, and its white plaster crocheted with sprays of ivy leaves. It had window boxes of pansies and draping blue lobelia and a tiny garden with yellow roses smiling through stout iron rails. It was a building that welcomed you, solid, warm and friendly, and saying 'Come on in; it's good to see you,' making you feel as safe as when your granny had held your hand.

Lizzy pushed through the mahogany and glass revolving doors to

America! As sure as she had been to the cinema in Balham Odeon, it was New York. The place was plush. It had warm colours, dark panelling, and an astonishing amount of art. The four-foot figure of a youth carved in ebony was better than the Venus de Milo, in that it had only one broken arm. In a display cabinet a polecat with a freshly killed pheasant was being challenged by a fox: beautiful and savage, a tour de force of taxidermy, exposing nature in tooth and claw. A range of artwork was on the walls, exhibited with no regard for theme or style. Oils, photography, watercolours, some accurately depicting views Lizzy had just seen, others abstracts, modern thoughts in tortured colours, crying out to escape from where they were hanging. She was enveloped by smells—onions, steak, beer, and tobacco—and the tinkling of china in the restaurant, glasses in the bar.

It was impossible for her to resist sneaking a closer look at some of the framed photographs. A man in a tall hat was towering over a dwarf in a military uniform: 'Physical Giant. Patrick Murphy of Killowen with Major Tom Thumb'. A pen portrait of a beautiful young woman, 'Teresa, from the Elverton Marriage Case, 1861' and 'Lassaras Leap', the castle at Narrow Water she had just passed in the train. 'Monument to a Warrior, The Ross Memorial' caught her eye: a spectacular obelisk against a backdrop of mountains and trees.

There was a reception desk with a telephone, a ledger and a brass bell, and, in the spirit of the place, she give the button on the top of it a solid dunt with the heel of her hand. It was a call for attention which instigated an alarm way beyond that which could be expected, a shrill clatter that unnerved Lizzy and brought a short, robust man down the wide staircase to the left. He was more than robust; he was a benign juggernaut, a man fortunate enough not to appear elderly, but to carry power though being 'up in years'. He fitted the ambience of the place so well, you never doubted that the hotel was his. He wore a salt and pepper tweed suit, his tartan bow tie giving him the appearance of a British bulldog in an American dog show. As soon as he had clapped eyes on her, he gave an exaggerated shocked gesture, a feigned buckling at the knees and clasping of the end of the banister, as his eyes popped big and round and wide, comical against the way he formed a tightly puckered mouth. Then, with his free hand, he made a great circular flourish, a request to Lizzy not to speak, while his head moved slowly from side to side, pondering, studying, and timing his 'Would you be anything to the McGrains?' line.

It was a question so exactly telepathic, so out of the blue, so corresponding to her 'He's nothing like I imagined, but could this be the "Bog King"?' that she was momentarily taken aback. His question (perhaps because of the strange environment) challenged her, stung her even, and she found herself bristling, lifting her head to look him straight in the eye and snapping, 'Yes. I'm Lizzy McGrain,' a flash of temper she instantly regretted, because, right in front of her, the razzmatazz left him. He seemed to slump, be vulnerable, even sad. Certainly he was no longer acting.

'Tom Cochrane. I was at school with your father,' he said, stepping across the carpet, shaking her warmly by the hand and disarming her with 'You're doubly welcome. It's wonderful to see you.' His hand now on the small of her back propelling her through the bar. Stopping to introduce a grizzled Paddy Sharkey, who confounded her with, 'I knew your father well, God rest him. Heart a' corn, heart a' corn. Fifty, sixty years ago, sure you'd a been only a wee cub at the time.'

Lizzy and Tom Cochrane sat at his corner table in the dining room of The Crown. 'Your father was right,' he mused. 'A clean break, putting the past behind him. That's the terrible part of it for some people: they're never happy, always yearning, looking back, making the very best of the worst of home. Singing about, glorifying, for heaven's sake, sod cabins and prudders and point. Do you know what that is?'

'No,' she replied. But she smiled and nodded and her eyes told him to go on.

'Potatoes dipped in salt. I don't think other nationalities do what we do. I don't think they look back at hunger, champ and onions, despair, and read something noble into it.'

Lizzy, famished, was distracted by the smell of fried eggs and bacon, as first the accompanying brown bread and butter arrived.

'Then, when you come home,' Tom Cochrane continued, 'all those adults you knew when you left, the ones you wanted to impress by staying away ... they're dead. And those who remain—they don't want to see you. What have you to talk about? Old times! It can stand one conversation at best. Their lives have been here; they've moved on, reared a family. You're only rambling about water under the bridge. You know nothing of the years in between.'

She knew it was because she was so hungry, but it seemed the most exquisite high tea: the crispest bacon, the unexpected tomato, the divine fried eggs. Even the bread and butter was exotic and gorgeous, as Tom Cochrane regaled her with 'Your father and I were in the "same book", that's the same class, in the old school. It's Drumreagh Hall now—they've built a new school since. It was Master O'Sullivan in our time. He'd taught in the hedge school.'

'Hedge school?'

'Well, they called them hedge schools. Parish schools; the independent schools of Ireland. You paid the Master a shilling a term for reading, a shilling for writing and one and six for reckoning up. It was the same building, but by our time it was called the National School. And it was free. That's why we all went. Down the road, up the road, over the mountain, over the river, there'd a' been fifty of us in all. You didn't go every day, but more or less till you were twelve. Well, whatever O'Sullivan was like in the hedge school, Jesus, Mary and Joseph, he was desperate by the time he got to us. He had the living life scared out of us. We were trembling for fear of him. He told us he had a rope in the cupboard to hang us if we done anything wrong. We believed him too! Certainly he battered us if we didn't do everything right. He shouldn't have been teaching; the man's nerves were in tatters, he was forever grinding a set of false teeth like a sick cow.'

Then Tom Cochrane's face lit up in a reflective smile. 'O'Sullivan was awful bad to big John Comerford; picked on him more than anyone, beat the ears off him, slapped his hands raw. Well, your father and I were there the day John's brother Pat came in. No ceremony, went straight up to the rostrum. He was about ten or twelve years older than John, a big rooskin of a fella. A bit of a gulpin, very at odds with the world. Went down to barber McCombe, shouted and roared, fighting mad, said he'd given John a bad haircut on purpose. On purpose!' The Bog King showed his gold teeth with the widest smile. 'Sure poor wee Hughie McCombe give everyone a bad haircut. He hadn't hands to bless himself. However. Whatever Pat Comerford said at the rostrum—and mind you he was no soft boy—it didn't take a flinch out of the Master. "Patrick Comerford," he bawled, "has had the audacity to come up here and complain to me for trying to lick some education into that dunderhead brother of his—the amadán." They were great words of O'Sullivan's, "amadán, dunderhead, hind legs". "Get up on your hind legs, children," he commanded, "and boo him out of the school. Boo him out of the school," he roared. "Get up on your hind legs and boo him out of the school."'

Tom Cochrane's eyebrows arched, his eyes twinkled and with a huge grin he beamed, 'And we did. We were all so scared of him, we jumped to our feet, your father and me, the whole school, John Comerford included. Boo, boo, boo, we shouted as Pat shamefacedly went out the door. It was a terror, wasn't it?'

Lizzy was comfortable in Tom Cochrane's company. He had the grace to refrain from wheedling questions, 'sifting' as her father would have put it, telling instead a recent story about Kate Crozier in Belfast for the general holiday. The Warrenpoint and Rostrevor general holiday, a day of civic pilgrimage, on the second Tuesday in September.

'There's not much to it,' Kate observed about Belfast on her return.

'But the zoo!' everyone asked. 'What about the museum? The trolley buses? Dinner in Woolworth's? Selecting what you'll have as you walk along the counter.'

It transpired that Kate had got detached from the group, and had spent the entire day wandering around the kiosks of Great Victoria Street Railway Station, unaware of the wider experience out on the city streets. And then with his head bent and his hand on his forehead, Tom contrived a quiet time for them to just sit there, before looking up and complimenting her: 'You're like your granny, and very like your cousin Maggie when she was young.'

Lizzy had a sound grasp of natural psychology. She knew esteem is best gauged when it is reflected through a second party. That children inevitably channel their parents' evaluations, and that the attitudes of lieutenants reflect the feelings of the chief. The hotel staff danced attention on Lizzy, customers, mortised to their stools, swung round and smiled, as she walked back from the dining room through the bar. And Paddy Sharkey, who showed every sign of intoxication, took off his cap, swung it above his head and growled, 'Good girl. The Stronghold.'

Knowing 'The Stronghold' to be an old-fashioned salute to Craigarran's history, she graced him with a bow.

She was in the best room in the Crown Hotel, one floor up, with a corner bay window that gave entertaining views of the square, the promenade, and the sweep of the mountains across the Lough. It was a suite with a cosy fire, embossed linen, and a four-poster bed. The chambermaid, a hearty woman in her fifties, brought a stone foot-warmer, fluffed towels and a flagon of hot water for the willow-patterned dish in the wrought iron stand.

'Will you have cocoa?' she asked Lizzy.

'No. No thank you.'

'Something stronger?'

'Oh heavens, no.'

'Hot milk then?'

'No, thank you. I couldn't face another drop!'

'Well,' the chambermaid beamed, 'I'll go down to the kitchen and have something myself.' And slapping herself on the rump, she chuckled, 'My figure will do them that's courtin' me now.'

As soon as she got the room to herself, Lizzy flopped on the bed, tired from her journey and overwhelmed with the hospitality she had received from the moment she had put her foot though the Crown's revolving doors. She drifted, exhausted, on recurring waves of elation, bemusement and sheer disbelief. How could Tom Cochrane have guessed who she was? She would never have thought that she would be taken to resemble anyone. She had no idea what Maggie looked like, though God knows Lizzy had sat through enough talk about Craigarran to last her a thousand lifetimes. Her mind was a swirl of thoughts. Was she smugly coy, secretive even, never to have mentioned Peckham Rye and Brother Anthony? Perhaps she should have said something when Tom Cochrane said, 'Your father was right—a clean break, putting the past behind him.' If only he knew.

She was back twenty years, holding her father's hand, walking down the corridor behind the monk. Everything was brown; his habit, his leather belt, his sandals, his rosary beads. The corridor was brown, even the handle of the door he turned to go into the little room. The room where she heard every tick of the clock, where she unconsciously inhaled the vapour from their incessant talk of home. Brother Anthony, with his constant letter-writing, was the font of all knowledge of Craigarran.

Her father was settling in the chair, searching for his cigarettes, saying, 'Well, any news?'

With so much talk of the Bog King, it was incredible that she had no idea that his name was Tom Cochrane. Was it that her father and Brother Anthony would have validated his success by saying Tom, or was it something else—a sort of pirate code, a sense that it wasn't gossip or loose talk as long as they never said his proper name?

She gathered together all the things she had heard about the man downstairs. He was from 'up in the Bog'. As a child, she had imagined a tall stately figure, a royal, with a white beard, ruling a vast upland kingdom. A happy kingdom, where as the clock ticked she would drift through a domain of thatched cottages, Shetland ponies and children always at play—images at odds with what was actually being said.

He was a hawker in Glasgow selling suit lengths; he had a café in Pittsburgh and had acquired a secret recipe for ice-cream—classified information that intrigued Lizzy's father and Brother Anthony. 'Ice cream, be the hokey' they delighted to interject, while recalling the Bog King's prowess as a showman. Drumming up a crowd, lifting a navvy on a broad-mouthed shovel, hoisting a barrel of beer above his head. Tom Cochrane had a special party piece. Clasping a broom stick at each end, he would repeatedly jump forwards and backwards over it—gymnastics joyously spectacular for such a squat man. Then there were whispers, words mouthed, things half-said. He had courted an older woman in America who had left him a fortune. He was involved in some skulduggery in Detroit where he bribed the authorities and escaped over the border into Canada, clasping a suitcase of bonds and money which (until he got home) he never let out of his hand. And her father was always saying, 'It's a terror.' And Brother Anthony would respond with, 'Boys, O Boys.'

Then, on the very edge of sleep, Lizzy was amused to think that while she may have looked like the McGrains, she might actually turn out to be like Aunt Rose in Bexley, a gnarled elf with a taste for Turkish cigarettes and gambling. Would she end up reading neighbours' cards and teacups, and tippling Bow Bells gin?

It was a beautiful summer morning as Lizzy walked round the baths corner and out the Rostrevor road. The panorama of nature, landscaping and architecture was, if anything, more impressive than it had been the evening before. Her very being was warmed by the heat of the sun and by her sojourn in the Crown Hotel. Tom Cochrane had made much of her, by coming down early from his suite to join her for breakfast. He wanted to drive her out to Craigarran, almost insisting that she get in the car, and only with the stoutest assurance that she was unhurried and looking forward to the walk did he reluctantly let her leave on her own, accepting no payment for the room, and telling her over and over how welcome she was.

It was a calm day, but Lizzy had the unconscious feeling of the wind at her back, as she strolled at an easy pace out the coast road. The tide was coming in, and every fifth wave, a little more forceful than the others, would run far enough up the shingle to reach the bottom of the retaining wall. Then, delighted with itself, it would celebrate with champagne bubbles for having got so far. Here and there stretches of yellow sand were exposed, interspersed with seaweed growing on rough granite rocks, the bladderwrack moving up and down on the tide like matted hair on grotesque gargoyles' heads; wise old heads, contemplating the wooded slopes of Slieve Martin, the crags of Slieve Foy, and the fine residences and mature gardens, which had recently blossomed, to ornament the shore.

Schooners, fully rigged, sailed past, eventually disappearing on the horizon as they crossed the bar, a narrow channel between the mountains which allowed them to drift from this enchanted place to the open sea. Their mirror image, with curls of white water at their prow, came gliding back on a plumped pillow tide. It was the Glens of Scotland on the Côte d'Azur, where motor vehicles and horses and carriages of all types promenaded; a place where holiday-makers politely greeted each other, and waved to fellow sightseers on passing jaunting cars.

Delight after delight drew her along, one wonderful garden after another. A stream running in woodland, a dome of rhododendron, its canopy purple and green, its supports cool, dark and intertwined. A girl and her beau rowed close to the shore. This was the domain of Captain James Pointer—a society in which he could swagger and fritter, where the mistress organised the servants, and dinner parties, and rubbers of whist. Unaccountably, Lizzy felt liberated. She knew what she wanted. She wanted a house in Albert Road, in the terrace just off the Common. A home with a little garden at the front, a bay window in the parlour, and a square of leaded glass in the front door.

Her attention was now drawn to an explosion of muscle and a clatter of shooing and chain, as a black horse pulled a cart, piled with seaweed, from the water's edge up the shingled shore, The carter, his left hand on the front tram, his right at the horse's head, tripped perilously close to a driving front hoof. It was a distraction of images that stayed with her as she strode through the delights of gardens and shore, until the monument—the obelisk from the picture in The Crown, the sterile fountain, that when she got there was anything but destitute of ideas, It was an extravagance in cut stone, rearing from a promontory on the land side of the road, Fenced by spectacular 'Buckingham Palace' ironwork, terraces of granite steps, thirty yards wide, climbed in flights and landings, until, from its high altar, the great pillar thrust to the heavens for a further forty yards. This was a memorial on a grand scale, a salute from an empire that said 'Monument to a warrior, Major General Sir John Ross'. But important and all as he was, Ross's fame must not have reached Craigarran, because Lizzy's father had never mentioned him, never once breathed a word about this architectural monstrosity that would be a landmark in any capital in the world. She climbed the steps to read the inscription on its plinth—'Major General Ross fell victorious, Baltimore, Maryland, 1814'. It went on with reams about him incised on every side of the great square base, and a solitary schoolmasterish figure whom Lizzy encountered as she walked round enlightened her with, 'He was an outstanding British soldier, campaigned in Belgium, Egypt and in the American War of Independence. Do you know that he burnt the American forces headquarters in Washington, and when they whitewashed the charred remains to boost morale, Major General Ross indirectly gave the residence of the United States president its name?'

Lizzy sat on the steps in the sunshine and thought, how many names 'fell victorious' will be listed on monuments from the present war? In spite of herself, she shook her head and smiled. It was the strangest thing; her father had talked of every little stone in the Clornies, every crevice in the Holly Rock, and had never once mentioned General Ross's monument, this landmark of landmarks, piercing the sky before his very eyes. Somehow his culture deigned that it meant nothing to him. She was certain that he had never even climbed the steps, never read the inscription, never thought it worth his while.

She got up and read on: 'The officers of a grateful army which, under the command of the lamented Major General Ross, attacked and dispersed the American forces ... His well-earned fame is also recorded by the monument erected at his grave in Halifax, Nova Scotia'.

She further marvelled that neither her father nor Brother Anthony had ever mentioned this historic military figure. Here was a

Rostrevor man who, as it said somewhere on the plinth, had a plaque in his honour in St Paul's Cathedral, and her father and Brother Anthony had ignored him, while talking endlessly of another local who had gone to America and come home with a recipe for ice-cream.

Lizzy tripped down the terracing. This view, this place, this ozone, compelled her to breathe deeply and feel alive; to almost skip a little farther around the headland and be pleased by her first view of Rostrevor village. A slightly elevated entity of spires, turrets, and sloped slate, a composition of pastel colours in a warm silk-screen print. It had a settled look to it, snuggled as it was beneath the mountains, in the curve of the bay. It was a village in full make-up, powdered, painted and camouflaged, with a profusion of trees. Lizzy knew exactly where to turn: just before the seven oak trees gracing the square, at the often referred to 'corner of the town'.

And what a corner! A T-junction directed her up the valley and away from the shore. A boulevard of townhouses and aristocratic terraces, their nameplates—The Anchorage, Glen Alpine, Lisnarran—suggesting shipping, spring walks in Switzerland, and rents from fertile acres in County Meath. Again, she had no idea there would be such houses, no idea that this stretch of the road would be dignified by their perimeter walls. They were beautiful. By turns, warm sandstone and whitewashed mortar inlaid with arched brick masonry, that was the public face of each property, its extravagance proclaiming tranquil wealth within.

She was gaining on a tall stooped figure, an unseasonal overcoat hanging from his dowager's hump. He was shuffling along, his boots unwieldy. Blind Ned Gilpin, it dawned on her. There had been talk about him too. In his bare feet, he knew every cobble of the loanin between Carrigs and Sliver Roe. When he was at home with his mother, Lizzy had heard, he could milk a cow, churn, do anything she put him to. In faded blue writing somewhere in an old dusty ledger in the back of Lizzy's mind, there was a footnote. Ned Gilpin had had a liaison; maybe two. And that wasn't the half of it. His mother kept him in petticoats until the day she died. By that time he was a big strapping fellow, maybe thirty-five, middle-aged even, running about in a shift, seemingly with a highlander's disdain for underpinnings. It wasn't only his feet that were bare. 'Sure the breeding of them,' her father would say. 'Every man of them had to have two women and every woman of them had to have two men.'

When his mother died, with nobody to look after him, here he was 'in pension lodgings', a sad figure, tapping and listening, and feeling every crack, pebble and root as best he could. Away from Carrigs geographically, he might as well have been in Timbuktu, so strange his route, his ear cocked for a familiar foot, a voice from up near home. He was alarmed at the step of her passing, his head held high, his white stick pathetically poised. Her heart went out to him. The blind stallion broken, she thought, as, calling out 'Good morning', she moved on.

She was on the outskirts of the village now, putting an inch to her step and no longer sauntering. The road was shaded and flanked on both sides by mature deciduous trees. She passed the gatehouse at the entrance to an estate, then a crescent of common ground which hosted a spring van with a lurcher tied to the wheel, and a child crawling out from under the canvas of a gypsy tent. Through the trees, the ridges of the mountains drew curves for her, as she passed several more excesses in wrought iron, and a small house-cum-shop on the very edge of the road. Then she could see the bridge and hear the river. Instead of crossing it, she took a moment to look at the water before, as naturally as if she had done so all her life, she walked up the road on the Drumreagh side.

And as the road began to rise, the country changed. Gone were the big houses, the planned gardens of exotic plants, the positioned oak and chestnut. Gone too the motorcar, the thoroughbred horse, the velvet-coated Jersey cow. Now it was simple homes, and subsistence farms divided by hedgerows. Small fields of tillage, a shorthorn cow, and increasingly more sheep.

And, like the country, the people changed perceptibly, from enterprising recent settlers, to ancient established tribes.

The throng and friendly greetings of Warrenpoint and the Shore Road were reduced to a woman with a basket who eyed Lizzy suspiciously, nodded a quick greeting, and walked on. From over the half-door, and from the fields, they monitored her. A man taking a moment to lean on his scythe, a woman straightening her back from lifting hay after him, her thumbs pressing into her kidneys, her neck stretched to heaven, automatically looking down her nose. Lizzy didn't feel hostility, but she felt the country's reserve, a guarded scrutiny, and again her doubts came flooding back. She should have written, told Maggie she was coming. Wallowing in the guilt of being presumptuous, of arriving unannounced when—'O Gawd. O Gawd!' she whimpered, petrified by the sight of a 'demon', framed between the whitewashed pillars and open green and white wooden gates. It's escaped, she thought.

The goat, sensing her a stranger, reared on its hind legs, arched its neck and pounded an imaginary foe into the ground. Repeatedly it stood up, its huge horns threatening, its eyes flashing, chilling her to the bone as it leered and licked its lips. Lizzy couldn't have been more frightened by a lion or a gorilla standing at the open door of its cage in a deserted passage of the London Zoo. She could neither go on nor go back. She knew she was being silly. The goat was probably harmless, but she couldn't stop the fear, the panic, and now the profound relief as a little girl of eight or nine, noting her predicament, ran from the house, loose-limbed, hair flying, body pitching, arms waving, to be affectionately thrown around the goat's neck. It was a wonderful moment for Lizzy and she walked on, holding the centre of the road, nodding her thanks, and accepting the open friendship in the child's brown eyes. The little drama said so much. A girl in a gingham dress, sensitive to the fears of a stranger, yet protective of the idiosyncrasies of the family goat. Up at the half-door the girl's mother nodded a greeting, as a dark-haired boy of two or three, dunted (not unlike the butt of a goat) her thigh with his head. A wee ruffian sporting the traditional petticoat—a ruse to fool the fairies, who were apt to spirit off a fine son and replace him with a changeling, an undersized crabbed child.

Quietly Lizzy walked, musing about the huge boulders built into the stone walls and banks on either side of the road. She longed to talk to those who had put them there, surprise them about her world, and learn more about theirs. She would translate 'The Horseless Carriage', a part of Columcille's Prophecies, talk about the wireless and chloroform, and listen as they related to her the pattern of their lives. Individual stones demanded her attention. They had a presence; some pleased with their position, others were grumpy and uncomfortable, afraid to fall. Cropping living rock providing a foundation for independent brethren who had been crowbarred and marshalled into position by her ancestors. Great chunks of the earth's core passively sitting there, registering everything that went by— sights, sounds, smells: settled moss-encrusted receivers, could science ever extract from them the messages they held?

At Roark's Bridge, a clear stream of water ran under the granite slabs, its bed of flat rock deep in a gully camouflaged with native trees. Lizzy went over and put her hand on the boulder that fortified the bridge. It was smooth and warm, an elephant's head of solidified lava bursting out from the bank, the matriarch of a herd that huddled under the ground. It had the marble hole in it where her father had placed hazelnuts to be cracked, and was the theatre where the nine-year-old Pat Flaxi, with a brand new penknife, had cut his wrong index finger and could still hold a pencil on arrival at school. It was a noble attempt to avoid writing duties, which failed because, in front of awestruck classmates, he naturally held the knife in his right hand to incapacitate his left.

A little farther and a woman had brought her husband tea to the field. They sat on the headrig. An unfettered horse picked in the hedgerow and a baby kicked its legs in the air, cradled in the horse's collar on the ground. Then Lizzy recognised the Holly Rock. Two gnarled bushes, black green and determined, their talons cushioned by heather as they doggedly tried to squeeze the life from a mansion of stone. Wild holly, with multi-fanged, wax-coated leaves, their teeth stripped, snarling at everything and holding their ground. Two sisters, Lizzy thought, not beautiful but, in scrabbling at the world, curiously fulfilled.

At the junction of the loanin and the road, Lizzy stopped and looked at the clachan below. Craigarran, the capital of a kingdom that had torn at her late father's heart. John Wilson's and her Aunt Maggie's houses were a long stroke of burnt amber, her father's house was at right angles to them over a stream fifty yards to the north. Three thatched roofs in close proximity, yet positioned in such a way as to give each privacy. The fourth feature, a walled garden, a bridle path distance from the gable of Wilsons' house, was a circular stockade of granite boulders, settled and purified a millennium before the houses were built. A cashel with a spring and a blackthorn clasping a natural altar, Craigarran's magic amphitheatre—Pulnafrog. Apart from the new gate and pillars, everything was exactly as her father had described. She was reassured to recognise the stone ditches, the fields, the cropping rock, the thorn bushes, and the meanderings of the stream. And she raised her eyes to look at Carrigs on the opposite mountain face, below it the fairy bailiwick of The Clornies, Sliver Roe on a lower contour to the north, and the walled bridle path running from her father's house to Coolnafrankey on her side of the valley floor. Now she knew why her father had never mentioned Warrenpoint or the Shore Road. Its grandeur meant nothing to him. This is where he settled his mind's eye, concentrating all his energies to convey Craigarran to her.

As Lizzy turned down the loanin, a young man was working with a dun horse in the field to her left. It was not the solid plodding powerhouse that she associated with farming, but a more spirited animal, a more subtle breed, concealing an acrobat's muscles under a light velvet coat. There was a fluency in their work, gliding up and down the drills, to turn effortlessly bottom and top. The horse performed a pirouette, as the plough, with the man holding it, pivoted as if on ice, to begin a thrust down the alley of the drill, never deviating from a central line to avoid trampling the foliage and causing damage to the crop. Always a consistent wave of rich dark soil flowed with them; crumbling loam to nourish and cosset green potato stalks. It was a circus act, intricate and difficult, made to look easy by enduring practice and a bond built between man and horse.

Down on the street between the three houses, an old man was sharpening a scythe, leaning over it, calling folk to muster, as he played a hornpipe with the stone on the blade. A little farther back, a woman of similar years was scattering oats to feed hens behind a gate. Lizzy knew they were John Wilson and Maggie McGrain. At the bottom of the loanin, she neither walked up to them nor made an effort to speak, hypnotised, irresistibly reeled in by the line cast from her people's door.

Confidently she swam with it, never doubting that it would admit her, as she put her hand on the latch. A touch with her toe on the bottom, a dunt with her knee farther up, and the door opened for her to step across the threshold of her future, and of her family's past. Instantly, with a sweep of her eye, she knew everything was in place. Even the smell was how she had anticipated it, a faint mixture of lime, tar and dry earth. She recognised the hearth, the crook and the fanbellows. Only the melodeon on top of the dresser, laughing down a welcome, took her by surprise. She thought it had been lost, appropriated by someone in the clearing out of her father's London flat. She had asked the landlord, and the removal people—Sawers of Streatham; everyone but Brother Anthony. The sight of it at the same time lifted her heart and made it sad; and in the energy-sapping emptiness she felt when she thought about her mother and father, was whisked a gnawing guilt. She should have contacted Brother Anthony and thanked him, not got caught up in a mindless bitterness and recrimination, blaming her feelings of isolation on childhood visits to a monastery in Peckham Rye.

It's lovely, she said to herself; it's really lovely. She walked round the kitchen and the bedroom, touching every artefact, sitting at the fanbellows and composing herself, then giving the wheel a practice turn on a non-existent fire.

Long before Lizzy had reached the head of the loanin, Mick, John and Maggie had seen almost the same thing. From the rise in the road at the Holly Rock, one had seen an interesting woman, the other two a pleasingly dressed girl. At a leisurely pace she moved between the hedgerows, and automatically turned down the loanin, as if she had done so all her life. Seemingly walking a familiar path, she stepped lightly over the stream and, without hesitation, walked into Owen McGrain's house, summoning Craigarran to attention, and demanding a lull in its activity until she came out. She had the type of figure that would grow stocky, rather than plump, and she wore a grey fitted costume with black boots. Her hair, beneath a summer bonnet, was in a no-nonsense bun, and while her gait was not restricted, she seemed to have, if not stones in her shoes, at least sand, giving her the slightest limp.

Lizzy left the door open behind her, and walked back over the stream and up to where John and Maggie were coming together at the iron gate, unconsciously sidling up to each other, too dumbstruck to say yet a word. The three now stood and faced each other in a triangle that fenced hesitancy, recognition and time. They all knew one another, though the base of the triangle and its apex point had yet to be joined. It was a confrontation in the purest human way, where the second of silence seemed to extend to infinity, before John spoke. Very slowly he said, 'You're the daughter of Owen McGrain.'

He had the tone of a botanist, recognising the shoot from a rare and exquisite bulb; surprised by how instantly recognisable it was, allowing a pause to savour it, then reaching out to touch it. Lizzy found her hand lost in his outstretched grizzled palm, her soul calmed by the familiar timbre of his words. It was in that instant she knew what she found so appealing about Tom Cochrane. Why she was so comfortable listening to him. He too had the inflections, flavours and tones of her father's voice—an accent little modified since these Gaelic speakers began adopting Elizabethan words. Theirs was a dialect nurtured over generations in a small settled society with its own *ceili* houses and hedge school.

'Indeed you are,' said Maggie, not giving Lizzy time to speak.

'Indeed—you—are.' And she opened the gate wide enough to draw Lizzy in by shaking her hand in a wholehearted clasp.

An arrival such as Lizzy's is seldom met with storybook whoops of emotion and cries of 'I'm pleased to be here' and 'God bless you, you're welcome, child'. The atmosphere is quieter, more restrained, and before either party can quite grasp what has happened, a defining moment has arrived and passed. In Lizzy and Maggie's case it was the handshake, a clasp that sparked counterbalancing energies, and defined them both of equal force.

Maggie turned on her heel and signalled Lizzy to follow her into the house. It wasn't an obvious signal, like a hand movement or a smile. It was more intuitive. It struck John Wilson as being similar to the rite of the new horse joining the established herd on the mountain. There is an interactive display of strutting, wheeling, posturing, before subtle inflections of head, crest and croup assimilate the outsider, and the pageant moves on.

All this he pondered as the notion dawned on him that this was the first new blood into Craigarran for at least two hundred years. For centuries, matches had been struck between neighbours, breeding stock drawn from Cleomack, Sliver Roe, Carrigs, like seed potatoes a woman was thought best to flourish if she was brought down from a harsher habitat a bit farther up the road. Owen's daughter had a halt in her step, she was English on her mother's side, but she resembled the McGrains. No doubt she'd be a hardy wee sort, short in the kidneys, as tight as tuppence … but what was he thinking of? She'd stay for a few days, if Maggie kept her that long, sort out something with Dinny, maybe even leave instructions with Seamus Walls to sell the farm. Either way, there'd be little auctioning on it. Who would bid against Dinny after him having it all the years? He would inherit Maggie's as well. John Wilson shook his head and went back to the house. What else would a London girl do with a farm?

Lizzy sat on the first chair she came to, a no-nonsense kitchen chair at the bottom of the table near the door. She felt self-conscious of her rigid posture and of the lack of the normal trifles of hospitality from her host. Maggie, a resolute figure, went direct to a blue dinner plate, one of a set standing on their edges on the second shelf of the dresser. She tilted it forward and took from behind it a very grand buff envelope about one foot long and four inches wide. Holding it against her heart, she swivelled, took the few paces back to face Lizzy, and, as dramatically as a courtroom judge, placed the document on the table at her right arm. The precision of the drill, and the slap of the weighty envelope on the table, left Lizzy startled, and momentarily taken aback.

'I had this ready for Owen … for your father,' Maggie said. 'But now I can give it to you.' Standing square and erect, and hardly allowing a moment to elapse, she continued. 'Go on, girl, take it. You're very much your father's daughter. It's the deed of your farm.'

Quietly Lizzy reached over, lifted the envelope and held it on her lap. She could feel her heart pounding, but she knew she must show no emotion. Something told her to say nothing, that a 'thank you' would be too trite. That this was a very peculiar game of cards, where points are won by the calm acceptance of a once-in-a-lifetime, dealt face up, winning hand.

It was an old woman's kitchen, cluttered. A child would have thought that it held all the treasures of the world, that amongst the books and magazines and bric-à-brac there were wonderful secret things. The back table was a rummage of paraffin lamps, clocks, delft dogs—all broken. So were the statues, several of Our Lady, a couple of the Sacred Heart and one of Bo Peep. The top of the dresser was a hardware store and, down on its main counter, washing its face and grooming its coat, tempting someone to 'put their boot in its arse' sat a supercilious black and white cat. It was a house very few got into, and if they did, this seat at the bottom of the table next to the door was as far as they got.

Maggie put an egg in the wee black pot, poured in some water from the kettle on the crook, and shoved it into the embers of the fire. There was no small talk, no comments on the weather, no 'how was your journey?', no invitations to come on up to the fire and don't be sitting down there at the door. Not that it was an awkward silence; it was a respite after the thunderbolt of the buff envelope, when

Lizzy could recuperate by watching Maggie get the table dressed, focusing on her floating a flour bag tablecloth in the air and allowing it to settle, fetching blue willow pattern crockery from the dresser, and jangling the cutlery from the drawer. She marvelled at the innovation of ornamenting a linen flour bag, of opening it out, boiling and bleaching it, and picking threads from the weave to form a lacy design. The technique was foreign to her. Somehow the artist had created an elaborate spider's web in the centre and semi-circular loops of the same pattern around the outside. Then Lizzy turned her attention to the crockery, to the three figures with lanterns crossing the bridge in the Chinese scene, and the cutlery, where she noted the wear on the bone handle of the knife and the spoon.

In silence Maggie took the farl of soda bread from the back window, poured tea from the pot, and with a big spoon spirited the boiled egg from the black tin, across the floor—popping it in the egg cup and promptly cutting off the top. Only when she took over the jug of milk and the pat of butter with the primrose print did she speak.

'Will you be staying in my house or will you be staying in your own?'

'I'll stay over at home,' Lizzy found herself saying. Even as she spoke, she was surprised by the finality of her reply, and astonished that she should have used the word 'home'. Here she was at half-past eleven on a June morning calling a small country cottage in a new world her home. The house she had only just clapped eyes on had now been confirmed as hers. She wanted to tear open the envelope and examine the deed, see what it looked like. That piece of Craigarran her father had always talked about, had lived and breathed, was now hers. She owned it! She tried to suppress the groundswell of euphoria, which, like a mixture of champagne and brandy, welled up and warmed her. And with it guilt about her delight in possession. To allay it, she did what she always did when she wanted to distract her thoughts: she concentrated on the maze of fire escapes leading to the communal quadrangle at the back of the flats in Clapham North.

None of this was lost on Maggie—the composure, the not losing the run of herself, the not trying to fill the silence with, God forbid, nervous giggles or gushing words. The girl with the English accent was a woman in charge of herself, and, to Maggie's quiet satisfaction, a McGrain woman, well fit to be in charge of the deeds of her farm.

Lizzy wasn't a picky eater. She buttered half a soda farl, sprinkled a little salt on her plate, and alternately dipped her spoon in it and scooped it in the egg. She was thankful that neither the distinctive flavour of the egg, nor the tack of the butter, were too foreign to her taste. Maggie still said nothing, busying herself in the kitchen, while Lizzy, conscious not to be too obviously watchful, nevertheless saw her take two flat folded brown paper bags and a flimsier white one from the table drawer. Then Maggie went over to two sacks at the bottom of the dresser, rolled down their tops, and from them measured a bowl of porridge meal into one brown bag, and three bowls of flour into the other. In the bag with the porridge meal, she cushioned four white eggs from a dish on the back window, and tore up the white bag, malleable paper for tiny containers, bulbs of butter, sugar, salt and tea. This was a rite of separation, a ceremony that may have had its roots in the ancient laws of Ireland, rules that Craigarran still adhered to. Two farls of bread, a can of milk, a bucket of coal, Maggie methodically counted out eight red-headed matches and tore a skelp of striker from the box, clear bold statements that from now on Lizzy was on her own.

⌒

With the provisions wrapped in a flour bag cloth, the bucket and the tin, Lizzy walked through the gates, down the street past Wilsons', and over the stream. A procession of intent, a tense running of the gauntlet which left her drained, elated, and pleased to close the door. But only the half-door. She would have dearly loved more privacy, but didn't want to fly in the face of tradition and close the big door as well.

It was the deed that excited her, the fact that she would get to open the brown envelope and look inside. She savoured it for a moment, pulling a chair up to the table, drawing out the manila folder and smoothing it with her hands. 'Land Registry of Ireland. Folio 40364. County Down. Leslie McCall, Registrar of Deeds'.

Methodically she turned the page. Stamped and dated and under the heading 'Deed Possessory' was her father's name, 'Owen McGrain, Craigarran, Rostrevor, County Down'. She leaned back in her chair.

All those years of paying rent on two rooms in Clapham. Did he know that he owned the farm? Surely he must have. Yet she was almost certain he would never even have prompted Brother Anthony to enquire from home. Pride, thinking he was disinherited, perversely hoping that he was, showing them he didn't care, using his bitterness as fuel. She stopped there. It was marvellous of Maggie to take charge of everything, probably knowing how he felt. She had negotiated it all. Who else in the country would have thought of getting a deed and registering it in her father's name? Maggie could just as easily have put her own name on it. Even now, had she said nothing, not given her the deed, Lizzy knew that in her wildest dreams she never would have thought of inheritance. Maggie could have kept it, and she already would have been strolling to a new horizon, bowling along in innocence, somewhere on the Shore Road.

She returned to the document, and looked farther down the page: 'Date of First Registration, 18 June 1916, Barony of Iveagh, Upper (Upper Half), County Down'.

What would her grandfather have thought? She allowed herself a wry self-indulgent smile. 'The Englishwoman's daughter owns it now.' Then she turned her attention to the portion of Ordnance Survey map attached. She looked at the red line outlining her parcel of land: a stout authoritative line going round the six fields, the gardens, the house and her street north of the stream. She liked the number her property had been given; 27881 was a sequence of digits she felt boded well. There was a pecked green line showing the right of way. It came down the loanin, it went to the well in Pulnafrog and, having rounded the gable of Wilsons' house, proceeded down the back fields to the Stepping Stones, and up to the Far Road. Then she noticed the red line ran down the centre of the river. She owned half the river!

There was something about owning half the river—something invigorating. Certainly she didn't see it as an additional sliver of useless marginal rind. She saw it as nature, laughing, talking, stepdancing past her ground, and it was hers! Of course it was ridiculous to think you owned a river, to think you owned land, but she had custody of it; and, with her finger, she followed the outline of her farm on the plan—every elbow and curve of the defining red line. She touched the centre of each field and counted to six, and calculated the total area—eight acres and three roods. Unconsciously she also tapped Cullinatee, Wilsons' wee field directly behind her house, and smiled, recognising the awakening of greed, with the feeling that it too would fit in nicely with hers.

Lizzy explored the house. Dreamy confirmations of what her father had told her about it turned to a practical audit of things she would need. Down in the bedroom she struck one of the matches to light the Sacred Heart lamp. Its ruby globe and burner a petit figure eight, which sat beneath the picture, and brought even on this summer day a special warmth to the lathed bed and the two chairs. Up in the kitchen the drawers of the dresser revealed cutlery, the cupboards at the bottom pots and pans, paper nibbled to chaff, and the droppings of mice. She would need bedclothes. Cautiously she pulled down the settle-bed that stood against the back wall of the kitchen. It transformed effortlessly from a bench-seat to a box-bed. Lizzy was delighted to find its construction so tight and perfect, its seams so flawless, that it had excluded even the smallest mouse. Inside was a horsehair tick, two blankets and flour bag sheets. She took them out, shook them, and aired them over the chairs, continuing to look, to search and come to terms with things, oblivious to the fire of rumour she had sparked in Craigarran's surrounds.

In a community only ever visited by those who were locally born, her arrival had caused interest and excitement that was second to none. How long would she stay? Had she already left? Stories of her background became more outrageous as the day wore on. She was married. Her husband was dead. She had actually fought in the war. Henry Sterritt caught the mood of the townland by cupping his hands to his mouth and shouting, 'Lizzy's home! Lizzy's home!' while children whispered, 'She has a wooden leg.' And over in Sliver Roe, Joe Marley credited Father Bennett with saying, 'In the circumstances, I am very concerned she may attract that element of English society that indulges in the practice of nudism.' On hearing that she was the spitting image of Maggie, Stephen Flavin growled, 'Another conapscious wee hure!'

Mick Wilson went on 'mouldin' spuds', the mare turning at the headrig and footrig to his quiet command of 'come up round', drawing the plough up and down the drills, the dark soil somehow dampening his spirits and putting a weight on his heart. The arrival of Owen McGrain's daughter had inexplicably disturbed him. It was a damp sponge soaked in gruel, lying heavily on him. He felt embarrassed and vulnerable. Under the mocking eye of his neighbours, she had stepped over the stream and drawn the power from him, this Englishwoman with her own farm.

John Wilson, too, felt the wind of change. Resigned, he shuffled round the gable of the house and sat on the armchair stone on the outside of Pulnafrog. The loneliness was on him. He missed his wife, but Mary Catherine was gone. In Luke's case it was the anguish of not knowing if he was living or dead, never hearing from him, from the day he had walked up the loanin and disappeared off the face of the earth. Apparently he was working on flying machines in Pittsburgh; Packy Hannah said that one of the McAnultys had been talking to him there. He could see him, not a day different from when he had put the shoeing on the slipe: happy with the hammer, battering in the rivets, bracing the wings to the carriage, as he constructed one of the newfangled machines.

Luke had always liked machinery. When he had gone away first, he had worked on the pile-engine on the Glasgow docks. He had hands on him for anything. He was in his element making the wheelbarrow with Jimmy Moore. Even Maggie said, 'He's the only mechanic we have' when he spliced in a bit of new timber and tightened the hinges on her half-door. That was the sort of him: let him at the hardware, but don't send him down the fields to look at a ewe lambing. John eased himself forward a little more on his walking stick. He shook his great head slowly, and with a smile, murmured, 'And for God's sake, don't ask him to clip sheep.'

From his new position, John could see just that little bit farther round the corner of the lane. There was a dead rabbit lying on the centre of it, just where the face of Pulnafrog reared to ten foot of stone-faced wall. A weasel flashed out, a ripple of ginger, black and gold, catching the sun and the rabbit, to inch it closer to the wall. A tiger with an elephant, it got down on its haunches and pulled in a short sharp burst of concentrated energy, before scurrying back. Only with a flashing overlap did John realise that there was more than one, a band of warriors, each taking it in turn to dash into the open and wrest back the enemy. How far had they transported it: six feet from a burrow on the opposite bank, or energy-sapping yards from the open plain of the back field? He had often seen them race after a rabbit, grab it by the throat, and swing in a graceful pendulum of death up on to the rabbit's back—a hideous circus act that careered across the field, until, in a grotesque surrender, the rabbit falls.

The weasels were all out now, six or seven of them, a concentrated effort, dragging the rabbit quickly through the door into their fortress wall. No wonder there were so many myths about weasels: they could put their tails in their mouths and whistle up an army, a seething mass of terror to strip your flesh. And they were devious. When John was a child, he would always refer to them as the 'Ws'; he was afraid of drawing them to him by a full mention of their name.

Luke had no idea of the pain he had caused. Rosie waited every day for the letter; then, when she was sick, she took to holding his school exercise book, comforting herself, looking at his handwriting, putting her palm on it, lightly stroking his dark curls. At first there would be word from Sliver Roe, Carrigs, The Alt. Somebody would mention him in a letter, saying that they had seen him: Sauchiehall Street, Broomielaw, The Bronx, Queen's, at ever increasing intervals, four, five, six years apart. Alaska, New Zealand, the waves of the world. He was one and a half times longer away than he had ever been at home. Sometimes it seemed a lifetime, sometimes just yesterday, that he had been throwing stones at the rooster on the street. He was a bugger for throwing stones.

John sort of knew why Luke had never written. The first few weeks had simply slipped away in the excitement. Then it was like not going to Mass. You're there all your life; you stop for three Sundays, and you never go back.

Coyles' house on the Far Road was, at a distance, the most impressive in the townland. A two-storeyed Georgian structure with a slabbed roof, it incorporated a byre, a stable and a loft. Built by the landlord for his agent in the days when each farm paid rent, it had a commemorative plaque engraved above the front door: a perfectly chiselled ellipse cut into the granite enfolding the words 'Batt Estate 1803'. For all its architectural grandeur, there was no more land to it than to any of the neighbouring farms. A stripe of cropped pasture that ran from the bottom of the mountain to behind the house, then from below the road to the river, where it marched Lizzy's land: seven hungry fields and a hotchpotch of gardens, crags and holms. Eleven acres, so starved of cover, the Creator had taken a second look at them and, feeling he had been mean-spirited, deigned to compensate by coating the skim of soil with mossy grass, and facing it to the morning sun.

The brae was so clean and pleasing and naturally manicured, you thought it had had work done to it, something that could never be said of the house. It was a squire's residence in terrible repair; a building that had never felt the oxygen of whitewash, a sorry flagship of chipped mortar and boarded windows, sinking in a sea of dung. A spreading, oozing cesspit enveloped the front of the house, desert yellow when it dried in high summer, reverting to putrid diarrhoea for the rest of the year. Warm weather turned it into a vast restaurant emporium for cruiserweight insects, bluebottles principally, which, having eaten, naturally withdrew to the house. There, their bellies distended, they lounged on dust-cushioned ledges, rifting and farting in a harem of luxurious boudoirs, blissfully oblivious to the threat of barbarous spiders intent on snaring them in their webs.

Inside the main hall was shared accommodation between humans and animals, its décor harking back to grander days: stout furniture broken and crudely nailed, a glass press with shattered panes. The banqueting table had been cut and colloped, vandalised, yet, battered and bruised, still stood defiant in the centre of the floor, its six legs supporting an acre of hardwood, engraved, chamfered and extravagantly deep. A tour de force in bog oak. There was a set of exquisitely decorated carver chairs, chipped, broken, heart sorry they had escaped the guillotine in France. One particularly pathetic aristocrat had been sentenced to stand on three legs with a cobbled paling post for a fourth. The hearth and surround were black and crumbling and there were squares of mud where tiles were missing off the floor. At all times a raftry of animals drifted about: six inbred dogs, two goats, and even Dinny's mother, Alice, wouldn't know how many cats. A houseful of four-legged playboys, confident and swaggering, American in their deportment, they had been through Ellis Island and been given citizen cards. Even the cow was a national, sharing a dormitory with Dinny and his mother Alice, nonchalantly entering by the front door, skirting the corner of the kitchen and sloping down to the low room, a right of way established when Dinny had initially brought her in six or eight times before a first calving. He was keeping an eye on her and didn't like going out in the dark.

God knows, it was no place for a *ceili*. Dinny, the fire, the mother were all too cold, the three of them sitting in line, withdrawn from the warmth of the rest of the house. The biggest crowd they had had since the father died—not just neighbours but more or less the spread of people who would go to a dance in Drumreagh Hall. Well, a bit older than that, and without the women of course. Solid, decent, respectable callers, they made no effort to entertain. But the Tailor was entertaining them, telling yarns, holding the kitchen in the palm of his hand. Someone had mentioned Maysie Corr.

'She's a powerful woman, Maysie,' he started. His tone was steady, low and authoritative, as he leant back in his chair, hooking his thumb in his belt and allowing the audience a space to accept him on stage.

'A great woman. When the doctor came out to Barney that time, he prescribed a box of wee brown tablets for the pain in his back. Done Barney the world of good. Well, whatever was left of them Maysie took herself; as a general pick-me-up, but more than anything not to waste them. Done her the world of good. So understandably, and in the light of such dispensary, the next time she was down in the town, she called in to get another box. A full box for herself!'

The Tailor was in his element. He had the kitchen charmed. His delivery was by times detached and introspective, by times warm and personal, drawing everyone to him, involving them, as they raised a smile and willed him to lift them further, and make them laugh.

'The doctor was reluctant to give her the tablets. "Is there anything wrong with your kidneys?" he asked. "Cripes, no," said Maysie. "Sure I could lift the screenings off the road."'

The kitchen exploded, erupted with the shrapnel of animals fleeing from the roars of belly laughs that relieved the tension felt at being so unwelcome in the house. Even Dinny and his mother suppressed a giggle, while the Tailor feigned detachment and allowed himself only the merest hint of a smile.

[113]

Then, warming them down as it were, the Tailor arched his back and grimaced, feigning great pain, before continuing, 'When Barney Corr was a child, he was sent home from Scotland to his granny—Minnie Finnin. It ended up with just him and his Uncle Paddy in the house. The Finnins always thought themselves a cut above buttermilk and, when Barney told Paddy that he was marrying Maysie, Paddy thought she wasn't a good enough match. In a bit of a consultation between old bachelors, Paddy mentioned his misgivings to Mickey Downey. "Well no matter how bad she is, she'll be better than the two women we got," says the bold Mick.'

Despite all the host's efforts to get them to go home—no fire, no tea, not even a bucket of spring water and a clean tin for any man choked with the druth after eating salt herrings—the people kept on making craic. 'Maysie's not a bit soft,' said Joe Doran. 'She worked Finley the solicitor.' They all knew the story, nodding for it to be told once again. 'Consulted him about Terry Polin using her street as a right of way to the mountain; said she'd call for an answer the next fair day. When she did, Finley had the whole thing looked into. Papers, maps, deeds, whatever, and discussed it with her for half an hour.'

Joe settled himself well in his seat to tell the rest. 'Maysie listened to it all, got up, thanked him and was about to go. "That will be half a crown, Mrs Corr," oul Finley says. Maysie took a few moments to consider, and then nice and pointedly asked, "Whatever for, Mr Finley?" "It's for my advice," he informed her. "Ah, that's alright!" said Maysie. "Thank you very much, Mr Finley, but I'm not taking your advice."'

They all smiled warmly and loved it, a point scored by one of their own.

In the lull that followed, people took to watching the antics of a solid grush of a black dog resettling himself under the table, pivoting on his haunches, and using his back leg to furiously scratch his neck. In the clouds of dust and mites which followed, he further performed with grabs and snapping at his own posterior, to cause a movement of flecks and specks to deposit on the milk in two uncovered crocks.

[114]

Alice and Dinny knew exactly why everyone was there. Now that Lizzy was home, they wanted to hear all the news about the Coyles buying the farm. It was, of course, not for open discussion, but something to be talked around, as each in turn went over an event of the day. Seeing her first at the Holly Rock, Maggie had invited her into the house. Some of them hadn't seen her at all. Sammy Nesbit said, 'She'll not breed policemen, but she's a tidy wee sort.'

Through all the speculation, Dinny and his mother remained on their pedestal, separated from the floor, hunched and uncomfortable beside the embers of a dying fire, every so often shifting themselves a little as if they were going to bed, and hoping it would prompt everyone to head home. But it didn't. Conversation had broken up into little groups. Some did, some didn't think Lizzy would stay, but all agreed it would be only for a short time. Legal minds colluded and whispered 'Maybe Maggie inherited the farm.'

And just when the Tailor was regaling them with awful things that could happen in a *ceili* house—like putting the cat in the churn, and how he had watched Pat Hooey flick cinders into the porridge pot at Dinsmore's, and then oul' Jemmie crunch through a bowl of it, and him without a tooth in his head—the door pushed open, and in a flurry of tics and ramrod-backed twitches Stephen Flavin came in. He was paralytic.

'Well, Dinny, did you ask her?' were the very first words out of his mouth—a query that had a startling effect on everyone. It was pertinent certainly, while at the same time fascinating and repulsive, and caused Joe Doran to sit bolt upright, raise his eyebrows and purse his lips. 'You'll need to be quick, ye boy ye,' Flavin further chided. 'A few drinks in his belly and a bottle of whiskey,' and pointing out of the open door in the general direction of Craigarran; 'we all know the sort of yer man.'

Holding the floor as he was, Flavin had a very unnerving habit of stripping his teeth at people, putting them in mind of a cur of a collie or a cornered brute of a rat. 'It's between the two of youse for her,' he continued. 'You and Mick the Talaigh. In the name of God, make a decent woman out of her and get a hoult of Pimple Head's farm.'

It was all too much for Alice. Openly saying 'Pimple Head' insulted the memory of Uncle Pat. With remarkable agility she was amongst them and, in a shooing hens exercise, fluttered her apron to a litany of guttural gibes. 'The devil take yis. God's curse on yis. Have yis no homes to go to? Away with yis and let decent people get to their beds.'

And in a clatter of chairs and boots, they were out on the street and the big door closed behind them, and Stephen Flavin walked over to the low side of the road and, sounding in the dark as if he could challenge Maysie Corr in the water pressure department, said something very vulgar about how it used to be.

He could buck them as quick as they pushed them in under him, and now needing to be over the bar of the gate least he pish on his boots, whereas formerly he needed to be under the bar of the gate least he pish in his eye.

Everyone pointedly ignored him as Joe Marley cautioned, 'Young Pimple Head's going to have to marry the Hairy-Arsed Schoolboy because Alice and Maggie have made the match.'

Lizzy, oblivious of it all, took the tick and blankets that had been airing on the chairs and put them on the bare boards of the bed. It had been an eventful day and she felt tired, when suddenly it struck her that she was all alone. Not isolated in the way she felt in the crowds of London, but central to all the ghosts of her family's past. She knew she would never get to sleep because she would be frightened by the shadows in what was now a strange room. But she tightened the sheets around herself, put her heel on her fears, and told every ghost in Craigarran that the house and farm were hers.

The moon spread a soothing mist of whiskey over the country, lulling Lizzy and those who had her on their mind. Dinny, wishing that she would leave; Mick, wondering would she stay; and John

Wilson eased his pains by recalling weddings, funerals, dances and children playing skittles when he was a boy. He thought of the warm, contented and comfortable things of his past. Maggie, however, wasn't looking back. She was drifting into sleep while planning the erection of whitewashed pillars and iron gates, just like her own, over at Uncle Pat's; visualising deeds, pondering which side of the stream was the red line on the map, and, as was her custom, saying at least two decades of the rosary on her beads, as she contemplated the joyful—or was it the glorious?—inconvenience to Mick, him having to open and close the gates every time he wanted to go over to Tievegorm.

As she lay motionless in bed, it was the silence that struck Lizzy first, then a distant sound of birds which seemed only to highlight it more. Consciously she allowed the space to settle on her. White light and air held by thatch, earth, a door, a window, and lime-washed walls. Other than a slight tilting of her head, she never moved, experiencing the aerated feeling of excitement and apprehension. She was delighted with her inheritance and equally pleased at how well she had slept. And without a further thought of what she would ever do with it, she visualised her farm. The sun shone through a division in the curtains and caught one of the ornamental wooden globes carved on top of the posts at the bottom of the bed. It highlighted the concentric circles in the dark, varnished grain. She raised herself and swung her two feet out on the dry earthen floor, sitting for a time on the side of the bed and enjoying the childish pleasure of sliding them from side to side and then back and forth. It was not like walking barefoot on the barren sand of Margate; this was planting herself firmly in fertile land.

Dressed, she went up to the kitchen and opened the big door. The country was in the intensity of its summer bloom. She knew all the landmarks, albeit as line drawings that were now filled with the detail of colour, smell and sound. The flower on the whin was the most luminous yellow, the rushes so deeply green they were almost black. Ravens coughed and soared on the mountain face, wheeling round the cliffs she knew were the Spallick Rocks. In the lilac bush a pair of yellowhammers and a bumblebee played hopscotch; in the field ewes and lambs bleated, and over at Wilsons' old John was brushing a horse. The country was a stage set with an orchestra, and the drumbeat that caught her attention was the rasping, munching rhythm of a cow. Where the sun caught the point of its shoulders, it changed the black in its coat to oiled blue. Lizzy could see the cow's tongue. Like an outstretched hand covered with shore sand, it circled and sheared thick, green, broad-leaved grass, unfurling in its wake a swathe of vaguely yellow wet ground, and a smell that the half-door was no barrier to: a mixture of digested vegetation, fresh milk and thick liquid summer dung—a scent so familiar to country people that it would soothe and reassure them, while overwhelming anyone brought up in the town.

There was no one on the street when she went to get a bucket of water, a pause in the rhythm of Craigarran which allowed her to have Pulnafrog all to herself—to open the little lattice gate and feel its latent power; a force she quickly realised that was capable of reversing its polarity. And if you tried to draw from it, it would draw from you, and she put aside her desire to tap its wisdom and simply filled her bucket and went over to the thorn bush. It too had a force field, and she didn't resist the temptation to kneel on the flat stone, put her hands on the gnarled roots, and in the sunshine be reconciled with the spirits of Craigarran and the enigma of Pulnafrog. Contented, she picked her way back through Wilsons' ducks and a nuisance of a friendly dog.

'I don't like the look of that,' Alice Coyle declared, as she caught sight of the Englishwoman gathering sticks and picking flowers. 'She's settling herself.' And she watched Lizzy walking the fields and stooping to pick a buttercup, a sprig of heather, a bachelor's button, and hold them in a posy in her hand. On the Flat Stone at the top corner of the Smoothing Iron, she sat down. Alice had no way of knowing what Lizzy was thinking, but it was a history of which she too knew every part: the field names; where the potatoes were the year the crop failed; the corner where the cow had twin calves; and the brae in corn where John Wilson had swung the first scythe in the country. The Smoothing Iron, Lizzy thought, was the perfect name for this little triangular field. It was already her favourite, and with such a view.

Now she was looking at the Lough, where her granny's sister, Alice's cousin Biddy, had sat on a boat becalmed for a week, going to America all those years before; really in a limbo between a life left behind and a life unknown. Granda Pat went out in a rowing boat to replenish the bread she would have eaten from her supplies. Men, women, boys, girls, mostly from the country, sitting there gazing up the valleys, eyes transfixed, where parents, sometimes lovers, hearts scalded, looked back in a protracted goodbye. Fear, shame, pride, farms mortgaged, tickets paid for, like soldiers charging in battle, they screamed silent cries and, in their despair, willed on the ship. Some people couldn't resist going down to the shore, calling out their own and their loved ones' names, and in so doing lashing all hands. Biddy's mother never left the house for the whole week, containing her sorrow, denying herself sight of the boat by day or a glimpse of its lights by night. It took with it any pleasure in her view of the Lough.

Walking back to the house, Lizzy was met by Wilsons' dog. A black and white collie, wagging its tail, dipping its head and waltzing from side to side. When it got closer, its antics lifted her heart and made her smile. She had never had a dog—always felt they were to be avoided, like their gross stools on the paths of Clapham Common—but she knew she had at least part of one now. Every movement in its sleek form asked to be her friend. It bounced before her, its two front feet thumping the ground, and its head touching its paws. Then it spun and frisked a little away from her, and directly came back. And when she welcomed it with an encouraging 'Good boy', it tried to answer with excited, high-pitched yelps. Though fully grown, it had a pup's energy and playfulness, and like a servant bowing in front of a potentate, it escorted her back to the house.

With the fire lit, porridge and a boiled egg in her belly, and her bag on her arm, Lizzy pulled the big door behind her and went to the town for provisions. Dressed in the only clothes she had, a pinstriped cotton suit, she stepped out to face the country as tar-brushed smoke from a freshly banked fire signalled that she would be back. She said good morning to John Wilson, waved her hand at Maggie, and ignored a crouched 'Rodin Thinker' examining a plough—Mick. It was a 'they didn't speak to me, so I didn't speak to them' state of affairs, that solidified twenty yards of clear fresh country air. They were both attracted and, frightened of rejection, they hid behind a rampart of vulnerability and pride. Even the dog didn't know what to do. The collie stood sheepishly, tilting his head, for all the world expressing guilt that he wasn't with her, but feeling compelled to stand by Mick now.

At the junction of the loanin with the road, the view down the valley was different to that from the Smoothing Iron and the Flat Stone. The hip of the mountain now blocked out the wider bay at Carlingford and the line of sight was the Monument and Warrenpoint. Trees, mixed pasture and fertile drumlins rolled to the Lough, and Slieve Foy reared from an apparent horizontal line on the other side. Sunshine highlighted the colours in the vale below her, contrasting with the brooding shadows cast by the mountains, the day before, on her way up. Then the country had seemed to be appraising her; now, with the authority of being a shareholder, she was comfortably appraising it back. Again she was shyly observed and politely greeted, only this time everyone knew exactly who she was, and assumed that this was the end of her stay.

'Up the road for buttermilk, down the road for brandy,' they sang. Two barefooted boys in short trousers, carrying full cans, the liquid splashing and turning the tied muslin lids from snow white to pale grey. 'Drumreagh is a dirty hole, Knockbarragh is the dandy.' She had heard it before, sung by her father, a ribald taunt jeered at school to start a townland war. Again they sang it. Shy and mischievous, they were surprised when she stopped. 'Is it buttermilk? Where did you get it?' she asked, and, making an allowance for their bemusement at her accent, pointed at the cans. They were momentarily flummoxed until 'Mrs McShane at the bottom of the hill', they chorused, fresh-faced and keen to help, making amends for the rudeness of the song. 'She's just churned,' one confided. 'You have to pay for it if you go all the time, but we're friends of hers and we're waiting for our cow to calve,' the other chimed in.

Evidently they were brothers. Lizzy smiled as the younger boy took a butt of a cigarette from his pocket and balanced it behind his ear. Not to be outdone, his senior rattled matches and, with an air of 'A houl ya! That's the sort of boyos we are', they swaggered off.

With her distinctive gait, and a slow easy stride, she walked on down the road between the whin blossom that daubed golden yellow fingerprints in the hedgerows and delicately perfumed the air. At the Dark Place, a giant palm oozed resin from a hatchet-cut to its bark: an oval of smooth inner flesh which cried great dark tears, telling the world of its pain. Beneath its boughs, a donkey, a spring van and a goat rested, while a human form in a bundle of old clothes tucked itself foetally in a tin barrel. 'We start with a goat, and we end with a goat.' Lizzy recalled her father's words, and wondered what painted wagons, horses, landscapes and people had the tinker put through his hands between then and now.

As she left behind the quizzical extended family that formed society in Knockbarragh and Drumreagh, others' curiosity about her began to wane. She felt the anonymity of the city in what was really a small village with only a few shops—a place with a nucleus of locals but which was used to strangers in and about the town. It wasn't a country village in that it had more or less disregarded its farming hinterland and existed solely on urban trade. Rostrevor was commercially self-sufficient in the coastal crescent from the Monument to Killowen: a pleasing entity of trade and culture with an architectural confidence that stood easily with the oak trees in the square. It struck Lizzy as odd that she should have skirted it the day before, turning directly up the Craigarran Road. Like salmon in The Pots, had she too an instinct guiding her directly home?

She stopped at the Remembrance Garden, a poignant tribute to those who had fallen in the war. A meticulous grid of tiny crosses set in manicured grass, a parade ground framed with roses, each little cross representing an extinguished youth. Here, as elsewhere, wealth did not cushion a family's loss.

She could have been in Bond Street as she admired the chocolate biscuits in glass-fronted display boxes, in Sinton's shop, and fine silks and fashions in Armstrong's Bazaar. In the square, almost canopied by oak foliage, a bay window proclaimed 'Help the Red Cross'. The front drawing room of a superior three-storeyed, redbrick, semi-detached home, which afforded an outlet for Women's Institute arts and crafts. Here watercolours signed by Olive Swansea vied with crochet and boys' Fair Isle pullovers with horses' heads on their chests.

A young man in a deerstalker and tweed suit came out of the door of the house that championed the Red Cross. Tall and gaunt, he shook, shivered, and somehow stayed perpendicular as he held the railings, and gyrated down the three granite steps. As if he were a wooden puppet, invisible strings further propelled him to a seat under the tree. A great sorrow rolled over Lizzy. Mustard gas! Now the window had a new meaning for her, and she bit her lip, ashamed that before today she would have thought that Rostrevor's inhabitants had fought only 'a drawing room war'.

Everywhere she was treated as a professional person, her accent marking her as either a nanny, a private tutor, or housekeeper in some privileged home. But she was none of these to the elderly man in the brown dustcoat, who greeted her so dramatically as she stepped inside his door. He was sinewy and bald, wore a pair of wire-framed glasses and had a presence that cautioned: trifle with me at your peril.

'A very good morning to you, young lady,' he began in a voice that made no pretence to be his own. It was a contrived Sandhurst voice, theatrical and gushing. 'Am I right in assuming you are the very lovely Miss Elizabeth McGrain?' And before Lizzy had time to respond, he was round from behind the counter and clasping her by the hand. 'It was a wonderful funeral for your father. A great turnout.' He declaimed:

[122]

'*Breathes there the man, with soul so dead,*
Who never to himself hath said,
This is my own, my native land!

'Sir Walter Scott! One very decent man, and so was your father.

'*And town and tower and cottage*
Hath heard the trumpet blast.

'Horatius! Your father would have been very proud. His homecoming was a muster to the Stronghold. Maggie and John leading the cortège, town and tower and cottage behind them. He's a bit of a pedant, but our new parish priest spoke very well. Eloquently. Metaphors, similes, drawing the comparison between your father's welcome back to his earthly home and the welcome he'll receive in the Kingdom above.'

With the words 'Kingdom above', he leaned right back and very slowly raised his outstretched palms and rolled his eyes, looking towards the distemper peeling on the ceiling and focusing far beyond.

'Father Bennett even contrived an excellent faux pas at the offerings. Couldn't have done more.'

Lizzy found it very difficult not to laugh. The man had all the characteristics of a Shakespearean actor, coupled with the antics of a music hall comedian on the Old Kent Road. He was a natural performer who couldn't resist a curtain call, even to an audience of one.

'The Vinegar Man', Geordy Lyons, presided over a faded empire: three blocks of Bridge Street, dozing between Sherwood's Pharmacy and Morgan's Corner House. It was a premises that had come to have a cold tea wash about it, twilighting the timbered décor of the hardware shop, a store with a 'last day of the sale' feel to it, its counters and shelves randomly scattered with end-of-the-line wares. This was what 'H. Lyons & Son, Carter and General Merchant' had retreated to, an atmospheric depot relying almost exclusively on packages left by the bus. Drawn back from an expanse of vacant real estate, forgotten behind the peeling Times Italic script over the double doors to the yard. Here, through an archway that even in daylight was brooding, stood a terrace of deserted workshops, stables, stores and lofts. Moss settled on the cobbles, myriads of wild flowers seeded against the walls, and broken windows gave glimpses of the accoutrements of the coach builder's trade. These coffins without lids and wheels of carriages were a haven for ghosts, who stepped back into corners, and gave a signal for long dead pall-bearers to tiptoe across the floor above.

Geordy owned it all. It was his birthright, a 'mess of pottage' that sapped his ambition and instilled in him a whiff of snobbery, all the better to indulge his obsession for the literary arts. He devoured poetry, ate crosswords, and was a leading light in the local dramatic society, where he demanded to be typecast. His forte was the evil army officer who delights in evicting destitute orphan families from their homes—wanton mischief that ordains a terrible comeuppance, and justifies the final act, the death scene where he can writhe and moan on the floor, a consequence of having spectacularly cut his throat with a wooden knife, and, as the curtain falls, for verisimilitude, he can spit his very own concoction of mulched tomatoes, carrot and blood oranges on to the stage.

All this enterprise he cultivated, while his business, like the paint on his premises, was falling about his ears, heroically neglected, sacrificed on the altar of theatre and drink. For reasons best known to himself, Geordy Lyons brought the character of a benign Captain Thunder into his real life, presiding over what he called the bus depot and directing his nephew with small deliveries in a pony and cart. It was hard to get a word in edgeways as he continued to tread the boards. He was a man who had indeed let his business collapse, but had the strength, the steel tempered in the white heat of village scrutiny, to forge his own place. He was more than an actor; he was a teacher, quoting lines from the classics as well as from parochial plays, so complete in himself that he needed neither approval nor applause, but he challenged us by his existence to look within ourselves and choose our own path.

'I would like you to collect a trunk from the station in Warrenpoint,' Lizzy eventually got to say.

She was met with a wild stare of mock surprise, and a reply in a voice even more polite than before. 'Yes, as you decree, dear lady. I will have one of our best operatives see to it right away.' Then Captain Thunder walked over to the shelves and from between a box of washing soda and a globe for a hurricane lamp, he took down a small brass urn.

'Perhaps I could also have a stone of flour and two bags of coal,' Lizzy continued, but the man in the dustcoat was concentrating on the urn, setting it on the counter, unscrewing its top, and delicately shaking some of its contents onto the palm of his left hand. It seemed to Lizzy like a mixture of ground cinnamon, pepper and snuff, which he touched and moved very lightly with his forefinger, before meticulously brushing every speck back into the jar. It was hard to ignore him, but Lizzy did try and she started to examine a quart tin can.

'In some societies they sprinkle the dust from their ancestors' ashes over their food,' he said in a voice that again caught her attention, because this time she knew it was his own. 'This is the remains of Major Pilkington,' he continued, solemnly tapping his finger on the restored lid of the brass urn. Then, after a pause, and in a new voice—polite North Down—he added, 'Cremated in Roselawn and transported from Belfast on the 5:20 bus. Great big robust fellow; there he is now in the palm of my hand. Humanist, used to live in "Carpenham", and requested in his will that I go up there, sprinkle a little of him on the lawn and fork the rest into the ground under the forsythia bush. Bit unsure about permission. No family. Wife predeceased him. Didn't want to be buried with her. Neither of them took to double harness—an element of kicking over the traces. We have all sorts here; don't know what attracts them. Spiritualists tapping tables, Druids who couldn't so much as bless themselves without casting the runes. Chap in the other day from New Zealand. Cooneyite he was. Seems it's a popular form of Christianity in the Antipodes. Dear Miss Empson, now she was a naturist. Her remains were peppered over the market garden. That was her wish. But not before a bit of a to-do. Young Maurice, tidying up, and not knowing the nature of the ashes, threw them on the fire. Dear lady, she got burnt twice.'

Whether true or not, Lizzy could see he loved to tell it, concluding with a wonderful raffish smile.

'I'd like to pay you now,' Lizzy said, trying to keep the transaction as normal as possible, and was relieved to see him concur and take from under the counter a duplicate receipt book, carefully putting in a sheet of carbon paper, and writing all the items in an exquisite and elaborate hand, crossing 't's, dotting 'i's and putting serifs at the end of every upward stroke. 'I suppose by now you've met St John,' he ventured, lapsing into his actor-producer voice. Then, handing Lizzy the piece of paper, he looked her directly in the eye and, with a mischievous grin, continued, 'Lady Macbeth caged in, her dogsbody Dogberry, and of course young Lochinvar.'

'And who am I?' asked Lizzy pointedly.

'You, dear girl,' he said without hesitation, 'are the Cailin Brea, the Queen of all Craigarran and the Rose of Sweet Drumreagh.'

She gave him a knowing look, smiled and said 'Thank you' and, having paid him, took the can with her and left the stage.

'You're for the Upper Parishes,' he ranted, this time in a Scottish accent.

'My heart's in the Highlands, my heart is not here. My heart's in the Highlands, a-chasing the deer.' She could still hear him out in the street and even across the square, pronouncing 'High' as 'He', and lapsing into Robbie Burns, 'Wee, sleekit, cowran, tim'rous beastie, O, what a panic's in thy breastie!'

At the Dark Place, the tinker had sloughed off his barrel and was crouched over the beginnings of a fire. He had all the appearance of a grounded raven with a broken wing: cold, vulnerable, too caught up in his infirmity to notice her go by. A little farther on, she stopped and glanced through the ironwork of Carpenham gates. In the distance, at the end of the gravel drive, was a period residence, its roof a multitude of chimney stacks and sharp angles, cutting into the sky like a dragon's back. The garden was an arboretum where the cool of the smooth-barked beech, walnut, oak and monkey-puzzle contrasted with the heat of the forsythia bush. A horticultural triumph, huge concave strokes of nature's distemper brush, dipped in golden yellow and swept joyously to the sky. Major Pilkington had no doubt planted it; he'd be happy there.

Biddy Drennan's shop, at the fulcrum of country and town, enticed Lizzy in for a box of matches and a packet of cigarettes. Inspired by the maxim 'a yard of counter is worth a farm of land', it was in the front room of a very small house, where, had the door opened out, it would have obstructed passers-by on the County Road. Efficient in so far as her shop was also her kitchen, Biddy had an advantage over Woolworth's in that she could serve her customers while getting on with her work. An enterprising woman, about five years older than Lizzy, she had been widowed in Scotland and had returned home with a daughter and two sons.

'I thought you were from the Hydrove yesterday,' she called, as she sat at her kitchen table surrounded by the paraphernalia of commerce and beckoned Lizzy in. It was said in such a familiar way, direct and warm, and reaching out with an openness of spirit that made it easy to push back the half-door, step behind the counter, and dispense with the formality of even shaking hands.

'Hydrove?' said Lizzy, settling into a chair and turning her head sideways to look under her hat.

'Yes, up at Knockbarragh House. That's what the Germans call it now.'

'Germans?' Lizzy again queried, sounding as if she only ever spoke in single words.

'Yes, they've piped water down from the lake on top of Slieveban and are callin' the place a health resort. You take the waters. Seems people are goin' to come from all over the world.'

Inside Lizzy a great anger was building. 'Germans!' she snapped. 'Just up the road! Were they allowed to stay here? During the war?' Each group of words was spat out with a venom that she could see puzzled Biddy. Somewhere between 'Carpenham' and this shop she had crossed a barrier into another world. From poppy gardens and military salutes to a zone that knew little of, and cared less about, the war. The youth of Drumreagh and Knockbarragh had fought and died in the mines of Pennsylvania and the slums of New York. Their country was this valley; their patriotism glowed directly in the tiny mountain farms.

A striking figure came in for a packet of cigarettes. Tall and elegant, outrageously painted and powdered, he had a cream gabardine coat draped over his shoulders, a silk scarf at his neck and a rakish wide-brimmed hat. Tottenham Court Road, Lizzy thought, as, in a froth of effeminate flourishes, he gushed, 'Lovely to see you, Miss McGrain, and, as always, lovely to see you, Mrs Drennan. You've brought the good weather with you, young lady,' and he very daintily paid for his purchase from a lady's purse, pirouetted and was gone. It was a performance that, to Lizzy's astonishment, didn't even warrant a raised eyebrow from Biddy.

'Ian Cambry,' she said very matter of factly. 'Bit light on his feet … They're vegetarians,' she continued, turning back to the Germans in the Hydrove. 'Keep to themselves; grow all their own food. They even have their own priest. He works away in the fields—just like an ordinary man.'

'Cremates his congregation,' smiled Lizzy.

'You were in The Vinegar Man's,' Biddy retorted. 'Geordy Lyons. You know, the Bus Depot. Did he do his party piece—the death scene from *Terry's Kate*? Such a set-to, squirmin' and kickin', him right down on the floor. It's a mercy you were spared that.'

They were comfortable together, forging a friendship, not by asking questions, but by equating answers and general talk, celebrating their compatibility with nods and smiles.

'Part of the Hydrove's treatment is fastin' for a day and takin' hot seaweed baths. They eat a lot of Carrageen Moss boiled in milk.

Bridget Morgan's the cook in Cloonevan on the Warrenpoint Road; says that a woman there eats nothin' else! Not another bite goes into her mouth, whatever her ailment. Never gets out of bed. Married even in bed, has a scraw of children, all on Carrigeen Moss boiled in milk. Nothin' to do with them up at the Hydrove. Always lived on it. Bridget tells me that when it's boiled, it's put out in the icehouse where it cools to a jelly. The woman has it for breakfast, dinner and tea. Eats it with a dollop of blackcurrant jam you have Mick Wilson beside you.' A reflection so blurted out in error, the whole sentence so run right in together, that both women laughed.

Biddy didn't think it worth her while to do any more than pull over the half-door, as she set out to walk Lizzy the first quarter of a mile of level road, talking of London and Glasgow, of a kingfisher under the bridge, a heron in the meadow, and the lobster quality of crabs' toes.

'There's a lot of crosses in the Remembrance Garden,' Lizzy said.

'Yes. God save people, they all went from the big houses, and them that had links with them.' And then there was a pause, and whether purposely or not, Biddy went off at a tangent. 'The Missioner left a picture of the Sacred Heart to be given to the next couple to marry in the parish. There hasn't been a wedding for three or four years; they won't even join the Pioneers.'

'Pioneers?'

'Yes, the Pioneer and Total Abstinence Society. They abstain from alcohol to honour Our Lord's thirst. They meet in a hall dedicated to Father Mathew. He must have started it.' And with a smile and nodding her goodbyes, 'Arthur Keenan says there's them in it who's not yet in the asylum,' she set off back to the shop.

On her own again, the road rising, Lizzy couldn't help but ponder all that had been said. For some reason she felt a little uneasy. Should she have been more guarded? No. She had said nothing. But still the feeling persisted. It was that she wasn't ready for Biddy's apathy. The Germans and the people in the big houses were both equally removed from her and she viewed them just the same.

McShanes' farm sported a rose garden. A bit of colour between the gable of the house and the road, which simply didn't exist above the Holly Rock. An artificial rouging no doubt deemed unnecessary, in the face of wild primrose, bluebell, thorn blossom, heather and whin that flourished farther up the road. Mrs McShane, like the garden, was welcoming, a homely matron who met Lizzy's 'Could I have some buttermilk please?' south London accent, with an 'Of course you can. Come in. I'll scald that new quart tin' Scottish burr.

Lizzy knew the Scottish accent was almost indigenous to the valley, such was the toing and froing to Glasgow and the Lowlands. Children were often born and partly educated in Scotland, before an inheritance, or a natural yearning for native heath, called the family home. She watched Mrs McShane take the black kettle off the crook, pour the boiling water into the new tin, and be struck by something else. There were no introductions. No one ever said who they were, or asked who you were. Here was a community where everyone knew everyone else, knew everything about them, and where the anomaly of a stranger's particulars would be assimilated into the great public register within hours.

'Were you in Biddy's?' Mrs McShane asked, and, seemingly knowing the answer, continued, 'Ran a lodging house in Pollockshield; the whole country stayed with her. She's the heart a' corn. Had her own troubles; lost two men. Was there any sign of Arthur Keenan about the place?' And again without waiting for an answer, and in a sort of resigned 'Sure what does it matter?' voice, added, 'I suppose they're just friends.'

'Biddy had two husbands already' appeared in big capitals on the blackboard of Lizzy's mind. Two husbands! And in the way Mrs McShane said 'just friends', it didn't mean Arthur Keenan and she were relatives; it implied there may be an element of company keeping in his earnest 'helping out'.

The dairy was a small detached whitewashed stone building at the side of the house. Perfectly clean, the interior had the fresh smell of wholesomeness, and a colour scheme that ranged from pale yellow to the whitest white. A dash churn and covered crocks sat on the floor, and prints of butter glistened on linen-draped shelves—the accoutrements and stock-in-trade of a home-based creamery that Mrs McShane marketed with a sales pitch that would do a stallholder in Petticoat Lane proud. First she presented a taste of butter on a silver knife. 'Do you think it's too salty?' she asked Lizzy.

'No, no. Not at all.'

'Not salty enough?' was her next concern.

The upshot of all this was that a little rosy-cheeked Drumreagh woman had turned the buyer-seller relationship on its head. It was Lizzy who had to reassure Mrs McShane of the quality of the product before she was allowed to buy it and continue on up the road.

There is nothing like a purpose to put a spring in your step. Lizzy had the buttermilk and butter, and with it an almost primitive need to get down the loanin and into her own house to begin to bake bread. As she hurried up the road, she went over her mother's recipe, recalling the metal ornamentation on the front of their Thornburn range. She was back in Elmhurst Mansions, in their flat on the second floor, looking at the smoke, and redbrick of Clapham North, and the iron steps zigzagging down to the communal yard. Her mother was making not griddle bread but pancakes, greasing the hot plate with butter, and ladling out the mixture from a yellow delft bowl. There was a red and white checked cloth on the table, plates and syrup, the warm smell of baking, and thousands of tiny white bubbles on the top of each pancake that was ready to be turned. The three of them were happy—her mother, her father and herself chiding each other as they waited to claim and devour each delicacy coming off the fire.

She was jolted from her daydream by a movement up at the Holly Rock, a distraction that was Wilsons' dog coming to meet her, bursting with a welcome, and wagging its tail, warming her heart and making her wonder how it knew the exact moment to leave Craigarran. She put both the can of buttermilk and her bag safely up on the ditch, and, stooping, clapped her hands and patted her knees, exclaiming 'Who's a clever boy?'

Paddy Magill, thinning turnips in the field below the road, couldn't help but witness the interplay, and, kneeling up straight, thought there's a bit more to her than beer and skittles; Dinny's not shot of her yet.

The afternoon sun was shining through the open door, its beam defined by pollen and dust, as Lizzy gave the wheel of the bellows a turn, linked the griddle on the creel, and left it to warm on a smouldering fire. In a brown crockery bowl, she made a blend of two cups of flour, half a teaspoonful of baking soda, and a pinch of salt. Then she began pouring in a half-pint of buttermilk and stirring the contents with a wooden spoon, taking care not to let the mixture get too wet, putting a shake of flour on the table and, with sleeves rolled up, tipping it out: a pliable oblate granite ball to be quickly kneaded with satisfying grasps. That's enough, she thought—too much will spoil it—as she cleaned the dough off each finger in turn, adding it to the bulk and flattening it out with the heel of her hand, patting it, making a disc nine inches in diameter and one inch deep, to be cut into quadrants and slipped (each one reforming the circle) on the griddle, which had been lightly dusted with flour.

It was very gratifying for Lizzy to be making her own bread. The smell of its cooking wafted through the kitchen, bringing a lived-in feel to the house. She sat by the bellows, spinning the wheel and adding individual sticks to the fire: seasoned whin stalks, as thin as your little finger, as thick as your arm. She wondered about the heat—was the griddle too hot?—busying herself turning the farls, stooking them, and lightly squeezing each one to see was it fozy or firm. She mused that her father had always liked a good hard crust; he'd talk about a 'bannock of bread', and she put the farls down flat again to give them additional time to harn. Finally she decided to take them off the heat, and place them in the back window, sitting on a white linen cloth. It seemed to take an eternity for the bread to cool, so, to fill the time, she boiled the kettle and dressed the table. Then, splitting a farl, and satisfied that it was cooked right through, she thickly buttered it and relished eating it.

One week slipped into another, with gathering sticks, whitewashing and making Craigarran her home, and while Mick Wilson's posturing was vaguely disconcerting, she felt secure and enjoyed the freedom of being left alone, to wave occasionally to Maggie and to acknowledge an unobtrusive 'Well, girl' from Dan Shannon and John.

Biddy Drennan's shop was her diversion, where (Mrs McShane was right) Arthur Keenan did spend an inordinate amount of time. A polite head gamekeeper sort of chap, presentable in worn tweed jacket and clean dungarees, toiling quietly in the vegetable garden and maintaining the etiquette of staying outside the shop.

'I'm surprised you've been spared "The Foxes",' Biddy said, and, as if to underline her clairvoyance, not two evenings later Rosie arrived.

'Our lassie says will you come over and have a look at a coat?' she said by way of introduction. And from the way she jigged about and didn't come inside, it was obvious that Lizzy was required to come with her, and she was expected to come now.

'It's to see if it's decent enough for me to get another season out of,' Rosie said, as Lizzie followed her past Tievegorm and along an ever narrowing loanin to a display of honeysuckle and foxgloves around Shannons' street. This was Coolnafrankey, a quaint grange of neglected buildings and dishevelled thatch.

'Sure there was no cause for you to be runnin' over, fussin',' May greeted her, a smug turning of the tables, that Lizzy unknowingly countered by reaching down to pat Sailor, saying he was 'a diamond dog'.

Together, in their regalia of layered pinnies and crocheted shawls, Rosie and May had a gnarled symmetry, May with the distinguishing feature of a gossamer goatee beard and a stubbly moustache.

'Do you see much of Anthony Green?' she asked Lizzy and,

without waiting for an answer, said, 'A monk! He couldn't be a priest you know, because he must have been a father in his own right.'

'Oh, fathered children,' Rosie affirmed.

Then in an onslaught of scurrilous dialogue, the two old sisters proceeded to pedigree the country, each revelation concluding with 'It needs to be said. It needs to be said.' Lizzy realised she was just the catalyst, and they spurred each other further to 'Owen Roark's children weren't his own, because they had dandled him as a baby and he didn't have the wherewithal to father a family, and Joe Marley was a son of John Lydon, because he was impish like Lydon, and not like another Marley in the house.' And the sisters rationalised this by relating that when a mare is brought to stud, the groom takes great pains to introduce the stallion to her, ensuring that in the act of being covered, the mare's attention does not wander to some swayed specimen in the distance, because from that nag the genes would be drawn.

And through all this, Sailor posed, and Shep slouched, and Lizzy looked round the kitchen, noting the steps climbing the side of the chimney breast to a second-floor room, and over by the settle-bed the stake and chain for the cow. All the while she wondered why 'It needs to be said' and how such a nice man as Dan Shannon could have two such harridans of sisters, a quandary she was delighted to put behind her when he came in to quell the furore and, without even a mention of the coat, allowed her to go home.

She saw him coming. He was about three-quarters of the way down the loanin—arresting, hypnotic, blind. The sight of him changed the green and pink of a beautiful Craigarran evening to the monochrome, concrete outside Field Hospital No. 2, Le Havre: columns of young men, each joined at the shoulders by outstretched arms, each a link in a human chain, dragged from the ship of youth by the anchor of war, going, but never again seeing, home, banished to a black tunnel where they must stumble without a chink of light. The blind man was led by a boy of eight or nine who was giddily swinging from his charge's left arm, more a hindrance than a help.

As Lizzy moved closer to the window to follow their progress, John

Wilson came into sight. He was rushing to meet the blind man, and, in forgetting his own affliction, resembled a rigid primate that had only learned to walk. Lurching from foot to foot, he swivelled forward to grasp the visitor by the hand, shake it excitedly and clap him on the arm. It was such a welcome that the exuberance of it rolled over the stone ditch at the corner of the loanin, over the stream and over Lizzy herself, its energy propelling the cripple and the blind man up the burnished rocks of Craigarran Street, and into Wilsons' house.

'You'll have Dark Dan with you,' John Wilson greeted her, as she crossed the stream the next morning on her way to Biddy's shop. 'If it's not imposin' on you, he'll go as far as Roark's loanin—that's his next stop.' Up at the gate, her charge was talking to Maggie, a woman more in jail than ever as she put her hand through the railings, slipped something in his pocket and touched him on the arm. Then Dark Dan stepped back a pace, braced himself as he turned, and headed down the street.

He was a tall, raw-boned man of between fifty and sixty, wearing a distinctive wide-brimmed felt hat and a grey double-breasted overcoat. He had powerful, well-formed bare feet. As he came forward, he sensed Lizzy and hesitated, and she, noticing how clean he smelled, reached out and took him by the arm. There were no goodbyes. John from the street and Maggie from the gate reverently watched the young woman lead him past Pulnafrog and up the loanin—he had his rosary beads in his hand. A man who had seen so much before, and after, the veil of cataract had been drawn over his light blue eyes, he enfolded her in his serenity as he quietly breathed his prayers. She sensed he liked women, and couldn't help walking close to him, leaning against his arm, spicing his meditations, and warming him with guilt for allowing the proximity for the quarter mile they shared. Already a child was running up the field to take her away from him. Sensing it, he stood and announced that 'A fox took a hen from a woman that had no hens, and gave it to a woman that had hens,' and as he spoke his head rose a little, his blind eyes seemed to twinkle, and he looked to the horizon, a little above the

Craigs of Mullaboy. And Lizzy wondered had his conundrum some Old Testament significance or had Dark Dan simply got a bit mixed up?

Biddy thought no more of Dark Dan than she thought of the other harbingers of high summer. In fact, she thought less of him. Less than the bumblebee hitting the window, the swallow swooping under the arch of the bridge, the blossom on the whin. Certainly she thought much less of him than of Arthur Keenan, gently shaking the onion bulbs and bending down their tops.

'Pilgrim Dan,' she said dismissively, to Lizzy's, 'Do you know the blind man who came and stopped in Wilsons' last night?' 'The blind tramp,' Biddy continued. 'He never comes down this far. Kilbroney, Drumreagh, Clontafleece—that's his run. Crossin' the county, collectin' for Lough Derg. He has houses to stay in. Out in The Close, Craigarran, over in Ballybot. I don't know why they keep them. There's "The Weatherblade" comes about April. Wait till you see her! Hair like a thorn bush. The "Talaighs" give her their kitchen. Seems she does her washin' and such. She's away before they get up. Mick wouldn't disturb her. If he's out and John's in bed, he climbs in the room window.'

'Lough Derg?' said Lizzy, trying to draw Biddy a little further on Pilgrim Dan.

'Aye, it's in some godforsaken place in the north-west of Ireland. A lough that has an island in the middle of it. Lough Derg I presume. He's collectin' to build a chapel and Stations of the Cross, and lodgings for pilgrims. Well, maybe not so much lodgings. Seems you go out on a boat to it, and fast, and stay up all night, and say your prayers.' Then, with a smile, 'Something like the Hydrove I suppose. Only,' and she gave a really big smile, 'there's a cave with "The Divil" in it. A howlya—the Germans never would have thought of that. And Dark Dan tells everyone that after two days when you're comin' back and the belly's droppin' out of you, you feel so good that all hands sing their heads off in the boat.'

Then she started to talk about Craigarran. About Mick's sister, Rosie, married down in Carcullion, and his brother Luke, who never wrote. 'He's supposed to be flyin' an aeroplane in America,' she quoted, twinkling her eyes and smiling to show a set of fine, even teeth. 'And your Great-Aunt Sar' Ann,' she continued.

'You're not going to tell me she's flying an aeroplane in America,' Lizzy teased.

'No, she married the Earl of Bicipsy.' Lizzy laughed. 'No, honestly! She was supposed to be a great beauty, anyway. Red hair. Sure oul' Tommy McAllenan, a friend of your own, actually went to see her. Pennsylvania, I think. "I'm at the right house," he said when the butler opened the door and he could see Sar' Ann's portrait on the mansion's wall. He's makin' up for his sins. He's like a boyo who done something awful,' Biddy mused.

'Who?' said Lizzy, and Biddy looked her in the eye, tilted her head mischievously and said, 'Pilgrim Dan!' and both of them laughed, quickly muffling their amusement as a small boy arrived.

'Five Woodbine, Biddy, and mark them on me Ma's book,' he ordered. A four-stone bundle of dark-haired energy and devilment, a precocious scamp who put the cigarettes in his pocket, and with a dismissive nod and a 'Right now, missus,' in Lizzy's direction, was gone.

'Wee Vinny McArdle,' Biddy said, as she walked a bit of the road. 'An oul-fashioned crab if ever there was one. An imp a the Divil. Would you believe that monkey's an altar boy, has to get cigarettes for his asthma; seems it's good for it.'

'I hope he didn't think we were laughing at him.'

'No. You couldn't be up to that playboy, throwin' balls of horse dung at the Germans going past yesterday. The breed of The Foxes. His mother's Bridie Shannon; Oul' Dan's his grandfather, Rosie and May's his great-aunts.'

For the entire valley, it was the biggest day of the year, bigger than Hallowe'en, bigger than Christmas, bigger than when the mare foaled. It was the last Friday in July, the Warrenpoint fair. For many, it was when they made whatever money was made that year, the day they sold the wether lambs. A morning of big breakfasts, white shirts, clean dungarees, barking dogs, shouting men, and bleating, separated ewes and lambs.

Wilsons' sheep were already gathered down from the mountain and convenient in the field behind the house. After a bowl of porridge and a cup of tea, but before washing, changing and the big fry, Mick, with a bit of help from his father and Trojan work by the dog, cornered all the sheep between the gate at the back of the house and the wall of Pulnafrog. There he caught each rough-headed wether, and lifted him over the cashel wall. A six-foot barrier, sometimes breached with a snatch, sometimes with a clean and jerk, but always at first repeated fruitlessly, since the isolated lamb in the holding would inevitably panic and make a supreme effort to jump out, trampolining up from behind the wall, and landing on the platform of the cornered stock. However, with a bit of perseverance and by getting the first few in as quickly as possible, the wethers for Warrenpoint were settled and penned, and the ewes and ewe lambs spirited away and for the time being secured in the far field behind the house. That done, the two men walked contentedly back for their breakfast, weighing the quality of that year's stock against the previous year's prices, and pondering what was the least they would take for the lambs—an evaluation that continued as John put the frying-pan on the fire and leant over with his stick to give the wheel of the fanbellows a turn. He carved a wedge of dripping from a white bowl, added it to the legacy of melting gravy, and laid on strips of bacon, before frying eggs and the day before's soda farls. All the while Mick bustled, preparing to get washed, shaved and changed into clean clothes for the fair.

The commotion outside, not just at Wilsons', but on the mountain and along the loanin and general surrounds, had Lizzy up and about that bit earlier. With no knowledge or reverence for the rituals of the day, she took the enamel bucket and walked over to the well. Conscious only of the green going off the bracken, she skipped over the stream, and indulged herself in that happy void of being free of thought. Just as she took the tin hoop off the little hazel gate and began to pull it back, she realised there was something different. In a ripple of wool and horn and vigour, there were sheep in Pulnafrog, bunching together, focused on her. Horrified, hesitant, never before having been that close to them, she stood with her hand on the gate in a hypersensitive seizure that magnified the sheep, the gap she had created, the smooth granite boulders and, in her peripheral vision, the reaction of Wilsons' dog. From comfortably reclining on warm cobbles up at the door, he was transformed into a neurotic caricature of himself, startled and shaken. You're doing something awful, he conveyed. You're committing a reserved sin. You're violating that which is sacrosanct. In the name of Jesus, you're opening the gate to Pulnafrog.

Then she was in a cinematography production. It was a horror film; the organ was pounding and the projector was going too fast. The lambs were dashing towards her; she could hear the rattle of a chair being bumped off a table, and a guttural urgent shout, 'For God's sake, woman, don't let them lambs out!'

It startled her, the power, the force, the naked command of it; a great bell, the clapper ringing in her head. Mick was at the door now, his shirt collar rolled in; he had shaving soap on his face and a towel dropping from his hand. The sight of him overwhelmed her with a sense of apprehension and embarrassment, and added to her helplessness.

Like Lot's wife, Lizzy crystallised into Craigarran's own pillar of salt, experiencing that awful moment in a dream, when your terror demands flight, but you can only stand. The lambs dashed for the opening, a solid pliable cumulus cloud with horns, pushing past her, buck-lepping round the corner of the wall and down the gable of the house. Leaving the hurdle a-kilter, they careered out into the beyond. Mick Wilson was right behind them, accelerating with the advantage of a downward slope in the street. Pumping his arms, lifting his knees, driving with his hobnailed boots, adjusting his stride for the gate and clearing it at speed. He never faltered, braces flying, shirt-tail flapping, and being overtaken by the dog. 'Get ahead! Get ahead!' he shouted, but it was too late. The wethers had already raced across what was in any case a narrow field and had burst through the hedge, to be back with the ewes and ewe lambs, instinctively burying their heads under the flanks of their mothers, and dunting them mercilessly to confirm that it was time they were weaned.

In the immediate aftermath of the furore, John Wilson came shuffling down the street to where Lizzy was still standing rooted at the gate. He was nodding and smiling and in the warmest way said, 'Sure, it's all no harm; you weren't to know. He'll get them back.'

Of course I wasn't to know, she could have screamed at him, her temper fuelled by her disappointment at not having closed the gate, and a boiling anger at something else. That … that toerag Wilson, with the first words he had ever spoken to her, should have the audacity to shout! She wanted him to have a lot of trouble getting the lambs back. Shouting at her! Snatching up the bucket, she fired the gate wide open and, to his words slashing at the drums of her inner ear, purposefully walked to the well, filled her bucket and returned slowly to the gate—in such evident bad temper that a subdued John Wilson knew to keep his mouth tight shut. A McGrain if there ever was one. It would be hard to keep the saddle on her, he thought.

Mick and the dog were again taking the flock up the field. He walked quickly and determinedly, while the dog, sensing the nervous tension, crouched and shimmied and used all his power of eye to keep the sheep in a tight bunch. Lizzy never moved from the hazel gate as Mick cornered them, lifting each six-stone lamb by rump and horn over the wall. His father in the cashel held the first, then the second, springing and somersaulting on the end of each arm until he was able to let them go as a third and fourth quickly followed, to an ever-increasing company that welcomed each new arrival, and put aside all thoughts of even thinking about jumping out.

Lizzy did not want to vacate the company either. Square-shouldered and square-jawed, she glared as Mick lifted each lamb over the wall. She let him be under her scrutiny, defying him to ignore her, noting with relish the fresh sheep dung on his new trousers and on the arm of his white shirt. That satisfied her, and, with a toss of her head and a swirl of her skirt, she picked up the bucket and swaggered back to the house.

Mick Wilson was part of an exodus that swept down the mountain lanes, swelled along the Shore Road, and poured into the square in Warrenpoint. It was a surge of energy created by small flocks of hill sheep, purposeful men, and attentive dogs, a fluctuating ribbon of black and white, here and there becoming ragged, as lambs looked for ewes and darted through open gates into gardens of floral delights. Pet lambs were a particular problem. Bottle-fed by women, they were as iron filing to a magnet for anyone in long clothes; drawing the flock behind them, they tore directly at elderly dowagers, sending them scurrying back into their houses. Gardeners, ladies in silk dressing gowns and retired military personnel were inevitably involved, registering outraged protest, as enthusiastic dogs, barking and snapping, tried to get out the intruders. Forgoing the niceties of shepherding, they harried their charges through goldfish ponds and flowerbeds. It was genteel pandemonium. Householders stood on their verandas, barked abuse at indifferent drovers and, in an assertion of rights, commanded the gardener to leave the gates unclosed.

Dinny Coyle always sold his lambs at home, quietly, almost secretly, to Paddy Brophy, a dealer from Warrenpoint. It was a transaction well out of the public eye and allowed him to add a shilling in the telling of the price. He had enough dogs to deserve an animal charity's funding, yet he still had not (even if he had wanted to) got one good enough to drive out sheep. All in all, the Lamb Fair was torture. Dinny didn't want to go, but he didn't want to stay at home, and his predicament was further compounded by Alice pushing him forward and dragging him back. To her, he was fifteen, not forty-five. She was still (because he had never left home) very maternal. A great phrase of hers was to 'pass yourself', meaning socialising with an easy grace. Dinny was to go out and be affable, but he wasn't to be drinking, gambling or coming home late. In short, his watchword was to be 'uninvolved'. Drunken scuts, gougers, bookies' runners were all to be avoided; he had so many instructions, Alice should have given him a list. She had particular venom for skilts, brazen hussies of seventeen or eighteen from Rostrevor or Warrenpoint, whose ardour should be cooled with a good dose of soot and buttermilk—cunning opportunists who would set their eye on Dinny, recognise him for the catch he was, and spirit him away. Girls who would inherit a wee bit of a farm, or failing that, had a dowry and the kudos of coming from a good farm, weren't so bad, and just at the moment, right at the back of Alice's mind, neither was Lizzy McGrain.

Yet, after all the agonising of would he or wouldn't he?, Dinny, as always, would take out a few old ewes, tied with a grass rope, in the stiff-wheeled cart. Blessed by a downpour of holy water and a litany of incantations, a sartorially eye-catching, short, pugnacious man in a bowler hat and black tweed coat set off for the fair. He did not stand in the cart, as was normal, but sat on a straw bolster, encased by the tied sheep and his dogs, Carlow and Toss. These towsers greatly resembled their master, and to a lesser extent a particular strain of Iberian bear. The three ensconced behind a placid Clydesdale, a strikingly awkward-looking horse with a big moose's head.

At Coles Corner, it was normal for those going to the fair to avoid the residential seafront of Warrenpoint and divert up the back road— a practical convention with which Dinny never complied. He continued along the shore, past the guesthouses, the Balmoral Hotel, and the homes of the moderately rich, his bowler hat a little above the sides of the cart, his head level with the horse's rear. He looked neither to left nor right, seemingly oblivious to the charms of the waterfront and the surprised stares of residents taking their morning stroll. This was the world of the promenade, where those described in the *Picturesque Journal* as 'treading on the heels of the aristocracy' could parade and savour measured lungfuls of sea air. It was a place to dress for, to see and be seen, and to be entertained. The new swimming pool, its stout perimeter walls capturing a bowling green-size square of the Lough, had a labyrinth of disinfected facilities, and a diving board that drew a certain type of healthy exhibitionist to show off. There were the foreshore activities: rowing boats for hire; hardy individuals bathing in the open sea; and, on the raised beach, a small gaily painted wooden café, where racy young people could have tea, cakes and ice-cream.

On the dock side of the swimming pool, but still well within the confines of Georgian architecture, pristine shoreline and public park, a Bentley pulled up: a car of such understated pedigree, it overshadowed its more vulgar sibling, the Rolls Royce. Gardiner, its chauffeur, knew this and, with proper bearing, he left the controls to come round and open the passenger door, allowing Lady Margaret Elmsmore and her entourage to get out. Here was a woman who, far from treading on anyone's heels, felt it her ordained right to tramp on their heads. A true aristocrat, a first cousin of Queen Victoria once removed, she thought nothing of telephoning Irwin's emporium in Warrenpoint and demanding that their greengrocery department have a message boy deliver a single tomato to her 'at once'.

Lady Elmsmore was a grande dame with chiselled features and a splendid equine nose, evolved to balance a pair of spectacles a little more than halfway down, an ornamentation that, far from softening her appearance, intensified her authority, whether she raised her eyes to look over them or knitted her brow to look down. She wore a marled tweed costume that would never be in fashion, yet would never be out of style. Classic in design, it was perfect with the stout brown brogues, at odds with the tartan tam-o'-shanter, and as sublime as anything would be with the exquisite fox shawl. It was a fur that made you feel warm even looking at it, its colour glowing blue black on oak brown. The pelt conferred power and dignity on its wearer, giving her a presence whether she was shopping in London's Bond Street or in a small provincial town. Not that Lady

Elmsmore needed any boosting; she sat on the Board of Police Commissioners; she was treasurer to the Royal Society for the Prevention of Cruelty to Animals, and, only because of her sense of duty, was something very big in the Girl Guides. This was a woman who knew her breeding, stud fees and all.

Lady Elmsmore did not like children, a bias she highlighted by borrowing a sixpence from Gardiner, a pittance for an RSPCC collector, before, on the afternoon of that day donating £80 to a donkey sanctuary, at a gathering in the Crown Hotel. Dogs and horses were her preoccupation, the more obscure strains of the Kennel Club occupied her villa, while pure-bred Arabian stallions and mares had the run of her estate. 'A place for everything, and everything in its place' was her motto. 'Children were to be seen and not heard; gentlemen were in the army; ladies running the home front; and never let it be forgotten: breeding will out.'

Lady Elmsmore had a choice of dogs to walk: pugs, miniature black and tans, King Charles II spaniels, golden retrievers—all with their papers. On this particular day, it was the turn of the miniature black and tans, and she had six. She held what looked like six long-legged rats on fine leads, three in each hand. These smug little toffs flanked her in red coats, trotting along on spindly legs. They were a foil, delicate beside her solid figure, and in their bearing were every bit as aloof and aristocratic as the lady herself. A septet commandeering the pavement, showing the populace that God was in his heaven, their betters were in authority, and all was well with the world.

The sight of the miniature black and tans vitalised Carlow and Toss. With their muscles ravenously enhanced and the hair standing on their backs, they stripped their teeth and, using Dinny and the sheep as a springboard, catapulted, spitting and snarling out of the cart. They were terrifying in the way they floated: front legs spreadeagled, fangs glistening, hair swirling, two chilling crossbred mutants, seemingly part werewolf, part rabid baboon, and part flying fox.

'Come up, yis bastards! Come up!' Dinny roared. His further rash of expletives dwindled to a pious aspiration of 'Oh my Christ', as his mind, a blur of images, piled ballast after ballast on his heart. They were going to coup the woman, take the legs from under her. Oh sweet Jesus, Mary, and Joseph, this was going to be a fiasco based in a butcher's shop. 'Ahhh!' he rasped.

But all the bellowing in the world wouldn't have changed the barbarous conclusion, nor would the yapping of the miniature black and tans, ensconced at the back of their mistress's legs. What did change it, what actually saved them, was the presence of the Siberian fox pelt shawl, lifelike and beautiful, which slipped off Lady Elmsmore's shoulders and swung in front of her as she shuffled back and bent forward in an instinctive action to protect the little dogs. The lure of the shawl's movement thankfully distracted Toss, riveting him momentarily, before an explosion of bile projected him snarling and spitting on the back of the fox's lacquered head, pulling Lady Elmsmore forward, securing a foothold on her costume, wrenching the shawl over her tam-o'-shanter, and lashing it into the ground. Then Carlow, too, was on it, both dogs rending their quarry piteously apart. But it wouldn't part, wouldn't give them a piece each, as old enmities boiled to the surface, with each sibling now wanting it all for himself.

Lady Elmsmore wasn't normally frightened of anything, but she was terrified of Carlow and Toss. Suddenly she was a fragile matron on the slippery slope to hysteria, startled, and now further unnerved by the sight of Dinny clambering to get out of the cart, pitching forwards and backwards, his lower limbs encased in the straw bolster, his upper body constrained by the ewes.

'Ahhh!' he guldered, as he struggled and threw all humanity to the winds in punching the sheep in the belly, driving them away from him and creating enough space to get to his knees. Here was Lady Elmsmore's childhood nightmare, a genuine Grimms' Fairy Tales troll! She was transfixed by him. Someone was whitewashing the inside of her stomach and she started to scream in a high-pitched contralto that was at first almost inaudible. 'Oh, oh,' she whimpered, 'police, police. Stop them, stop them. Look, look.' Then she started to hyperventilate, gasping, 'Look at the horrible little man!'

By now Dinny was beside her, trampling the fur at its point of tension, and widening his stance as he shimmied each hobnailed boot ever outwards, in an effort to prise off the dogs.

'Where is the constabulary?' Lady Elmsmore was now trumpeting and the two Miss Parkers were unfortunate enough to be drawn into the mêlée as they passed.

'Do something!' she ordered them. 'It was my grandmother's, the Duchess of Württemberg.' And, in case that didn't impress them enough, 'Her Royal Highness the Duchess of Württemberg! Trapped in Russia, cured in Paris, it has a pure Rhineland silver clasp. Can't you at least get Gardiner?'

And then an amazing thing happened. As if realising that she had lost the run of herself, breeding did out. Lady Elmsmore drew back from her hysteria and, becoming the calm, aloof commander, ordered the Miss Parkers to form a defence. This transformation wasn't lost on Dinny. The new state of affairs further alarmed him, spurred him to step off the fur and reach down and snatch Carlow and Toss up under each arm. The dogs were still holding their quarry as Dinny lunged at the spokes of the big wheel, gained a foothold, and in a final act of desperation, tipped himself and the whole caboodle on top of the sheep and into the well of the cart.

There was now a lot of attention being given to Lady Elmsmore. A circle of wives from Victoria Terrace and Slieve Foy Place gushed across the road to console her, sidelining the Miss Parkers, who showed remarkably good sense by continuing their stroll.

Mrs Neill, the chemist's wife, was not so circumspect. Misreading the situation by bringing over tea and biscuits, she was soundly rebuked with 'Such nonsense! Return to your mistress at once.' But concern for the black and tan miniatures was permitted. After all, it did show a proper leaning to the RSPCA, and Lady Elmsmore did tolerate that … for a time. She examined each little dog, calling it by its name and enquiring gently if it was hurt. It was remarkable that she could distinguish between them—Festus, Jacob, Mabel—and convince each one that everything was alright, 'Mamma is here now. There, there, the horrid man has gone.' There was never a word of the perpetrators, who no doubt had been exonerated under the ruling that 'there are only bad owners, never bad dogs'. Given Lady Elmsmore's lead, the crowd became very maternal. Mothers who couldn't wait to spirit their infants to a nanny gently lifted Isa, Titus and Zoë (albeit at arm's length) and reached them to their mistress for her to comfort and reassure.

Like the Miss Parkers, Dinny used the arrival of the powdered wives to smokescreen his getaway. Still holding Carlow and Toss, he shook the reins on the Clydesdale's back, and the old horse duly moved on. Butter wouldn't melt in his mouth, as, with his big wise head moving from side to side, he rounded the Baths Corner, passed the municipal gardens and went on up Queen Street towards the fair.

Lady Elmsmore, now right back to herself, rounded on the company with, 'What are you doing with my dogs? Keep back. Will you dreadful people go home?'

By the middle of the day, Warrenpoint square was a vast patchwork quilt flanked on one side by the docks, and on the other three by the commerce of the town. A quilt that lay on a restless sleeper, its patches of sheep and cattle pulled by the rise and fall of the schooners in the dock, a rhythm that further shivered the stipple of horses, people and dogs. Only the stalls were steady, canvas islands in a lapping tide. It was a pageant painted in primary colours and orchestrated in animal sounds. Fissures opened as men flashed horses, and closed again to swallow the ubiquitous dogs. There were collies everywhere, tied to carts, disciplined beside their masters, and running wild. Add to that a sprinkling of town dogs, amongst them Canon Empson's boxer, Simon, cavorting with a whippet, and Captain Codd's Kerry blue.

The air was full of the pungent smell of mulched animal dung and urine, fried herrings from the eating houses and, depending on where you were standing, the fragrance of a fellow human being, kippered in tobacco and preserved in natural oils, seldom having washed in his life. Even this early in the day there were men roaring, sulking, grabbing each other by the lapels and then shaking hands, drunk. It had all been too much for them; they had to hide somewhere, and, not being used to alcohol, it could have been behind as small a barrier as two bottles of stout. It shielded them from the unease of being off their own dunghill, and helped them cope with the exotica of the woman with Tourette's Syndrome shouting terrible vulgarities at the two black men making their way through the crowd, back to the docks. And there was something else about the fair, something permeating the whole thing. It was the merest hint of revulsion at our betrayal of stoic, bewildered animals, an immoral veil that hangs over everywhere they are bought and sold.

Constable Cavan traversed it all, meridians up and down, parallels over and across, and then he walked in circles. A big, raw-boned man with a commanding presence, further empowered by a truncheon and a gun. With his wide shoulders and hair just protruding from under the back of his helmet, he had the look of a vulture. His hair was like oiled feathers, cut square and raised slightly over the shaved nape of his neck. He was a poker player hiding his thoughts, concealing a busted flush, pretending to be holding a full house.

Constable Cavan's thoughts were out at The Lodge, Lady Elmsmore's estate at Rathcoole on the Rostrevor road. In his mind he was in the drawing room looking through the bay windows at the rhododendron clump, the dolmen and the meadow rolling down to the Lough. Old Lennon, the gardener, was pruning exotic shrubs and quoting their Latin names to a nipper, while the Arabian horses fox-trotted round the ancient monument just outside the wooden fence. This was the best location in Ireland to bury a chieftain or build a house. The room reeked of camphor, its mantle only partially smothering the smell of the dogs, as her ladyship, flatulent as ever, her head back, her glasses on the end of her nose, looked at the portraits of two army captains on the wall. Young men, clean-shaven and idealistic, had been photographed formally and identically framed in gilt. 'Shot themselves over me,' she barked. Her shooting stick pierced the carpet, her wide beam supported by the leather cradle as she introduced the unfortunate men to him. Every time he was called out, he had to listen to her account of how she had rejected a marriage proposal from each captain, and how they in turn had done the decent thing and shot themselves in the head. It was a story she would relate with relish to everyone, from Jones the grocer's message boy, to Wolsley the Commissioner of Police. Constable Cavan let it settle on him for a moment, and considered how strange it was that she should take such pride in these tragedies in her past. Well, at least she's making one man happy—the one she never married, he thought. Lady Elmsmore had his heart scalded. She was one cantankerous, self-centred, dyed in the wool 'hure'; a pedigree bitch who treated everyone as if she owned them, and considered the RIC to be her private force. He tried to block out the incident at the previous year's British Legion parade on Summer Hill, but it was embossed too deeply. He had been standing under the sycamore talking to four or five players from the silver band, when she humiliated him by using her stick to tap his helmet, poke his uniform, and signal for him to put out his cigarette. Well, at least today she wasn't inspecting his appearance or introducing her unfortunate suitors. She was too flustered, her heartbeat still not quite settled after the kerfuffle on her walk. 'Ghastly, ghastly, you poor darlings,' she kept consoling the black and tan miniatures. Everyone in the house was around her: the maids, the butler, Gardiner the chauffeur; even James Lennon was standing, cap in hand, uncomfortably in the hall. Her 'poor darlings' were being consoled with hard-boiled eggs mashed in cream, its ambrosia dripping obscenely from each dog's moustache. She was rattled, the wind out of her sails, and so reduced to whining. 'A horrible rough man, with two huge mongrels and an ungainly horse and cart; an unshorn savage attacked me and the piccaninnies and absconded with the fox fur stole and clasp.'

Dan Cavan pondered how 'black unlucky' he was. The fair was full of unshorn savages; he couldn't even ask her for a fuller description, she was such a high-falutin' queen bee. Why was it always he who had to do the dirty work? What about young Menary and Summerfield? They were the boys being groomed for higher office, attending church services with her and Commissioner Wolsley, and slipping up the greasy pole of promotion with Bibles under their arms. It was pointless asking questions at the fair, futile expecting help; Cavan knew that. He understood it because he was part of this clan, he was their kith and kin, now forever isolated with a uniform and a gun. The Great War, government, his authority, it all meant little to the people from the hills. For a thousand years they had ignored invaders, defeating each wave by looking inward and clinging to the wreckage of an elaborate social life. He could see John Wilson arriving, driving a splendid cob that filled the shafts of the fair's stoutest cart. Hardly an unshorn savage and hardly an ungainly horse. It was the sort of animal kings and emperors were depicted as riding: powerful, stylish, solid black, with a luxurious mane and tail. It was a settled horse, easing confidently through the traffic with a velvet touch of the rein; controlled, steadied, manoeuvred by an elderly man whose arthritis dared him to budge in the cart.

In his heart of hearts, Constable Cavan did not want to know who had scarpered with the shawl. He was repulsed at the thought of actually finding it, dreading seeing a hair of it looking out from under an old top coat or a hessian bag on a cart floor. It was an incident he would have enjoyed, if only he had not been involved. Most people in the fair would not want a fur shawl; they wore wool, tweed and linen cloth. They would not, even if they had been sent it from America, put it on. Why had someone taken it? Dan Cavan didn't even go up to the hay market, didn't give a glance to the hen man, ignored the carts with tarpaulins, smiled to himself at the thought of it snuggled beside a litter of pigs. And then he saw his old neighbour Seán Og Taggart, and TAGGART'S FISH MERCHANTS painted in green on the white tailboard of his tricolour-themed fish cart.

You son of a bitch! Seán Og glared at him.

You impudent little bastard! he glared back.

The wet marble of the fish cart's counter was an ocean of bile between the two men.

'Herrings, alive and their eyes open; pipes in their asses and them smokin',' Seán Og cried, and as Dan turned away the fishmonger further goaded, 'You took the soup with your eyes open; licked their asses and them gloatin'.'

Seán Og's play on the Cavan 'herrings alive' catchphrase wounded the constable with a vulgar scorn that triggered a great anger, a venom that gripped some organ behind Dan's navel and clawed right up his innards to deep within his chest cavity. He wanted to turn around and grab the little bastard by the front of his shirt, twist it in a tourniquet, lash his open hand back and forward, back and forward, five, ten, fifteen times, across his face. He wanted to reinforce every slap with 'Who was the smart-aleck who tarred "Dan Cavan took the King's shilling" on the shore wall at my mother's door? I couldn't go to her funeral. My own mother's funeral! I had to sneak over the fields behind the house to see her in her coffin. Smuggled in like a criminal. To her wake!'

The cry of 'herrings alive' had demeaned Dan Cavan, tugged at the carpet of his own respect, and reminded him forcefully that he was Judas Iscariot in his home townland of Ballytra.

Fuck Lady Elmsmore, he screamed to himself, clenching his fists and gritting his teeth as the tension climbed up the muscles of his face. The whole parcel of bastards, the Sergeant, Seán Og Taggart and Wolsley were a shower of shite, he thought, and he began to feel a little better and walked on.

Earlier, Dinny too had walked on, his face a study of tics and pouts as he visualised himself at the next month's Petty Sessions where, in a setting of mahogany and distemper, he confronted the judiciary and gloriously undermined the proceedings by putting his hand on the Bible and swearing before God that he had never been at the fair. And to this end he turned the Clydesdale up Meeting Street and, keeping his head cool and his feet warm, skirted the activities and, in avoiding the coastal road, by quiet country lanes—slipped home.

As you had neighbours on the bog, you had neighbours in the fair.

[151]

It had nothing to do with those who lived beside you; they could come from another valley, another religious persuasion, but, by some process, evolved over generations, they sold their stock next to you. This was an assembly of the old and the young, the rich and the poor, which was testament to Fortune's rise and fall. If neighbours in the fair were once close kindred, had shared grazing, or joined forces with one horse each for ploughing, these ties may have been in the past. At the bottom of Duke Street, Wilsons, Sintons and Boydes held their sheep in a grid of pens provided by the urban district council, while Donnans, a little behind them, scorned the hurdles and tied ten late lambs in a line to the railings outside the Masonic Hall. Each family followed its own ritual. Paddy Flynn, twelve stone of swivelling, nervous energy, always kept his sheep on the pavement, coating it with skitter just outside the door of McAlonan's Lady's Dress Shop.

From the corner of the pen, Wilsons' dog supervised his charges, transmitting just enough authority to ensure that they were standing with their heads up facing him, photogenically at their best. Mick Wilson, on the other hand, was not quite at his best. He was uncharacteristically uneasy over the business with Lizzy McGrain. It weighed on him like a fall of snow on the branch of a whin, and it was only the wind of people's attention that shook it off. He had none of the aggression that often accompanies men when they are unsure of themselves, when they are in a crowd, and concealing the stress of having something to sell. He was comfortable; he knew he had good stock and that he would make a sale. There was always a friend coming over to talk, acquaintances to greet him, and children, ever quick to detect composure, wanted to be around him, justifying their presence by touching the horns of his sheep and patting his dog.

Never a man for courting popularity, Mick kept an eye on the lambs, listened out for prices from other deals and, knowing the folly of selling too early, or holding back and leaving it too late, assessed the day's mood. He was, however, in the difficult position of having a possible client, a man who had always bought from him, but who might not have come to that year's fair. It was a matter of holding off other buyers by feigning detachment and projecting an aura of not yet being ready to sell, much as a woman keeps a surfeit of suitors at arm's length, neither encouraging nor discouraging them, ever conscious that one may be a best second option. So Mick stalled. Until he could see the man from Jerrettspass almost sneaking through the crowd. That was the sort of him—apologetic, inoffensive, a middle-aged man with the appearance of an office junior overlooked for promotion and never expecting to get it, even though he had diligently filed cards and filled in ledgers for twenty years. He wore a long faded gabardine coat, and proclaimed the weakness of poor eyesight and a bald head by sporting a pair of glasses, and forgoing a cap. Beside him a creeping collie bitch glided on a rope. Mick considered how deceptive the man's appearance was; you would never think he was someone at the fair to buy lambs, a prosperous farmer with forty acres of barley stubble on the drumlins of County Armagh. A strict Protestant who disdained chit-chat, he went direct to the wethers and, holding the bitch back a little, checked their condition by putting his spread hand firmly on a couple of backs, sampling them: at the shoulders, on the saddle, and just above their rump. It was a hand that had seen plenty of work—big, with powerfully developed fingers and a claw-like thumb, a hand with such assured capability, it seemed at odds with the rest of the man.

Then he stepped back, pushed up his glasses with the middle finger of his left hand, and, shyly looking into the ground, asked Mick, 'What will you take for them?' His was a high voice in a sing-song accent, distinctive in the way that speech develops to highlight separate but coexisting communities. It was a dialect neither rural Belfast, Ulster Scots, nor southern brogue. It was Jerrettspass baptist fashioned over generations and peculiar to one townland on the border of Armagh and Down.

'How did they do with you last year?' Mick asked. It was a cordial enquiry that invited a bit more from the encounter than the purely monetary transaction of buying and selling lambs, an overture firmly placed in abeyance with the Jerrettspass man's 'Fairly well, fairly well' reply. Mick, fearing that some well-meaning lug could come over and spoil the deal with a mêlée of spitting on hands and clapping them together, said: 'Taking one with the other, there's nineteen lambs in it, and I'll have to get twenty-six pounds.'

The buyer wanted to be asked a price he considered to be fair, so he could put his hand into his right inside pocket, take out the little black purse with the silver clasp and, without bother or fuss, pay what he was asked. It was a ritual well known to Mick: the buying for the asking price, the purse, the money meticulously picked out by the big rough hand. Then there was the matter of the Gospel tracts. Taking them reverently from his left inside pocket, certainly not hiding them, but careful not to taint them with an unseemly flourish, he solemnly asked Mick if he would accept them, and had he recognised as his Saviour the Lord Jesus Christ. When Mick took the tracts too quickly and said that he had, the Jerrettspass man seemed disappointed and sceptical, even sad, because it was his way of extending friendship; of more than that—of showing genuine concern for someone he saw as spiritually starved.

In silence the two men marked the lambs, adding to the flamboyant red of Craigarran a sobering stroke of lowland blue. Then, at a lull in the traffic, they opened the pen gate, and directed the lambs, skipping, down Charlotte Street: a bunch of vibrant white lilac, outstripping their liberators, until at the fire station the Jerrettspass man slipped the rope off the bitch, signalling his willingness to let her take it from here, just as the wethers decided to jump a low place in the golf links wall. Instantly she was after them, taking advantage of their bunching at the sight of the golfers, a momentary gathering of resources preparatory to them scattering through the hundred acres of mounds and hollows, trees and sheughs, doctors and dentists, on the course.

Mick feared a debacle, but the collie was focused. Disregarding people, traffic and an ugly brute of a black Labrador, she tore down the main thoroughfare, up a side loanin and hurdled a high place on the perimeter wall. It was a fantastic outrun. She was in amongst the golfers, ignoring them, brushing past trousers, hypnotising men, women and wethers from her viewpoint in the bunker sand. Ears pricked, head on the ground, shoulder-bones raised, she crawled forward, her power compressed. Sometimes, like a statue dance, she held up a paw in mid-stride, her attention never leaving the sheep, controlling, cajoling, responding to the Jerrettspass man's every low whistle and shout. And then she had them as, en masse, they visibly surrendered and she guided them back over to the gap in the boundary wall, and further pressured them to jump it again.

What Mick liked about the collie was her power of eye, and how her breeding kept her always the perfect distance from the stock, pacing right up boldly to move them on, knowing instinctively when to hold back. He turned, put his hands in his pockets and smiled as he felt the religious tracts. They reminded him of his own religious instruction: the penny catechism, the priest examining his class for Confirmation in Drumreagh Hall.

'What is perjury?' he was asked.

'Totakealockofloavesorbreakafalseone,' he confidently sang out.

'Slower,' said the priest. 'Slower.'

'To take a lock of loaves or break a false one.'

'To break a lawful oath or take a false one!' the bishop's representative corrected him sternly.

And indeed, in looking back, he had to agree that, while it had the same rhythm to it, the content was different from his interpretation of a church edict chanted around the class and learned by rote.

Looking over his shoulder, Mick could see the Jerrettspass man, the bitch at his heels, the lambs in front of him, striding out the broad road.

What if he had had his penny catechism? Mick thought. What if he had had his rosary beads? Could the Jerrettspass man have accepted them as readily in return? It's a funny business, the religion business, Mick decided. One man's cherished beliefs is another's pishogues, even an affront to God. He had often seen groups preaching on the promenade on a summer's evening, one fellow giving his testament: a very ordinary-looking chap confessing to extraordinary excesses in his past life, proclaiming years of drunken revelry and outrageous dalliances with women. In short, he seemed to have been constantly presented with the type of God-sent opportunities that Mick felt cheated to have missed.

Then he thought of how he had done a bit of missionary work himself. Well, not directly, but at Mass he had joined in the prayers for the conversion of England and as a boy he had been involved in the black baby campaign, where the whole school had brought in halfpennies and pennies to ... he had to think what. To vaguely ransom an African child from the jaws of its debauched life. The whole thing was going very well, until someone planted the seed in Tommy Heaney's mind that since he had brought in the most money—ninepence halfpenny, or something like that—the child would actually be coming home to him. Yes, to his house, to run about Heaney's street, throwing stones at the hens and balls of horse dung at the people going up the road; in short, doing all the things a normal child would do. The contributions petered out for a while after that, only to be revived when the eight-year-old Joe Marley, even then a great one for starting a rumour, said that the black baby was a big lump of a fellow who could be put to work doing all sorts of drudgery, and he would have a lion with him to eat all the dogs about the town. So the children made great lists of people's dogs that needed devouring, and unappetising manual duties like sheughs that had to be cleaned, and started to bring pennies in again.

Mick could see, from the far side of the square, his father and Tom Cochrane outside the Crown bar, drinking and eating in the stiff cart. They even had an onion box on which to rest pints of porter, half-ones of whiskey, and a plate of sandwiches that had been brought out. It was a sight to make him smile: two old men oblivious of everything, happy in themselves, up on stage, and rummaging about in the past.

'Terry McPolin. Do you remember him at school? A big rooskin of a fellow; Red Skull we called him. Even then, he had a bit of a moustache and was starting to grow hair, of all places, on the rims of his ears.' John Wilson was telling it, recalling for both of them 'Mrs

McVeigh, or Miss Tuite as she was then, asked the class, "Now, boys, I want to know what you have all read,"'

Tom Cochrane raised his pint and, knowing full well the outcome, developed the biggest, roundest smile. Both men had a heightened sense of well-being, and were wondering why they didn't do this more often, as both felt the first flush of drink.

'We all tried to say something,' John continued. '*Robinson Crusoe* by Daniel Defoe. *A Tale of Two Cities* by your man. When it came to Terry, God save us, Miss Tuite was foolish enough to ask, "And what have you read, McPolin?" "Please, Miss," Terry said, "I have red hair on my arse."' The two of them, savouring the memory, smiled and pondered what to do next: sip whiskey, eat a sandwich, down some porter, light a pipe or smoke a cigarette.

'"What do you think we married you for?" he'd say to the brother's wife when he wanted a clean pair of socks. Don't know if he's living or dead; he went to America! Never came home. I remember his father taking him to school on a rope.'

'No! I don't remember that, but I do remember "There's two bastards in this townland and our Terry's the both of them." That's what they said.'

'*A Tale of Two Cities* by Charles Dickens. That's who it was,' John remembered. 'Wasn't it good of her to buy it for us, and out of her own pocket? "It was the best of times, it was the worst of times." That's how it started, and so we in compositions for ever after would start with, "It was the wettest day, it was the driest day." "He was the biggest man, he was the smallest man."'

'She was from Ballyhaunis. We were her first class. Is she living yet?'

'I wouldn't think so. I don't know.'

Mick kept them in his sight, slowly making his way towards them, nodding to this one, speaking to that. As he got close to the cart, Tom shouted at him, 'What about that woman I sent you?'—a jovial challenge that drew attention to the platform party and to Mick.

'The McGrain girl. And there's a bit of a dowry with her. I believe she's come into the farm.'

[157]

John was surprised to see how much the remark rattled Mick; how it was met with nothing more than a tightening of a smile. 'What will you drink, men?' he said, his tone clipped; more than that, it was cold and final, drawing a line under the banter and rebuking the two playboys in the cart. Tom, particularly, felt chastised, with the feeling of somehow having insulted a friend, while still knowing that he had said nothing wrong. He felt he was only making much of Mick, and anyway what was the world coming to if you couldn't take a bit of a rise out of a single fella about a girl? And with the taste suddenly off everything, slowly he raised himself and, steadied by a hand on John's shoulder, mumbled some excuses and climbed out of the cart.

Mick too was chastised; he was heart sorry he had spoiled everything. What in the name of Christ had come over him to be so sensitive? He should have been bigger, but he was unaccountably hurt, and, more than that, just for a minute he was angry that someone should imply that he would be interested in Lizzy, just because she had come into a bit of land. Unconsciously he was defending her. She was an independent woman, fit to stand beside anyone. She didn't need a legacy; she was a handsome woman, a catch for any man.

A grown man and his father living together can comfortably subsist on a pittance of talk. Mick grabbed the dog by the scruff of the neck and the fold of flesh between leg and flank and threw him up on the cart. Then he counted out the money to his father and took back a ten shilling note for himself. 'He's added me to the list of those he prays for,' he said, passing up the two religious tracts, and leaving the old man stoically looking at them in the gouged crater of his hand.

John Wilson looked at Mick walking away from him, his shoulders swaying, weaving through the fair. It wasn't like him to shout at Lizzy, and now to be cold to Tom. He was only ever like that when he had pigs to kill. John knew he hated it, the brutal drama that happened in everyone's street. Six or eight men signalling their intention, holding their frantic squealing victim belly-up, its soft throat inviting the knife, its death-throes transmitting terror to the next unfortunates in the sty. Mick killed them on his own, cajoling each pig to the slab of flat rock at the back of the carthouse, and channelling his disgust in an explosive sweep of the long-handled hammer and a silent dispatch with the knife. He was chillingly efficient: shaving the pig's hair with kettles of boiling water, and effortlessly suspending it (by a stick through the sinews of its back heels) from a convenient sycamore bough. Purposefully he positioned the wheelbarrow to catch the entrails as he opened its belly, and, having separated the liver and the heart, he cleared everything away, all the blood and hair from the killing stone, before attending to the next subject in line. Afterwards he was himself again, contentedly eating fried liver, and showing every sign of a man at peace with the pig's ghost.

But we don't even have pigs at the moment, John Wilson mused, lifting the reins of the cob.

'Minnie Cardwell, come out and fight like a man.' It was anything but threatening. Mick could hear the voice plaintively drifting down the cobblestones of Wheelbarrow Lane. The repeated invitation to fight was bewilderingly like a weak pet lamb bleating for a bottle of milk.

Gurrie Ford whinged it, as, lying in the gutter, he addressed his challenge to a little old lady, six stone of seasoned sinew and bone standing resolutely at the top of two granite steps. Minnie Cardwell, the barmaid, bouncer and septuagenarian proprietor of the Windmill Bar, had thrown Gurrie out. When Mick reached down to help him up, he could hardly believe a man could be so limp; there was no substance to him, a bag of giblets, his nerves numbed, his muscles pliable, no doubt preventing injury when he fell, and underlining Arthur Keenan's great maxim 'There's luck in drink.' Gurrie had no idea on God's earth where he was; to further quote Arthur, 'he didn't know if he was punched or bored,' and he had a disturbing imbecilic grin on his face and not a flicker of recognition in his unnaturally focused, big blue eyes. Helped to his feet, he couldn't control his legs, and like a plucked chicken held by the neck, he collapsed when lowered to the ground. Mick didn't know what the hell to do with him, but settled for dragging him over the footpath and sitting him down on the cobbles, propped up in the corner between the steps and the wall. It was an act of charity that didn't go down well with Minnie—who considered it to be consorting with the enemy—so Mick had to turn sideways and gently squeeze past her to gain entrance to the bar.

It was a premises not unlike the owner herself: smoke-cured, ancient, compact and dark, where Tim Rogan and Packy Price were working like billy-o, serving drink behind the bar. Although customers, they had left their pints for the prestige of being seen at such demanding work. Uninvited and certainly unpaid, they were now important people, with everyone trying to get their attention, in an atmosphere of revelry floated by just one name: Dinny Coyle.

Mick was a time coming to terms with it. As far as he could gather, Dinny had been involved in some nonsense at the Baths Corner, a scuffle with Lady Elmsmore of all people. Trying to rationalise it, he first wondered could it be something to do with her ladyship championing the RSPCA? No, dog licences more likely, or not having a nameplate on the cart. Whatever it was, Dinny had done Trojan work. He had somehow 'struck a blow for Ireland's freedom'; snippets of his heroics were to be heard everywhere. He had knocked down her ladyship, thrashed Gardiner the chauffeur, stolen an expensive fur coat, and got Carlow and Toss to savage her pack of little black and tan dogs. Cavan the policeman was reported as telling someone that she was in a bit of a state out at The Lodge.

'An unshorn savage.' He could hear someone mimicking a genteel voice. 'Down from the hills to plunder our little town.'

'He put his boot in Gardiner's arse,' someone else said.

Arthur Keenan and Joe Marley, tethered to the bar like goats, knew no more about it than Mick. 'Something to do with Lady Elmsmore, Dinny, and a load of dogs,' and even as he said it, Joe couldn't let it go at that, reporting, 'She wanted him arrested for not enlistin' in the army and fightin' in the war.'

'He was badly missed,' mused Arthur, as Mick ordered a drink for the three of them and leant against the bar. But he couldn't settle, throwing the pint quickly down his throat, and to Arthur and Joe's glanced 'what the hell's wrong with him?' he said a curt, 'I'll head out the road, men,' and was gone. Out past Minnie, now affronted that he was leaving, over the sleeping Gurrie, and up the cobbled lane.

What under God had took him into Cardwell's anyway? he thought. He wanted a bit of solitude, not a load of codswallop about Dinny; he wanted a few minutes' peace to think about Lizzy McGrain. He had the clearest, crispest image of her. A woman, four-square and resolute, radiant in the morning sun. By God, she was a new presence in Craigarran, standing with the white enamel bucket, asserting her presence, planting her hands on her hips and challenging him. And he allowed his mind to dwell on her white blouse, black skirt, and haughty air.

What the hell was she doing, purposely letting the lambs out anyway? Well, not purposely, but, God in heaven, she had made no effort to keep them in. And at that he stopped himself, smiled and said out loud 'Have a bit of sense.'

He loved the shore when the tide was out. There was more to see: shingle and sand, cockle and mussel beds, and seaweed growing on the rocks, a diversity of colour, ranging from green algae and blue cockles through to chocolate bladderwrack. A meadow without grass, but just as fertile and supportive of life; a milky way of scurriers and exposed shellfish that seagulls took advantage of: plucked, carried them up into the air, and dropped them to splatter in broken shells and tasty morsels on the rocks.

Why had she not by now gone back to England? he mused. Surely she had a life there, a boyfriend, and at that he felt a twinge just at the apex of the 'V' his ribs made in his chest. The thought had stabbed him like a three-foot icicle broken on a winter's morning off Spallick Rocks. He had galloped up the mountain to find a sheer precipice on the other side. What if she had a man? What if she was

[161]

married? Sure, with English people you wouldn't know. They have no religion. Look at that case out in Killowen. The poor old parish priest had been cajoled into marrying two English visitors, and then it transpired that the groom, a Captain Elverton, had been married before. He was not even a Catholic—it was bigamy! All hands trailed through the courts. Didn't the newspapers call the Sacred Heart Church in Killowen 'the Elverton chapel' to this day?

No, she would have hardly stayed this long in Craigarran if she had somebody. Not for weeks. But what if he was a soldier away in the army? Maybe she was just passing her time. No, there would have been letters, and anyway Biddy would have known. And with a great sense of relief, Mick said out loud, 'Christ, if anyone would know, Arthur would know. Sure Biddy must know every turn of her. Isn't she always down in the shop?'

He liked the rise and fall of the seaweed at the water's edge; how the tide lifted the young olive green strands in a curved buoyancy that reminded him of the gentle sway in a woman's hair. What was he thinking of? Lizzy McGrain was no more thinking of him than ... She was a woman of property, an independent woman, getting on with her life, while he was just a glorified flunkey on his father's farm. Still, she was a lassie to think about, and he warmed to musing how she wore her hair pulled back in a bun and had pale buttermilk skin. It was thick skin; now that was different from thick-skinned. Hers was deep, unwrinkled, clotted cream, stretched without one furrow across her brow. What was she like in her bare feet? he pondered, and visualised them plump and bonny, with a flaw in one toe that gave her the halt in her step.

He could hear the throb of the engine as the coal boat came up the Lough. It was moving surprisingly fast, crouched in the water, almost to the words THE OAK printed on its side. At its prow two crests of water rose, driving out from each side of the boat in powerful waves that ever reduced, to become a ripple tickling the seaweed here and on the far shore. Ulster and Leinster, a boat with the power to unite Ireland, Mick thought, and he laughed to himself and went back to concentrating on Lizzy McGrain.

Her foot didn't hamper her in any way; she could skip over the stream and carry a bucket of water. Down at the river, she didn't always use the stepping stones; it was a couple of good jumps to cross at the Gorum Rocks. At that, his solitude and musing were interrupted when Peter Magill stopped to give him a lift in the new petrol engine lorry, a shining dark blue horseless carriage, dedicated to W. LYGETT (BUILDER) with a beautifully signed front board. Mick would rather have walked, but the dual feeling of curiosity and not wanting to offend Peter made him accept the lift. Opening the door and stepping on to the running board, he savoured the trembling of the chassis and the smell of leather seating and warm oil. This was a force that scorned fatigue, sweating through its harness in a race to inevitably replace the horse.

'Too bad about Dinny. It's the whole talk of Warrenpoint,' Peter began. 'He's a desperate man.'

Mick looked quizzically at him, admiring the effortless co-ordination of his hands and feet, pushing levers, pedals and handles, smoothly getting them started, while he continued to chat.

'Beat up two policemen, ripped Lady Elmsmore's coat to shreds, and choked every one of her wee dogs. Killed them like rats, I believe; grabbed them wherever he could and whiplashed them to death. Strangled them and broke their backs.'

Peter was in full flow. 'People are saying that the lease may be up on that big house he lives in. It might well have reverted to her. That house could still be hers from the days of the landlords. You see, she could be evicting him. He's supposed to have got a boat to Omeath. Overpowered Cavan and took his gun. I believe he's joining Davy Lairy. He's escaped from jail you know, with a raftry of German prisoners of war.'

'My God,' said Mick, wondering how anyone so gullible would have brains enough to drive a lorry.

'A terrible flight of a stairs,' said Peter. 'A terrible flight of a stairs, but it could happen to anyone. Sure look at that Doctor Jekyll and Mister Hyde—something much the same. I read about it in a book.'

Well shot of Peter, Mick walked across the shingles of Rostrevor

Square, past the horse trough where children were splashing each other, under the tree and into Riley's grocery store and public bar. It smelt good. Somewhere in the shadow, an exquisite moth fanned the aromas of tobacco, porter-smoked ham and settled dust. Delightful luxuries wafted in the air. He ordered a bottle of stout and a whiskey, lit a cigarette and, not for the first time, looked at the framed photograph of Giant Murphy and Tom Thumb—a pint of ale and a glass of rum, on the distempered wall. There was something very decadent about having the mahogany and brass, the glass optics and ivory pumps all to yourself, he thought. Your own bar room, your own barman and your very own thoughts of Lizzy McGrain.

At the counter he thanked Brendan, paid him for the drinks and, with a quiet step, a gesture of limiting conversation, went over and sat at the fire; down in the body of the church as it were, well away from the altar where the minister was polishing glasses, burnishing them with white linen and methodically holding them up to the light until, satisfied, he put them on the shelves. Brendan understood the signals a man gives when he wants to be left to himself. Politely he retreated to the grocer's shop. Mick absent-mindedly turned the bellows wheel, spinning it quickly, letting it go, and slowing it down by touching the leather pulley lightly with the heel of his hand.

She's tough, not afraid to stay on her own, he thought. Strange to come to Craigarran after London and the war in France, but not half as strange as five Sundays and never going to Mass. Her limp. He smiled to himself, enjoying the image of her glowering at him, shoulders back, chin out, buttons right down the side of her skirt.

'We'll join you, Mick.' It startled him; he was so deep in thought, he hadn't noticed Billy Canavan and Pat Stimes up in the shop. 'We'll take the bad look off you.'

Mick got up from the corner to face another onslaught about Dinny Coyle.

'I hear your neighbour and the two curs tackled her ladyship,' Billy shouted. 'It'll not do her a button of harm. Amint I right? Amint I right?' Billy, for all his peevish aggression, was inclined to be unsure of himself and liked to be on your side. 'Do her the world of good,'

[164]

he continued, before changing tack and swinging into 'Wasn't it a shockin' business down at the Foresters' Hall? A calamity!'

Mick's heart sank, for if there was one thing worse than a hape of nonsense about Dinny, it was a hape of nonsense about the Foresters' Hall.

'Toby Moyle—he'd skin a flea for a halfpenny; he's hunger's mother,' Billy ranted, 'sneakin' about upstairs to get a few shots on the new billiard table. Waitin' until everyone had left. Wouldn't pay for a game—miserable hure.' Then his face changed to a look of shocked concern. 'He could rip the bloody cloth!'

(Billy loved the Irish National Foresters—the band, the banners, the marching; the merits of wearing a sash, as opposed to a collaret.)

'Then, when he came down and found the front door locked, laced the boots into it—the bottom panels were matchwood—before poor oul Tommy Rodgers could get out of the lavatory and open the lock. Panicked. Panicked, I tell you; thought he was in it for the night!'

Pat had another round of drinks up in front of them and Billy took a couple of mouthfuls to sustain himself before bursting on.

'He's suin' us, the skitterin' bastard, for not payin' him "infidelity". Off work with bruised shins, bad cess til him. That's what we do, you know'—Billy was solemnly taking the opportunity to extend the recruitment drive to Mick. 'You pay threepence a week and get a half-crown benefit if you're off work. But, sufferin' God, man, claiming benefit for puttin' your boot in the door of your very own Foresters' Hall. Honduras mahogany. The very best. It's the mother; she wants the money. Bitch o' hell! Went to see Ballintyre the solicitor in Kilkeel; not content with one of our own.'

Billy was secretary of the Rostrevor branch of the Irish National Foresters. He liked writing everything in the minutes, liked telling people to put it through the chair.

'They'd have shot him for it, took him out and shot him for it, if he'd panicked in the war. Only for me speakin' up for him at the extraordinary committee meeting, it wouldn't only be one hundred years' barrin' he'd be lookin' at. He'd be barred for life.'

[165]

Pat didn't seem to see any irony in that, and it was the best Mick could do to nod sagely by way of a reply. All the while Billy went on legislating, marking time with a bent forefinger as they supped their drinks. He was back to Dinny again. 'I believe she had four or five ridgebacks with her; they were just matchsticks to him—rended them limb from limb.'

Mick was sick of it. He didn't know how Pat put up with Billy, but couldn't get out because Brendan was now giving all his attention to the new bacon slicer in the grocer's shop, clamping the ham and spinning the wheel to cut gossamer shavings of opaque red. It was impossible to signal to him, bad form to shout, and, if anything broke his concentration, you would not want to be responsible for a barman who has lost a hand.

There is an art of extracting yourself from company without causing offence, a studied, casual manoeuvre, lulling everybody into complacency before you pounce. It is at that moment when there is a harmony in the gathering, when we are all equal in the eyes of God and the eyes of man, by having bought the same amount of drink— it is then that we must scuttle the opposition and stymie their attack.

Mick finally caught Brendan's attention, ordered a round of drinks and, in just a fractionally lower voice, a half-bottle of whiskey which he put into his pocket. Then, keeping a little ahead of Billy and Pat, he anticipated the penultimate moment just before either of them could order, and disengaged. He got sharply to his feet, drained his glass, placed it crisply on the counter, and, with a firm 'Goodnight, men,' was out the door.

Drink affects people in different ways: from getting so relaxed, they sleep in corners; to being over-emotional; to wanting to fight. In Mick's case, he was just a bit more of himself: more laughs, more fun, more ready to sing a bar of a song or give a step of a dance. He was cordial, a man other men liked drinking with, never losing the run of himself, always sound. But this was a different evening; it was an occasion when he was engrossed in his own thoughts, contemplating Lizzy, his father, the ground around Craigarran, and his brother Luke. He wasn't dwelling on them, more marvelling at their fleeting

[166]

appearance in the balmy void of his mind. He was a little drunk, and allowed himself to be more so, not like at a wedding, a christening, or at a wake, where he was making much of others. For once, he made much of himself, enjoying the mechanics of his own being, the spring in his step and the satisfying pleasure of feeling alive. Round the corner and up the Drumreagh Road he glided, speaking to everyone while keeping detached, buoyant on a river of alcohol. Occasionally he put his hand in his pocket and uncorked the half-bottle of whiskey, fuelling himself for the next mile.

At Roark's Bridge he could hear ewes on the mountain, unsettled, bleating for lambs sold in Warrenpoint fair. It was, he presumed, an intermittent mist that would rise in the morning, while his people's bleating for Luke was a deluge without end. He had vexed himself, rolled back the thatch on a pit of anguish and could not get it closed. A bilious yeast fermented in his stomach as he pondered his father's endless waiting for the postman, a melancholy watch that activated images of a lost child, in the loanin, on the stepping stones or at the Holly Rock.

Mick sat under the thorn bush in Alt na Taggart, the mountain field above his house, and looked down on the country in the setting sun. Again he uncorked the bottle and, still thinking about Luke, pondered how he himself had never written a letter in his life. He lit a cigarette. The sun rested on Craigarran, its rays skimming the mountain and leaving Coyles' house on the Far Road a charcoal drawing in the shade. His own street was highlighted in colour: everything from Maggie's gates and pillars to the stones in the carthouse wall.

But it was on Lizzy's house that he focused. It was a hypnotic composition of thatch, wood and stone which beckoned him, pulsing a warm invitation to its door. He pictured her looking wonderful in her white and blue print apron, baking bread, a fire in the hearth, a kettle on the boil. He was mowing in Theogoram, she was taking tea to the field. What would they talk about? He was sick of 'news', pishogues about Dinny and Toby Moyle and the door of the Foresters' Hall, and his father going on about whether to break up the Carnaun Field for potatoes or to reseed it direct from lea. He wanted conversation, for Lizzy to bathe him in her English accent, using the unfamiliar words he'd overheard like 'marsh' and 'brook'. He wanted her to smile at him and say 'Mick'.

He took the very last mouthful out of the bottle and slid it into a space between a gnarled thorn root and a piece of cropping rock. Then, from a sitting position, he rocked backwards, kicked his legs in the air, put his two hands on the ground and sprang forward to land upright on his feet. 'What is "Lizzy" short for?' he said out loud. 'What odds if she doesn't go to Mass.'

When Lizzy McGrain saw Mick Wilson coming down the loanin, she knew he was drunk. He wasn't staggering, twiddling his hands or sucking his lips back over his teeth the way some men do, but there was just the merest change in his persona which shouted out to her: Mick Wilson's drunk. She found herself peering out the window to keep him in her sight, pressing her cheek against the glass at an oblique angle as he got to Pulnafrog. Her heart jumped. He wasn't going up his own street! With a light skip, he crossed the stream and came over towards her house. In a fluster, she dashed from the window, threw a white cloth over a cup and two plates in the washing-up basin, and sat, with apparent composure, on the wicker and wood armchair at the side of the fire.

Out in the street there was the commotion of him making his presence known. An exaggerated rattling of his boots and greetings of 'Hello. It's a grand evening. How do?' Then there was a tap on the big door, a quiet 'Are you there? It's only me,' and the half-door was pushed open.

He blocked the light for a moment as he stood, got his bearing, smiled, and planted himself in the first convenient chair. Lizzy was not in the least put out. Instead, she had the faintest hint of a self-righteous warmth that he had the manners to admit his coarse outburst, and that he thought enough of her to apologise. As she looked at the elegant way he was reclining, he could have been a flamenco dancer or a matador, comfortably sprawled with his right elbow on the table, his left leg stretched across the floor. Even drunk, he had an athletic power, not a restricted brute force, but more the lazy grace of a very big cat, at ease on a balmy evening in a favourite chair.

He turned and straightened himself, raised his eyes towards her, and in a clear tenor voice said, 'Will you marry me, Lizzy McGrain?'

It was like a bayonet stabbed right into the central point between her ribs. She clutched the spot, sharp and scalding. That this selfish prig, who knew nothing about her, could just walk into her house and say such a thing, violate her being with a childish whim, outraged her. He knew nothing of the challenges that others faced, nothing of white feathers, of extreme danger; he hardly knew that there had been a war. Loneliness, illness, even rejection, had not touched him, and hence the hurt in others was something he could not see or understand. She had never felt so angry, so ready to fight, to scratch and bite and claw Mick Wilson. In that instant, almost before he had finished speaking, she glared at him and spat out the word 'Yes!' It was her way of insulting him, her way of belittling him, of putting her heel on his proposal and showing him that it was trite. Abruptly she got out of her chair, stepped over his sprawled feet and, slamming the door behind her, took refuge in the bedroom.

In the silence that followed, she heard three distinct things: the sharp creak of a vacated chair, the scrape of the big door being closed, and Mick Wilson walking past the window, going home. Even if she had wanted to, she couldn't cry. Enveloped in a terrible weight, she felt empty inside, and weary at the end of a long, emotional day. His shout from the kitchen when she had let out the lambs had remained with her. She could not get it out of her mind. No amount of gathering sticks, of baking bread, of trying not to look for him coming down the loanin would make it go away. He was spoiling everything, making her unwelcome, and her vexation deepened as she mulled over how much he restricted her. His lounging about the street every morning meant that she could not comfortably go to the well; she had to wait to see where he was working before she could venture out. 'Him and his two Chinas!' she spat. She was sick of them and, still with all her clothes on, without even taking off her boots, she pulled back the blankets and got into the bed. Clutching the bolster and curling up into a tight ball—his voice still reverberating in her head, first shouting at her, then proposing to her—she fell asleep.

Mick Wilson felt awful; he always did after too many drinks, but this time (albeit on an empty stomach) he had only had about the equivalent of a bottle of whiskey, an amount he would not normally consider excessive; but he did feel bad. He was queasy. He had a sore head, his mouth felt full of a mixture of sheep's wool and dry straw, while his nerves, normally thick mooring ropes, were now delicate, taut silk threads. However, it was his brain that hurt the most. His head was in a big black thorn bush, which he was too dispirited to come out of. Instead, he forced his mind to divide three score and ten years by twelve, and equate his age to a month of the year. It was a game he had played to comfort himself since he had been February. He was late May now, almost June.

What possessed him? What in the name of Christ was he at? Jesus, he felt guilty, guilty and ashamed. Should he go back over? What could he say? He could hide. No, no. He could 'cut the rope next the neck'. It was a phrase of Charlie Rosin's, good rest to him, who would often take the easy way out and snig the cow's tether, rather than take the trouble to unravel a knot. If only that bastard Luke would come home from America, Mick thought. He had no idea what Luke looked like, but a figure in a camel hair coat and a wide-brimmed hat was shouldering a huge trunk down the loanin, and he, Michael John Wilson, with hand luggage and a ticket to New Zealand, was meeting him going up. Lizzy McGrain thought he owned Craigarran. He only had the flat field, the bank and the wee holms of Theogoram. His mind's eye settled on the hiker he had met on the mountain: a useless 'hure' in thick woollen socks pulled up over tweed trousers, sporting a couple of gansies and a pair of good leather boots. A big soft pompous shite, preaching at him—how lucky he was to be gathering sheep at Loug e dubh, and how he admired the simplicity of his life. A very condescending bastard, ramming platitudes down his throat.

Mick knew that dabbling in a bit of vague matchmaking was not the sort of thing he would normally worry about. Having a few drinks and flattering a man about his daughter was one thing (sure, if nothing else, it drummed up a bit of trade) but 'asking' the woman herself—now that was a whole lot more. He had slept badly, the sweat was breaking out on him, and he mopped his chest with a sheet from bedclothes that were uncomfortably askew. Out on the street the sun cast shadows, gradually illuminating the plough, the upturned cart and the whitewashed walls. It warmed the dog, the cobblestones over at the stable and the greater expanse of hard blue clay. He could hear his father shuffling about; it was well past his time to get up. Mick pulled the blankets over his head and stayed in bed.

The sun was also shining on the two-storeyed edifice of Dinny Coyle's, on the entire length of the Far Road, and on Constable Severs, his helmet and his bike. The policeman felt clammy and wondered if he was getting a summer flu. He had trouble opening his shirt collar; the button he had pulled through with a hairpin was far too tight. It was a wild goose chase, four miles up into the mountains to question Dinny Coyle. Did they expect him to find Dinny's mother sitting at the fire in Lady Elmsmore's stole, with its silver clasp? It was that devious bastard Cavan. He could imagine what he had said: 'Out of my jurisdiction, madam. Needs to be dealt with in Rostrevor. Easily solved.'

Constable Severs's new uniform was an added irritant. The material was so coarse and heavy, it was like wearing black chimney pots over his long drawers. Everything was wrong. He felt weighed down with all his accoutrements: pencils, notebook, tory-whistle, truncheon and gun. At Purgatory, even though it was a flat part of the road, he leant on his bike and walked. 'Pinicky,' a boy shouted, and to the suppressed giggling of children and further cries of 'Pinicky', a hail of horse dung rose from behind the thick thorn hedge.

Archie Severs would never make inspector, never even make sergeant, but he was the smartest boy to come out of Lurgancanty and Upperlands National School. He had gained first place in the entrance exam for the Royal Irish Constabulary, and contemporaries who were now Superintendents liked to put that from their minds, along with any obligation they should feel at having taken their first step up the ladder with their boots placed securely on Archie's 'long head'. True, he was easy-going and short of that leadership quality of blind commitment, but he was a man who could see very far, and understood better than the children themselves why they were championing Pinicky.

Constable Severs liked Pinicky. He admired the free spirit who lilted for dancers and respected a yellow yorning's nest, while, twice a year, on the seventeenth of March and fifteenth of August, in a most ingenious and definitive way, showed that he cared not a fig for the rule of law or the authority of the land. Clean-shaven and dapper, this nine stone of peasant drank three bottles of stout and three whiskies in Morgan's Bar, and in full view of everyone walked direct to the barracks. There, with alarming athleticism, he proceeded to run up and down outside the front railings and give vent to his nationalism with high-pitched yelps of 'Comeoutandfight'. It was a challenge that made a laughing-stock of Constable Lanny, who was silly enough to run after him, an error of judgement that coincided with a mysterious posting to the back of beyond, when he compounded the folly by reporting the incident and requesting armed back-up to go to Roosley and arrest Pinicky at home.

Archie Severs, on the other hand, knew that Pinicky's republic was Knockbarragh townland and he contained the revolution by standing at the barracks door, acknowledging the demonstration, and doing nothing more.

'Pinicky, Pinicky,' the children shouted. 'Ta me go maith, Chuig ar la,' and the road was littered with more horse dung as Archie jumped on his bike. He hated having to leave the village and its familiar people. Country folk ignored him, moving away from the half-door, stepping behind a hedge. No one ever spoke.

But Dinny was watching, watching and waiting on the high ground of Mount Pleasant, ploughing out a few drills of early potatoes in the three roods against the mountain wall. He could see the uniformed figure jump on the bike at Purgatory, a place of confinement from which no wayward animal could escape: a distant crown of thorns, thought Dinny, wherein they must remain, until their souls are purified and they may look at the face of the Lord.

On the policeman came and, between the jigs and the reels of mounting and dismounting, eventually arrived at the house, where, with some ceremony, he leaned his bicycle against the wall and disappeared under the ridge tile, beneath Dinny's line of sight.

Archie Severs couldn't have known, but the presence of four or five hens and a rooster contentedly picking on the street signalled that Dinny was not at home. Because Dinny hated the hens. He persecuted them with a venom. Their claim to an undivided share of his street infuriated him. The rooster's aloof posturing, while the hens single-mindedly foraged, drove him to distraction. 'Hins, hins,' he'd shout, running to scatter them, flapping his coat, driving them up on the dunghill and, in his enthusiasm, continuing to follow them until the dung was over his boot mouth. It was an unusual phobia, and all the more so since he was highly tolerant of other people's poultry and ate a lot of eggs.

Dinny's mother was at home. Surprisingly pleasant and helpful, calling the policeman 'sir', and pulling the half-door behind her to keep in a ferocious menagerie of dogs, cats and goats, before spoiling it all for Archie by taking him to the corner of the house and pointing to Dinny and the horse at the mountain wall. There was a contrived sweetness about her, a smug detachment in never asking why the policeman wanted to speak to Dinny, that left Archie with no option but to climb the steep hypotenuse of mountain land. Dripping with

[173]

sweat and panting for breath, his lungs burning, he clambered up the stone ditch and through the thorns at the bottom of the top field.

The constable's appearance triggered the second part of Dinny's plan. He left the horse with the sock of the plough buried in the drill and struck out over the mountain wall.

'Hello!' Constable Severs found himself gasping. 'Mr Coyle, I'd like a word with you.'

But it was futile. Dinny was ignoring him, and had left just the right distance between them to cite a hearing impediment, if he was accused of failing to halt. Outmanoeuvred, Archie wondered how he had ever thought of Dinny Coyle as an old man. He was probably a good deal younger than himself. In his late thirties or early forties, he deceived you with the clothes he wore, the way he spread his feet, his crabbed demeanour.

It was heavy going across the rising ground of Slieve Moyle, a punishing obstacle course of big stones, clumps of heather and bitter, wind-sculptured whins. Wicked runts, with talons that (even through the uniform) scrabbed the legs off Archie, as he tried to keep his feet on sheets of smooth wet rock. Dinny was effortlessly maintaining his distance in front of him, and Archie began to feel that his laboured breathing was generating a wind for his quarry's back. The thought struck him to shoot, wing the cur at least, but it was an aberration that only stayed for an instant, smothered as it was by the dawning of a plan. Not even quite a dawning, a pinhole of light on the far horizon of a dark sky. Instead of climbing, Archie veered gently, almost absent-mindedly, down, back through the blackthorn and stone ditches, trying to minimise the pressure on the joints of his knees, as he formulated his thoughts.

Sifting through Cavan's telephone conversation, he settled on 'my informant told me'. His informant was Roddy Folin; an unfortunate who had a weakness for following the fire brigade, and trying by broking tittle-tattle to ingratiate himself with the police. However, given Lady Elmsmore's description, he didn't need Roddy Folin to tell him that the unshorn savage could only have been Dinny Coyle. But why? He would no more steal anything, no more accost yer woman (and for a fox fur stole) than fly. It was a conundrum. Why hadn't Cavan arrested Dinny? As the thought settled gently on Archie, it all became clear. He couldn't arrest Dinny, because Dinny Coyle hadn't gone to the fair. And the sleekit burghers, from Cavan to Wolsley, to the High Chief Justice because it had certainly been reported as high as him, at least—had washed their hands of it, and handed (as Archie told himself) poor gormless Archie the poisoned chalice of demanding that Lady Elmsmore come to Rostrevor barracks and identify Dinny, before the case could go on.

Archie Severs was freewheeling down the Far Road, the wind gently wafting under his helmet as his spirits waltzed to the tick, tick, tick of the Raleigh's back hub. He took his right hand off the handlebar and patted his notebook in the pocket over his heart. He had got the statement. Dinny's mother had testified that it couldn't have been Dinny because Dinny wasn't at the fair, and Archie knew that she knew what he was doing, as she read the statement before carefully signing 'Alice Elizabeth Coyle' underneath it. It was a signature in a steady bold hand which chastised Archie, because he thought she was illiterate and would sign with an 'X', and he would have to write beneath 'Alice Coyle, her mark'.

The tick of the Raleigh hub was a percussion driving the sweet lyric of his thoughts. This would push it back on the bastards, give them something to think about, and he smiled as he thought that he would suggest it might be someone from Ballyholland, or ... better than that: he would prompt Cavan to tell Wolsley to inform Elmsmore that it was probably an opportunist up from County Louth. Jesus, that would put them all mad. Elmsmore hated the people of County Louth, called them the 'fadgies', wanted them all horsewhipped; while Cavan was just paranoid. He was from Omeath; and couldn't go home, his mother and father had been pilloried when he had joined the RIC. And Wolsley, hadn't he been hunted out of Cork? Such a set-to if he were to suggest it, a whole new trend of thought which tickled Archie Severs and favoured Dinny Coyle, who not for the first time was lucky with the law. Only the previous year he had stood in the dock of Warrenpoint court, and in answer to the charge that his dog had worried one of Susan Poland's ewes, had said, 'Sir, my dog might have been seen grappling with a ewe of Susan Poland's in the gutters of the Eel Hole—but he didn't put her there. Sir, my dog had simply catched her by the wool at her neck, and was only wrestling with her, because he was trying to pull her out.' It was a homily in a grave monotone, delivered with such gentle sincerity, by a man with a small halo washed in the centre of his face, that Justice of the Peace A. J. Sinton had let Dinny off.

Lizzy was buoyant. After a good night's sleep, she felt completely different about the proposal. It was now an episode that made her somewhat giddy and inclined to laugh. Certainly she had no intention of holding Mick Wilson to his offer of marriage, but she was glad she had said yes. It was the most delightfully idiotic thing— exquisitely romantic. Mick Wilson's drunken, childish proposal had inexplicably pushed Captain James Pointer into an irrelevance in her distant past. He would never have done anything so reckless, so vulnerable, and so gallant. Pointer's courage was bounded by military tradition. He would have cut his throat for the regiment, but not so much as pricked his little finger for anyone else. She felt warm about the proposal, curiously uplifted, and thought of it as a very pleasant secret which she could always keep.

Leisurely she ate breakfast and decided to go to the shop, stopping every so often in her preparatory chores to question what was making her feel so good. And then she would savour it. The image of Mick Wilson sprawled on the chair just inside her door. The light striking his forehead, his long lashes shielding his blue-grey eyes, and his feet at every angle to his flamenco dancer's legs. Even when she was ready for the town, she couldn't stop tinkering: brushing the hearth, washing dishcloths and hanging them on the line, laughing at herself for being so scathing about Mick's cronies,

Arthur and Joe. They were lovely, always friendly. Arthur was polite and reserved, while Joe was a scallywag you couldn't help liking, bursting as he was with rascality, his eyes dancing in an owlish face. He had called her every variation of her name from Miss McGrain right through to Beth.

From the garden she wondered what the dark figure was doing walking a constant one hundred yards behind Dinny Coyle on the far hills. It was the strangest sight; they were like two black sailing ships caught in a constant breeze, neither able to pull away from the other, nor for the time to turn back. Then the second of the two vessels changed tack and, catching a crosswind, sailed back down to the house.

Wee Vinny McArdle was also watching Constable Severs. After instigating the shower of horse dung, he left his mates in Purgatory and slipped over the river to the Drumreagh Road. Idling on one of the last days of the school holidays, up over Roark's Bridge, past Craigarran, and down the next loanin to his grandfather's and his grand-aunts', Rosie and May. They were dancing with bad temper. The Oul' Fox was standing at the dresser, laying down the law. 'Be my song,' he was saying, 'I'll go over.' And he struck his fist on the timber and rattled the plates. 'And by God, John the Talaigh will brierd that ditch. Upon my soul there'll be no more of his sheep in with us! Where's me stick, Rosie ... May? Me stick.'

And, to wee Vinny's delight, and to a hornpipe of bad temper from the two pishmires, his grandfather lashed and beat the foxgloves and honeysuckle at the start of the wee loanin that followed the contour to Wilsons' door. And Vinny was with him, walking proudly just half a pace behind, because it was too narrow for them to be quite abreast. Two men ready to fight, greeting the 'new woman', as his grandfather called her, with a 'Hello, girl' and straight up to John the Talaigh, scuffling weeds on the street.

'Well, John, tis a grand morning,' his grandfather started, and was greeted in return with, 'Ah, me sound Dan.' It wasn't the fighting talk Vinny had expected. Not to put too fine a point on it, it was all wrong and very disappointing. Surely they should at least have been kicking each other on the shins?

[177]

'This is a great man you have with you,' the Talaigh said, and, to Vinny's sinking heart, his grandfather replied most cordially, 'He's all that.' Then there was a lot of talk about the weather and the balance of the spade the Talaigh was scuffling with, and about Severs following Dinny from Mount Pleasant, before his grandfather said very quietly, 'We'll have to do something about that ditch,' and the Talaigh said, 'We will, Dan, we will.'

And then they talked about scour and warbles, and blight and maggots, and one hundred and one things Vinny couldn't care less about, before his grandfather again said, 'Hello, girl,' as they passed the new woman's on the way home; where May and Rosie were fit to be tied, waiting as his grandfather again startled Vinny with, 'By the sufferin' Christ, I told the Talaigh,' and the two women danced on the floor as he regaled them with the terrible threats and dastardly retributions he had ordained. 'Beat him!' he growled. 'I'd beat him with my cap. Doesn't know how lucky he is to be scufflin' over there with only his shirt stuck up his arse.' And in no time the sisters had eggs and bacon on the pan and were looking very favourably on Vinny, who undoubtedly had played a big part in the fight. And his Great-Aunt May went down to the room and got him a cigarette to smoke after 'the tay'.

For Lizzy, the morning slipped into afternoon, and it was now too late to go anywhere. Besides, she didn't want to break the magic that she felt about the house. She was afraid to go to the town, afraid to trust herself not to tell everything to Biddy when the two of them got talking in the little kitchen behind the shop counter. Engrossed in her own thoughts, she gave a start when, out of the corner of her eye, she noticed the two girls framed by the posts of the open door. It was like a life-size print from a popular painting. Tall and willowy, the girls wore full-length cotton dresses of identical design, one fashioned from a remnant of predominantly red flowers, the other mostly blue. Both had the same nut-brown hair, straight, shoulder-length and cut in a fringe. They stood nervously side by side, each with their hands prayerfully joined in front of them, their index fingers apologetically tipping their lips. They could see that they had startled her, and when she jumped, so did they. There was a moment of distance before Lizzy broke it and invited them in.

It was a telling moment for Lizzy. She would never have believed herself to be superstitious, but now she knew she was. Not the commonplace things, like walking under a ladder or saying 'white rabbits' on the first morning of a certain month, but the very Irish belief that certain people can bring you luck. It was such an old-fashioned thing that she rationalised it by telling herself that she simply had a feeling that the girls meant her very well. They were her first real visitors (not counting Mick) and they came through the door like principal dancers in a ballet, performing a delicate and shy pass.

'Ma says will you come over for a *ceili*, maybe tonight?' the two said in unison, as they shifted from foot to foot, keeping their gaze demurely on the ground.

'I would really like that,' Lizzy said. 'You are very welcome. Please sit down.'

It was a pantomime, the sisters like two nymphs: flustered, exquisite, beautiful, bumping together, smoothing their dresses and jumping to their feet again as both tried to sit in what Lizzy now thought of as 'the drunken flamenco dancer's chair'. Their names were Madge and Mary-Agnes Finnegan, they told her, and they were living with their mother and father and brother Peter next to Dinny Coyle on the Far Road.

'We're cousins of Mick's,' they kept saying in delighted unison, as if that made them important. Two almost identical sisters of fourteen and fifteen, whose presence brought home to Lizzy a realisation that while Craigarran was a second language to her—a language of fields, lanes and crops, coupled with breeding and history—it was only a knowledge of an older generation who had now almost completely gone.

Lizzy put a spoonful of leaves into the tea-drawer and wet them with boiling water from the kettle on the crook. Then, having given the little tin pot a swirl, she sat it on the edge of the hob. She knew the girls wanted to stay, to be friendly, grown up, and to talk.

'Did you see the policeman out with Dinny?' Mary-Agnes asked.

'He had a bit of bother with Lady Elmsmore and had to come home early from the fair.'

Lizzy didn't want to appear to question the girls, but she gave a genuine look of surprise.

'His dogs bit her dogs and mistook her scarf for a fox'—'Shawl,' her sister corrected.

'Poor Dinny,' Madge said. 'He loves his dogs. "Where's my wee favourites?",' she mimicked in a gravelly voice. 'That's what he calls them. He also likes to think he's home from America. "A'll be mighty beholdin' to you ma'am." That's the sort of thing he says.'

It was a very good American accent, and Madge's eyes twinkled as she delivered her party piece. 'A shemozzle in the Bronx.'

'Hins, hins, hins,' said Mary-Agnes, and the two of them laughed.

Lizzy was struck by how much the girls knew about Dinny. In London she would have had no idea about the people in the next flat. She was also struck by how clever the girls were, the bit of mimicry to draw her attention away from the policeman when they felt that they may have said too much.

'Arthur Keenan was in our house when we left,' Mary-Agnes said. 'He looks up words in our dictionary—words he's heard Father Bennett'—'Canon,' Madge corrected— ' … words Canon Bennett used at Sunday Mass. He was looking up "incorrigible". Arthur says, "He could only have been talking about Stephen Flavin,"' and in a parody of the judiciary or maybe even the clergy, Mary-Agnes quoted '"bad beyond correction or reform".'

Lizzy took cups from the dresser and a tin of biscuits from one of the cupboards, thinking how the girls' upbringing had been so different from hers. Theirs was a close-knit communion of culture, place, family and friends. They had no interest in the vote, certainly not in the war, and they were free from the bondage of standing or class; complete in themselves as long as they could tie corn, bake bread, and milk a cow.

Then she realised what Mary-Agnes and Madge really wanted to talk about. With wide-eyed enthusiasm, they introduced it in a flustered duet.

'Do you see much of Mick? He's always being asked to stand as godfather for a child. We come over to brush his suit and polish his shoes when he goes out dressed.'

Lizzy could see the two of them, delighted with themselves, one standing on a chair whisking specks from his collar and shoulders, the other directing from the floor.

'He's going to enter the mare in the big race at the Tup Fair,' Mary-Agnes gushed. 'Sometimes when he's coming home from the forge and he's had a sup of drink, he just lights out across the fields from the bridge. Jumps all the ditches.'

'It's out of all latitude,' Madge added, and for their amusement she got to her feet and struck a very stiff pose. Then, sounding remarkably like John Wilson, she said, 'It's out of all latitude, Mick. You were lucky not to break the mare's neck, if you didn't break your own.'

Lizzy enjoyed listening to them and encouraged them to talk on.

'He has to go over to Shannons' first thing on New Year's morning. They want Mick to be their "first-footer". May is his godmother. Nobody would go next or near Shannons' house until after Mick's been in. Normally it's alright to be first in, as long as you're not a woman or somebody with red hair. But May chased Tommy Roark, and he's as black as the ace of spades, because he called one New Year's morning before Mick had arrived. They're shocking freakish about the new moon. It's not lucky to catch a first sight of it through the window, and they be running in and out looking for it for days. "God bless the moon and God bless me"—that's what they say when they first clap eyes on it. "God bless your work"—that's what Mick always says when he arrives on our street and we're milking the goat or the cow. It's what you're supposed to say.'

Lizzy could see that they thought the world of Mick, making him the object of their girlish romance and wearing their hearts on their sleeves in a way that (even at their age) she never could have done.

That evening, as Lizzy walked down the fields behind Wilsons' house, she could see the girls waiting for her on the Far Road, jigging about, exploding to run down to meet her at the Wee Holms, and jumping out of their skins with skips and dances, to escort her up to their house. Susan and James Finnegan met her, stepping right out on the street, accepting her quarter of tea, and shaking hands. Susan was tall and clean-limbed in a floral pinny, while Big Jim was a full head shorter in a black waistcoat and starched shirt. They were an eye-catching couple and not just because of the unconventional difference in their height. Susan's bobbed hair and no nonsense dress-sense contrasted sharply with Big Jim's handlebar moustache and cock-of-the-walk style. His moustache was truly exquisite, remarkable in that it was what you would expect from a cosseted Indian Rajah, rather than the extravagance of a farmer on the Knockbarragh hills. And just when Lizzy was wondering how in the name of God he maintained it so well, he spoke. In the deepest, most resonant voice she had ever heard, he said, 'You're welcome. You're welcome.' It was a voice that vibrated from a vast internal cavern, a voice with a Scottish inflection, evoking thunder in the Great Glen. Repeating 'You're welcome, you're doubly welcome,' and with arms outstretched in a gathering gesture, he ushered everyone into the house.

Lizzy stepped across the threshold, and said, 'You have a lovely home,' noticing the wood-panelled ceiling and the table dressed for the evening meal invitingly pulled out to the centre of the cement floor. The door to her left was wide open, and although Biddy had mentioned him to her, she hesitated at the sight of Peter in the bed, until Susan touched her arm and all five of them went down to the room. They wanted her to meet him, to show her at once their tragedy and their pain.

'Peter was kicked and left for dead,' his mother said in a resigned whisper. 'He was hired down below Rathfriland and got set upon by a gang.'

None of the others spoke since her voice alone conveyed the shock and bemusement of them all. Peter's head was swathed in bandages, with only the oval from his temples to just below his mouth exposed. He had the appearance of a soft-boiled egg, shelled and distorted to its maximum, between the thumb and forefinger of an imaginary hand. His mouth was horribly drooped on his right-hand side, and when he looked up at Lizzy and nodded, it was a disinterested look from pain-glazed eyes. She had thought herself impervious to shock, yet, standing in the midst of this family group, she could easily have cried. Bending down, she gently brushed his bandaged face with her cheek, an impulsive gesture she knew she had brought from France.

Back in the kitchen, Lizzy was ushered to her seat at a table set as painstakingly as colours in stained glass. The linen cloth, chinaware and stainless steel cutlery underpinned two prints of freshly churned butter, and a dozen farls of barely cooled soda bread. Susan ferried boiled eggs, and amid gentle fussing Lizzy noted the clean lines of the table, chairs, and settle-bed, the marquetry in the high dresser, the delft dogs, and the framed print of Landseer's 'The Monarch of the Glen'. James sat affably booming at the head of the table; it transpired that he had worked for years in Scotland, mostly as a ships' boilermaker on the Clyde. Bad digs and cold porridge sandwiches had a particular place in his affections. He recalled lodgings so cramped that guests had to climb in and out of windows to sleep in beds occupied in a rota of eight-hour shifts.

A foot on the street caught her attention, a step that she knew was Mick Wilson's, even before he came in the door. And from the way the girls looked at her and smiled, they too knew it was Mick, a jaunty figure who portrayed the faintest hint of surprise as he gave a general greeting of 'How do?' and went down to see Peter in the room. Lizzy knew he hadn't expected to see her, and she felt confident and vaguely amused that he was at a bit of a loss. He self-consciously took off his coat, threw it on the chair and rolled up his sleeves. Then, like a footballer grasping the leather case of a ball, he cupped Peter Finnegan's bandaged head. Immediately a huge release of tension evaporated from the house. Susan began to seem younger, and James visibly relaxed. It was a responsibility lifted, a moment each day when their burden of anguish was carried by someone else.

From her seat at the table, Lizzy had the clearest of views. Mick wore a grey flannel working shirt with no collar, and as he leaned forward, his braces cut into his shoulders, pulling the cloth down to expose a crescent of pale white skin at the nape of his neck. The view was so tantalisingly immodest that she was obliged to look away, but inevitably to now and again look back. She rationalised that this therapy had little directly to do with the immense physical effort, little to do with the moulding pressure (after all the bandages were doing that); it had to do with the prestige and standing of Mick Wilson, his voluntary confinement, and the temporary equal footing of both men. In the war, no amount of modern medicines would have saved Peter. In the field hospitals, patients were managed as though they were on a parade ground. Wounded men, roused for bed linens to be squared and pillow tabs aligned (just because it was a particular minute of the day), never saw anyone they knew, and were exiled in a regime where the nurses were run off their feet, with little time for personal contact, never mind personal care. Here the Finnegans simply accepted that Mick would be over at teatime. For the best part of a year he had been there, soothing Peter, while they got on with their evening meal.

'As God's my judge, what about the policeman trying to catch Dinny on the mountain?' Susan began. It was a nonchalant opening of the top button on social reserve, an inclusive gesture to make Lizzy feel at home. 'It must have been an awful set-to with him, Lady Elmsore, Carlow and Toss, and all the wee dogs. And the fox fur! Had to take it home with him. Seems Toss ripped it off her back.'

'I was down at her stables with Paddy Magill,' Big Jim offered. 'The time Paddy was drawing dung to the gardens along the shore. Such a figgairy. She would stand out in the yard and watch every forkful we threw on the cart. And it was dear—sixpence a load. "Would you take fourpence a load?" Paddy asked her. Well! she flew at him like a clucking hen. "That's not ordinary horse manure," she shouted. "It's pedigree; pedigree horse manure!"'

They all smiled, as Susan tilted her head and looked coyly at Lizzy, implying that the story may have been just a little risqué.

'He's not a bit soft, Dinny,' Big Jim continued. 'Very long-headed—and so's Archie Severs. Sure you know he didn't want the bother of it. Dinny's a bag of weasels. He let him off.'

Lizzy found it hard to concentrate on the conversation. She didn't want to appear ill-mannered, but she was irrevocably drawn to watch the spectacle down in the room. Mick too was talking. 'Dinny showed a clean pair of heels to Severs,' she could hear. 'Some way I don't think we'll see Alice out in the fur scarf.' Quiet, random talk. 'It's been a long drawn out spell for you, but you're overin' it, Peter, and you're comin' into a good fortnight. Things heal better on the dark side of the moon.'

For Lizzy the image of the two men in Finnegans' low room was the antithesis of war. It was purified humanity, and hypnotic. She looked back and back again to Mick's elegant awkward pose, holding Peter's distorted head, a discipline that must have made his sojourn seem like an eternity. She watched captivated, until all too soon it was over, and he stood, said, 'That'll do us for now, Peter' and with a hand gesture and a 'Right, everyone' was gone. It was a departure of almost indecent haste, not lost on the two girls, who, smiling knowingly to each other, transmitted, 'It's Lizzy McGrain.'

Mick's foot wasn't off the street when Susan went over to the dresser and took out a small leather purse: pear-shaped, its texture worn to soft pigskin, its imprints faded, its whang fingered to delicate liquorice at its reefed neck. Reverently she opened it, and slipped into the heart of her hand a smooth, light brown, polished stone, an exquisitely grained medallion pierced through the arc of its polar parallel. The cure for migraine passed from the mists of antiquity, druid lore, adapted to Gaelic Christianity, a relic with a prayer. 'In Ainm an Athar,' Susan began, gently holding the burnished surface to Peter's temple, whispering a litany beyond comprehension, an incantation conferred by rote through a thousand years.

It was one of the most sacred things Lizzy had ever seen. She felt a shiver in her legs, in the muscles on each side of her spine and down her neck. It was the realisation that these people had such a pure faith, they expected their prayers to be answered. They felt that close to God. They were at one with Him, as Peter, his lopsided

[185]

alabaster face glowing with the radiance of a child, quietly drifted off into a contented sleep.

'We're delighted you could come,' Susan said, returning to the table. Her demeanour implied that Lizzy was the busiest and most important woman on God's earth. 'The girls have been … we've all been … very excited; you must come more often now that Peter's on the mend. Mick's great with him. He's as good as a nurse.'

'Mick got a lovely shirt in Rathfriland,' Mary-Agnes said.

'With starched collars,' Madge confirmed.

Then the two of them, realising the irrelevance of their outburst, looked shyly into the table as Susan smiled and registered an idea. Nodding it to Big Jim, and prompting him to clear his throat, lean back in his chair, fold his arms, close his eyes and sing.

> If I was in Rathfriland, and looking far and wide,
> I'd see the purple heather on the Mourne mountainside.
> I'd see the town of Belfast, and the far-famed Bessbrook mill.
> From that little town in County Down.
> Rathfriland on the hill.

Walking up the fields behind the house, Mick Wilson felt better. After his initial surprise at seeing Lizzy, he was delighted to sense her eyes on him, and, as he held Peter Finnegan's head, know that she was no longer upset. From feeling bad, he now felt good. He had only picked at food all day and he was hungry, his mind was full of how lovely she looked, and how he would fry himself a slice of bacon, a soda farl and a couple of eggs. Playfully he kicked a 'bouckanborough' and watched the rainbow-ribbed fungi splatter into the air. 'New Zealand,' he murmured, and with a wide smile and a giggle to himself said, 'Maybe I'll not go after all. I'll wait a while yet!'

Lizzy and the girls waltzed down the rough-sloping ground to the

Wee Holms. It was a *ceili* tradition to leave your visitor part of the way home. Madge and Mary-Agnes were quieter now, taking her into their confidence, pressing their fingers to their lips as with wild stares they led her through the undergrowth and off the beaten path; their gestures conveying not so much the need for silence, as the need to appreciate the importance of the special secret they were about to entrust. Pushing branches with their raised forearms, they proceeded, careful to ensure that the saplings didn't spring back and 'cut the face off' the next explorer in the line. Bending, squatting, shimmying through tall whins, thorns and hazels, they reached a clearing and a solid double drystone wall. A rampart of broken toffee—granite, basalt, sandstone, crowbarred and shunted, gathered and carried. 'It's where Dinny hid the stole,' they whispered. 'Our march ditch; we saw him put it in the wall.'

They were peeping through the boulders now, from a dark wigwam of shade to soft daylight. 'We've marked it with a bit of crockery,' they whispered. 'We can reach through and get it from this side.' Then, forgetting Lizzy, 'Go on, Madge, put your hand in.'

'No. You do.'

'No!'

Both girls shivered and giggled with excitement. 'It might be a weasel's nest.'

Lizzy could see Madge brace herself and grasp the nettle, her face a study in terror, as she slid her arm into a cavity between the boulders of the wall. Mary-Agnes was now on her hunkers, navigating; 'Just a bit farther to your right. You've got it!' she gasped. 'It's a parcel. It's wrapped in sort of leather, greaseproof paper,' and both of them knelt, ashen-faced, opening the package on the ground. A little detached from her companions, Lizzy felt uneasy and responsible, with the slow dawning that they would never have extracted it if she had not been there.

The fur was indeed beautiful, glowing in russet shades of fresh husked chestnut, contrasting with a flashing northern lights silver clasp. First one, then the other, of the girls tried it on. It sat square on their shoulders, proud and defiant, snarling with its teeth, staring with its eyes and showing off its claws. A garment that would pulse dignity and wealth in the environs of Bond Street, yet mean very little in Craigarran and be pretentious at the Crossroads Dance. The foxfur was a useless encumbrance to the Finnegans and so far removed from Dinny, he hadn't even thought to give it back.

'Ma will be looking for us,' Mary-Agnes said and, to Lizzy's nodded approval, they re-parcelled the treasure, and in an act of final benediction, tossed their marker to the elements, and interred the pelt in the wall.

An eventful day, thought Lizzy, relaxed in the chair, smoking a cigarette, drinking a cup of tea, and tipping the wheel of the fanbellows to spark an ember in the fire. She recalled Mick Wilson with his back to her, his braces gathering the shoulders of his striped collarless shirt; the bitter sweetness of being in Finnegans'; the joy in the kitchen; Big Jim singing; the anguish in the room; Madge spinning the marker, a crown of white and blue willow pattern crockery turning Dinny's stole into a legend, a Siberian fox, his neck adorned with silver, forever crying and haunting the rough ground at the Stepping Stones and, joining forces with the Black Pig in the Wee Holms. And, with a smile, she whispered Susan Finnegan's favourite edict—'As God's my judge'—and made ready to go to bed.

It startled Lizzy when Maggie, out of breath and flustered, burst into the kitchen. 'Get Mick, get Mick,' she spluttered. 'Don't just stand there! Run, you girl you. Run.' She had her sleeves rolled up and was very excited, and Lizzy's first thought was that John Wilson had died. It was that sort of commotion. After all, Maggie seldom came out from behind the gates, let alone over to Lizzy's house. 'Run, run!' she shouted and, taking her own advice, dashed back out the door.

Lizzy felt compelled to follow, and was relieved to see her quarry burst past John as he shuffled down the street. He, composed as always, a mahogany door propped up by a stick, said, 'Like a good girl, Lizzy, run and get Mick. He's mowing hay in the river field, and Maggie's black cow is starting to calve.' And while he said it quietly, there was a hint of urgency in his voice that was further conveyed by the gates being opened to cries of 'Run! Run! Run, pigeon, run.'

Maggie tore at her pinny and scurried up and down in a performance that did indeed excite Lizzy and, just as strongly, Wilsons' dog. He was right tight on her heels, getting away from the commotion, round the corner of the gable and down the back fields.

Lizzy could see Mick, knees bent, shoulders crouched, mowing rhythmically, painting the field in alternate strips of olive and lime-green. With his proximity to the river, she would need to shout, but she couldn't. It was the silliest thing. She tried a very timid 'Mick, Mick,' under her breath, then a louder 'Hello, hello, yoo hoo,' but it was inaudible. Her vocal chords had involuntarily seized. She was unable to let Mick Wilson know she wanted him, even for something as indirect as Maggie's cow. But the dog had no such inhibitions, scampering on ahead. He caught Mick's attention, and Mick, now seeing Lizzy's hesitant beckoning, fired away the scythe and exploded into a bounding run. Lizzy knew his presumption and his evident distress allowed her to shout, 'It's only Maggie's cow.' But he couldn't hear her, and she accompanied her shouts with 'keep calm' hand movements. And in her excitement of shouting and allaying his anxiety, she couldn't help but think how much her voice sounded like the woman on the jellied eel stand outside the Thomas à Becket pub in the Old Kent Road, yet she still called loudly, 'It's all right. It's OK!' and didn't care.

He came up to her smiling and, understanding her message, gave a relieved 'Is this the next of it?' roll of his eyes; as neither stopping to allow her to get into step with him, nor hastening away, he purposefully strode on up the hill, creating a space between them that was reluctantly occupied by the black and white dog. All their apprehension had unfairly descended on him. He looked sheepish, not sure where he should be, closer to Mick or, looking back at Lizzy, closer to her. The three of them, heads down, silently speeled up the back fields, along the gable at Pulnafrog, and on up the street, where Lizzy automatically followed Mick through the gates and round to the garden at the side of Maggie's house. To the harsh reality of … what was she doing here? What in under God had possessed her to run on willy-nilly after Mick Wilson, instead of sensibly and sanely going on over to her own house? But it was only a moment's recrimination before she forgot herself and was caught up in the drama, like everyone else.

The black cow was standing in the corner, calving; engrossed in her exertions, her head down, back humped and tail up. With each contraction she gave a low moan, stretched her neck and compressed her sides. Lizzy could catch a glimpse of protruding glazed porcelain hooves. Maggie was in a panic, shivering, her head particularly, fluttering on the mainspring of her neck, her hands wringing in her pinny, her entire frame a tortured study in uncertainty about what to do. John Wilson, by contrast, leaning on his stick, was ballast steadying the ship. Mick stood beside him, and between the two of them, so did the dog.

'Just go over and settle her, Maggie,' John said. 'See if she'll lie down.' The words transformed Maggie, like a measure of laudanum. They stopped the shaking and brought her to herself. They calmed Lizzy too, and sparked in her a great yearning, a more intense reproduction of the feeling she had had when the Finnegan girls had arrived at her door. She wanted them to be lucky. This time she was the visitor; she carried the burden and desperately wanted to be 'lucky' herself; not to be the stranger who brought misfortune, and to be forever associated with things going wrong. And as she stood with the cow, the Wilsons and Maggie, in Maggie's garden, with every ounce of her being she willed things to go right.

Maggie quietly went over to the cow, and inoffensively lifted her right hand to scratch the bones on the animal's rump. Then in a lilting whisper she sang, 'Tar as now a chroi, a chroi, a chroi. Tar as now a chroi, a chroi … ' Strange words to Lizzy which registered as a Gaelic milking song, a hypnotic lullaby that soothed the cow, and prompted her to, front legs first, sink slowly to the ground.

Mick stooped and, almost on tiptoe, went over to catch the protruding feet, pushing his hands forward to grip the knuckles just above the front hooves, making a dent for himself in the grass with the heel of his right hobnailed boot, and showing the sparables as he stamped out a divot to resist the pull. Then she could see the muscles on his legs and the sinews on his forearms and neck tense, as he began to apply a steady pressure to extract the calf. John could give no help, but Maggie was right down on her knees, pushing back the flesh under the cow's tail, exposing the calf's muzzle, as they strained in a desperate battle to get it out.

'Just hold steady, Mick. A steady pull,' John said. 'Give the cow time; she's doing well herself.' His voice was a reassuring drone, but even Lizzy, who had never seen a cow calve before, knew this was a tense time. The calf was big. The cow was doing her best, stretching her head and neck almost in a straight line, her lower jaw straining to the sky as she pushed and rocked, groaning in her exertions as the calf's head emerged. Grotesque and beautiful, highlighting a Rubicon crossed, as Mick pulled with all his might and Maggie, now almost flat on the ground, wedged herself between him and the cow. She was pressing with both hands, creating restraint, desperately trying to push more taut, tense, inflamed flesh back, at her wits' end to somehow manipulate a restricted aperture over the calf's shoulders and chest.

This was a pivotal moment in the battle to deliver the calf safely. John Wilson's stick quivered frustrated immobility, and circumstance slapped Lizzy in the face and told her it was no good standing back and silently crying 'O my gawd!' She was needed and something pushed her and she stepped right into Craigarran, dropped onto one knee and grabbed the calf, her hands just below Mick's, firmly clasping the white tallow of its feet, her strong left ankle placed firmly in the ground. Mick's strength and proximity surprised her. He was like a magnet and she was in his field of power. Not quite touching, there was a paper width between her shoulder and his, but a thousand paper widths could not have stopped him fluttering iron filings against her heart. She dug deeper with her left foot, gripped

[191]

and pulled and flexed herself. They were bringing forth the calf's neck and chest.

Suddenly the cow, with great agility, got up and, rocking backwards, could easily have fallen on Maggie, had Mick not let go of his holding, thrown his shoulder against the cow's rump, and, like a child with a ragdoll, caught the prone figure by the pinny and lifted her back.

'Pull down,' said John Wilson, as the force of gravity, nature and Lizzy slowly extracted the calf's hindquarters—a delivery prevented from a haphazard fall onto the ground by a timely cradling from Mick. It was a fine red heifer, a calf glistening with vitality and raising its head for the cow to lick.

A great sense of achievement gripped Lizzy; she felt lucky, proud to have cleared the void, and to have sprung forward to claim the prize of acceptance by gripping the calf's wet ivory feet. Maggie too was delighted, not flustered as before, but full of a positive energy as she circled, admiring the maternal instincts of the cow, while congratulating everyone. 'Good work, good work!' she clattered, 'Thanks until you're better paid.'

Lizzy was the first to wash her hands in the dish of warm water which Maggie had put out. It was part of the ritual—that, and a cup of tea. They observed it quietly. She felt a better balance between her and Mick as they ate the soda bread and rhubarb and ginger jam, walked round to look at the calf, now on its feet, and returned home through the gates, as Maggie again called, 'God bless yis, and thanks 'til you're better paid.'

Summer was drifting into autumn. The children were back at school, their activity telling Lizzy what time of the day it was, as, still in their summer uniform of bare feet, they laughed over the Stepping Stones and went up and down the loanin, to and from the Far Road. She could hear the exuberance of their play, a tonic filling the country with life, as from half a mile away they celebrated their lunch in the schoolyard. And she was busy with the small, delightful chores of daily living—the cooking, cleaning and going to the shop, where Biddy knew everything, brokering gossip and living up to Joe Marley's name for her—'The News of the World'. It was impossible to go into the shop and not come home without a bulletin of some kind.

'Seems the Germans up at The Hydrove are coming out of themselves. The Tailor, droll as ever, remarked that it took him a week to realise that he had been insulted, when one of them said, "You have much better taste than your delightful wife." Geordy Lyons is again at loggerheads with Canon Bennett, taking exception to his "simple carpenter theme". "And who should God choose for the earthly father of His son?" the Canon preached. "Saint Joseph!" His tone was dismissive. "A tradesman, a simple carpenter, the lowest, humblest of men." An analogy that stung Geordy into branding Canon Bennett "a galvanised prig". As a young man, Geordy had served his time as a cabinet-maker, and in his own estimation was anything but "the lowest and simplest of men". And one of the McCumiskey girls has a new bicycle, and on taking it in and leaning it against the dresser for her granny to see, the old woman laughed and chided, "Sure God love you, child, how could you go down the road on that? It can't even stand by itself!"'

All this and talk about Mick Wilson, Biddy finding it easy to tease Lizzy, though she knew nothing of the proposal, and in her heart Lizzy found it exquisite to act a little coy and go a little red. Was it any wonder it was the setting for the dream, the location of the delightfully enriching experience she brought back from her sleep? Her mother and father were sitting comfortably behind the counter in Biddy Drennan's shop. Lizzy could only marvel at how well they looked. She knew they were dead, but in a parallel world of reason it didn't trouble her one bit, as she lifted the counter and joined them amongst the paraphernalia of the grocery trade. Just the three of them, sitting placidly behind a veil of white linen dyed with onion skins—or was it tea leaves?—which filtered a setting sun and bathed the room in sepia light. Lizzy felt contented, knowing she was in another dimension, in a limbo between this world and the next, where all three could rendezvous, comfort one another, and then move on.

For some reason she said 'Richard of York gave battle in vain,' and her father answered, 'Yes, the colours of the rainbow.' And then he said, 'The other months curse a fair February and that makes them bad.' And turning to her mother he said, 'It's fine; the Lord's Prayer is fine.' In the dream a great sense of enlightenment welled up in Lizzy: she felt serene, reclined in her chair and noted how their Elmshurst Mansions' Thorburn range was now installed in Biddy's shop.

'Perhaps you'll visit his grave,' her mother whispered as a gentle draught of consciousness fanned Lizzy awake. She felt elated. Every line, every image from the magic lantern show still remained: clear, defined, sharp. But its meaning was slipping. Like that hint of honeysuckle on an autumn breeze, it was tantalisingly drifting away, demanding that she concentrate, frantically trying to skim butter from a dash churn, as the lid went down on the staff and the profound relevance of the words, which she had understood in the dream, was lost. But it did set her thinking, pondering the meaning of their fractured conversation and prompting a visit to the graveyard, 'a Christian duty' not widely practised in Clapham North.

Lizzy found solace in Kilbroney cemetery, a walled sanctuary, removed from the cares of the world, where St Bronagh's ruined monastery and freshly whitewashed holy well were at the centre of plumbed Christian headstones and irregular pagan slabs. The word 'McGrain', chiselled deep in a fine granite pillar, caught her attention, and, with a surge of pride, she wondered how long it had stood there to mark another Craigarran under a canopy of tall trees.

'Good girl yourself. You found it. Did I startle you?' James Scullion shouted, as he made his way towards her. 'He's restin' at the south side of your grandfather. I gave a hand at the diggin'. Young Wilson and me, and one of the "The Parchies". That fella Marley done nothing. It was lamentable. A useless calderer if ever there was one, shilly-shallying about readin' the headstones. Sat … over … there …

and … drank … every … drop … of … the … whiskey … Maggie … sent. A selfish gorb if ever there was one. I remember the oul' pair's funeral, your grandparents. I was workin' for Mayburys'. They owned "Applecroft" at the time. I seen the two hearses goin' past. He got divorced, you know!' And, seeing Lizzy's puzzled expression, 'Young Larry Maybury. Tommy Green the carpenter read about the whole thing. He was fixin' chairs up in Mayburys' attic, and I was helpin' him, when he found the divorce papers. I mind it well; they were tied with a red ribbon. I had to tap the rafters with the hammer, pretendin' we were working, while he read out the whole case. God between us and all harm, it was an almanac of mortal sins. They don't like their dead buried too deep, the Craigarran people. Like to keep them well up, close to the sun.' Lizzy could see there was no need for her to say anything; the pensioner was in his element, rattling on about everything, as a self-appointed high priest in local lore.

'There was a big tree here beside the monastery, and at the time of the Viking raids the nuns hid the bell in it. And hundreds of years after, on a wild night, you could still hear it ringin', I declare to me Christ, and people thought it was a ghost. And then it stopped, and there was no word of it. Even them that talked about it was dead. And, whisht, till you hear, about one hundred years ago the tree fell down. Could a' bin the big wind of '39, and they found the bell in the fork of it, and the clapper separate. It had rusted up at the tyin', fallen out.' He paused for effect. 'No sound you see! St Bronagh's Bell. It's now down in our own chapel. Go in, strike it three times, you'll get your wish. An awful stormy night in February. The other months curse a fair February and that makes them bad. That's an oul Craigarran one. A good February stands fornent a bad year.'

Content that he had provided a valuable service in leaving Owen McGrain's daughter better informed, James Scullion put his hands behind his back, spread his fingers out at his kidneys, and walked slowly up the path. Lizzy stood there and knew that her father was in the right place, that his bones should rest in this rath, with his people, while her mother's rested in Highgate cemetery's formal gridlines. And she rationalised the dream as telling her that each from

[195]

their own place had now joined again, had gone back into double harness in a ceremony at the fulcrum of both their worlds—the Lord's Prayer and Biddy Drennan's shop.

Lizzy felt it must have been a dreadful February because it had turned out to be such a good year. Every day was a good day, even when it rained. She liked it in Craigarran, liked the bizarre symmetry of the place; how neighbours and friends balanced it, and how she and Mick Wilson were now talking. She even enjoyed the way Maggie ignored her and stayed resolutely behind the gates. The Bee, as people called Maggie, was delighted with the heifer calf. John Wilson said that it created such a ball of work that Dinny had been seconded full-time. They had trouble at first getting it to drink from the bucket, but by encouraging it to suck their fingers and then submerging their hand in the milk laced with linseed oil, all was now well. Lizzy could see Dinny and Maggie forever escorting it across the street, one on each side in a shuffling waltz, both with a hand on its shoulder and flank, carefully pushing it through the wee gate into the garden, giving it a while in the sun, and before it got a founder, taking it back.

The morning activity on Wilsons' street allowed Lizzy to contrive when to go to the well. Her coming back with a bucket of water always coincided with Mick harnessing the horse. 'How do?' he would say, and she'd reply, 'Good morning,' and leave down the bucket. And he'd smile at her and lean against the mare, prompting a peevish display of jealousy as The Dun swished her tail, gathered her flanks, and threatened him with laid-back ears and snapping teeth. And he'd give Lizzy his bemused twinkling 'Is that the next of it?' look, while she, to justify lingering, always said, 'Isn't the weather heavenly?', prompting him to give an even bigger smile and say, 'It is.'

And Lizzy, not wanting to move, still lifted the bucket, stepped over the stream and walked on, saying to herself for the umpteenth time that week, 'Are you courtin'?' It was a question that, when put to her in London, used to embarrass and confuse her, and require a confidence-sapping 'No!' Now those three little words were an exquisite private indulgence. 'Are you courtin'?' she'd say to herself, and immediately feel giddy and glad, and whisper 'Yes'.

Even if she hadn't known the importance of the second Wednesday in October, the dog would have told her that it was a red-letter day; a very special morning when it was not expedient for him to wait as usual to meet her on her way to the well, but imperative that he come over and inform her at the house. 'It's here,' he proclaimed, putting his head round the open half-door and excitedly bowing and snuffling his message, while ever-mindful of the etiquette of keeping at least one of his back legs outside.

'What are you telling me? What are you telling me?' Lizzy urged, until his yelps and contortions became so painful, she had to lift the bucket and follow him out, allowing him to soothe his tongue-tied frustration and lead her to the force field over the stream. Immediately she could feel it: a storm of electrical pulses radiating from John, grooming the tup tied to the horseshoe in the wall; from Maggie, unusually inquisitive behind the gates; from Dinny behind her; and from Mick, just disappearing into the stable with a bucket of corn. Her empty enamel bucket seemed to conduct the energy, and she countered the insulation of the cork handle by allowing the curve of the metal to rest against her thigh. There she held it, to get the full benefit of its stimulus, as she hurried to the well in Pulnafrog. Never thinking to inspect its surface for a daddy-long-legs or a spider dangling from within the cowl, she scooped a bucketful of water, splashed out the top three or four inches, and carried it back. Back to

[197]

the force field and the daily routine of meeting Mick, who, without his usual prop of the mare, stuffed his hands deep in his pockets, shrugged, smiled and said, 'Well, what do you think?' It was a very jaunty 'Well, what do you think?' and Lizzy couldn't resist a 'Well, what do I think of what?' to take the wind out of his sails and chastise him to a more subdued, 'The race. They're reviving the Cloughfadda Race.'

Resigned to the fact that she had never heard of it, much less had any interest, he again shrugged, smiled, and, at a loss, said, 'It's a lovely day.' Lizzy, realising that he had no idea how much she had sifted the Finnegan girls and Biddy, teased him with a mischievous, 'Ah, the race. The race at the fair in Hilltown. Round the big stone in Polands' field.' She countered his startled expression with a smiled, 'You'll be fine.'

While the Warrenpoint Lamb Fair carried with it the anxiety of providing a major part of the hill farmer's yearly income, the Tup Fair in Hilltown was free of such mundane restraints. It was a gathering of tribes where people felt they were amongst their own, comfortably away from the prying eyes of the regimented classes; men exchanged tups from the year before, for one to breed in the year to come. Often the deals had been done before the fair—genetic qualities balanced, differences in monetary values agreed—leaving only the actual exchange of the sheep to happen on the day, when, without the penance of being linked to livelihood, Hilltown square had the full exuberance of a medieval fair. An opera with a cast of hundreds, in a rich mix of goodwill and ill-will, alliance and enmity, and drink. It was a gathering that had the country's bloodlines running through it: almost every man jack, apart from the hawkers, were in some tenuous way related to everyone else. And they knew it.

The Polands of Sliver Roe knew that their great-granny's sister had married a Gallagher from Benagh, and the Gallaghers knew that, through the Polands, they were related somehow to the McAtamneys of Drumcrow. This inevitably led to an almost frenzied bout of jollification and no doubt contributed to Flavin's aberration when in 1915 he sold his good grey cob. It was a great block of a wee shilty that could hunt, or work in any harness, 'a real nice sort' that he had no intention of selling, but which he was unlucky enough to be offered, and take, good money for—a roll of white fivers that fuelled three days in the horrors of whiskey, an overnight stay with the constabulary in Rathfriland, and a further week's convalescence in The Clornies, when he came home.

It was a custom of Flavin to eat all his meals in the carthouse, so every bite he put in his mouth had to be carried out—a foible that would intensify at the birth of a child or in the aftermath of an affray. Then room service would have to be extended half-a-mile uphill to the rocks, blackthorn and bracken of the fairy domain. These sabbaticals could often last for as long as a week, and that particular one, after his selling the grey cob, became known countrywide as 'When Flavin was sick in The Clornies, after the hooves got stuck in his throat, the year he drank the cob'.

When Lizzy heard the rattle of the hubs and the grinding of the big wheels on the gravel and stone, she went out to see Mick go up the loanin with the dun mare. Geordy Lyons' description of him as Young Lochinvar came to her, and, she smiled at the set of him with his leg up on the front board, the reins loose in his right hand, standing erect in the cart. Tied beside him, its head level with his hinch, was last year's tup. It reminded Lizzy of a pure white musk ox, a foe for wolves to fear on the tundra, such was the sweep of its horns and the breadth of its back. It was tied tight against the front board of the cart, its wool rippling to the ground as it shook its head. A mountain of a sheep, proud and resolute, pulsating energy, capable of smashing the timber to matchwood, had it the leverage of taking a few steps back. The dollop of fresh red keel on the point of its shoulders gave it added height and width, and stamped the Craigarran hallmark, the crimson war bonnet, that was Wilsons' coat of arms.

Then, suddenly, from nowhere, a song came to Lizzy. Henry Fearon's song her father always called it, as slowly, vaguely. 'This ram he had a horn', unfolded. Then ...

This ram he had a horn; it reached up to the sky.
'The angels built their nests in it,'
You could hear the young ones cry.
It's a lie, it's a lie, it's a most confounded lie.
If you had of been in the same shibeen,
You'd have said the same as I.
It's a lie.

There was much more to it, but she couldn't remember the words, only the joy of the chorus, 'It's a lie, it's a lie, it's a most confounded lie', as she watched the mare showboating: snorting, arching her neck, tossing her mane, and taunting the muscles on her flanks as she drew the cart with an easy grace, up the steep incline of the loanin. Sometimes, just for the fun of it, she would drive her shoulders into the collar, jingling the links of the draught chains and lifting the big wheels off the ground. Then, hitting the broad road, she again flexed herself, powering instantly into a fast trot, and as the raised eyes in Craigarran looked on, Mick eased her back, steadied her to a jaunty swagger, his soothing 'Easy girl, easy' carrying to John and the dog, to Lizzy and to Maggie, who, for all her enmity was now at her most animated behind the gates. She may have been an old woman, but there was a shine off her as she stood, head up, back straight, shoulders square, bursting with pride. A natural-born warrior, there was very little scraping of the surface to make Mick's fight her fight. Before she was willing him to thrash his opponents in the fashion of a superior bringing discipline to the rabble—with a holly rod. 'Give them the holly, and plenty of it,' she murmured. Then she turned and went into the house.

Lizzy didn't yet go into the house; she allowed herself to be drawn a little way over the bridle path towards Coolnafrankey. Edging along, keeping Mick in her sights, craning her neck as he slipped past the Sliding Rock, the School, and out of view at McKevitt's Stream. But she could still hear the cart and, as she became aware of the rattle of another coming up the road, and of a yet farther away one on Sliver Roe loanins, her excitement began to rise.

Even back in the house, she couldn't settle herself. Hilltown … Hilltown … Hilltown. Mary-Agnes and Madge loved to say 'Hilltown' much as Balham girls loved to say 'Up the West End'. It made them both seem worldly and smart. Mary-Agnes and Madge never stopped talking about the place. 'The boys from Hilltown will be at the Crossroads dance. They're great dancers. Mick is a great dancer, but he step-dances. The same as Red Pat up in Carrigs, much as all the old people do at a wake. But the Hilltown fellas, they know the new dances: "The Siege of Ennis", "The Sweets of May". They can swing and spin and lift girls off their feet, and they can waltz!'

Hilltown parish was a valhalla that started four miles up at the crossroads at the ridge of the mountain, and swept down the great glens of Lindseys and Carcullion into the town. For the Finnegan girls, it was a romantic hinterland, with more young men than would thatch a house. And while Lizzy got further jizzed up by Roark's trap stopping at the top of Shannons' loanin, Oul' Dan flannelled, 'Sure I thought youse would come with me,' and the two sisters danced with delight. May, who hadn't left the house in years, and Rose, who didn't even go to Mass, suspended belief to a further 'By the Holy, I thought youse would have come.' And they looked at one another and went down to the room, and took him up a further half-crown that he feigned no heart in taking, such was his disappointment. His heart scalded at having to leave Coolnafrankey without them, he edged out the door to a further 'Youse won't come. That's a terror; that beats the band' before straightening himself to march up the loanin and squeeze in beside Tommy Roark in the 'bird's nest' trap.

On the Far Road, Dinny was pacing the kitchen. 'If there's one place I don't want to go,' he lamented, 'it's the Tup Fair. The accursed Tup Fair. I-do-not-want-to-go. I could certainly do without that. But I need to be there and … ' It was the preliminary dirge

Dinny had to recite, and indeed perform, before going anywhere: an elaborate denial, a litany that Alice inevitably brought to a close by saying, 'Sure, go on. Pass yourself. You're up to that time of day, you need to mix with the people.' This encouragement was followed by a stern warning that he was not to be drinking and, above all else, he was not to be talking to 'skilts a' girls'.

Lizzy had no such rituals or limitations. Free of a parochial restraint that the Tup Fair was now a man's occasion and passé for women, she pulled the big door after her and was away up the broad road. Venturing farther than before beyond its junction with the loanin: to look from a different angle on Coolnafrankey, contemplate its faded grandeur, marvel at the ambition of its stout entrance pillars swathed in fuchsia, its gnarled orchard, and the brooding quality of ornamental trees now intrusively canopying the house.

She recalled snippets of her father and Brother Anthony talking about Coolnafrankey. The Shannons had been high earners. On coming home from a spell in Scotland, one of them had asked his mother to hold out the bottom of her apron while he filled it with sovereigns. Another had made a fortune in America, but also brought home with him an unquenchable thirst for corn mash whiskey. When drunk, he would proclaim, 'This one-horse town sure gives me the blues.' Though learned far from the Sliding Rock, this idiom still voiced his inability to resettle where the mountain swept down to his doorstep and (apart from the plots gifted to the parish) steadfastly held back the advance of arable land.

Leckan More surrendered two plots. One from antiquity, a site for a garden and a hedge school, now renovated and divided into a residence for the master and a meeting hall, and beside it the latest acquisition, a fortified square stamped in the heather for a playground, toilets and school: a statuesque building, tall and wide-shouldered, giving girls and boys a classroom each, with a high ceiling and a window of cathedral proportions to enlighten their studies within, and their daydreams without. It was a school which even wanted to educate Lizzy as she passed. 'Six fives are thirty, six sixes are thirty-six, six sevens are forty-two' the building cried, and she looked high on the porch to read the stamp of authority 'Drumreagh National School 1912 AD', chiselled in the wall.

With the times tables ringing in her ears, Lizzy stood for a moment at the old building, her father's school, and it was he and Maggie and the Bog King and others who were singing their tables; and layered behind that was whispered Gaelic from generations past.

The country above the school was different. Going up the road, you no longer had the views of the Lough, the lowland valley, the monument, and the spires of Rostrevor and Warrenpoint. Nor had you the eye-catching copses and clusters of farmsteads. From here on, it was a very gradual rise of brooding heathland, bounded on each side by the mountains and stretching in the distance to the crossroads at the ridge of Gruggandoo. With each contour, the fields became less fertile and the colours changed to browns and purples and infinite barren greens. Here and there paddocks had traces of lazybeds, desperate attempts to grow potatoes in only inches of cover soil. Lazybeds was the euphemism for the back-breaking toil of placing double rows of seed potatoes on the ground and covering them with a parallel width of cut scraws. A rash of tiny squares of boulders and turf sods whispered of homes where people had once struggled to survive, where the Famine had struck hardest with families dependent on potatoes, unable to grow corn. This was known as 'The Wasteland', a tweed shawl on the shoulders of a big handsome woman who was always sad, pining for lonely beings in Glasgow and New York, sons and daughters forever separated, kept from a mother they could constantly hear beseeching them to come back. But they couldn't come back to this landscape—as pleasing to the eye as medieval tapestry but as low in nutrient as a hank of dyed wool.

For some reason it brought to Lizzy's mind Clapham Junction and the hands of a clock, one at nine and one at three. A quarter past nine, or a quarter to three—it didn't matter—Clapham Junction and The Wasteland were opposite each other on the dial of a clock, registering places where people survived. The Junction was a rabbit warren of narrow streets, tunnels and tiny red-bricked houses, a domain in the depression below Clapham Common, where a hive of humanity scurried in a perennial smog. The place gave the impression of being underground, a labyrinth of dark passages inhabited by a sub-species bonded to the gargantuan tangle of railway tracks. It always seemed to Lizzy like one of the better parts of Hell, where the damned were still allowed to enjoy themselves; still allowed their grimy pubs, betting shops, dance halls, and diversions of every sort.

The road was now just a gradually rising track, a ribbon of gravel through heather, rowan, rushes and bog. It was a landscape no longer worth fencing, its sparse dwellings crouched close to the ground, roofs of deep coarse thatch, fortified by cross-ropes and weights of suspended stones, with one recently renovated cabin, a bolt-hole for a returning emigrant, Mickey Morris, where, Biddy had told her, he had avoided conscription and sat out the war. The concept made Lizzy uncomfortable. No longer sure of her convictions, she looked at the energy of the dwelling's whitewashed chimney, its vegetable patch and chicken run, and saw a green shoot in a land dispirited by old age and isolation, an austere beauty subsidised by money earned and sent home by people yearning from afar. And, as if to underline to her that there was more to The Wasteland than its spartan appearance, a hare skipped through the bog-cotton and sat on the road in front of her. A clean-limbed, confident athlete, strikingly beautiful, taking her under its scrutiny and giving her a feeling of mysticism tinged with pleasurable fear.

When Lizzy got to the ridge at Gruggandoo, a whole world opened up. She could immediately see why the Finnegan girls were so excited by the thought of a crossroads dance. With such a diversity of country radiating from it, it had conversely to draw dancers from a range of families and social circumstances. It was a spectacular view. To her right, expansive uplands stretched to the tors and ridges of The Mournes, to her left were the peaks of the Ring of Gullion, and behind her Slieve Foy sheltered Carlingford village and the Lough. Ulster's heartland lay in front of her, with its fertile plains, mountain ranges and towns. She could see Rathfriland first, perched on a drumlin, almost at her natural eye level. Then closer to home, right beneath her, Hilltown village—a compact clump of well-slated housing at the end of the Brandy Pad. This focus of the eighteenth-century 'run' of wines and spirits cadged across the Mournes from the smugglers' caves above the tideline at Maggie's Leap was where 'a glass well filled and running over' became known as a Hilltown measure, and the mountains met the lowlands at a meander in the river Bann.

The ground fell away quickly from the crossroads, the land ever improving, as the track careered down the northern face of Gruggandoo. Heather quickly became grass, wetlands were transformed to sheer dry pasture, and the fiddle changed tempo from slow air to lilting verve.

There were more people on the road now. Lizzy could see them in front of her, in groups and pairs and singles, holding their distance, giving each other a bit of privacy in the general serenade of horses' hooves, laughter, muffled conversation and draught chains.

A sudden vamp of accordion music made her turn and look behind at another stiff cart, one perfectly proportioned to suit the donkey drawing it over the skyline. The musician must have come up from Ballyvalley, and on the highest contour was knocking out a tune, one that reminded Lizzy of the Marie Lloyd song 'My Old Man Said Follow the Van, and Don't Dilly-Dally on the Way'. She had never thought of it as a marching song, but it was perfect for going down-hill.

I dallied, I dillied, I dillied, I dallied,
Lost my way, and don't know where to roam.

A movement alerted her—a head comically popping up and down from behind a whin. She could see him, but not, she knew, before he saw her: a slight figure jigging an empty bucket, stepping in and out of a little wooden gate through which he had been feeding a calf.

Prairie dogs, Lizzy thought; he was exactly like the little fellows up on their hind legs at their burrow in the London Zoo. They were instinctively on the lookout for predators, while he was habitually looking for news.

[205]

'You're late,' he greeted her. 'Your neighbours—young Talaigh, Tommy Roark and The Oul' Fox—are all away afore ya. There's only "Sprickeldy" behind you. Did you hear him give a bit of a belt on the melodeon? He always does that coming over the top. You're McGrain from the Back Side. There's very few "weemen" go to the fair now. I'd say you're for the fair.'

He was a very active man, though well into his seventies, and he celebrated his blessing of good health by being jovial and outgoing. Falling into step with her, he said, 'I hear you're from London. Then you'll know Pat Bradley, a neighbour of ours who's over there now.'

Lizzy found it hard to tell him that, in a city of eight million people, not only did she not know Pat Bradley, she had not even known who lived next door to her. But she warmed to her new acquaintance and his air of innocence as he regaled her with chit-chat along his home stretch of the Mullagarra Road.

He said, 'You were in the war, they tell me,' and, not waiting for a reply, continued, 'I wrought down in Magee's,' pointing to a neat farm in the Vale. 'Young Pat Magee married on one of the Talaighs. People here always married on weemen from the Back Side.'

Lizzy mulled over the terms 'wrought', 'married on', and 'Back Side' and found herself looking down at the farmstead where Mick's older sister Rosie lived, and assessing, by the buildings and the size of the dunghill, how much land Rosie owned. It was an instinctive evaluation that brought home to her how much of a countrywoman she had become.

Then, without asking her who she was, he introduced himself as 'Sailor Drennan: never smoked nor drank nor bothered with women myself.'

'Strange for a sea-farin' man,' Lizzy teased, and the Sailor took a skip of a step and recited: '"It's I that am the captain of a tiny little ship, of a ship that goes a-sailin' on the pond." I always said that poem at school; that's why they call me The Sailor. Sure I never was farther than Hilltown in my life. Well, Rathfriland and Rostrevor,' he corrected himself. 'Hugh Barney Arthur O'Hagan was in the same book as me and his poem was "Tukesbury Road" and he got nothin'' but Tukesbury O'Hagan to the day he died, God rest him! The Vinegar Man's a terror for the poetry and that sort of thing; he's a far-out relative of mine. His mother was a Downey from over at Crotlieve. She was ... now let me see, what friend she'd a been. Well, no matter, anyway, he's some boy. Fair skarred the pish crossways in half of Hilltown hall when he cut his throat in the play. Lying kickin' and squealin' on the stage like a stuck pig, coughin' up guts and gorbich, and frothin' at the mouth. He played a Redcoat. One bad bastard. *Terry's Kate*—that's what they called the play. The parish priest had them come down and perform here. You see them crowd in Rostrevor are always puttin' on plays. Then, for fear that wasn't bad enough, Oul' Dick Martin played Kate's father, Terry, naturally enough. He was mad drunk. For the graveyard scene, the stage was set out with pasteboard headstones that Dick was supposed to tip with his stick and say something like, "Ah, good rest to you, Mary, me darlin' wife." But he couldn't conduct himself, he swiped and lashed the headstones into the people sittin' in the front row.'

At a half-open swayed wooden gate, The Sailor was becalmed. Old ghosts told him to hold his whisht, as he crossed the cobbles and grass of Rathmay bawn. He was the last of his bloodline, threading on thousands of years of occupation, to a house quietly sinking into another layer of this historic site.

Lizzy felt warm and sad and somehow drawn to him as she left him behind. Walking the final stretch to Hilltown, she pondered how, far from looking for news, it was an audience The Sailor wanted, fresh faces to appreciate an old man's uninterrupted talk.

The road was now bounded by blackberry, rosehip, sloe and rowan, and, through them from the direction of the fair, Lizzy could hear a megaphoned announcement: 'Every man with his horse and cart will start here at the square. Then you'll go down the street, over the

Bann Bridge and out the Cabra Road to the loanin at Rooney's meadow field. Jim Traynor's standin' there with a big white flag. Go down the loanin and, once in the field, take the horse out of the cart. The rules clearly state that, there, you must ride your horse bareback and that no one is to be ridin' with collar and hems. Leave the harness and light out for Cloughfadda, the big standing stone in Polands' field. You can jump the ditch or go through the gap down at the river, whichever you want, but round the stone you go. Then back to your cart, hitch your horse, and head full steam for that white line Charley Hagan's painted in the square. Mr McCartan of McCartan's Close has put up a prize of five guineas! It's somethin' his father before him always done. Now there's somethin' I want to say to youse spectators: keep well back, keep well back! There's no call for runnin' ram stam all over the place. Youse can see all you want from up here.'

Lizzy, turning the final corner in the Mullagarra Road, could see Hilltown Square, with its church tower and fine Georgian inn, and in the middle of it Big Ned McFadden roaring instructions, 'out in his figure', as Biddy would have said, in his shirtsleeves and braces, standing on the platform of a four-wheeled hay wagon, with a loudhailer in his hand. Certainly no one had to tell Lizzy he was enjoying himself, this doubly fat master of ceremonies, surrounded by enough people (albeit primarily men) to fill the sets for a great four-acre *ceili* dance. A dance that was at that point in the proceedings when the music has stopped and the revellers are left to their own devices, shouting, jostling, searching for new partners, and in some cases, having found them, practising their steps. The more rumbustious grabbed each other by the shoulders and swung in a 'Siege of Ennis', while reserved types tripped out in a 'two-hand reel'.

This was a gathering of farming clans spiced with traders: apple sellers from Armagh, herring men from Kilkeel, and hawkers of cloth and cadgers of tin cans from God knows where. An assembly predominantly grey in colour, stamped with a red and white stipple of horned tups and horses and carts. It was for these horses and carts, driven by spirited yeomanry, that the race was run. Heavy chariots, designed to traverse rough, unmetalled ways, with five-foot-high wooden wheels: all shod, pinned at the nave and buttered with axle grease, to give a movement and sound as distinctive as a grandfather clock. Pulled by horses in stout harnesses: collar, hems, britchen, straddle, belt and braces issue that had been dubbined and double-checked. These steeds had ploughed and worked the land all year, but had that extra bit of fire in their breeding to show presence in a jaunting car, speed and pace in a trap. They were an extension of the men themselves and an expression of their zest for life.

As Lizzy approached the gathering, part of the crowd on her side of the square turned towards her and clapped and cheered. Then just as she was beginning to wish that the ground would open up and swallow her, a middle-aged man in a donkey and cart passed. Sprickeldy! A gaunt emperor in a black overcoat, inclining his head to accept the plaudits of a jocular crowd who were raising him to the level of a fully-fledged contender in the race.

As the ten starters lined up at the far end of the square, one outfit was so obviously, blatantly, advantaged, it laughed at the other nine. It was a spirited chestnut hackney, posing between the shafts of a light spring van. A rig, advertising 'Portadown Linen', which had in attendance three of the most celebrated gougers from that town. This was a team with the look of mongrel dogs clubbing together to worry sheep, an amalgamation of the worst possible bloodlines—a terrier, a boxer-labrador and an Irish setter. The three essentially disparate individuals were Midge Curtin in the gig, a journeyman jockey; Cob Horan at the horse's head, a spasmodic prizefighter; and Dollar Donnan at the tailboard, a part-time freelance bookie and an all-time polished rogue. Dollar was the brains of the outfit, an effortlessly charming matinée idol, collecting money, handing out tickets, and constantly calculating permutations to give himself even more favourable odds.

Mick Wilson was about six stands away from the bookmaker, his hand resting on his mare's withers as he talked to more than a dozen well-wishers and friends. Joe Marley was one of them, saying that at the far end of the Square 'Sprickeldy' had been clapped and cheered before the crowd had lifted him and the wee donkey and cart and passed the whole caboodle over their heads. It was an implausible story, drolly undermined by The Oul' Fox, who never batted an eyelid, but said very sagely, 'It's the God's truth that man speaks.' The casual observer would have noted that the craic was all taking place along the sides and back of Wilsons' cart; certainly no one was drifting along the front. The dun mare was standing quietly but had an unsettling tendency to drop back her ears and strip her teeth, cautioning the unwary not to stray too close. She had an aura about her—a peevish, sleeked malevolence—as she stood, not presenting herself like the hackney, but relaxed and detached: head low, shoulders slouched, pastern bent to allow the point of her off back hoof to rest at right angles to the street. It was almost as if she was trying to play down her condition, but was unable to disguise the glisten and sheen of her coat.

'Stand well back. Stand well back or there'll be wigs on the green. Well back. Clear the street. Clear the street,' Big Ned shouted. 'Let the dog see the rabbit! Give them plenty of room. I appeal to you, in the name of God and all in heaven, give … them … room.'

He loved to hear the sound of his own voice and have such influence. A passage like that ordered by Moses in the Red Sea opened in Hilltown Square.

'I'm going to give you your orders,' Big Ned roared. Then, pointing at the competitors, 'Not yet! But the next time I say "ready, steady, go," you're to be off.'

Mick Wilson stood upright in the cart, lightly raising the reins in his right hand. It was as if he had told the mare that she had acted long enough, and she, agreeing with him, became transformed from a surly, settled nag, to a focused, athletic horse. In the blink of an eye she was sculptured. Big, fit and powerful, more defined even than the chestnut, as she bunched her shoulders in the collar, tightened the chains on the trams, and crouched on the starting blocks, ready for the race.

Cob Horan was holding the hackney's bridle.

'Ready!' Big Ned shouted. 'Steady!'

At that moment Cob let go of the hackney's bridle and ran in front of the other horses, waving his arms and flapping his coat. It was a plan of Dollar Donnan's to give his horse an advantage, a course of action Cob Horan jettisoned when it came to obstructing the dun mare. And indeed discretion was the better part of valour, because when the hackney took off with a high stepping style, the dun mare gathered herself, got right down on her haunches and leapt forward, putting her head over the backboard of the spring van, fusing herself to it, as down the street the two of them accelerated, the chestnut horse and the dun mare: coupled carriages of a runaway train.

Midge Curtin had journeyed a long way to the Cloughfadda Race. He had come from a promising apprenticeship in Watson's Yard in Ballynahinch, from the Curragh, Epsom Downs, The Keystone Track in Philadelphia, The Hawthorn in Chicago and less noteworthy venues in between. At thirty-seven, he carried with him the scars of being warned off in England, and banned from the United States in a judgement (over pulling horses) that involved being deported and branded with a tattoo. Now he was moving in the shadowy world of sporting trysts, mêlées on the periphery of the likes of the Oul' Llammas Fair in Ballycastle, or the great gathering at the October horse fair in Ballinasloe. Unlicensed races of every kind were his bread and butter, where a stewards' enquiry was something Cob Horan settled in the back yard of a public house.

Midge was a cantankerous, conniving little pishmire, a skittering monkey with a God-given ability to get the best out of a horse. To this end, the instant the mare put her head over the tailboard, he instinctively repositioned himself, moving up to the kicking board, because a kicking board it would surely have been had he not redistributed the weight, countered the pressure, and thus prevented the shafts lifting to jiggle the straddle and agitate the bellyband under the chestnut horse. Midge was perched on his right hip, half-looking back, half-looking forward, his right leg curved painfully underneath him, his left leg stretched full out and perilously close to the jaws of the dun mare. She was a foreboding presence, adding to his simmering chagrin at Mick Wilson casually surveying him from the raised platform of the traced cart. A less seasoned campaigner might have done something foolish: tried to kneel up, to stand up, might even have tried to kick the mare, but, as it was, Midge let the hare sit. He didn't unbalance the van, he didn't endanger his leg, but instead settled for a pragmatic interlude where he suffered the pain and kept a tight grip on a skittish horse.

Big Ned had been right when he had said that they could see the entire race from the square. Every yard of the crescent running down Bridge Street, over the river and out the county road to where Jim Traynor stood with a big white flag, was visible. It was even possible to see Jim's backward-at-coming-forward demure, as he stood sentry at the gate to ten acres of prime after-grass sweeping down to the banks of the Bann. This field and the one north of it, where the Cloughfadda stood, were separated by a trimmed thorn hedge, a barrier cultivated generations before from sloes pushed into a thick straw rope and planted in a perfectly straight line. The composted straw provided warmth and nourishment for the germinating seeds, which resulted in a five-foot high, four-hundred-yard long steeplechase jump. This obstacle could either be faced straight on or avoided at its gap with the river's edge.

'Three to one on the chestnut, two to one against the mare. That's a wager of three pound to get a pound on the stepper, but it's only one pound to get two if any of you feel like backing ... your mare. Last round up now!' Dollar goaded. 'It's three to one. No. I'll make it five to one against any of the rest.' And as the chestnut and the dun turned into the ten acres of Rooney's Meadow, Joe and Arthur and half of Drumreagh and Knockbarragh, but not Dinny, rose to Dollar's challenge and put a further, if somewhat smaller, bet on Mick Wilson because the mare was still tight behind the hackney, while all the others were strung well back along the road, including for some reason the prizefighter, following after them, at a laboured jog.

'What the hell's the gorilla doing joining the race?' some wag beside Lizzy shouted. But his words fell on deaf ears, coinciding as they did with Mick and Midge starting to unhitch their horses and the crowd beginning to realise the extent of the skulduggery and the advantage the Portadown men held. Vexed that they could be taken for such gomerils by scuts from the lowlands, they stood numbed as Midge Curtin unhooked a cleak on each shaft, pushed back the light cart, and in a fluid movement pulled all the harness over the hackney's head. It was 'trotting tack', a combination of joined leather straps easily removed in one piece, and, while it flustered the chestnut and Midge had to hold tight to the leather reins, by the time Mick had loosened the dun's bellyband, the hackney had been manoeuvred alongside the wheel of the spring van, and from there Midge jumped on to his back—a smooth and practised procedure, ensuring that a highly strung animal was kept well clear of any disruption caused by the arrival of the other carts.

It was all happening in slow motion for Lizzy as Midge galloped down the field, along the river and through the gap into the big meadow beyond, silencing Hilltown Square, as Mick, rooted, worked at the cart, tipping it up, moving the mare forward and using a length of timber as a prop to keep the shafts in the air. He loosened the britchen, unbuckled the straddle, but seemed to take an age with the collar and hems.

Midge was almost at the dolmen, a fluttering jack-in-the-box astride a horse that drummed the ground with fast pumping strides. He was in agony, balancing precariously on the jarring ridge tile of the hackney's spine, spitting venomous vulgarities, lost for a saddle, calling on all in heaven to curse the committee who had decided that this part of the race should be run bareback. He dreaded particularly the slightest decline, where his groin would be jarred by the acute withers of the hackney horse, his blasphemy changing to prayers of relief with a rise in the ground.

In time, the crowd in the Square got a voice again, a whisper rising to a murmur as supporters began shouting, sounds that merged into a boisterous chorus. The more serious shouting were Christian names, surnames, horses' names, parish names, townland names, and, of course, Mick's name—names that fused into a driving war chant that in Lizzy McGrain's mind was all for Mick Wilson and the dun mare.

[213]

As soon as the mare was clear of the harness, she took off. Crouched on her powerful flanks, she leapt forward, her ribs a fettered mainspring released. Ten hundredweight of muscle, sinew and bone powered after the hackney, now rounding the Cloughfadda Stone. Mick had her by the mane, using the momentum to give one bounce with his feet together and propel himself in a perfect arch on to her back. It was a manoeuvre that would have made a weasel proud.

Straight out across the field they went, Mick leaning forward, his hand on the mare's withers, his head on her neck, coaxing, focused on a low place in the thorn hedge, directly between them and the dolmen, the shortest distance between the two points—a straight line. The mare was flying, her ears back, her neck outstretched, reaching for the meadow, reeling it in. Only at a chain's length from the jump did Mick lift the reins, gather her, pick the spot of sheugh, hedge and ditch, and let her go. She rose, driven by the power of her hindquarters, to soar effortlessly into the next field.

Two sods gouged from the ground flew into the air.

'Come on the Stronghold,' the Bog King roared. Lizzy looked over to him. A rhinoceros, in a camel-hair coat, clenching his fists in front of him, as Dan Shannon beside him coolly looked through brass-encased binoculars. They were an expensive commodity that no doubt belonged to Tom Cochrane, an increasingly animated Bog King.

Midge Curtin had to go back the long way again, looping down the field to return to the spring van through the gap between the river and the end of the hedge. The hackney, a trained pacer and no doubt someone else's expensive horse, did not jump. Not that Midge wouldn't have tried to 'brush him' through the thorns if he had to, but the little tactician knew the risk was unnecessary because he was so far in front. And, indeed, in yardage he was, although Dollar, from the vantage point of the square, was beginning to tend towards being the very slightest bit uneasy. He was taking an interest in the race now, his chiselled matinée idol's features raised under his soft brown hat. The cut of his tweed suit showed as he squared world-weary shoulders, and the leather of his light brown boots creased as he got up on his toes. He could see there was now a bit of activity back where Midge had left the linen van. A mêlée in the flustered efforts of tail-enders hurrying to get carts, horses and harnesses disengaged. Dollar looked pensive. Had he detected the strong smell of pigs from a cart with a folded tarpaulin in it, he would have looked perturbed. As it was, he stood with his index finger tipping his upper lip, and allowed himself an expression of weary concern.

Midge hadn't the luxury of being either pensive or concerned. He was like a skipper in a small boat, battling a rough tide back-washing off a harbour wall. He couldn't get the thoroughbred moored. Even when he was off his back, he struggled to settle his horse, to calm him and get him to stand. He knew it was the smell of pigs that had spooked him. Now he was frightened of the van itself, even the leathers.

'Pig's shite!' he snarled and, as if this wasn't bad enough, Cob Horan hadn't arrived.

But Midge Curtin wasn't a man to be easily beaten and, holding the end of the leather reins, he threaded them through the harness and tried to put it back in one piece over the fidgeting thoroughbred's head. This proved to be a disaster. Midge was too short, and his natural instinct to jump up only further agitated the horse. He was shying back, throwing up his head and twisting, casting the harness into a clatter of buckles, rings and leather, suspended on the reins. The horse was now snorting and showing the whites of his eyes. Midge could not get the harness on by himself; hot coals of tension burned in his chest as, seething, he waited for Cob. Dollar watched the whole set-to, his handsome poker player's face blank as, composed again, he became reconciled to how little he would win if his great plan failed.

And while Dollar calculated odds and outgoings, a tiny pulse of optimism was stirring in the crowd. They could see Midge's predicament, and their roars and yells of support were now only for one horse. Lizzy's heart was pumping.

Mick Wilson was coming straight back. He had circled the dolmen like a perfectly thrown boomerang. The mare was showing glimpses

[215]

of the Curragh, the Pony Express, the Galway Plate, and Mick was a part of her, a lithe extra power supply, moulded to her back. She was fearless, ignoring a grey and a sorrel plunging towards her, as again she cleared the thorn hedge and devoured Rooney's Meadow, back to the paddock that held the carts. The area was a cauldron of movement and boiling emotions, to which a lumbering out of breath Cob Horan had just arrived. Among all the activity, the dun mare stood exactly as she would on Craigarran street. Mick quickly put on the harness and backed the mare into the cart. The partnership of long days ploughing, opening drills, just standing beside one another, came to the fore. Now it was the hackney, Cob Horan and Midge, who were behind. The three of them were flustered and fidgeting, Cob was an exhausted buffalo that Midge, a voracious hyena, wanted to tear apart.

The rules of the Cloughfadda race were neither overtly stated nor written down. They were accepted—like being a man of your word, respecting women, and saluting anyone in 'the cloth'. It was a race for one man and his horse. That was sacrosanct. This tradition had never before been broken but Cob and Midge were dirtying their bib by unashamedly working together, yoking the hackney and propelling him after Mick, gaining on him, as the mare, driving her shoulders into the collar, sliced the big wheels through what was now mud and gutters, and powered the cart to a better footing on the broad road. Then, just as Mick's mare left the quagmire and her feet hit the hard core, Mick jumped out. He hopped over the side, closed the gate and completed the manoeuvre by springing onto the back tram. The shafts lifted, the bellyband tightened, and, as the mare broke into a trot, he was back in position and gathering the reins.

It was a sobering moment for Jim Traynor, an innocent marshal, delighting in holding the big white flag. He froze, registered his horror by widening his eyes, and, in doing nothing, did quite well. Because Jim created a blank canvas for himself, and on that he could paint whatever he liked for the rest of his life.

Mick's bit of sharp practice stole a march on the Portadown men, who had to break the pacer's rhythm and stop, while Cob footled at the makeshift wooden hurdle before ripping it off its hinges and bad-temperedly firing it into the hedge. Midge didn't wait for him. He drove the hackney through the gap and spirited the horse at full stride down the road.

The cumbersome harness and the stout structure of the cart restricted the dun mare. A vehicle built to draw loads along potholed loanins and uneven ways is no match for a spring van in a chariot race. The heavy chain jumped in the groove of the straddle and the traces rattled on the shafts as Mick stood astride the fulcrum, balancing both mare and cart, not letting her break into a gallop, equating every tension, striving for an equilibrium while keeping her at a steady trot. The hackney was now in contention but, with the rattling and clattering of rims, naves and chains, was reluctant to pass. The chariots hurled up Bridge Street in an explosion of savage energy. The blood-engorged muscles of the horses were now defined in slashes, as the hackney and the dun, with nostrils flared, manes flying, eyes wild, threw out their front hooves and strove for new ground. Both drivers were now doing everything by doing nothing, motionless, trying to levitate to gain an advantage, willing their horses forward, Mick standing, Midge static, a composed elf sitting on the side of the cart. Just when it seemed the hackney had overcome his initial hesitation, and Midge was about to urge him to pass, Mick dropped the end of the rein on the mare's rump; not a flick, just the merest tip.

It was as if he had scalded her with a white hot iron bar. From trotting at full stretch, she bunched herself, every muscle on her neck, chest and flanks further defined as she sprang forward in a gallop, lifting the cart and bouncing the two shod wheels on the road. The piece of timber used as a crutch for holding up the shafts leapt over the tailboard. The hackney veered to the right, Midge automatically checked him and Mick had won!

Somewhere midway through his jump from the cart, with one hand on the mare's rump, and just before his hobnailed boots hit the ground, Mick looked directly at Lizzy McGrain. His steel grey eyes locked right into hers and twinkled a greeting as she smiled back, lifted her right hand and twiddled her fingers in a silly little wave. His was not a surprised flicker of recognition from a random glance; it was concentrated eye contact, telling her he knew exactly where she was in the milling crowd; more than that, it was telling her he was glad she was there.

Lizzy was elated. This was a Craigarran victory and she was part of it. Standing at her full height, she couldn't help taking a deep breath and feeling proud of her association with Mick Wilson and the dun mare.

She couldn't join the others who congratulated the victor, shaking his hand and slapping his back; it was too public for Lizzy. Instead, she pushed quietly through the crowd, purposely hiding from Mick, slipping across the road and into the snug of the Primrose Bar. This was a little room to the right-hand side of the front door, a place with a railway carriage feel to it, eight feet long, six feet wide, and sheeted with dark wood. It had a mahogany table in the middle, flanked by elongated, upholstered chairs, tall sofas thickly padded and covered with embossed corduroy, the pattern was cows' licks in sweeps and circles of red. The bottom two-thirds of the window to the front street was fitted with a frame of tightly woven green wire mesh, embossed with the words 'Primrose Bar'. A lace curtain afforded those who were sitting close to it, on the inside, a clear view of the square, while those outside, even on the footpath, couldn't see in. It was a very private boudoir, a warm faded parlour, with a tiny confession box shutter that allowed a woman discreetly to order a drink from the public bar. Here the words 'whiskey', 'brandy', 'porter' were whispered in an exquisite litany of forbidden sins.

The little room had one other occupant—a woman so obviously Romany, she could have had 'tinker' tattooed on her forehead and 'gypsy' on both her arms. A plumply Mediterranean matron, with dark brown eyes and a placid, fleshy face that was an etched calf-skinned cover on the pages of her past. This woman had been a great beauty; her bangles, rings and necklaces pulsed high grade gold. Smithed gold! She sat in flowing robes like a Hindu goddess, a woman with an air of deity who had a wicker basket at her side and a glass of whiskey and a pint of porter at her hand. Lizzy nodded to her and sat herself by the window, looking out at the commotion in the square.

Mostly she looked at Mick, laughing and slapping the mare on the neck, as he loosened the chains to take her out of the cart. The mare was back to slouching, the dun colour of her coat showing black, brown and yellow, highlighted with sweat and froth. She could have been dipped in oil and decorated with cream, such was the consequence of her effort. A do-or-die winner, flicking her ears, arching her neck, snapping her teeth, and step-dancing on the spot.

Arthur Keenan and Joe Marley were behind her, Arthur supervising Joe tying what Lizzy assumed to be the new tup to the wheel of Wilsons' cart. She could see Dinny Coyle bobbing about and looking at them from various places in the anonymity of the crowd. He was too wise, too cautious, even to celebrate Mick's win, and just as Lizzy was pondering how being too wise and cautious can hold you back, a corridor in the crowd allowed her to spot Stephen Flavin lifting Sprickeldy out of the donkey cart. Of course, she thought, that's what it is about Sprickeldy—he can't walk—and she instantly warmed to Flavin as he carried the musician as naturally as if he were his own child into the Shamrock Bar. He was the best man in Ireland ... well, after Mick, she mused ... to do it. He had an arm round Sprickeldy's shoulders, another under his bent knees, while the accordion, the troubadour's flagship, was still strapped to Sprickeldy's chest. But it was Sprickeldy's legs from the knees down that stayed in her mind; they were pathetically inclined together, dangling, and very long.

Now the crowd shifted again and, as Lizzy's line of sight was lost, her attention rested on the driver of the stepping horse. Away from the glamour of the elegant chestnut, he was a gnome gnarled with bad temper, spitting sulphur and trying to get talking to the man who was running the book: a sleeked grandee, ostensibly ignoring him while graciously accepting tickets and paying money from a bus conductor's bag. There were more horses now crossing the white line, as men patted them, laughed, shouted and shook hands. They knew that winning wasn't everything. To have successfully taken part was a good selling-point for any horse, a good talking point for any man. And nobody was talking more than Jim Traynor, now down at Heanin's Corner.

'You see, I was the Marshal. I had to have my head well screwed to the ground. What with me havin' the flag, I couldn't be seen to do anything. But I shouts to Mick, "The gate, Mick, the gate. Close the gate." And he lights out of the cart and throws it shut and he's back in again without the mare breakin' her stride. Well, Holy Mother O' Christ, God forgive me for takin' His holy name in vain, but the roars and the bawls of Horan. The bawls of that man.'

At this point, Jim's eyes widen, his chin drops, and his mouth opens in innocent shock. 'The "f"s and slews out of him—it was badger's breath. I was goin' to say "Rein in your feathers", but I just stood there. Only God knows what he called me. I couldn't make it out, but it wasn't good, something about "from arsehole to breakfast-time". Then yer man with the steppin' horse left him. The "f"s and the slews. I houl ya' Collie Doyle wasn't afraid of him. He tried to stop Collie, but you know the sort of Collie—he'd a drove over the top of him. Well, you should a' heard him then, into the "f"in' and slewin' again, and the breakfast-time thing. The next fella, I don't know who he was—must a' knowed him—give him a lift.'

Lizzy took special pride in Mick knowing everyone, shaking hands, laughing, throwing up his head, giving his 'Is that the next of it?' smile. He is 'Young Lochinvar' she thought, as 'The Vinegar Man' and 'The Sailor' shook hands with him and clapped him on the back. Then she started going over in her mind how many of the crowd she knew. Six … seven … when: 'You're on the shore of good fortune' startled her. It was the gypsy woman, whom Lizzy had quite forgotten about, in her preoccupation with the events of the fair.

'I'll tell you more about your voyages, past and present,' she continued, 'when you put silver in my palm.' It was a voice with a most unusual resonance; a woman's voice all right, but one with the timbre of an operatic bass. It reminded you of distant thunder on a summer's evening, a harbinger of warm weather that threatened lightning and unwanted rain. Every accent in Europe seemed inflected in it; it breathed generations of travel; it could have negated the difficulty at Babel; it transcended tongues. 'You're very lucky with the final man in your life,' it teased.

And Lizzy smiled, looked the gypsy woman in the eye, leant forward just enough to invade her space, and said, 'I don't want my fortune told.' It was delivered slowly and firmly, yet she hoped inoffensively, by mustering an accent of concentrated Bow Bells. It was now the gypsy's turn to smile.

'Al' right, loves,' she countered, and in that moment she could have been a stallholder at the Elephant and Castle, as, with a rattle, the sliding doors on the confessional opened and a racket of voices, music, singing and tinkling glasses escaped. A waft of blue-grey smoke carried the scent of tobacco and warm worsted clothing through the opening, and then the face of the barman appeared. Young and angular, with such a startled look in his eyes when Lizzy asked for a tawny port, she immediately followed with, 'Perhaps a brandy instead.'

'A brandy then,' he repeated, his framed face visibly relaxing, putting her in mind of a young cleric taking his first confession, an innocent chap relieved that his dread of a heinous reserved sin being foisted on him turned out to be only the slightest touch of a misdemeanour. His confidence restored, he passed out the measure as the gypsy woman took a sip of her whiskey and a long draught from her pint of stout.

There was an air of tranquil equilibrium in the snug, the women neither challenging nor submissive, comfortably not talking, in the way of very close old friends. Lizzy occupied herself by staring out of the window, while the gypsy was lost in her own exotic thoughts. The fair seemed to be a forum where everyone had the opportunity of doing something—talking, buying from the stalls, assessing a tup's age by looking in its mouth. It was interacting humanity which appeared from a distance like a newly ploughed field, the banqueting table for a vast squabble of magpies and crows.

'I see a child in London, a girl in uniform, and a woman in a farm of land,' the gypsy whispered—an involuntary murmur, as she crouched, trance-like, over the dregs on the bottom of her glass. Then, slowly, she roused herself, hooked her basket on her arm and, as she got up and turned for the door, her dark brown eyes caught Lizzy in her gaze.

'He won't be badly beaten, not with the horse,' she said—a proclamation of reassurance which, as she emphasised the word 'horse', put a shiver from the nape of Lizzy's neck to the top of her head. It was like a thousand wrinkles rippling on her scalp, a legion of caterpillars racing to her crown, which immobilised her until long after the gypsy woman had gone.

'He won't be badly beaten, not with the horse.' Over and over Lizzy repeated it, but what did the prophecy mean? He wasn't beaten! Was there to be another race? And in her mind she began to rationalise everything. How much did the gypsy woman really know? Did she know anything, or was her fortune-telling just tinker's guile? Perhaps she had seen her wave at Mick outside? A woman with no rings, now captivated at a window, intently watching every movement of Mick and the mare. Like a detective, Lizzy went over the clues—her cockney accent and could there have been the merest hint of French in the way she had said 'brandy' or 'tawny port'? Out in the throng of the street, Lizzy could see the mare, her head drooped, her ears back. Unharnessed to just a bridle, she was impersonating a giant lathered greyhound as she walked up and down after Mick. It was all very watchable, so she decided to have another brandy before going home.

Not ten paces away, through the little 'confession' door, Alfie Synge was contemplating a more permanent home. In a scene reminiscent of his maudlin dirge about death at her father's wake, he was now confronting the weighty philosophical question of old age.

Squeezed in a corner, oblivious to the whole pub, he contemplated his pint, his whiskey, his pipe; now and again he would take to examining the lines on the palms of his hands. Not a blessed soul was listening to him as he quietly recited his lament.

'Life's long when you look forward, short when you look back. It's a rotten, rotten, thing, old age, a detestable thing in man or beast. In a horse, great holes above his eyes, and a hollow in his back, stiff with sidebones. A young colt's dancing, jumping out of its skin, couldn't hold it. A dog, a sheep the same. Wee lamb, skipping about the ditch; old ewe, a crow's nest of bones and pain.'

Then he brightened and smiled before lamenting more. 'When the priest asked Stephen Flavin about the father and the ignorant gulpin said, "He's eatin' like a horse, and dungin' like a horse, and pishin' like a horse," that's a good sign of anybody. It's a testament to their health. They're tough people the Flavins. There couldn't have been much wrong with him. And even at that, he died! The years were there. Oul' Paddy Flavin had a big funeral, but what does it matter how many's walking up the street after you, if you're the one in the box? And we're all for the box. We're falling through the thrasher as the mesh in the riddles gets tighter—until we're all caught.'

As the conformity of not wanting to be seen courting in public lifted off Mick, it settled on Lizzy, and she began to feel out of place. She could see him scanning the crowd and sensed that he was looking for her, as, standing on his toes, he partly camouflaged his intent by looking over the mare's mane. That was it she thought; she didn't want to be part of his entourage, didn't want to share him, and when the crowd shifted to block his view, she slipped out on to the street. Shadow-dancing with the drunks, she circumvented the carnival, discreetly making her way round the square until she got to Toner's shop—a family grocery—where she treated herself to ten Wild Woodbine cigarettes, a box of matches and a novelty of the fair—a thick slice of buttered currant bread.

'That's Sprickeldy on the accordion,' the woman said, as she arched the inside of a brown paper bag to protect the butter on the barmbrack. 'He's playing "Rathfriland on the Hill".'

Outside again, Lizzy almost furtively distanced herself from the shenanigans of the fair, and the accordion music drifting from the Shamrock Bar.

On the high tract of Gruggandoo, she sat on the Mass Rock, a solid table of stone at the side of Mullagarra, and marvelled at the energy of the water thrashing past. A brook, skipping down the mountain, prancing along a chute of sandstone and shale, pure hydrogen and oxygen, full of itself and lilting just for her.

'I'm 'Enery the Eighth I am, 'Enery the eighth I am I am. I got married to the widow next door. She's been married seven times before.'

Basking in a sound that brought her back to familiar haunts in London, she ate the buttered currant bread, scooped a draught of water from the stream and lit a cigarette, pursing her lips and watching the smoke form a translucent sculpture in the soft mountain air. Hilltown was below her; she could see its spire and the dark gathering in its square. She closed her eyes, still feeling the brandy, as she inhaled deeply and again saw Mick on the mare, leaping the hedge at Rooney's Meadow on his way back from the Cloughfadda Stone. She knew all the landmarks now. Smoking reflectively, she recalled the image of Mick, suspended in mid-air, his hand on the mare's rump as he looked directly at her.

'He won't be badly beaten, not with the horse,' came to her, but she shook her head and put it out of her mind.

Mick walked the mare up and down the cobbles of Mill Row, brushing her down with a folded hessian bag, never letting her stand to get a founder as the day cooled. Even when Hamilton McCartan, dignified in a black suit and felt hat, presented him with the five guineas, Mick kept the mare on the move. He held the driving-reins gathered in loops in his right hand, and stood at the mare's head, easing her backwards and forwards, as she champed on the bit and beat out a tattoo on the cobbled stones. 'One hundred per cent. One hundred per cent,' Big Ned bellowed. 'The genuine article, a real one. One hundred and ten per cent. A real nice sort. Not the like of her in the whole of Ireland. I'll go further than that—not the like of her in Hilltown today!'

At this point in the litany, Mick led the mare across the street and through the arched entrance at the back of Taggart's grocery store and public bar. A livery yard, as clean as a whistle, whitewashed and tarred, without a wisp of straw on its cobble-paved floor, it was an enclosure with a terrace of outhouses extending from the main building along the boundary wall. Six pristine compartments, starting with the urinal at the pub's back door, then four loose boxes and finally an open shed, stacked with bottles of hay. It had a pump, an elaborately moulded wrought iron totem, capping a well, a pace and a half from the second stable wall: a short, stout, armoured warrior encircled with gleaming buckets, who delivered pure sweet water to 'jingle the teeth in your head'. The yard was a draw for Taggart's: it was a 'stand' for travelling stallions and a place for countrymen to stable, or even tie up, a horse. It had an aura. It was the sort of place where a very settled bachelor, the sort of boyo who went to eight o'clock Mass on a Sunday, who attended the full week of the Men's Mission, could secure the pony and trap and go in for a drink while waiting for his mother, having politely driven her to the Women's Mission, or indeed, to twelve o'clock Sunday Mass.

All this was very much Hilltown, a town that was more a countryman's town than Rostrevor, and while Craigarran's parish was undoubtedly Kilbroney, Hilltown's business and social hinterland certainly extended to Biddy Drennan's shop. Here people understood clatting praties, pulling flax, shigging corn, and you could buy soft red rope to langle sheep or a globe for an Aladdin lamp. And if you really wanted something good—a top quality scythe, a suit length or a pair of 'sparable' boots—Rathfriland stood proud and honestly Protestant on a drumlin two miles farther on. Hilltown, though steeped in history, had the feel of a frontier town, a trading post where a slow waltz on a fiddle was forever played. It was where Craigarran had always sent her men to buy and sell, and to sing, dance and drink whiskey in Taggart's bar. Mick led the mare into the stall and continued to rub her down with a handful of dry straw. Short, brisk strokes on her neck and chest, long and flowing on her back and rump; absent-mindedly at her kidneys where she threatened to spin, lash out and flail him to the wall.

But he ignored her gathering flanks and switching tail; his mind was elsewhere, filled with clear images of Lizzy McGrain. The little wave, holding up her hand and tinkling the keyboard with her fingers, warmed him more than winning the race. He should have gone over, spoken to her, claimed her in the eye of the fair. If only he could get talking to her on his own! That was the trouble; there was never a minute's peace. His father, Dinny Coyle, Maggie McGrain, the whole bloody country was trailing after him. There were no dances; the priests were against them, denouncing them from the pulpit as 'an occasion of sin'. It took a wedding, or on a grander scale a wake, to stir up a bit of jollification. You could have craic at a wake, but, even then, everybody was looking at you. To quote the caption on the bottom of the 'Stations of the Cross': 'The vulgar gaze of the rude and scoffing multitude.' And every girl in the country had joined the 'Children of Mary'. Running about in blue robes, like nuns; their most important rule was that they could not walk or talk or have anything to do with anybody in the courting line after sunset. In the name of God, Mick pondered, was it any wonder nobody was marrying?

Feeling much better that he had cleared that off his chest, albeit to himself, Mick went over to get a bucket of water and a bottle of hay for the mare. Some gaunch had written 'Póg mo thón' in black pencil on the newly whitewashed wall. A clever bugger whoever he was, because it was written in a beautiful Irish script, small and perfect, and was just big enough to be seen from the pump, but you had to go over to read it. Mick smiled, wondering how is it that everyone knows the Irish for 'Kiss my arse'?

There were eight pubs in Hilltown, and every one of them was packed. Taggart's was a standing sheaf of humanity, from the front of the grocery shop, through the pub, to the door that led to the yard at the back. If the assembled bodies had been corn, they would be tied too tight to ever dry. Mick got a welcome as soon as he pushed inside. And that was only from the first twenty men packed into five square yards of sinew and bone, welded to the back door. The revelry meant that those farther up had no idea what the commotion was about, and only when they pushed and squeezed and fought their way to get to the 'yard' did another reveller know he was there. Pub time is different to ordinary time and packed pub time is different again to that. All the good feelings from the crowd are lumped together and, in some 'loaves and fishes, tongues of fire' way, deposited in their entirety on almost every head. In it, an elephant's lifetime passes in the heartbeats of a mouse. Mick got in step with the company in the space of a pint, a whiskey, and another pint that somebody placed before him with a reassurance that 'Man doesn't live by prayer alone'.

Through the orchestra of raised voices, Mick could hear a fiddle being played and a song being sung. Two distinct parties in close proximity, celebrating, with neither the player nor the singer acknowledging that the other was there. The fiddler was hammering out a jig, while the tenor sang a slow air. Yet they complemented each other like porridge and buttermilk, or heather rustling beside a mountain stream. But it was the singer who held Mick's attention with a distinctive voice and a familiar song.

It seemed at first an ordinary voice, a voice sheltered from reality, kept at home with its mother, and now, for the first time, abroad. Since it was open, kind and vulnerable, you were concerned for it, worried that it would be taken advantage of and somehow fail. Sheltered by a veil, it was only when it lifted that you realised how extraordinary it was, how it had brought a harpist with it and a sage to tell you that things are truly beautiful only when you grasp that they must end.

Red Pat sang in a slow, exquisite drone. He was in his seventies, with no longer a strand of the hair for which he was named. The song was 'Capall an Rí' (The King's Horse). Mick had sung it himself, and he could even remember being at a wake in Carrigs when he was a child and some old woman singing it in its original Irish form.

> *If the Fairy King of Gruggandoo should grant me wishes three:*
> *A farm of land, a crock of gold, a schooner to sail the sea.*
> *I'd tell him he could keep them all, if he would grant to me:*
>   *A treasure more than all of them, Capall mear mo croi.*

Mick ordered two glasses of whiskey and, holding them above his head, started to push towards Red Pat, up in the grocer's shop. He eased past Dinny Coyle, an unpleasant man in drink, past the prize-fighter who was drinking porter and eating pickled eggs, and through the door in the central partition between the bar and the shop, where Dollar Donnan raised his whiskey to him, allowing the glass to tip his brown felt hat.

> *I want a horse that has the courage and that special turn of pace.*
> *To pull a cart and carry me in the Great Cloughfadda Race.*

Mick knew that Dollar had won money on the race, but if the hackney had been first, he would have won a great deal more. Round him, on both sides of the partition, were as many as twenty men from the low country, men who had no doubt backed Midge Curtin and had lost; a competitor who, peevishly disgruntled, had waited for Cob Horan to come back before he threw the most vicious tantrum ever seen on Hilltown Street. Unable to contain himself, dancing with bad temper while still holding the reins, he squealed, 'That was the slackest, fuckin' uselessest bit of work I ever seen.' Then, reverting to an incomprehensible stream of bad language, he jumped up on the spring van, forced the hackney rudely through the crowds, and down Rathfriland Street, heading for home.

> *Like the one you gave Cu Chulainn, to win the warrior test.*
> *About sixteen at the withers, and good width across his chest.*
> *He'll be well up on his pasterns, and have a curve upon his crest.*

[228]

Red Pat and half of Drumreagh and Knockbarragh stood and sat round an upturned tea chest in the front corner of the shop. Mick pushed towards them, and reached the whiskey over to the singer just in time to join him in 'It'll be a mare with courage, and that special turn of pace/That I can take to Hilltown and win the Great Cloughfadda Race.'

The Clornies—five acres of Celtic wonderland—gazes at Craigarran from the corresponding contour on the Knockbarragh side. It is a domain of indigenous trees and blackthorn, camouflaging a rath, randomly positioned standing stones, and vague courtyards paved with strewn masonry, suggesting a civilisation from farther back. Red Pat lived in a well-maintained, single-bay thatched house, on the ridge just above it, and if a horse and dog were closest to his heart, the fairies in The Clornies were next to that:

'This time of the year in the late harvest,' he started, in an accent fashioned when commerce decreed that native Irish speakers use English words, 'upon my song, the mist would roll back. It would peel back from the centre like you would sned the top of a turnip and pull back its skin, and it was as clear and glistenin' as the flesh underneath. Here was me standin' on my own street, and right fornenst me, upon my song, as that whiskey glass is in my hand, the fairies up to all their diversions in The Clornies Forth. Their castles—consider the great cathedrals of icicles on the coldest winter mornin'—hanging from the spallick rocks. Well, they were like that, only pointin' up the other way. They had their own rainbows, trees and streams, and the moon would concentrate itself on their world. But the landscape was just a place to gallop their horses and run their dogs. They had a funny breed of horse, a bit smaller than you would expect in proportion to themselves.'

Red Pat turned his head and thought for a moment. 'About fourteen fairy hands, but powerful, great blocks, fierce hindquarters and flowin' manes. They had temper, every one of them. A fairy wouldn't keep a horse if he hadn't that bit of spirit, the blood. You know, in spring, when you see lambs sportin', ten or twelve of them comin' together and crowdin' on a flat rock, then burstin' away in random directions, like a handful of chaff caught in the wind—well, the fairies were like that, gallopin' on their horses, making them prance and dance, but never goin' anywhere, just wheelin' about. I suppose they got tired of it after a while. And their dogs—Irish wolfhounds nearly as big as themselves—always walkin' at their heels, at their shoulders more like. Sometimes they'd let them sport a bit, but not very much.' Red Pat took another sip. 'The music, I never could see anybody play. It's funny, I can't remember the tunes, but it was poteen goin' straight into your veins.'

Mick had to go to 'the yard', and put his hand lightly on Red Pat's shoulder as he left. The place was still packed, but not as crowded as before and he felt good and well with the world. The men from the low country were still drinking on both sides of the partition, and increasingly they were becoming a thicket of curmudgeon between the grocery and the bar. Dollar Donnan was there and beside him Cob Horan, and next to them, though not in their company, was Dinny Coyle. Mick pushed through them all.

Just when he was two steps past Dinny, when his head was full of the dun mare, Red Pat's singing and images of Lizzy McGrain, he heard Dinny say, 'The English pagan! He's going to marry the cripple for her money, so he'll get the farm.' It was spat at him, not whispered or mumbled, but announced for all the place to hear.

He stopped. Mick then and there wished he had walked on, but involuntarily he had stopped. 'Going to marry the cripple for her money, so he'll get the farm.' That's what cut him, and what silenced everyone, as the words rang through the rafters of Taggart's bar. Mick could hear the dry sound of his fingers rubbing on his palms. How he wanted the words to somehow be inhaled, for plates of time to overlap and, in so doing, make them never to have happened. For to confront them, and Dinny Coyle, was to make the words never go away. But, just as one wave receded, another, laden with sand and splintered rock, crashed against the harbour wall. 'Pimple Head's granddaughter,' Dinny Coyle continued. 'The crippled English soldier's home.'

Mick turned. Dinny had his back to the bar and was leaning

forward with a drunken leer. He knew Mick would not hit him, that a perverse moral vanity would stop him engaging in man's normal impulse to lash out. Dinny knew he could say anything; it never crossed his mind that he may have pricked a new and particularly sensitive nerve when he had slighted Lizzy McGrain. Suddenly Dinny's coat tightened around his back and particularly under his arms, and his feet were no longer touching the ground. Mick had lifted him by the lapels and was holding him against the bar, right up where he was able to sit on the counter, first feeling silly, and then debilitated with fear. Mick's steel grey eyes flashed malevolence; in them Dinny could see not one, but a tribe of primeval men in a frenzy of violence, a ferocious sub-species powerful and blood-splattered, their huge eye teeth dripping offal as they rejoiced in savaging a squirming victim lying on the ground.

Then, as quick as it had flared up, the anger was gone. Mick let him go, left him to sit on the bar and started to turn away. But he had only half-turned, his shoulders hadn't even followed his head, when Cob Horan hit him—a swinging, clubbing blow—just above his right eye. Mick's head spun, his legs buckled, and he dropped, smashing the bridge of his nose on the mahogany bar. But the counter that broke his nose also broke his fall. Automatically he had his hands on it, he was on one knee, his head languidly drooped, almost touching the ground. It was limbo: no pain, no feeling, detached from the staccato fall of blood dripping from his nose and pumping from above his eye to splash first, and then to run in crimson rivulets on the sandstone tiles. In his peripheral vision, he could see the horrified faces of Dollar Donnan and Dinny Coyle. He could see the backdrop of other faces, and directly above him, a little to the right, Cob Horan, nostrils flared, chest out, posture proud. Cob's neck was swollen over his collar; he was now a caricature of a brutal schoolmaster, decreeing 'That'll teach you not to close gates, my boy!' A smug and self-satisfied figure, sated with drunken arrogance, looking down.

Mick sprang to his feet, half-spun, and struck out with a straight left that caught Horan in the mouth. It was the action of a cat, the natural repositioning of the predator to strike again. Then, his feet

[231]

firmly planted on Taggart's tiles, Mick swayed back and unleashed a fierce looping right hand, a thunderbolt that hit the prizefighter, crashing through his plasticine nose and rubber lips and exploding on the square jutting point of his jaw.

It was as if a firmly rooted ashplant had been pulled back and let go, an ashplant of such substance that it carried an anvil on the end of it, to strike with such power that it rattled every bone and sinew in Cob Horan's frame. He shuddered, but he didn't fall. He couldn't fall. Like a single stalk of oats cut at the base, he was held up by the rest of the sward. The men from the low country were round him, surging forward through the partition door from the grocer's shop, to join the others of their crew in the bar. There was enough room for the three or four ringleaders to throw punches and kick at Mick. All were delighted that a fight had started and that they could get involved. Here was a chance to vent their spleen on Mick Wilson, to blame him for everything: the money they had lost and their general umbrage with the world. Individually they probably meant him little harm, but collectively they were murderous animals that wanted him dead. A wave of kicking, clawing, punching humanity engulfed Mick. It was a threshing machine, its flails moving relentlessly forward, pushing him back, as he put his forearms in front of him for protection. He could recognise a lot of them, knew their faces, if not their names, as the wave came on. One man in particular was leading the mob, his face contorted with gleeful malice as he swore and screamed and egged them on: dehumanising Mick with screeches of snake, rat, badger, even buck-goat and sow-pig. These he prefaced with 'dirty rotten', interspersed with the most vulgar expletives, great mouthfuls of slobbering obscenities to spray the crowd.

Mick, still facing the mob, was driven out of the back door and stumbled into the yard. He kept his feet as best he could, but they were overpowering him, as, crouched and unsteady, he retreated along the outside of the urinal wall. He knew he mustn't fall over the buckets, mustn't be trampled, and instinctively he turned and sprang for the space between the pump and the graffito, striving for the stable door. Vulnerable now, his back to the pack, he flicked up the latch and pulled it back, as the pump and buckets gave him a moment's respite before the mob were onto him again, scrabbing his coat, pulling his hair, trying to kick the feet from under him as he dived through the opening and between the legs of the dun mare.

'The dirty rotten bastard,' the ringleader screamed; 'we've got him the bastard,' and he grabbed the edge of the door. Applying every ounce of his incensed fury, he wrenched it fully open, clearing a four-foot space for himself and his half-dozen triumphant thugs who were in an instant transformed from a pack of hounds at their feral zenith to whimpering mongrels and frightened curs. Cowed pups, repelled by the aberration in front of them, were desperately clutching at each other in a frenzy to withdraw.

The mare, her mane a cockscomb of fluttering raven's wings, was terrifying: black, avenging, glowing with evil and throbbing with equine vice. She was doing a sword dance over Mick Wilson's sprawled frame. It was a dance where the metal of her shoes not only moved up and down, raising sparks from the tiles, but propelled her forwards and back, attacking and defending, ready to strike. Her ears laid flat back, she snorted, showing the whites of her eyes and, as part of her dancing steps, raised her off-front cannon to the height of her chest, swivelled the hoof at her pastern, and fired it straight out, piston-like, to pierce the space between the posts of the open door, drawing her shoe back to strike the ground (inches from Mick's kidneys) in perfect time. It was a dancing with death, a desperate Russian roulette, that made the mob gasp 'O Jesus, please stop,' as, horrified, they watched her snapping teeth, her lashing front feet and the spectacle of the man they had been pursuing about to be trampled to death. From wanting to kill him, they now wanted to save him, but they were too afraid. Even the bravest among them cowered back or squeezed themselves against the walls on either side of the door, a respite that allowed Arthur Keenan and Joe Marley to get down the yard.

'She'll do him no harm, if you leave him alone,' Arthur shouted, as the two of them pushed and pulled at the assailants, exhorting them to 'For Christ's sake, keep back!'

In the silence that followed, the mare stopped dancing, delicately moved sideways, and started to sniff and nudge at Mick. The demons had left her; it was for all the world as if she was pampering a new foal, rousing it, encouraging it to get to its feet. The transformation quelled everyone. The men from the low country, chastised, most of them ashamed, slunk off, not back into Taggart's, but out of the yard, either to find another pub or to head for home.

Mick got to his feet. He was sore and bleeding, but he looked worse than he was, nodding his old mischievous smile as he straightened himself and stepped out of the door, barring it behind him, and never giving a second glance to the mare.

⌒

Rosie McAlinden had nursed in Dublin, married a Doctor Keyes who had played rugby for Ireland, and had come home widowed with a daughter by the age of twenty-five. This alone would have made her life remarkable. What made her exceptional was that her achievements as a district nurse so far overshadowed this momentous chapter in her life that it relegated it to a footnote in the public mind. She was a matriarch, a figure of such standing that it never entered anyone's head to ask how a girl from up above Drumreagh School had got to Dublin, been trained, married a rugby international, and, above all, had come back to be Hilltown's district nurse. The question seemed absurd because Nurse Keyes was so self-evidently the district nurse, so fully formed even from the first that no one could see her as anything else. A stout woman, now in her fifties, dressed in full nurse's regalia, from the top of her head to the hem at her heel, she exuded the confidence of a woman who was midwife, general physician and locum surgeon to a district of respectful children, women and men.

When Arthur Keenan and Joe Marley escorted Mick into her dispensary on the Rathfriland Road, she received them with the professionalism for which she was renowned. Nurse Keyes exercised a studied stoic taking charge of the situation, in a surgery, where she treated small boys as men and men as small boys. This was a woman who extolled the virtues of champ and butter, porridge and milk, and the fumigating properties of smoking a cigarette; who thought nothing of publicly reprimanding the roughest gouger, should his behaviour or language not meet her standards, and, if he was under thirty, reminding him that she had expected much better when she had brought him into the world.

Nurse Keyes sat Mick on the wooden chair in the centre of the distempered room, and with what could only be described as disdain, motioned for Joe and Arthur to wait outside. Slowly she put on her spectacles, taking her time to examine Mick as she fitted the wire frames behind her ears, before stepping forward to pluck at a clean piece of linen on his bloodstained shirt, giving him a withering look to convey that she thought his spoiling the garment was the greatest injury of all.

Washing his face, she started at the top. With a tiny needle in the shape of a new moon, she put five stitches in the wound above his eye; five no-nonsense stitches. Mick could see her drawing the thread through, knotting it and clipping it, much as a man would when sowing a bale of wool. Then she sandwiched his nose between her joined hands and realigned it, securing it in place with a strip of sticking plaster that ran from cheek to cheek.

'Is the rest of you alright, after your fall?' were the first words she spoke: an enquiry in a polite, slightly affected voice, which admonished him and carried with it a pretence that her delicate disposition could never envisage anything so uncouth as a fight in a bar; a pretence she then put behind her to show how much a Drumreagh woman she still was, by acknowledging Mick's thanks with a mischievous boxing stance, and a word of advice.

'Carry your right hand a bit higher, young Wilson.' This was followed by a consolatory, 'You did better in the race.'

Mick Wilson stepped inside Taggart's bar, took a couple of short snorts up his nose, and every man in it knew he was not subdued by the fight. There was aggression in his cavalier stride as he passed very close to Cob Horan, who, like a bullock at a manger of hay, was standing against the bar.

Cob never moved. His mouth was cut and badly swollen, the whole effect made worse by a mottled stubble of porter and tobacco stains and the remains of pickled egg. He was isolated and downhearted, his willingness to leave well enough alone registered by Dollar Donnan's 'Good man, Mick.' And Mick, back with his friends, knew that while he could have done without the belt in the mouth, he would get over it, whereas Cob would find it more difficult. He was a bully, who saw himself primarily as an enforcer and hence didn't have the luxury of dismissing a pub brawl as a folly that would fade. And no sooner had he thought that than he felt priggish and remembered another line on the bottom of one of the Stations of the Cross: 'Children of Jerusalem, weep not for me, but for yourselves and for your children,' and he determined to put it all behind him. He drained what he knew was one of his whiskies from the top of the tea chest, and lit a cigarette.

The dun mare powered the cart, Red Pat, Mick and the new tup along the steep track on the face of Gruggandoo. She had a spring in her step—she was going home—and only repeated murmurs of 'Steady, girl' prevented her from breaking into a trot. Red Pat was mad drunk and had to be kept an eye on, lest he fall out of the cart. Not obstreperous in any way, good-mannered always, sober or drunk, but he would try to stand up, to point or, more alarmingly, to shake hands with ghosts along the way, greeting people long gone. He shouted some of their names, others he whispered. The road was lined with them: a guard of ever-present holy souls. Pat could see lights in houses that were now only tumbled stones, turf glowing in kitchens of briars and nettles, where he had danced, supped porridge, and sung. Even the family names he spoke had been lost to the country, replanted and vibrant in places far beyond. He shouted the pedigree of horses rolling and sporting in the grassy clearings stamped in the heather, and acknowledged a 'grey woman' floating from a thorn bush in Altnataggart to a rath at Mallaghmore. For Pat, ghosts were spiritual beings, friends and relatives, spending a time drifting close to us before finally moving on.

Fairies were something else—small people in another dimension, in a world he could sometimes see through a door of fractured light. He viewed them quite naturally, accepting them as he did the waxing and waning of the moon or the rotation of the stars. If he did try to rationalise them, they were in a limbo, curiously trapped in a world without struggle or desire. His language was now increasingly falling back on prayers he knew in Irish, whispered bits of his old catechism, snatches of scripture and poetry he had learned at his mother's knee.

'A thorough Matilda, but there it is, the dawn on the hills of Ireland,' he quoted, and, reaching out to touch the stones in the wall at the Sailor's gate, he declared them 'as lovely as delft dogs. Ad Deum qui laetificat inventutem meum … Rathmay,' he whispered, and Mick was glad Arthur Keenan wasn't with them. What with the ghosts and the prayers before Mass, and Red Pat's mysticism, Arthur, being so freakish, would have needed a bottle of holy water and a priest.

At Carrickari, the circular mound at the crossroads with a view over a dominion of townlands, Red Pat began to sing. He was sitting in the well of the cart, propped between the sideboard, the front board and the new tup. He sang his heart out, occasionally putting out his hand and patting the mare's rump. Mick didn't understand a word of it, but it was beautiful and melodic; a delivery in slurred Gaelic, the man and the song from another time.

Below them the country was washed in blue black ink. The dun mare was coasting to Craigarran, Red Pat was snoring, and Mick was looking down the valley to the lullaby of the mare's step and the gentle grind of the cart's shod wheels. The Cloughfadda race was far behind him, distanced by the curtain of Dinny's words and the mêlée in Taggart's bar. He felt quiet in himself, made lonely by the Milky

Way, the Harrow and the Plough. He was tired, but he could turn it into a dull aching pleasure when he directed his mind to thoughts of Lizzy McGrain. Dressed in gingham, she was stopping to talk to him at the bottom of Craigarran street. The enamel bucket with the cork handle was by her side, and he allowed himself the added pleasure of softly singing to himself Maggie's song, 'When you held my hand and smiled at me, and we danced at Sliver Roe.'

'Whoa, whoa, steady now. One more step, one more.' Red Pat was opening drills with some fanciful horse. And then he must have been singing to himself, because he mumbled 'Faint heart never won fair lady,' and Mick knew he was flailing himself, still tortured over Kitty Mackin. Mick would take him onto Craigarran (there was no one waiting for him) and Pat would sleep on the settle-bed, until a fierce pride would wake him before breakfast, and he'd go home. To Carrigs, visible now beneath a sky streaked with shooting stars—holy souls with their time served in purgatory, heading for heaven in their droves.

A 'bride's race!' Could there be an event more unsuited to her? Lizzy mused. The Finnegan girls had called and were jumping out of their skins, their thoughts of a dance at the crossroads forgotten, in the excitement of getting to run down the field at the back of Wilsons' house. The youth of the country had gathered to honour two young people from up in The Bog. It was such a beautiful warm harvest day that it would be churlish not to attend, but as soon as Lizzy rounded the gable of Wilsons' house, she felt it had been a mistake. A great weight rested on her. She felt out of place amongst the forty or so young people, in Geordy Lyons' words, 'from the upper parishes', and a few from the town, milling on the headrig of the field.

Like a group of chattering starlings swirling to their nests under a London arch, nervously they twittered their delight and embarrassment as they joined two by two, and followed the bride and groom down the steep grass field. Boys and girls holding hands and running for all they were worth, shouting and screaming and desperately trying to keep their feet. Demonstrating the elasticity of youth, they britchened on the few level paces of footrig, rearranged themselves; then, boys to the left, girls to the right, they walked back up, selected a new partner and began again. Couples were running constantly, sometimes falling, rolling over, being dragged, accompanied by the hysterical sound of youth being tickled to death. The Finnegan girls couldn't have been having more fun. Life was just beginning. They were tall daffodils delighted with spring.

Lizzy shook hands with the young newlyweds, a slightly built, sandy-haired boy and a dark-haired slip of a girl. They were both fair-skinned, the bride particularly. Her face was the deepest shade of cream and white, contrasting with her hands, oak-stained by sun and dark earth. Lizzy felt uncomfortable, self-conscious about her limp and lack of affinity with the group. She went over and sat on a long flat stone in the corner of the field, apart from everyone by at least ten years, and consoled herself by lighting a cigarette. She smoked it, not as an act of defiance, but as reflectively as a labourer would in a break from tying corn.

Then she saw Mick and knew how avidly she had been watching him from the first day she had arrived. Not consciously, but in spite of herself, she saw his every move: the way he filled a space, threw out his feet, swung his shoulders and carried his head when he walked. Now she could see that, like a bubble in a sealed jar that had been minutely tilted, he was marginally out of kilter. Dressed in good working clothes, he was perhaps a little more erect than usual; and, walking across the top of the field, he was just that bit too mindful of placing his feet on uneven ground. Keeping himself detached from the runners, he came towards her, smiling ruefully as she focused anxiously on his face. He appeared to be wearing spectacles, the lenses two crocks of cream into which treacle had been streamed. His lips were bruised and swollen and the slash of sticking plaster looked like an additional scar running from cheek to cheek. When he took a deep breath, he held his ribs, and Lizzy could easily have cried.

She sensed that Mick had somehow got involved in a brawl about

[239]

her. But instead of crying, she involuntarily laughed. It was a nervous expression of relief that led to her declaring, 'I don't like to run.'

'I was born with a spastic right ankle joint,' she explained. 'That means my right foot is one size smaller than my left.'

Immediately she was embarrassed. Why did she find it necessary to relate such a thing? It was the most personal of admissions that she knew was a complex mixture of reaching out to him while snatching an opportunity to air an impediment and get it out of the way.

'I don't like to run myself,' he smiled and, feigning a grimace, tapped his ribs. Gingerly he sat down, delighting her by dismissing her disclosure, and pretending he wasn't so bad by ham-acting worse than he was.

'I made a mistake yesterday,' he said.

'The fight?'

'No, no. That was fine,' he laughed. 'By not talking to you in the fair.'

'Not taking me to the fair,' she bridled, arching her eyebrows and giving him a playful glance.

'Well, no,' he said, and with a smile, 'I suppose you can't understand a word I say … Not talking to you in the fair.'

The 'bride's race' had a centrifugal force and the fact that the young people were caught up in it, enjoying themselves, left Mick and Lizzy by themselves. The country was at its autumn best. Below them the river flowed through a swathe of sycamore, scots pine, ash and oak; trees that galloped away from the watercourse, in places charging up hedges and gambolling in clumps. Splashes of autumn colour that were more recent in antiquity than The Clornies, which looked directly at them from the 'far face'. Viewed from Craigarran, The Clornies resembled the ruins of a monastic settlement embraced by gardens that had been untended for a thousand years. Red Pat was on Carrig's street high above it and to the north the sun reflected on the slated roofs and thatch of the remaining four houses in Sliver Roe.

It had been Kitty Mackin, Mick thought, who had thrown her arms round Maggie's neck at the railway station in Warrenpoint. Kitty

Mackin, the love of Red Pat's life. When he was drunk, he'd sing about her, about how he regretted 'lettin' her away'.

> *It's quartz that's in the Diamond Rocks,*
> *Sand in the Golden Pool,*
> *The sun's behind the mountain,*
> *A cloud blocks out the moon.*
> *I miss you, Kitty Mackin,*
> *Why did you have to go?*
> *You took the magic from The Clornies,*
> *And my heart from Sliver Roe.*
> *You were the levels in the loanin,*
> *The moss beneath my feet.*
> *It's only you I think of,*
> *Perched here on Carrig's street.*
> *Till the day I wear bog cotton,*
> *I'll regret you didn't stay,*
> *And that I was so faint-hearted*
> *As to let you get away.*

There could be any number of verses, always ending in 'Faint heart never won fair lady', as Red Pat flailed himself and looked into the ground.

> *In my heart where thorns are growin',*
> *I hurt and rue the day,*
> *That I thought I couldn't keep you,*
> *On Carrig's rocks and lea.*

It seems he thought that she would always be there for the asking, comfortably with him, until, out of the blue, Peadar Burns from the Point came up, and she was gone.

Red Pat was now walking across the field at the side of the house. The sun was indeed behind the mountain, its rays clipping him, shining on Craigarran and leaving him and the whole sweep of the

[241]

'far face' in the shade. He had a stick with him, not to cap a sheep, threaten a bull, or swing to cut the head off a thistle. He carried a stick because he needed the support; it helped him walk. Mick had never considered it before, but the sporting bachelor, *buachaill rua*, was an old man. You didn't think of it because Red Pat was such a mainstay, breezing out of Carrick, good-humoured, irrepressible, and you'd watched him all your life. 'Life's a weary puzzle,' he'd say smiling. And, as Mick pondered that, a weight anchored to his heart. It was a weary puzzle; we must never stop to thank God for the health and pleasures we have, it sours them, spoils them, steals the moment, squanders a gift intended to be selfishly enjoyed.

For a man grumbling about 'not having a minute's peace to talk to her', Mick had very little to say. Comfortable and contented, he and Lizzy idly looked at the country, both blandly blissful, while the couples in the 'bride's race' flashed up and down.

Lizzy wanted him to repeat the very words he had said to her, on the evening of the Warrenpoint fair. She knew every syllable, every inflection of 'Will you marry me, Lizzy McGrain?' She tried telepathy, putting each of the six words on a wave of thought and passing them to him, concentrating so hard that surely he must voice them back, but he didn't.

'Do you believe in fairies?' he asked her. Lizzy tapped the long flat stone they were sitting on, looked into the ground, smiled and slowly shook her head.

She could see he was lost for words and, wanting to help him, said, 'My father told me that in his grandmother's time a little man called for a can of oaten meal.' But he wasn't listening; he was furrowing his brow and biting the inside of his lip as, through knotted vocal chords, words struggled to get out.

'I have a brother Luke in America,' he finally blurted. 'I only own Tievegorm.'

The irrelevance of it scalded her. 'Do you indeed,' she snapped. 'Sure I thought you owned nothing at all!' Instantly she was horrified—she could have kicked herself—but Mick only laughed and continued, 'Luke's flying an aeroplane.' Inconceivably it broke the ice and he was looking at her, his eyes twinkling and mischievous as he added, 'as God's my judge,' and they both smiled.

Then he was serious again, and in his eyes she could see a calm October day, a tranquil autumn setting where she was happily tripping through dry leaves on Clapham Common, and contented still when the location changed and she was gathering sticks in the hazel groves along the river below Tievegorm. She could feel her heart glow as she thought of Mick smoking a cigarette at the fanbellows, while she read the *Evening Standard* on the opposite side of the hearth.

'Did you mean what you said when I asked you after the Point lamb fair?' he managed to stammer.

It wasn't quite what Lizzy wanted to hear, but it was near enough.

In the warm autumn sunshine, the ghosts of Craigarran flocked to them. They came, not as old embittered men and women, but as life-affirming ambassadors, with the humanity, the energy and the joy they too felt when they were in double harness and were young. They sat them on a pillow of freshly picked heather blossom to cushion the weight of their enchantment, and linked their arms around them, forming an invisible ditch of stone, sod and blackthorn. They brought oxygen to them, bolstered their hopes and wishes and, for a time, held their fears at bay.

Mick was very uneasy, waiting in the hallway of the parochial house. He had never had reason to be in the priest's home before, and was conscious that if he didn't count confession, or the words 'Good day, Father,' it would be the first time he had spoken to a priest. In a cavity behind the wall of his chest, he could feel the power of the place, the sense that from these cold chambers lives were ruled. He had asked to speak to one of the priests, but now regretted not asking specifically for the curate, Father Hicks. He would have been more at ease with him, but Miss Hanley, the housekeeper, had now disappeared down the hall. She was a short, gutty, middle-aged woman, dressed in a black and red floral overall. Its tyings wrapped around her middle accentuated her rump.

It was a big cold hall, wide and high, sparsely furnished with one chair, one small semi-circular table and a grandfather clock. There were two large pictures on the wall: a depiction of Christ rising from the tomb, and Mary being told she was to be the Mother of God. The one about the resurrection was to Mick's eye a bit overbearing. A triumphant Christ levitating, flourishing a red and white flag over unfortunate soldiers, trapped and maimed beneath rubble on the ground. He liked the angel one better. It was of a handsome girl with folded wings, on her knees submissively reverent to Mary, a hesitant figure and surprisingly marginalised. The artist had focused on the angel and the palace, and whatever about Saint Joseph being a carpenter and Our Saviour being born into humble stock, this event took place under a high, domed ceiling and on opulent terracotta tiles. But Mick really liked the idea of the angel being a beautiful woman. He had always visualised a man, a big white-robed authoritative figure, shouting down instructions—and then he wondered were they paintings or prints? Because it was a print that James Finnegan had brought home from Scotland: the big deer on the mountain, 'The Monarch of the Glen'.

Mick could hear the rattle of cutlery in the background and knew they must be at their tea. Nervously he made little circular designs on the thick brown oilcloth with the toe of his boot, conscious that he had arrived at a bad time and would have to wait. He tried to put out of his mind the heresy of equating this place with an ordinary parish home where a child would be given a slice of griddle bread buttered and sugared, almost for arriving on the street. A neighbour and even a stranger would long since have been forced to sit down for a cup of tea and a boiled egg.

After an eternity (during which Mick was about to slip out), Canon Bennett came tripping up the hall. In his urgent progression he gave the impression that he was so busy, it was an impertinence for anyone to take up his time. Now in his own domain, he was more than ever the past president of the seminary in Newry, more than ever the classical scholar. He was a don expecting 'students' arriving for tutorials to be well prepared, their treatises to the point. Certainly Bennett now liked to be addressed as Canon, a recent elevation that more than ever gave him a sense of his own importance and licence, if need be, to unfetter his caustic wit.

'Well, Michael, what can I do for you?' he intoned. The word 'well' was deep and resonant, authoritative and outdrawn.

Mick grimaced, shuffled his feet, put his hands in his pockets and tapped the floor.

'I'm … eh … thinking of getting married, Canon, and wonder what I'd need.'

'Have you a lady friend to begin with?' came the instant response as he ushered Mike into the front room.

'Yes, father. Lizzy McGrain, Owen McGrain's daughter.'

In a strict and regimented church, Canon Bennett was a wise enough leader to have no difficulty in occasionally following his flock, particularly if they were going his way, and he immediately assessed the situation as a God-sent opportunity to get himself out of a difficult spot: a solution to the problem of a single marriageable woman, living in a house of her own, in his parish, and not going to Mass. It would not have mattered a jot to him if she had lived amongst the gentry in the village, or on the Warrenpoint Road, but in Craigarran she was ensconced amongst his flock, a foreign woman, outside his influence. With the tips of his fingers together, and very much in the same tone as he had announced Owen's death to Maggie, he said, 'We'll get the necessary documentation from the friary in Peckham Rye.'

Mick didn't know it, but he had a lot to thank Canon Bennett for. This, after all, was the parish of the 'Elverton Marriage', where, on 15 August 1857, a very trusting Father Bernard Mooney married Theresa Longworth and William Charles Elverton, to spark a bigamy controversy that ended in the Dublin courts. It was an intrigue involving a Major from Cork, a gentlewoman from London, their very short stay in Rostrevor, and an unwitnessed marriage in the parish's outlying country church. To add to that, neither of the participants proved to be Roman Catholic, the Major demanded secrecy, and the old priest dispensed with the normal banns, believing he was sanctifying a civil ceremony that had been performed in Scotland some time before.

Little wonder the national and international press had had a field day, and crowds milled around the Four Courts when litigation subsequently ensued. It was a trial that had ended ignominiously, yet fate decreed that Theresa Longworth should capitalise on it and proceed to write a successful novel, *Martyrs to Circumstance*, based on her life.

In the light of all this, Canon Bennett had been painstakingly researching Lizzy's background. Continuing to correspond with the abbot of the friary in Peckham Rye, he further contacted the Catholic chaplain of the British forces in Le Havre and the Administrator of the Oratory church in London's Queensway—a parish with a catchment area extending to Holland Park. His intelligence spanned Lizzy's baptism, her infatuation with Boy Pointer, and that aloof officer's recent posting to Mombasa on the Kenyan coast. A girl from Mayo now held Lizzy's post in the Pointer household and a priest in the Queensway parish relayed in a letter to Canon Bennett that: Girlie Pointer's husband, a one-armed diabetic, had to have every bite he ate carefully weighed for him, and Mrs Pointer herself was so vain as to have her face rouged by an American who was preparing actresses for a cinematographic production on the Fulham Road.

Canon Bennett knew, insofar as it was humanly possible, that Lizzy McGrain had never been married before.

The great events of life have their own momentum, and time and time again Mick Wilson found himself touching his white shirt just between the third and fourth button down from the top. He would put his arms by his sides, only to find the middle finger of his left hand unconsciously tapping a spot, a place where he felt nothing, a space filled with hydrogen that feigned to lift him, to elevate him above Lizzy McGrain, who stood beside him, Father Bennett and Wee Vinny McArdle, who were in front, and Arthur Keenan and Biddy Drennan, who were behind. They were a small group. The autumn sunshine streaming through the stained-glass window magnified the vastness of the church. Mick couldn't help thinking that, considering the size of wee Vinny, their number was only five and a half.

He had an unreal sense of participating in an event centred on him, yet beyond his control, as he inhaled measured whiffs of incense, candle wax and carbolic soap. Never before had the ornamentation of ceremony sprung so clearly to him. The diamond patterns on the gold candlesticks vied for his attention with the purple embroidery on the vestments and the red buttons on the soutanes.

He turned his head a little to look at the woman to his right. She, in turn, turned left to look at him. She wore a short fitted jacket, a skirt that almost touched the ground, and stub-heeled boots—a very square-shouldered figure, composed, her face veiled beneath a pillbox hat. He could see the back of her head, her auburn hair drawn straight back, thick and shining, like frost and moonlight on a sheaf of oats. How little he knew of her. They had never held hands, never danced. He seemed only to know that she was thirty-one and he was twenty-nine. And they would get the picture the Missionary had left—the one of the Sacred Heart.